THE GHOST OF
IVY BARN

Mark Stay got a part-time Christmas job at Waterstone's in the nineties (back when it still had an apostrophe) and somehow ended up working in publishing for over 25 years. He would write in his spare time and (he can admit this now) on company time, and sometimes those writings would get turned into books and films. Mark is also co-presenter of the Bestseller Experiment podcast, which has inspired writers all over the world to finish and publish their books. Born in London, he lives in Kent with YouTube gardener Claire Burgess and a declining assortment of retired chickens.

@markstay
markstaywrites.com
witchesofwoodville.com

Also by Mark Stay

Robot Overlords
Back to Reality (with Mark Oliver)
The End of Magic

The Witches of Woodville series

The Crow Folk
Babes in the Wood

THE GHOST OF
IVY BARN

The Witches of Woodville III

Mark Stay

**SIMON &
SCHUSTER**

London · New York · Sydney · Toronto · New Delhi

First published in Great Britain by Simon & Schuster UK Ltd, 2022

Copyright © Unusually Tall Stories, Ltd 2022

The right of Mark Stay to be identified as author
of this work has been asserted in accordance with the
Copyright, Designs and Patents Act, 1988.

1 3 5 7 9 10 8 6 4 2

Simon & Schuster UK Ltd
1st Floor
222 Gray's Inn Road
London WC1X 8HB

Simon & Schuster Australia, Sydney
Simon & Schuster India, New Delhi

www.simonandschuster.co.uk
www.simonandschuster.com.au
www.simonandschuster.co.in

A CIP catalogue record for this book
is available from the British Library

Paperback ISBN: 978-1-4711-9801-4
eBook ISBN: 978-1-4711-9802-1
Audio ISBN: 978-1-3985-1324-2

Prin   ) 4YY

This one's for all the teachers wot taught and encouraged me to write words good. Not least (but not limited to) Mrs Godfrey at Duncombe School, Islington, Miss Molony at Woodville School, Leatherhead, and Mrs Wright at Therfield School, Leatherhead.

August, 1940

The Battle of Britain continues to rage, with Hitler's planned invasion of Britain, Operation Sea Lion, reliant on the destruction of RAF Fighter Command. The Luftwaffe prepares for *Adlertag* – Eagle Day – the first stage in the annihilation of the RAF. Meanwhile, in a small village in Kent, strange things are afoot in a farmer's barn ...

A BARNEY IN A BARN

Bertie Butterworth's Battle of Britain Diary

Friday 9th August, 1940

Started with distant gunfire in the morning. Air raid warning from 3–7pm. Big raid at night. Lots of flashes. Maybe twenty planes shot down. Think two planes crashed nearby. Must investigate. Made Spam hash today. Bit salty. Had a strange dream where me and Faye were riding bicycles in the sky. It was so peaceful up there. I wanted to hold her hand, but the wind kept pushing us apart. Can't stop thinking about Faye. I think about her when I wake up, I think about her when I'm fixing Dad's tractor, I think about her when I'm pulling a pint in the pub, and I think about her when I go to sleep. Is that normal?

Faye Bright's teeth rattled as her Pashley Model A bicycle shuddered down the bumpy coast road towards

3

the village of Woodville. The moon lingered, pale in the brightening sky, though the morning sun was already warm and the sea glistened. Waves beckoned her to hop in and splash about. Faye was tempted, though the beaches were littered with barbed wire and wrought-iron crosses and other such invasion defences, so a quick paddle was out of the question.

Faye was also knackered. Having just finished an all-night Air Raid Precaution coast watch with Freddie Paine, she was ready to curl up into a ball, duck under her bedsheets and kip the whole day.

It had been an intense evening. Faye lost count of how many planes tumbled into that same sea last night. At least twenty. The Luftwaffe bombers stayed high, and some of the fighters would come down and shoot barrage balloons like it was a game. Mr Paine seemed calm enough. Standing stock-still, gripping his binoculars, calmly telling her how he had seen the bodies of pilots fished out of the water the day before, all while the sky was lit up like fireworks night. Faye had always felt safe on ARP duties with Mr Paine, but last night was the first time she'd had the terrible thought that they might actually lose this war. She tried to shake the thought away, but it lingered even now like a bad smell.

Faye hadn't felt right for weeks. Not since that business with the Bavarian Druid Otto Kopp. In an effort to save three Kinderstransport children from a ravenous demon, she had been forced to take them across a magical threshold into an endless void. For some time she stood alone in that strange darkness with the moon, and its incredible ancient power had coursed through her. She could feel it still, fizzing in her belly and her brain as if waiting for something.

Faye rounded a bend and could see the bell tower of Saint Irene's Church poking over the tops of trees when Larry Dell ran out into the road and flagged her down.

'Faye! Faye Bright, have you got a mo'?'

Larry's farm was one of the biggest in the area. He mainly grew brassicas, hops and barley, and had recently dabbled in a bit of livestock, starting with a dozen sheep. Larry was a pleasant enough fellow, with a lower jaw that jutted out and an impressive dent in the top-right corner of his forehead. Rumour had it that he got the dent while leading a charge at the Battle of Ypres, though Faye's dad said Larry was kicked in the head while shoeing a horse and had never fully recovered.

Faye squeezed her bicycle's brakes and came skidding to a halt.

'Morning, Larry. Where's the fire?'

'No fire, Faye, but . . .' Larry squinted one eye and his jaw jutted out just a little further as if he hadn't quite thought through what he was going to say. 'There's something rather odd going on in one of my barns and I wondered if you might have a moment to come and take a look at it.'

'It's not another sheep with five legs, is it, Larry? What are you putting in their feed?'

'No, nothing to do with the farm, Faye. It's just I know what with you bein' your mother's daughter and all and consorting with the likes of Mrs Teach and Miss Charlotte—'

'Oh.' Faye raised her chin. 'That sort of problem.'

Larry nodded eagerly and smiled. Whenever someone in the village had some issue that might only be solved with the help of magic or witches, they would ask for that help in the most convoluted and pained way so that they avoided any mention whatsoever of said magic or witches. If they were to suddenly admit these things were real, then they would have to confront the idea that there was more to the world than their own existence, and their minds would be perturbed by the true strangeness of the universe, which could put them off their tea. And no one wanted that.

Since last month's incident when everyone had their minds controlled by a Bavarian Druid and a demonic dog stalked Faye and a bunch of scared children, the villagers could no longer avoid the truth that Woodville was a very strange place. And when strange things happened they would seek help from those steeped in strangeness. More and more they came to Faye, and she was beginning to like it.

Faye followed Larry off the road and down the winding, dusty path to his farm. Cabbage white butterflies danced around them, and sheep scrutinised the pair as they passed.

They approached a large barn on the edge of Larry's biggest brassica field. It was draped from top to bottom in ivy, and the word 'Ivy' had been painted above the doors by someone who was a dab hand with calligraphy.

'Ivy Barn,' Faye said. 'I can see why you called it that.'

'Oh no. All that ivy's just a whotsit. Coincidence. I name all my barns after, well ...' Larry trailed off and blushed.

Faye grinned and gave him a wink. 'Old girlfriends?'

Larry's jaw moved about like a cow chewing cud and he pointed to a distant barn across the field. 'There's Ruby, and by the farmhouse is Gladys, and I keep my tractor in Gustav.'

Faye blinked. 'Gustav?'

Larry nodded, his eyes drifting into memory. 'Spent a night in the trenches together. Both of us scared stiff. Me a Tommy, him a Hun, both farmers. Nice lad, as a matter o' fact. Pro'lly saved my life, I reckon. Anyway.' He shook his head clear. 'Here we are.'

They came to a stop before Ivy Barn's doors and immediately Faye felt an odd sensation. An unsettling vibration in the air. One that any normal person would steer away from. Faye stood her ground.

'Is this where those planes came down last night, Larry?' Faye asked, glancing back at the brassica field.

''S'right,' Larry said, a worried tremor in his voice. 'Hurricane and a Messerschmitt Bf 110. You can still see the damage they done to me field.' He pointed to a great gouge in the soil. 'I saw it meself. The pair of them crashed into pieces mid-air, then dropped out the sky like confetti. Made a hell of a mess. Most of the scrap I've got in here.'

Larry swung the barn doors open, swirling dust motes about and revealing a mess of mechanical detritus. Propeller blades leaning against the wall, a scorched section of a 110's fuselage, the glass canopy and bullet-riddled tail fin of the Hurricane. There were countless engine parts scattered across the floor, alongside unidentifiable lumps of scorched metal, and a machine gun with its barrel bent like a banana.

'Bloody hell, Larry, it's like an airbase crashed into a scrapyard. Are you, uh, are you supposed to have these in here?' Faye asked, noticing a few wheels in one corner, and an RAF pilot's wool-lined jacket draped over a chair.

'Army took most of it, but I managed to get this lot in my barn before they turned up.' Larry boosted himself onto the workbench next to the far wall. Behind him hung saws, hammers, chisels. 'So, finder's keepers, I reckon.'

'I'm not sure that's how it works, Larry, but your secret is safe with me. So what's the problem here?'

As she spoke, a chill prickled up her back, her breath puffed in the air and the summer heat evaporated. The back door to the barn slammed open and shut repeatedly. The timbers and planks rattled, shaking more dust into the air. A scythe hanging from a hook on the wall took flight, floating in space for a heartbeat before spinning directly at Faye and Larry.

'Blimmin' 'eck!' Faye piled into Larry, knocking him to the ground as the scythe's blade juddered into the barn wall where Larry's head had just been. 'Out! Quickly!' Faye grabbed Larry by the crook of his elbow, dragged him back into the sun and slammed the barn doors shut. Then came thud after thud as bits of aircraft scrap were hurled against the barn's walls.

'There's . . .' Larry gasped for breath. 'There's something in there. Though it didn't throw stuff last time. What do you reckon it is?'

The barn door juddered again as something quite solid thumped against it.

'Whatever it is, it ain't happy.'

'It's a poltergeist,' another voice said.

Faye squinted into the sunlight to see two familiar shapes striding towards them. One was pear-shaped and moved in dainty little hops, the other as slender as the blade of a knife and smoked a clay pipe.

'Mrs Teach and Miss Charlotte,' Faye said, wondering if the sudden arrival of her witchcraft mentors was a good or a bad thing. 'What brings you here?' she continued as the barn door was hit by something heavy and Faye and Larry were almost knocked off their feet.

'As if that wasn't obvious.' Charlotte raised an eyebrow.

'Rumours of some peculiar activity in Larry's barn reached my ears and we thought we would take the liberty of having a quick nose around,' Mrs Teach said. 'Looks like we're just in the nick of time.'

Faye turned to Miss Charlotte. 'What did you call it? A poultry-what?'

'Poltergeist.' Charlotte thinned her lips. 'An angry spirit.'

'A ghost?' Larry said, going as white as one. He crossed himself and backed away, leaving only Faye to keep the barn door closed against whatever was banging about inside.

'Larry, dear.' Mrs Teach took the poor man by the hand and steered him away from the barn. 'Why don't you pop home and put the kettle on? I think you could do with a little rest after all this excitement. A good nap might help.'

'The kettle! What about that thing in my barn? An angry spirit, you say? Angry with who?' He looked over to the scratch in the earth where the planes had crashed. 'Forgive me, O spirits. I didn't mean to nick your scrap metal. I throw myself upon your mercy and—' His pleas ended in a cough as Miss Charlotte blew smoke from her pipe into his face.

Miss Charlotte carried all kinds of different blends of tobacco with her for all sorts of supernatural emergencies. This one had the immediate effect of putting Larry Dell into a pleasant daze. Faye had learned the hard way not to get within puffing distance of Miss Charlotte.

'How about that tea now, petal?' Mrs Teach gestured down the path to where Larry's cottage could be found.

'Tea ... yes,' he said absently. 'I'll ... I'll put the kettle on. Nice cup of tea and bit of shortbread. Hmm.'

While he meandered his way home, Mrs Teach and Miss Charlotte stood before the clattering barn. Faye was still leaning against the doors as one heavy item after another was hurled against it.

'Are you two going to just stand there like a pair of lemons, or will you help keep this door shut?' she asked them.

'Perhaps it's keeping the door shut that's making it angry?' Mrs Teach mused.

Miss Charlotte rolled her blouse sleeves up. 'Only one way to find out.' Tying her long white hair into a ponytail, she gave the nod. 'Faye. Open the doors.'

POULTRY-GEIST

Poltergeist. The word rang a faint bell. Faye was sure she recalled mention of such a ghost in her late mother's book of magic. The book her mother Kathryn Bright (née Wynter) created in order for Faye to learn witchcraft after Kathryn died. The same book that was burned on the orders of Vera Fivetrees, High Witch of the British Empire, on account of the strict rule that nothing magical be written down. The rule existed in order to stop magical secrets falling into the wrong hands. Trouble was, it also stopped magical secrets getting into the right hands. Faye's education under Mrs Teach and Miss Charlotte was going at the speed of a not-very-magical snail, with only a few lectures on moon and sun magic and that was it. That said, you couldn't beat a bit of practical on-the-job experience and that's precisely what she was getting this morning.

Miss Charlotte gave Faye an impatient glare. 'What are you waiting for, girl? Open the doors.'

'Are you sure?' Faye had to raise her voice over

the banging and crashing coming from within the barn. 'I reckon if I open this barn door, we'll get a face full of aircraft engine parts or a scythe will lop our 'eads off.'

'We are prepared.' Miss Charlotte stood tall in her culottes and boots, producing a small pouch from within her waistcoat. She weighed it in her hand like a bag of sand.

Faye knew that Miss Charlotte was fond of magic powders. Black salt, white ash and blue dust were all in her supernatural armoury, along with the strange blends of tobacco designed to befuddle people's minds.

'Yes, dear, do open up and be sure to stand back.' Mrs Teach took a bundle of sage tied with string from her coat pocket and struck a match. She applied the flame to the tops of the leaves and began to waft it around, leaving little trails of grey smoke in the air.

A slat by Faye's ear cracked, sending splinters and dust spiralling. The banging was reaching a crescendo.

'Will you give it a rest in there?' Faye hollered at the poltergeist, her patience wearing thin after a long night. She turned to Miss Charlotte. 'Now?'

'Open after three.' Charlotte hefted her bag of powder like an Olympic shot-putter. 'One. Two. *Three!*'

Faye swung the barn door open, ducking and running for cover. As she rolled on the flaky soil, she covered her head, half expecting a propeller to come whizzing at her. She stayed that way for a few seconds before daring to look up.

The banging had ceased and the morning air was

silent but for a few blue tits having a chat and the gentle rumble of the breeze.

Mrs Teach and Miss Charlotte stood before the wide-open barn doors. Inside, the barn was a mess, but it was otherwise peaceful.

'Where's it gone?' Faye was the first to speak, though Miss Charlotte gestured for her to be silent.

Mrs Teach raised her burning sage and slowly walked over the threshold into the barn.

'Begone, spirit,' she said in a clear, raised voice. 'You are not welcome here.' Mrs Teach continued to mutter words unknown to Faye as she swished the sage around like a wand.

Faye got to her feet, patting the dust from her ARP uniform, and hurried to Miss Charlotte's side.

'Is that a banishing ritual?' Faye whispered.

Miss Charlotte nodded, then said out of the side of her mouth, 'Follow me, stay by my side, no sudden movements. Got it?'

Faye gave a thumbs-up. She and Miss Charlotte moved slowly in unison towards the barn. They stepped from light into shade and tiny droplets of sweat trickled down Faye's spine. It looked like a tornado had blown through the barn. As well as all of the aeronautical debris, the floor was littered with farm tools. Old paint pots were scattered about, and a ladder lay across the back door. On the walls, a rubber hosepipe and lengths of rope hung from nails.

The trio reached the centre of the barn.

'Has it gone, then?' Faye broke the silence.

Mrs Teach jumped and clutched at her chest with her free hand. 'Young lady, would you be kind enough to provide me with some kind of warning before you give me a heart attack?'

'Sorry. Only asking.' Faye pulled a face. 'Well, has it gone?'

'Shh!' Miss Charlotte raised her nose as if sniffing the air. 'I don't think so.'

'You know, it might just be scared,' Faye said.

Charlotte snorted.

'Who's to say if it ain't scarier actually bein' a ghost than not bein' a ghost?'

'It doesn't matter.' Miss Charlotte gripped the black pouch in her hand. 'It shouldn't be here and needs to leave.'

Faye looked around the barn. Dust drifted gently in the air and birds cheeped in a nest in the high eaves.

'Whatever it was, I reckon it's gone,' she said just as the barn doors slammed shut, kicking up dirt and straw from the floor, plunging them all into darkness. The only light came between the timber slats. The temperature dropped again and Faye had the sensation of ants crawling up her shoulder blades.

'You were saying?' Mrs Teach's voice tickled Faye's ear.

The timbers began to rattle and dust fell in jittery waves. The birds in the nest flapped about in a panic, looking for a way out, but there was none. Mice and rats darted from their cover and ducked under the door, skittering to safety outside.

'Form a circle,' Miss Charlotte commanded.

'There's three of us,' Faye said. 'We could do a triangle.'

'You know what I mean,' Charlotte snapped. 'Back to back, and face outwards.'

An unseen man's voice screamed inches from Faye's ears. Her heart pounded as if wanting to break out of her chest. Blood rushed in her ears. 'What the flippn' 'eck was that?'

He screamed again. It wasn't like a ghost in the films, all echoey and distant. This sounded like he was standing right next to her. His anguished cries became incessant and the hairs on her arms stood on end.

She felt another unnerving sensation. One inside her as the moon's magic warmed her belly.

'Oh,' she shouted over the racket. 'I don't like this.'

'I'm not sure we are meant to, my dear.' Mrs Teach swished her sage about for all it was worth.

Faye thought about correcting her and describing the strange stirring in her tum, but the only thing she could compare it to was a bout of flatulence she had last Christmas, so she kept it to herself as this didn't feel like the right time to describe magical wind to Mrs Teach and Miss Charlotte.

'Ladies,' Charlotte said, 'when I give the word, take one step forwards.'

'I'm not sure I want to,' Faye replied.

'Why not?'

''Cos I think it's right in front of me.'

Mrs Teach made a patronising mewing noise. 'And what makes you think that, sweetie?'

'I can see its eyes.'

It was true. Faye was facing the barn doors, and just within arm's reach, she could see two bloodshot eyes suspended in the air.

They blinked.

'Oh, friggin' 'eck.'

'Take this.' Charlotte gave Faye a handful of ash from her black pouch. It was warm and flaky and smelled like the tide was out at the beach.

'What is it?'

'Throw it in its face.'

The thing screamed again. The eyes were drifting closer.

'What will it do?' Faye asked, but Charlotte ignored the question.

'One step forwards . . . now!'

Faye took a step and flung the ash into the air.

The eyes snapped shut and the screams intensified.

Fay winced at the sound. And that feeling in her belly grew and grew. She was light-headed and she could see sparkles in the corners of her eyes.

Mrs Teach continued muttering her incantation as Miss Charlotte handed Faye the whole pouch.

'Again,' Charlotte ordered and they all took another step forwards.

Faye threw another handful of ash. The eyes returned, even redder and darting about now, accompanied by another agonised scream.

'I'm hurting it. I don't like it,' yelled Faye.

'It's the only way to convince it to leave,' Charlotte shouted over the screams. 'Another step. Now!'

The three women did so and were out of arm's reach now, forming either a circle or a triangle – that was a discussion for another time – and giving the ghost less room to manoeuvre. Faye tossed more ash before her. This time the flakes clung to the ghost and she began to see its – *his* – shape as he writhed, clutching the sides of his head.

'Back, go back to the light,' Miss Charlotte told it. 'We are the Hecate and you have no power here.'

'We're the what?'

'Don't interrupt, dear, it's working,' Mrs Teach said between incantations.

'Another step,' Charlotte said.

Faye threw more ash and the ghost wailed. 'I've got one more handful and that's it,' she said, looking up into the ghost's face.

He was a young man, not much older than her. His hair was lank, like he had been sweating, his cheekbones were sharp, his lips full and his skin milky-white. He looked straight at Faye, his eyes wide, reddened and streaming.

'Another step ... now!' Charlotte called out, but Faye stayed where she was.

The lad wore a tan flight suit with a pale yellow life jacket. He had three gulls on a patch on his arm, and a belt with some kind of bird on the buckle. Faye knew from looking through Bertie's books that this young man was a pilot with the Luftwaffe.

His mouth moved, but he had no voice. Faye could see from the look in his eyes that he was pleading with her to end the pain.

'You don't have to be here,' Faye said to him gently, her voice wavering as the moon magic inside her made her giddy. 'You can go any time you want. Go on. Go. Have a bit of peace.'

'Another step!' Charlotte cried again. Faye glanced back at Mrs Teach and Miss Charlotte who were getting closer and closer to the barn's walls.

Faye refocused on the ghost. Behind him, by the barn doors, a swirling darkness twisted in the air. It felt old and familiar. 'That way,' she said.

He turned and hesitated.

'I know it must be scary, mate. But I think your time is up. You can either stay here with this lot screaming and waving smelly herbs at yer . . . or you can find out what's on the other side.'

Faye had no idea whether he could even hear her, let alone understand her, but he lowered his head and nodded. He gave Faye a small, grateful smile before running to the barn doors.

The darkness ballooned and clung around the pilot like smoke as the barn doors swung open and daylight stabbed Faye's eyes. She closed them and let the warmth of the summer sun prickle her skin.

By the time her eyes had adjusted to the brightness, the ghost and the darkness were gone.

'Good work, ladies.' Mrs Teach's voice came from the far end of the barn. 'I think we've done it.'

Miss Charlotte started sniffing the air again. 'I think you're right. Good job. Well done. I'll send a report to Vera and let you know what she says.' She gave a little salute and headed back the way she had come across the bridle path on Larry Dell's brassica field.

'I'll let poor Larry know that his barn is safe.' Mrs Teach pottered off towards the farmer's cottage.

Faye watched them go and wondered if she should tell them what she had seen, and what she had felt, but what was done was done and the young pilot was gone now anyway. The odd sensation in her belly was subsiding already, and she began to feel like herself again.

She turned to close the barn door to find another pilot standing in the centre of the barn.

This one wore RAF blues. Half of his face was burned red and raw. He looked terrified, like a child caught skipping school, as he raised a finger to his mouth. *Shh.*

Faye blinked and when she opened her eyes again, he was gone.

DUCK ISLAND COTTAGE

On the edge of St James's Park in London is a small cottage. Built in 1841 in the style of a Swiss chalet, with magnolia plaster on its walls and terracotta tiles on its roof, it bridges Horse Guards Road with a small island on St James's Park Lake. There are those who will tell you it is home to the park's bird-keeper and hosts meetings of the Ornithological Society of London. These people are misinformed.

To be fair, the island is teeming with birds, including pelicans who regularly flap over to London Zoo for lunch. And members of the Ornithological Society of London do indeed have permission to meet in the kitchen extension from time to time, but they have no clue as to the building's real purpose. A few members have commented on the lingering rich aroma of rare herbs and spices, and the dining table with a pentangle carved onto its surface.

Those with a keen eye might note that the cottage is a short walk from Downing Street and a mere jaunt to the Cabinet War Rooms across the road.

Passers-by have been heard to say that it looks like the kind of cottage you might find in a fairy tale. One where a witch might lure children over with sweet treats before shoving them in an oversized oven.

While they might be wrong about the children and the oven, they're right about the witch.

The first resident of Duck Island Cottage was one Peggy Sage who designed the building herself, including tunnels to Downing Street and Buckingham Palace. Peggy – or Lady Sage as she became known – was the first High Witch of the British Empire to foster a new inclusivity with Prime Minister Robert Peel and Queen Victoria in order to better coordinate the witching community to resolve any magical threats to the Empire.

Some uncharitable types have suggested she just wanted a cheap London residence with a nice vegetable patch, but it cannot be denied that being a mere stone's throw from such mighty seats of power consolidated British witchcraft's place in the Empire's hierarchy.

As the sun set over St James's Park on a warm day in August, dipping below the tethered barrage balloons, Bellamy Dumonde, a warlock of some renown, found the current High Witch watering her lettuces.

'Vera Fivetrees, isn't this the most splendid evening?' he called, striding towards her with what he hoped was a friendly smile on his face. She would know that Bellamy was coming directly from the War Rooms, and the two Secret Service chaps flanking him in coats too heavy and long for the summer sent a message all of their own. 'Yes, yes, I believe it is,' Bellamy answered himself in a jolly and conversational tone.

Vera was no fool. After last month's debacle in that village in Kent she would surely know what was coming, though she masked her feelings well. She looked up from her vegetable patch with a calm smile, but he could see her gripping her watering can like a weapon. Bellamy wasn't duped by the bright summer dress she wore or the jolly straw hat on her head. Nor was he dismissive, as many of his contemporaries would be, of a woman with a Caribbean complexion. Vera Fivetrees was, without doubt, one of the most powerful magical practitioners in the country, if not the world, and as a result he was always cautious around her, never fully sure what she was capable of. It wasn't so much her magic that scared him, more the withering glares. They reminded him of Nanny. Bellamy fought the urge to cower like a schoolboy before her. He might be half her age, but he had a neatly trimmed beard and a fine three-piece suit and very good shoes. He was more than ready to take her place.

'Keeping the *Lactuca sativa* hydrated in this heat, I see.' Bellamy, hands behind his back, nodded towards Vera's vegetable patch.

'Why not call them what they are, Bellamy?' Vera said. 'Lettuces.'

Bellamy laughed. The tendons in his neck tightened as he clenched his teeth like a guard dog, and then huffed like a steam train climbing a steep incline. Bellamy Dumonde's laugh only lasted a few seconds, but it was enough to startle some nearby ducks, sending them paddling back into the lake.

'Can one help instinctively putting things into categories?' he asked no one in particular. 'No. One cannot. Lettuces are in the Asteraceae family, so they're technically daisies, which throws a whole new light on one's salad, does it not? Yes, yes, it does.' He was waffling. He did this when he was nervous. Couldn't help it. *Stop waffling, man*. But he didn't stop. 'Did you know, it's oh-so-slightly narcotic? Yes, yes, our friend the lettuce was called *sleepwort* by the Anglo-Saxons. There's something in the stems, I'm led to believe. And the Yazidi people of Iraq simply won't eat them at all. The Yazidi faithful were slain by the Ottoman caliphs in lettuce fields and to them the lettuce is like the poppy to us. A symbol of—'

'Bellamy,' Vera raised her voice. 'I'm sure you didn't come here to discuss the fascinating history of lettuce. If you did, I should like the opportunity to put the kettle on. If not, I'd like you to get to the point.'

'Ah, forgive me. I can get distracted somewhat. Yes.' He glanced at the two men flanking him, took a breath and did the necessary. 'I'm afraid I am the bearer of bad tidings, Vera.'

'Is it about what happened in Woodville?' Vera resumed her watering.

'I'm afraid it rather is. Is it about appointing blame? No. But there must be an investigation all the same.'

'Of course.'

'I'm on your side, Vera, I really am. And this is not a

26

decision we've taken lightly, hence the delay. But Otto Kopp ... you let him wreak havoc and then get away.'

'I thought this wasn't about blame?'

'No, no, it isn't. Of course not. Perish the thought. I know what a devious bugger he can be. But it is the duty of the Council of Witches to investigate such matters.'

'I am aware of the duty of the body over which I preside, Mr Dumonde.'

'Of course. Then you will also be aware that you will be ...' Bellamy found his mouth was suddenly dry. 'You will be suspended while the investigation is ongoing.'

Vera showed neither anger nor surprise as she continued to water her lettuces. Bellamy knew there were people on the Council who had been waiting for her to make a mistake and last month it had happened in that little village in Kent. A situation that got out of hand remarkably quickly. What started as an attempt to hex the Nazis' top sorcerer Otto Kopp ended with the possession of the entire village by the old Druid. Including Vera herself. Were it not for the actions of a young witch called Faye Bright, then all might have been lost.

'I understand.' Vera raised her chin.

'I'm most dreadfully embarrassed by this whole situation.' Bellamy wrung his hands together, then hurriedly put them behind his back. 'Should Vera Fivetrees remain as High Witch of the British Empire? Of course, of course she should. I would be first in line if that were put to a vote. But does her position raise her above the law in some way? I'm sure you would agree that it does not.'

Vera tipped the watering can, depositing the last drops over her *Lactuca sativa*. 'Am I under house arrest, then?'

'Ah. No. A decision was taken to politely request that you vacate the premises. Some – not me! – some felt that allowing you to reside in a house of such powerful magic would be akin to allowing Billy the Kid access to the armoury at Arsenal.'

Vera glanced at the Secret Service men behind Bellamy. 'You didn't think I would come quietly?'

For once, Bellamy neither posited nor answered a question. 'We've got you a room at the Dorchester. As places of incarceration go, it's top notch.'

Vera raised the watering can. Fast and deliberate. Both the Secret Service men's hands were a blur as they reached for the weapons holstered in their long coats.

Bellamy raised a hand to stop them. *Fools.*

'I see.' Vera smiled and handed the watering can to Bellamy. He was sure that she did so in such a way that some of the wet soil on the bottom of the can rubbed onto his suit.

'Look after this place,' she told him. 'The chimney was damaged by a bomb months ago and I'm still waiting for someone to repair it.'

'Leave it to me,' Bellamy assured her, knowing full well that there were neither the funds nor the resources to address the problem.

'This is more than a place of work.' Vera looked back

28

at the cottage. 'My mother was a friend of Lady Sage and the pair of them trained me in magic. The ancient obeah and Myal magics of Africa, and the witchcrafts of Europe. This place means everything to me, Bellamy. I will be returning soon.'

For the first time in their conversation, Bellamy detected a smidgen of doubt in her voice. If found guilty, she knew she would never see this place again.

Snug Gossip

Bertie Butterworth stood alone behind the bar of the Green Man, ready for anything that the publican life might throw at him.

Faye's dad Terrence Bright – landlord of the Green Man, Woodville's premier purveyor of Kentish ale – had agreed to give Bertie a trial shift a few weeks ago but hadn't held out much hope. Working in a pub required a savvy instinct for nuances of human nature that Bertie had never shown any aptitude for. A publican had to be gregarious, and Bertie was shy to the point of bashfulness. A publican had to listen to all kinds of nonsensical toot from their patrons with a patient smile, while Bertie preferred to stare at the clouds in his cider. A publican required an almost-psychic recall of every punter's preferred drink, whereas Bertie barely knew what day of the week it was.

But, put this normally shy lad behind a bar and a transformation as remarkable as a caterpillar changing into a butterfly would take place before one's very eyes.

As if someone had flicked a switch in his brain, Bertie blossomed into a chatty barkeep with an easy laugh and a memory for long and complicated orders that even astounded Terrence.

'The lad's a natural,' Terrence said to Faye, the pair of them watching Bertie pouring pints for a cluster of airmen. Terrence leaned closer to Faye and lowered his voice. 'Here's a thing. This afternoon, I had ... whotsit ... What's that thing ... ? That thing that other people have?'

'Money?' Faye ventured.

'No.'

'Clean underwear?'

'Bloody cheek. No.'

'A reliable memory?'

Terrence snapped his fingers. 'Spare time!' His face wrinkled into a smile. 'A whole hour.' The smile faded. 'I didn't know what to do with meself.'

Faye nudged him with her elbow. 'You know what you need?'

He shook his head.

'A hobby,' she said.

Terrence made a noise much like a toddler rejecting vegetables. 'I ain't got time for hobbies.'

'Clearly, you have.' Faye gestured to the hurly-burly of the pub. 'And you need a break from all this malarkey sometimes. Just a little bit of peace and quiet to give your noggin a rest.'

'I could stare at the wall. Does that count as a hobby?'

'Mr Hodgson collects Toby jugs.'

'What's the point of that?'

Faye shrugged. 'How about jigsaw puzzles, then?'

'Get out of it. I ain't a child.'

'Very relaxing. I've still got a few you can have. Pretty sure all the pieces are in the box.'

'And they can stay there.'

'Give it a go, you old grump.'

Their conversation was interrupted by the crash-ring of the till as Bertie slammed it closed. The lad flinched at the noise.

Faye ambled over to him as he wiped the bar down. 'Dad says you're a natural, Bertie.'

'I don't know how to explain it,' Bertie replied, before immediately contradicting himself and going on to explain at some length. 'Having the bar between me and someone else changes me. They're pleased to see me 'cos I get them a drink, and I'm pleased to see them 'cos I can get them a drink and make them happy. It's like a perfect circle of happiness. When I was working on me dad's farm I couldn't do right for doin' wrong, and he would never tell me what he wanted, he would just expect me to know, but here everything just clicks into place, like a jigsaw puzzle.'

'A what?' Terrence said as he joined them. Faye shushed her father and Bertie continued, oblivious.

'The punters ask for something, and I'm happy to give it to 'em. Does that make sense?'

'It does, Bertie, it does,' Faye said with a smile.

'Bertie.' Terrence raised a finger and pointed it over Bertie's head, where another cluster of keen RAF airmen had bustled in, eager for pints.

'Righto.' Bertie did a quick turn. 'Evenin', gents. What can I get you?'

Faye watched the lad who was born with one leg shorter than the other shuffle to the end of the bar where each airman greeted Bertie by his name.

Faye, for one, was grateful for his new lease of life. She needed more time to master witchcraft, and to figure out just what the blazes was happening inside her belly and brain, and that meant time away from working in the pub. It was a relief that Bertie did not hesitate to step forward and fill the gap.

They had grown so much closer since the strange events of the Summer Fair last month. What had begun as a pleasant day with Faye and Bertie stepping out and holding hands for the first time had been somewhat marred by Nazi occultist Otto Kopp. He used his extraordinary powers to control the minds of every villager in order to hunt down Faye and the children she was protecting. As first dates went, it was a peculiar one to say the least.

Since then, what with the constant air raids, the roaring trade of the pub, Bertie's shifts with the Home Guard, and Faye's magical training and ARP duties, they'd not had much spare time to talk about what happened. All Faye knew was she found herself wanting to see Bertie's smile as he came through the door. She loved hearing his laugh, and the way he scrunched his nose when he was thinking, and she delighted in watching him and her dad work together behind the bar.

And there were times when she wanted just to grab

the lad and give him a great big smacker on the lips. Faye had never before had any interest in boys or any of that hanky-panky, so this was a new feeling, and one she was surprised to discover was quite thrilling. But she and Bertie had so little time alone that the opportunity for a bit of passionate canoodling never arose. That was about to change. They had promised to make time to attend Reverend Jacobs' Social Evening at the church hall tomorrow, and after that they would go for a walk and on that walk Faye would take Bertie's hand and pull him closer so that her body met his and she would wrap her arms around him, pucker up and—

'Ahem.'

Faye jolted and turned to find that Mrs Teach and Miss Charlotte had her trapped in a pincer movement.

'Blimey, you were quick.' Faye pressed a hand on her chest to calm her beating heart. 'Did you see anything?'

'No.' Miss Charlotte raised an eyebrow in Bertie's direction behind the bar. He gave a little salute in return and began pouring a gin for her, a sweet sherry for Mrs Teach and half a cider for Faye.

'No?' Faye blinked and adjusted her specs, which were still steaming around the edges after her canoodling daydream. 'I know what I saw. There's another ghost in that—'

'Ladies.' Mrs Teach cut Faye off with a smile and gestured towards the comfy chairs in the snug by the fireplace. 'Shall we retire to a quiet corner? There is much to discuss.'

❧

'Tinkerty tonk and down with the Nazis.' Mrs Teach gave the toast, and her fellow witches raised their glasses. The pub was heaving now. A mix of RAF pilots and engineers from the airbase at Mansfield and local farmers and land girls slaking their thirst after a long day. The bustle and burble allowed the three witches in the snug to converse in a relaxed manner about their supernatural business.

'I saw him with my own eyes,' Faye insisted. 'He was an older pilot, about your age, Miss Charlotte—'

'There are few my age,' Charlotte said.

'True, but he *looked* about your age, or what your age would be if you were normal. And his face was all burned on one side. It was all red and raw and 'orrible, poor bugger. And he raised his finger to his lip and told me to shush.'

'I like him already.' Miss Charlotte smirked and took a sip of her gin.

'Faye, darling, we checked the barn as you requested and there's simply nothing there. No supernatural presence of any kind. Do you think . . .' Mrs Teach rested a gentle hand on Faye's in a gesture that was supposed to be kind but was more than a little patronising. 'Do you think this might have been one of your funny visions?'

Faye grimaced. Last month she had been plagued by visions that gave her blackouts. Mrs Teach called it 'magical puberty', but Faye hadn't experienced any visions since sending Otto Kopp packing. She withdrew her hand from under Mrs Teach's. She decided there and then not to tell them about the strange magical flatulence inside her for fear of more patronising mockery.

'No, it wasn't a vision,' Faye insisted. 'It was completely different. It was like he was right there in front of me.'

'Well, he's not there now,' Miss Charlotte said.

'P'raps you two scared him after what you did to that other ghost and he's too frightened to come out?' Faye suggested and instantly regretted it as Mrs Teach's face contorted into an expression of extreme haughtiness.

'Scared?' Mrs Teach's voice rose in pitch as she splayed defensive fingers across her chest. 'Of us?'

Faye was going to elaborate further, that the two women sat before her – one a white-haired witch at least four centuries old, and the other the village busybody who could make grown men shrivel with a flutter of her eyelashes – were somewhat intimidating, but Miss Charlotte interrupted.

'Look, this isn't important.' Charlotte waved at Faye the way one might try and shoo a fly. 'We have news.'

Faye sneered at Miss Charlotte's shooing hand. 'I don't care. What about my ghost? The poor fella—'

'Vera Fivetrees has been suspended,' Mrs Teach said.

Any thoughts Faye had about her ghost were bumped to one side. This was indeed big news. If Faye felt intimidated by her mentors before her, then she was positively paralysed with awe whenever she was in the presence of Vera Fivetrees, High Witch of the British Empire.

'We just received a telegram,' Miss Charlotte added.

'B-but why?' Faye asked, then thought, of course. The events in the village last month. 'Oh. Was it the whole thing with Otto Kopp controlling the entire village, including you two and—'

'No,' Miss Charlotte snapped. She didn't like to be reminded that Kopp had briefly got the better of her. She took out her clay pipe and began to stuff it with tobacco. 'It wasn't *just* that.'

'Vera had objected to putting a hex on Otto Kopp in the first place.' Mrs Teach leaned forwards, eager to impart some first-class gossip. 'She's always been keen to keep us at arm's length when it comes to getting involved in politics and war and such.'

'We will not become a tool of the army,' Miss Charlotte interjected.

'But the rumour is she was under pressure from some of her colleagues to make a greater contribution to the war effort.'

Miss Charlotte made a short grunting noise as she lit her pipe. Faye couldn't make out if she was agreeing with the sentiment or not, but she recalled that the older witch had been quite keen on hexing Otto Kopp when the idea was first mooted.

'There are those who think she was forced into giving the order to hex Otto,' Mrs Teach continued. 'And that in some ways she was set up to fail.'

'Oh, blimey,' Faye said. 'What will she do now?'

'There's to be an investigation.' Pipe smoke swirled slowly around Charlotte. 'In the meantime, she is

suspended and the Council of Witches has a new tem-
porary head.'

'What's her name?'

'Bellamy Dumonde,' Charlotte said, enjoying Faye's
puzzled expression.

'Is that a fella?'

'He is indeed,' Mrs Teach said.

'Are there fella witches?'

'Warlocks,' Charlotte said.

'I only asked.' Faye frowned.

Mrs Teach tutted. 'They're called warlocks, you
silly girl.'

'And how's that different from a wizard?'

'They're real, for a start,' Charlotte said. 'As we shall
discover when he arrives tomorrow.'

Faye felt a creeping unease. 'Why's he coming here?'

Mrs Teach leaned closer. 'He says he has a mission for us.'

'One that could change the course of the war.'
Charlotte pursed her lips, relishing the thought.

'Read this.' Mrs Teach took a telegram from her
handbag and handed it to Faye. 'The last line.'

Faye's eyes scanned the telegram. She read the final line
out loud. 'I am looking forward to meeting you. Stop. Not
least the most powerful witch I think I may ever encounter. Stop. Sincerely yours, Bellamy Dumonde. Stop.'

Faye looked up to find two supremely self-satisfied
faces, both utterly convinced that the 'most powerful
witch' mentioned in the telegram referred to them.

Faye sighed to herself. 'Oh, Lordy.'

BELLAMY DUMONDE'S GREAT PLAN

Bertie Butterworth's Battle of Britain Diary

Saturday 10th August, 1941

Apparently there was a siren this morning. Slept through it. Very distant gunfire all afternoon. Picked up a lovely blazer and trousers at a jumble sale for the show tonight. Faye and me are stepping out to Reverend Jacobs' Social Evening at the church hall. We're planning on going for a long walk afterwards. Faye said we could head down to the Old Roman Bridge and finally do some proper canoodling. I had to look that word up in Dad's dictionary. I can't wait!

An army truck came for Faye just after breakfast. Miss Charlotte was already sitting in the driver's cabin, and Mrs Teach was quick to bagsy the only other free seat.

Faye was happy to clamber in the back, if only to avoid the unspoken contest of knowing looks between the two older witches over who would be crowned most powerful witch by the new boss.

Their destination was Mansfield Airbase, the official name for a big field, a shed and a few biplanes that was a twenty-minute drive from the centre of Woodville. Faye rarely had a reason to come out here. The last time she could recall was just after war was declared when Bertie insisted they go and look at the Spitfires. All they saw was a sorry-looking Puss Moth biplane and a tractor that didn't look capable of long-distance flight.

The field today was quite different. Faye could smell it before she saw it. The air was so thick with aviation fuel, Faye feared that if Miss Charlotte lit her pipe their truck would go up in flames.

As they turned off the road they came to a checkpoint where guards inspected their papers. Faye looked through a flap in the canvas and gasped. The field was littered with craters as big as the truck, and the charred, skeletal fuselage of a Spitfire was being dismantled by a group of soldiers.

The truck started up again and headed for the heart of the base. They passed row after row of Hurricanes and Spitfires, some peppered with bullet holes, others with wings and tail fins missing.

The base had become its own little village, with the officers' mess, a water tower, storage huts, barracks, workshops, fire station and hangars.

They approached a cluster of tin huts, around which

sat dozens of RAF pilots in deckchairs. A few were reading newspapers and books, a couple were playing chess, but many of them were catching forty winks. Faye knew from speaking to the lads coming into the pub that they were going up three or four times a day into intense combat and were utterly exhausted. Their usual good cheer was getting strained and her dad even had to break up a fight between a couple of them last week.

The truck shook to a halt and Faye hopped out of the back. She hurried to the passenger door to help Mrs Teach down from the cabin. Miss Charlotte waved Faye's helping hand away and jumped down.

'This way.' Their driver gestured towards one of the huts and the three of them followed.

From above came the familiar growl of a Merlin engine and Faye looked up to see a black Spitfire with no markings bank over the trees at the far end of the field. It looked like the same specially adapted two-seater plane that Vera Fivetrees had arrived in when she helped clean up the mess left by the crow folk.

'This must be him,' Faye said, and they all stopped to watch it land. Faye could sense the disapproval of the fidgety young driver who probably had orders to squirrel them away in a tin hut, but he wasn't about to argue with three witches. 'How much do you know about him?'

'I've heard he's young and dashing,' Mrs Teach said with a flutter of her eyelashes. 'And full of *modern* ideas.' There was something about the way she pronounced the word 'modern' that suggested she didn't fully approve but was willing to give it a try.

'He's the one most keen to get us more involved in the war effort.' Miss Charlotte slid her hands in her pockets as she watched the black Spitfire taxi towards them.

'I remember you both telling me that was a bad idea,' Faye said.

'It probably is,' Charlotte replied. 'But I'm not sure there's any avoiding it now.'

'We should play the hand we are dealt,' Mrs Teach added.

The black propellers kept turning as the pilot hopped out of their seat. Faye tried to make out if it was the same girl who flew Vera, but they kept their flight cap on and were too far away to see. The pilot stood on the wing and helped Bellamy clamber out of his seat and to the ground. With a salute, the pilot got back in the cockpit and began to taxi towards the crater-pocked runway.

Bellamy straightened his tweed suit and gave them a jaunty wave. Faye was surprised that he was so young, and he half ran with his elbows pinned to his ribs, his forearms flapping about. He had a sprightly skip and an eager smile.

'Thank you, young man,' he told the driver. 'I'll take it from here.'

The driver saluted and marched back to his truck.

Bellamy Dumonde stood before them, legs apart, hands on hips.

'Do I spy the inestimable witches of Woodville

Village? I surely do.' He hurried to Mrs Teach first, shaking her hand. 'You must be Mrs Teach? Yes, of course you are. I have heard such remarkable stories of your youthful misadventures with Vera Fivetrees.'

Faye glanced at Mrs Teach, wondering why she hadn't heard of these youthful misadventures. Mrs Teach blushed and shook her head.

'That was a long time ago,' she said.

'Nevertheless, I long to hear more,' Bellamy said.

So do I, thought Faye.

Mrs Teach squeezed Bellamy's hand, waiting for him to formally anoint her the most powerful witch, but he slipped from her grip and moved to the next witch in line.

'And who is this standing before me? Can it really be the legendary Miss Charlotte Southill?'

Charlotte pursed her lips into a triumphant little smile, while Mrs Teach blanched at being passed over.

Of course Miss Charlotte was the most powerful witch, Faye reasoned. She was older by far, had much more experience, and magic seemed to come easily to her. And young Bellamy was in awe of her.

'It is my true honour to finally meet you, Charlotte – may I call you Charlotte?'

Miss Charlotte never let anyone call her Charlotte, but she gave a little shrug of consent.

'If half the stories I have heard about you are true—'

'They probably are.' Miss Charlotte's voice took a turn for the husky.

Bellamy shook her hand. 'We are blessed to have

you on board for this most vital operation. It truly will change the course of the war. And finally ...' Bellamy turned to Faye. 'This cannot be the daughter of Kathryn Wynter?'

'Er ... yes it can?' Faye ventured, wondering if starting a sentence with a question was now compulsory.

'Your mother was most remarkable. Was she the most dynamic of witches? She was not, but one who did everything she could to help those around her. Countless good deeds for her neighbours. And now here you are, Faye Bright. The young witch who took on Otto Kopp and won. You, truly, are the most powerful witch I have ever met. It is a privilege and a pleasure to meet you.'

Faye's feet took root in the ground. She could feel the radiation from the glares she was getting from Mrs Teach and Miss Charlotte, and she couldn't help but blush.

'R-really? Weren't nuffin'.' Faye wondered how much Bellamy knew about her mother and her good deeds.

'Oh, it was something, Faye Bright,' he told her. 'Something quite magnificent. And with proper training, you could be after my job in a few years.'

The words 'proper training' did something to the air around Mrs Teach and Miss Charlotte. The implied insult to their tuition of Faye created a kind of heat-haze of rage, and Faye glanced about to see if there was a bomb shelter nearby that she could duck into in a hurry.

'And just what is your job?' Miss Charlotte's voice came with a chill northerly wind.

'I'm glad you asked, Charlotte—'

'*Miss* Charlotte.'

'M-Miss Charlotte, of course.' Bellamy was flustered for all of a second, but Faye saw from the wicked smiles on the faces of her fellow witches that it pleased them. 'Pending an investigation of Vera Fivetrees' conduct during the Otto Kopp affair, I have been appointed the High Witch of the British Empire. If I may be frank, I don't rate poor Vera's chances. Her clumsy handling of the Otto Kopp hex left us dangerously exposed. Were it not for this young lady here, things might have been a great deal worse.'

Faye squirmed at the flattery.

Mrs Teach gripped her handbag. 'If you're going to condemn Vera, then you might as well throw us all in jail. Otto Kopp is not to be underestimated, Mr Dumonde.'

'Oh, I agree.' Bellamy frowned sincerely. 'But Vera is in a position of accountability and must be held responsible. Whereas you are ordinary witches.'

Ordinary. Mrs Teach and Miss Charlotte stood together like two sticks of dynamite ready to go off. Faye didn't think there would be a bomb shelter big enough to save her. She would have to emigrate to Australia to avoid the fallout from their wrath.

To Faye's astonishment, all that followed was Miss Charlotte clearing her throat. 'At least we know where we stand.' Her tone was civil and pleasant and yet it scared Faye more than the drone of a Luftwaffe fighter.

Faye found her voice. 'Why are you here, Mr Dumonde?'

'Why am I here indeed?' Bellamy asked. 'To stop the Nazi invasion of this country. And who will be helping me with this most important task? You three.' He was about to elaborate when a noise made them all turn and look to the sky. Half-a-dozen Hurricanes were coming in to land. Two of them had smoke trailing from their engines. 'And there's no time to lose.' Bellamy gestured to the hut behind them. 'I believe this has been reserved for our use. Shall we?'

℘

The hut was a flight briefing room, with a few chairs scattered about and the aroma of tobacco, damp and stale sweat hanging in the air. On the wall hung a map of the south-east of England and the coast of northern France, marked with the locations of airbases. The Luftwaffe ones were marked with swastikas. There were so many Faye shuddered to look at them.

They each took a seat. Mrs Teach sat ramrod straight with her handbag on her knees. Charlotte leaned back, crossed her legs and lit her pipe. Faye felt like she was in a school classroom again and felt the sudden urge to go to the toilet.

Bellamy stood before the map. 'I would remind you that you have all signed the Official Secrets Act and nothing we discuss here today is to go beyond these four walls. Is that understood?'

He got murmured yeses in reply.

'I'm sure it hasn't escaped your attention that the Luftwaffe has intensified its offensive in the air. Their plan is nothing less than the total annihilation of the RAF, thus clearing the way for an invasion by sea.'

Faye's stomach turned. This was all too real. Hearing about the war on the radio or reading about it in the papers was one thing, and doing her ARP duty and seeing the dogfights above was something else, but being told that an invasion was imminent in an RAF briefing hut had a dread weight to it. She had visions of Panzer tanks crashing through the village, destroying the bell tower, burning the pub. She shook her head clear.

'How can we possibly stop it?' Bellamy asked and, as usual, didn't wait for an answer. 'I have been working on a ritual. One I discovered in the ancient writings of the Filí, the keepers of ancient Celtic magic. This ritual is said to have repelled Caesar from successfully invading Ancient Britain. I believe that, with your help, I can use this ritual to repel the Nazis from invading us today.'

Mrs Teach and Miss Charlotte said nothing but fidgeted in their seats. They were unconvinced.

'Who wrote this down?' Faye asked. 'I didn't think anyone was allowed to write magical things down.'

'Opinion is divided on the subject,' Bellamy said with a knowing grin. 'I have made it my life's work to study what little magical writing remains. I have been lucky enough to read some of your mother's work, Miss Charlotte. Truly remarkable, if I may—'

'Hold your horses,' Faye piped up. 'Miss Charlotte's mother wrote down magical stuff for her?'

'Yes.' Bellamy nodded. 'I believe it was quite instructional.'

'I bet it bloody was,' Faye snapped.

'Can we discuss this later?' Charlotte said through gritted teeth.

'Yes, I think we bloody will.'

'May I continue?' Bellamy's arms were folded and he tapped an impatient foot on the floorboards. 'I think the imminent fate of our glorious nation is more important than any of our own petty squabbles.'

'Forgive us, Bellamy,' Mrs Teach said with a strained chuckle. 'You were saying?'

'From the poems of the Filí and Vates of the ancient Celtic tradition I have concocted a ritual that will not only cloud the minds of every Luftwaffe pilot in the sky, but could also see their aircraft dropping like stones. Is this ambitious? Yes. Yes, it is. And I can only do this with your combined help.'

'It sounds like a cone of power,' Mrs Teach said.

Faye vaguely recognised the term. 'I think I read about that in my mum's book. Of course, if I hadn't been forced to burn it I might have a better idea of how I can help, but there y'go.' She folded her arms and smiled insincerely, not caring for the glowers she got from her fellow witches. 'Don't look at me like that, Miss Charlotte. P'raps you can explain to me why your mother's book remained in one piece while mine went up in flames.'

Miss Charlotte looked away. 'It was a long time ago.'

'Ladies, please. Yes, Mrs Teach, it is indeed a cone

of power ritual.' Bellamy splayed his fingers across the map on the wall. 'One that will ensure that the Nazis will not cross the Channel. Has there ever been one this powerful before? I don't believe so. We will perform the ritual on the cliffs of Dover, beginning at midnight and bringing the ritual to an end at sunrise. Also – and this is most important – to ensure that we are able to produce as much magical energy as possible ... we will be skyclad.'

Mrs Teach's gasp was so sudden and mighty that it threatened to collapse the walls of the hut. 'We most certainly will not!'

Skyclad. This was another word that Faye recalled from her mother's book, but she had to be sure. She raised her hand. 'You ... you want us to do this ... in the nuddy?'

A Brief Discussion About Nudity

There was a long moment of awkwardness between the witches as the ghastly idea that any day now they might see each other's bits sank in.

'Of course.' Bellamy looked puzzled. 'That's what skyclad means. It comes from the Jain Dharma, one of the oldest religions in the world. The magical power that emanates from one's body must do so unhindered by clothing. Any kind of covering will impair the flow of energy.'

Faye had been considering asking Bellamy about her own magical energy flow, but she now decided that it would be a bad idea. There's something about a man eager to get naked that can put a girl off.

'Listen to me, young man.' Mrs Teach's tone became as hoity-toity as Faye had ever heard. 'If you think you can convince us to go prancing around in the altogether on the cliffs of Dover in the middle of the night, then you're off your rocker.'

'Worth a try, though,' Miss Charlotte said, blithely refilling her pipe.

'Why am I not surprised?' Mrs Teach pursed her lips. 'Any excuse for you to get your kit off.'

'There are plenty of witches out there who think magical energy is hindered by clothing.' Miss Charlotte glanced at Bellamy as she lit a match, adding a tang of phosphorous to the air. 'For certain rituals.'

'What sort of rituals?' Faye asked as Charlotte puffed her pipe into life. 'Like this cone of power thing?'

'Indeed.' Bellamy pressed a hand to the map on the wall. 'Performing this kind of ritual fully clothed is like putting a sock on a lightbulb. I, too, shall be skyclad if it's any consolation?'

'It is not!' Mrs Teach cried.

'Doing this fully clothed risks complete failure, and need I remind you that we are on the precipice of invasion.'

'You're on the precipice of getting a boot up your backside,' mumbled Mrs Teach.

'Beg pardon?' Bellamy angled an ear at her.

'I'm dead against it,' Mrs Teach said, loud and clear. 'I will have no part in it. There has to be another way.'

'I'm game.' Charlotte clenched her pipe between her teeth.

'Faye. What do you think?' Bellamy asked her.

Three intense gazes turned on Faye like search-lights. She was well aware that she had been nagging her fellow witches for more responsibility for some time, but they often dismissed her appeals and urged her to pay attention, listen and learn. She would burn with anger at being written off as a silly girl by these two, but finally they wanted to listen to her, and now the decision for a pivotal ritual that could change the course of the war had fallen into Faye's lap. Where the bloody hell was an air raid siren when you needed one?

Faye sat back and folded her arms. 'I'll be honest with you, Mr Dumonde, I'm always suspicious of any fella who asks women to get their clothes off for no good reason—'

'This will save lives, Faye,' he replied. 'It will change the course of the—'

'So you keep saying, but I've seen what these ladies are capable of, and they've always managed to do it with their drawers on. I reckon we should stay dressed . . .' Faye looked at the map. 'And get more witches in.'

Miss Charlotte hummed, which Faye took as approval.

Mrs Teach wasn't as pleased with the thought of other witches moving in on their patch. 'Now, let's not be hasty—'

'Why not?' Faye shrugged. 'We can't be the only ones who can do this ritual. What does it even involve?' She turned on Bellamy and pointed at him. 'If it's just us flashing our boobs at Luftwaffe pilots, I shall be very disappointed.'

'Certainly not.' Bellamy rested an offended hand on his chest. 'And, to reassure you, Faye, we do already have other witches coming.'

'Who?' Mrs Teach asked, tensed and ready to unleash a torrent of disapproval.

'Elsie Nichols, Ophelia Babbage and Dolly Greengrass.'

'Scryers.' Miss Charlotte released her pipe from between clenched teeth. 'Good ones.'

'The finest,' Bellamy declared.

'Scryers?' Faye recalled a brief mention of these in her mother's book. 'Aren't they like fortune-tellers?'

'A common misunderstanding, Faye,' Bellamy said. 'Scrying is hopeless when it comes to seeing the future, but it is very good at disseminating magical energy over the aether, which is essential for this ritual to work.'

Faye thought about asking what exactly the 'aether' might be, but she had a more pressing question. 'Just three witches? That it? Why not get every witch we know up on the White Cliffs of Dover? Give the ritual a proper wallop and we can all keep our pants on.'

'That's a splendid idea,' Charlotte said, and Faye felt a peculiar flush of pride. Miss Charlotte hoarded praise like a squirrel with nuts.

The feeling soon vanished when she saw the frown on Bellamy's face, and it occurred to her that she might just have narked off the new High Witch of the British Empire.

'Well, this would somewhat throw my plans into disarray.' He pinched his chin between thumb and forefinger.

Faye cleared her throat. In for a penny, in for a pound. 'With respect, Mr Dumonde, you're the High Witch of the British Empire. Someone I suspect will be spending every waking moment dealing with witches like us. Now, I haven't been witching for very long, and I only really know these two here, but if they're a typical example of your everyday witch, then I reckon you need to get used to the idea of your plans bein' in a state of disarray. 'Cos I can tell you from first-hand experience, tryin' to get this lot to cooperate is like herding bloody cats. No offence, ladies.'

'Some taken,' said Mrs Teach.

Miss Charlotte briefly removed the pipe from her mouth. 'Lots taken.'

'See what I mean?'

Bellamy hunched his shoulders round and continued to pinch his chin in thought. He stayed in that position for so long that Faye thought he'd had a funny turn.

When he eventually spoke, he did so with a small smile. 'I can see you are indeed your mother's daughter, Faye Bright.'

Faye's belly did a flip at the second mention of her mother. Had he met her? She was about to ask when he started pacing and the moment was gone.

'I think your proposal is an interesting one. On the one hand, more witches equal more power. On the other, more witches increase the risk of the mission's secrecy being compromised.'

'Are you suggesting we're all loose-lipped gossips?' Mrs Teach asked in a voice so sweet it made Faye's teeth itch.

'Heavens forbid, Mrs Teach,' Bellamy replied hastily. 'The Council would simply prefer witches to work in small cells to prevent any . . . unintentional disclosures of classified information. Standard operating procedure across the entire intelligence community these days. Nevertheless, I shall investigate the viability of conscripting more witches from other areas into our mission.'

'I have some suggestions,' Miss Charlotte said.

'Very good. Jot them down, if you'd be so kind. In the meantime, what do we do? We proceed as planned.' Bellamy reached into his tweed jacket and produced a parchment bound in red ribbon. 'Ladies, allow me to reveal my cone of power.'

Mrs Teach grimaced. 'I thought we agreed no nudity?'

∅

The three witches were deposited by the truck at the bottom of Gibbet Lane.

'I don't trust him,' Charlotte said.

'You don't trust anybody,' noted Mrs Teach.

'Him less than most.' Miss Charlotte crinkled her red lips. 'But ... it's a good ritual. It could work.'

Faye kicked at the flaky dirt by the side of the road, all churned up by the army trucks that cut through the crossroads. 'Has anyone asked Vera about this?'

'She would dismiss it as completely barmy.' Mrs Teach gripped her handbag so tight that the leather creaked.

'I'm not so sure.' Charlotte tapped ashes from her clay pipe on the grass verge. 'A cone of power – when done properly – can be incredibly effective. It's a question of piling on the magical energy, and if there's enough of us we could do some real damage.'

Mrs Teach took a step forwards, lips tight. 'I'm still not convinced that our magic has any place on the front line of warfare. We shouldn't get involved.'

'We are involved,' Charlotte snapped. 'Whether we like it or not. The most destructive force the world has ever seen is about to kick down our door, and I for one want to start kicking back. War is upon us, and we have the power to fight, which means that sooner or later we will have blood on our hands, either through inaction and allowing the suffering of others, or through taking the fight to the enemy and risking our own necks. I would much rather fight.'

'Me, too.' Faye clenched her fists. 'I mean, it scares me proper, but I ain't one for sittin' back and doin' nothing.'

Mrs Teach raised her chin. 'Never let it be said that I was ever one to shy away from a challenge, but let's not forget what happened with Otto Kopp. We put our head above the parapet and the whole village ended up under his power.'

'Not all of it.' The words had barely left Faye's lips when regret made her blush.

Mrs Teach pressed her fingers against her chest. 'Oh yes, let us not forget, Miss Charlotte, that we are in the presence of the most powerful witch that Bellamy Dumonde has ever met.'

Charlotte smirked. 'Indeed.'

'Oi, I didn't ask him to say that.' Faye wagged a finger. 'I knew you lot would get all funny.'

'Who's getting funny?' Mrs Teach looked away

from Faye. 'Just don't get any ideas above your station, young lady.'

'My station?' Faye's hands went to her hips. 'I reckon you two have made it clear what my station in this little coven is.'

'We're not a coven,' Miss Charlotte said.

'We're witches. There's three of us. I reckon that's a coven.'

'That word is an invention of anthropologists,' Miss Charlotte said in a way that suggested everyone should know this, not least Faye. 'You forget that I've been around long enough to see our profession become categorised like some sort of exhibit in a museum. I blame the Victorians. They went pottering all around the world, started labelling things, then putting the names down in bloody books, fixing them in place.'

'If we ain't a coven, then what are we?' Faye narrowed her eyes. 'You called us something when we were in the barn with the poltergeist. Higgledy-something.'

'Hecate,' Mrs Teach corrected her.

'That's it.' Faye snapped a finger and turned back to Miss Charlotte. '*We are Hecate*, you said. What's that?'

Miss Charlotte gave a little smile as she recalled her words. 'Oh yes, I did, didn't I? Hecate is an ancient Goddess. I like to invoke her now and then. She's often depicted with three faces or as three women – maiden, mother and crone.'

Mrs Teach stiffened. 'I most certainly am *not* the crone.'

Charlotte grinned. 'Don't worry. I'm happy to be

60

the crone. I am the eldest by some margin. You can be mother, Mrs Teach. A testament to your abilities with a teapot. Which I believe makes you the maiden, Faye.'

Faye's feet shuffled in the dirt. 'What does that mean?'

'Whatever you want it to, Faye. Don't let men with books define who you are.' Charlotte glanced up at the sun. 'It's gone noon. Get some rest. Lots of work ahead, ladies. Let us speak again tomorrow. Fully clothed, and ready for war.'

SCRYING TONIGHT

Jennifer Gentle had discovered that it was jolly easy to kill a witch. Dolly Greengrass, a scryer of some repute, was a trusting old soul and partial to tea and carrot cake. Jennifer simply had to lace a slice with the requisite amount of strychnine and sit quietly as the old dear gasped for breath on her living room rug. It was a crude way to bump someone off – Jennifer didn't have time for anything magical – but it was awfully effective.

Dolly's black cat joined Jennifer on the armchair, claws scratching at the antimacassar as she watched her primary source of food pass away in front of her.

'Don't worry, Dolly, dear,' Jennifer reassured her as she snapped open her silver powder mirror and applied a little lipstick. 'Just don't fight it, hmm? Not long now.'

How wrong Jennifer had been. It was an hour before Dolly stopped rasping and kicking her legs, and a further two hours for her to stop twitching.

If killing a fellow witch was relatively easy, albeit time-consuming, then getting rid of the body was a more complicated kettle of fish. At least it was dark. One of the benefits of the blackout, even in a city as busy as London, was that it allowed for all kinds of nefarious activities after sundown.

Jennifer's ambulance was parked in an alley behind Dolly's terraced house in Plumstead. She popped out of the back door, down the garden, past the outhouse, skipped along the alley and opened the ambulance doors. All around her were darkened houses. Their windows were criss-crossed with tape, blackout curtains drawn, and the indigo sky was swept by distant searchlights. Somewhere on the main road a couple chuckled as they made their way home, but their voices soon faded.

Jennifer had never been much good at creating a glamour to hide herself, but she had always struggled to be noticed anyway. If she ever attended a party, people would step around her as if she were a hat stand. Trying to get the attention of a waiter in a restaurant was a futile task for Jennifer Gentle. Teachers at school would forget her name. As would uncles and cousins. Even her mother referred to her as 'girl' more often than not. Now she could finally use that anonymity to dispose of her victims.

❦

Jennifer left the ambulance doors open, dashed back inside and returned soon after, dragging Dolly's strychnine-stiffened body and dumping it in a wheelbarrow. This was the most risky part of the whole evening. If someone were to stumble upon the scene it might just look a smidge unsavoury, what with Dolly being all twisted and contorted and such. Though Jennifer was sure that the combination of the ambulance, her charm and her First Aid Nursing Yeomanry uniform should be able to convince even the most suspicious of snoopers that she was helping a poorly elderly dear get to the hospital. If that didn't work, she had a cheese knife concealed in her cap that would make short work of anyone's jugular.

ẞ

Getting Dolly from out of the wheelbarrow and into the ambulance was no mean feat and involved a couple of planks, a long run up, and some choice cursing. When Dolly finally landed on the deck of the ambulance, the woman still had a puzzled expression on her face, as if she continued to wonder in the afterlife just what the dickens had happened. Jennifer had spent the better part of a fortnight getting herself in Dolly's good books, asking for advice on scrying, doing the old dear's shopping, helping around the house, and expertly teasing little nuggets of information from her about some secret exercise that the Council of Witches was preparing. Once she had everything she needed, Jennifer received the order from her sponsor. Kill Dolly. She was the third witch Jennifer had killed that month. All with the same skill in common. Scrying.

Scrying was one of those witching skills that had long gone out of fashion, due to its association with fake mediums and fortune-tellers, though truthfully it had very little to do with seeing the future. Jennifer loved how scrying enabled her to become one with the aether, that place beyond our plane where voices from the past, present and future would whisper to her like echoes of a dream. She would never feel alone when she was scrying.

Very few real witches practised it these days, but Jennifer found she had a knack for it and, despite her mother's protestations that it was a pointless and dying art, she became rather good at it.

That, and cold-blooded murder.

Jennifer closed the ambulance doors, but not before Dolly's cat darted inside. She thought about trying to negotiate with the thing, but in her experience, cats rarely listened and if this little girl wanted a ride with her late mistress then that was up to her.

Jennifer hopped onto the ambulance's driving seat and started the engine. It was an American ambulance – left-hand drive – which she had collected yesterday from the docks in Liverpool. The Yanks didn't want to get involved in the war, but they were happy to donate aid and ambulances via slow boats from New York. This ambulance wasn't due at the depot till tomorrow, so it was all hers tonight.

She liked life behind the wheel of an ambulance. No fuss, no distractions, just the road and a destination, which this evening was a nice spot a short distance upriver of the docks.

It had been Mother's idea for Jennifer to join the

FANYs. Mother was always forcing her to join things. The woman was what some had called 'a socialite', but Jennifer preferred a more honest term and referred to her as a 'drunken old sauce' within earshot as often as possible.

Daddy died just before Jennifer was born. Mother frittered Daddy's inheritance in no time on endless dreary dinner parties with toffs in black tie and gowns, boring Jennifer senseless with talk of fascism and annexing the Sudetenland, whatever that was. Jennifer became a dab hand at lip-reading at these affairs. Sitting unseen in a corner or at the end of a dinner table, interpreting idle gossip, seeing her mother make excuses for her daughter's silence, then, after a few too many gins, telling them what she really thought of Jennifer, which wasn't much.

Mother was always telling Jennifer to meet people, as if more dullards in her life was the solution. Signing Jennifer up for the FANYs was almost the last straw, but when she was assigned to ferry ambulances across the country – a drive from Liverpool to London and back again was not uncommon – she discovered that she quite enjoyed it.

Mother often enquired if she had made any friends there. Jennifer cheerfully invented entire cliques of Hilarys, Bettys and Rubys just to shut her up. It was when Mother started asking when she was going to meet a chap and settle down that Jennifer decided Mumsy had to go.

Mother had a touch of the magic herself and had

dabbled in augury in her youth, but she had never taken to it. Certainly not as much as she had to money or summer parties, gin and sherry. Mother's magic was slight, almost non-existent, through lack of practice. When she realised Jennifer had the power – and significantly more than she could cope with – Mother urged the girl to write to other witches.

'Find a mentor,' Mother had said, giving her a list of witches and their addresses. 'Have them show you the way and all that, because frankly, my little sausage, I've forgotten most of it.'

Jennifer wasn't surprised. Mother could barely find the kettle in the kitchen some mornings, weaving her way to the booze cabinet instead.

Being young and obedient, Jennifer did as she was told and wrote polite and formal letters to every witch on the list.

She didn't get a single reply.

Except one. That came much later. Years later. She didn't even recall writing to him, but he replied with such passion and enthusiasm and promises of power that she couldn't possibly say no. He was her mentor now. Jennifer never mentioned him to Mother. Mostly on account of her being dead.

Mother never understood what magic meant to Jennifer. To Mother it was an impediment to being accepted by people with estates in the country and expensive jewellery. A thing to be swept under the carpet. To Jennifer it was all she ever needed. A mirror, a quiet room, some blood and the power of the moon.

Jennifer had shown Mother the mirror that final night. It had been Jennifer's birthday, her twentieth, and she told her mother that she could see visions and talk with other scryers from across the world. Mother had scoffed, but when she looked into the mirror her eyes glazed over, never blinking, as Jennifer whispered into her ear. When the air raid sirens howled, Jennifer's mother went for a walk. She never came back. That had been Jennifer's best birthday ever.

⌀

Jennifer reversed the ambulance down the ramp towards the Thames. She ratcheted the handbrake into place and hopped out of the cabin. The summer night was chilly, and a damp, mossy aroma emanated from the old stone of the dock houses. Barrage balloons lined the river, the only witnesses to her crime.

Jennifer opened the back doors of the ambulance to find the cat licking its bits.

'Oh, I say. Have you no dignity?'

The cat gave her barely a glance as she continued her intimate grooming.

Getting Dolly out of the ambulance was somewhat easier as Jennifer simply shoved the woman out, letting her land with a hard crack, then dragged her contorted corpse down the ramp to where the lazy Thames slopped against stone.

Jennifer rolled Dolly into the water. The old woman floated away, and Jennifer kicked herself for not weighing her down with some bricks in her pockets. Ho hum.

One of the advantages of the war was that there was no shortage of bodies turning up in peculiar places. When Dolly was inevitably found, the police would start an investigation, but she would be just another anonymous corpse to add to the glorious dead.

Jennifer got back in the ambulance. The cat came with her.

⚶

She drove back to her lodgings above the Wellington Pub across the road from Waterloo Station. The sun was just rising as she locked the door behind her. As she tossed her FANY hat across the room, there was a scratching at the door. She opened it a crack and Dolly's cat zipped inside and made herself at home, curling up in an armchair.

Jennifer stood before it, hands on hips.

'I pay more for a room of my own, and I don't much fancy sharing with anyone else, least of all a wretched cat.'

The cat blinked at Jennifer and licked her lips.

'Fine,' Jennifer said. 'I'll supply milk, but you get your own food, understand?'

The black cat curled into a ball and closed her eyes. Jennifer wasn't sure who had benefited most from this negotiation. She had a nagging feeling that it wasn't her.

The dawn light crawled across the floor and the first trains at Waterloo began to rumble and chuff outside. Jennifer kept the curtains closed and pulled a rug from the centre of the room, revealing a chalk circle. She lined it with a black ash of her own making, then took a suede bag from a drawer and placed it in the circle, sitting cross-legged before it.

The world beyond the circle began to dull and fade away. She opened the suede bag, taking out an obsidian mirror. A slate of Mexican volcanic rock, it was the size of a small plate, black and shiny. She positioned it directly before her, then removed more items from the suede bag. She arranged two wax discs engraved with her rune and the rune of her sponsor on either side of the obsidian mirror. Between them, at the twelve o'clock point, she placed a gold disc the size of her palm.

She then took a small amber glass dropper bottle from the bag. It was three-quarters filled with blood – that of her sponsor. Essential for the communication she was about to make.

Jennifer unscrewed the lid, squeezed the dropper to suck up just enough blood, then oh-so-carefully ejected a bubble of it onto the gold disc.

She moved the disc onto the obsidian mirror. The little ball of blood rested there for a moment, then began to vibrate with the magical energy generated by the mirror. The magic would last as long as the blood fizzed. Mere minutes, so no time to waste. She closed her eyes and rested her hands on the wax tablets.

She heard a clock downstairs chime the hour. The pre-arranged time for her weekly communication with her sponsor. Scrying had many uses. Visions of the future and the past, projecting nightmares and dreams into the minds of others, and it also made for a jolly useful long-distance telephone.

'Hello, Jennifer,' a breathy Bavarian voice said, tickling her ear as if he was crouched directly behind her. 'Is it done?'

'It is.' A smile curled on her lips.

'Excellent. I knew you would not let me down.' Otto Kopp's voice oozed with a sinister joy. 'There are two more on the list. When will they be dealt with?'

'I'm already bosom buddies with both of them. Simply give the word.'

'The word is given,' Otto said. 'You must eliminate them today.'

'I beg your pardon?' Jennifer's voice tightened to a screech. 'You want me to bump-off two witches in a day?'

'By lunchtime if possible,' Otto said with the breezy confidence of a man who regularly murdered a couple of witches before breakfast. 'Once you have done as I ask, contact me again. Bellamy's little plan is already under way. He will call for you any day now.'

Bellamy. That unctuous little twerp. Jennifer couldn't wait for the day when she would see him writhing about as strychnine robbed him of his faculties. If that meant pulling a double shift, then so be it.

'Two in a morning,' she said. 'Consider it done.'

'Oh, I will Jennifer, I will,' Otto replied with an exhalation of joy. 'Finally we will have our revenge on those who have spurned us. Finally we will destroy the Council of Witches.'

LOSING ONE'S RAG

Faye and Bertie had known one another all their lives. They were friends. Mates. Chums. They were so familiar that, were one to fart audibly in front of the other, there would be chuckles and no recriminations.

That changed at the Woodville Summer Fair last month. Not only had they 'stepped out' as a pair for the first time, they had held hands, and Faye had even pecked Bertie on the cheek. Who knows where it would have ended up, were it not for the supernatural chaos that ensued?

Since then, they were still friends, mates and chums, but there was something else. Something new. A burning and passionate desire to fondle one another and plaster their lips together for a start. But they had been so busy – Bertie in the pub and the Home Guard, and Faye with her witchery and the ARP – that they hadn't found a moment to do anything beyond hand squeezing and suggestive winking.

Both hoped that would change tonight. The

Reverend Jacobs' Social Evening would be held in the village church hall in aid of the Motor Ambulance Fund. For one shilling and sixpence they were promised tea, biscuits, musical numbers and sketches.

Faye had promised Bertie the best night of his life. He started getting ready as soon as his shift ended. He had a hot bath, washed his hair with soft soap and had a proper shave. All the while his mind raced at the thought of just being with Faye. It didn't matter a jot what they did, just that they were together.

At a quarter to seven, Bertie shuffled into the saloon bar of the Green Man. Normally, Bertie's uneven legs meant there was little chance of him swanning in like some suave star of the silver screen, but tonight he wore a cork lift in one shoe, evening out his limp and giving him a little swagger.

Bertie had hoped that the pub would be empty, and that everyone would already be enjoying the Reverend's social extravaganza. But the Reverend had a strict no-booze rule after a punch-up at the last jumble sale, and so the Green Man was rammed with villagers getting a swift pint in before the festivities.

All eyes fixed on Bertie. He wore a cornflower-blue blazer that pinched his arms and flared about behind him like a cape. His trousers had been ironed with a crease like the blade of a bayonet and his shoes were polished to perfection. His usually straw-like hair had been forcibly flattened into a kind of bale atop his head, and he was scrubbed so clean that he had rediscovered long-lost freckles.

Mr Baxter was leaning against the bar and was the first to speak. 'Bertie, you've just reminded me I need to stick some more straw in my scarecrow up the allotment.'

This got a roar of laughter.

'*What are you lot laughing at?*'

A voice blasted through the saloon like a gale, silencing everyone in an instant. Bertie froze in the doorway as the speaker walked in from behind the bar, the heels of her shoes clopping on the floorboards. At first, no one recognised her. It was a girl in a pretty summer tea dress, complete with flutter sleeves and light ruffles of lace. Her hair shone and was neatly brushed and held in place with a clip. She might even have had a bit of lipstick and mascara on, but those who spoke of it later were so befuddled by what they saw, they couldn't be sure.

Bertie knew who it was. Though, for a moment, he thought he was dreaming. It sounded like her. She wore the same specs, and had the same narrow-eyed squint when she was angry.

It took him a few moments to find his voice. 'F-Faye?'

'Evenin', Bertie.' Faye smiled, revealing a smudge of lipstick on her front teeth. 'You look very smart.'

'You look grand,' Bertie said. 'That's a lovely frock.'

'It's me mum's. Bit tight around the bum, but it's all right, isn't it?' She gave a little twirl as the pub burst into cheers, and someone gave a wolf whistle. 'Oi!' Faye jutted out her jaw and pointed at the crowd. 'I ain't some sheepdog, so don't be whistlin' at me like one. Understood?'

As one, the crowd shrank back from her, nodding.

'Thank you, Faye.' Terrence was standing behind the bar, arms folded. 'I do love it when you terrify my cherished customers.'

'All I'm saying is if I want to wear a frock, I'll wear a frock, and I'll do it without the comments and whistles, thank you very much. And if Bertie makes the effort to look like a dandy, then we should tell him how smart he looks.' She stood, hands on hips, expectant. 'Well, tell him, then!'

The patrons all jolted in their seats, then narrowed their eyes, silent as they gathered compliments in their heads before delivering a jumble of murmurs in Bertie's direction. 'Very smart, I like the colour, nice shoes, Bertie,' and so on.

Faye gave the boy a wink.

'Thank you, everyone,' Bertie replied.

'That's more like it.' Faye took a step forwards and something crunched under her feet. She glanced down at the floorboards where jigsaw pieces were scattered far and wide.

'What's this?'

Terrence cleared his throat. 'I thought I'd have a go at one of them jigsaw puzzles you mentioned.'

'You're supposed to put them together, Dad, not fling the bits all over the place.'

'I must confess, I lost me rag with it.' He sneered at the pieces on the floor.

'How can you lose your rag with a jigsaw puzzle?'

'It's just putting a picture back together that some other twonk took apart. What's the point of that?'

'It's supposed to be relaxing!' Faye said, raising her voice.

'Well, it ain't!' Terrence yelled back.

'I can see that!' Faye hollered, making Bertie flinch. Everyone in the bar was gawking at them, wide-eyed. She took a breath and lowered her voice. 'P'raps you should find a different hobby, dear Father?'

'P'raps I will.'

'Good. We shall discuss it later, perchance?'

'I'll be counting the minutes, darling daughter.'

'You do that.' Faye turned to Bertie and smiled. 'Shall we?'

Faye extended the crook of her elbow and Bertie slipped his arm through it. He tingled at the very touch and never wanted to let go.

'I think we shall,' he said, and they strode out of the pub into the summer evening.

A heartbeat later, everyone else in the saloon hurriedly downed their drinks and scrambled after them, keen to see how this would turn out.

Terrence was left alone in the pub with his jigsaw pieces.

'Oh, ta la, then.'

REVEREND JACOBS'
SOCIAL EVENING

Faye insisted on paying her own one shilling and sixpence entry fee. Larry Dell was taking the money on the door.

'Evenin', Larry,' Faye said, then leaned forwards. 'How's the barn?'

Larry looked around furtively, glancing at Bertie, unsure if he should speak.

'You can trust Bertie,' Faye reassured Larry. 'He's seen some really peculiar stuff, haven't you?'

Bertie nodded and gave a little shudder.

Larry puffed out his cheeks. 'Tell the truth, Faye, I've not had the nerve to go back. My dogs keep barking at the barn like there's someone in there, and whenever I go near it, the place gives me the chills. Am I being daft?'

'Get a move on!' a voice called from behind Faye. She glanced back to see twenty or so folk from the pub queueing up behind her.

'You're not being daft.' Faye rested a hand on his shoulder. 'I'll pop over tomorrow morning and see what I can do.'

'Bless you, Faye. Bertie. Have a lovely evening.'

⌀

The hall was dominated by the proscenium arch stage at the far end, and Reverend Jacobs stood front and centre, giving his best Ko-Ko from *The Mikado*, singing about a little list, while Faye's fellow bell-ringer Mrs Pritchett played an upright piano that was almost in tune and sang along with the chorus bits.

Chairs were set out in rows facing the stage, and almost half of them had occupants, all listening politely and slurping tea.

Lined up against the wall were two tables with a tea urn and teetering piles of china cups, and plates of McVitie's afternoon tea biscuits. Faye and Bertie made a beeline for them, as did the pub patrons as they were herded into the hall. Never let it be said that the British public would ever pass up the opportunity for a cuppa and a biccie.

The bustle rather drowned out the Reverend, who not only raised the volume of his singing voice but also its pitch, putting him at odds with Mrs Pritchett's piano. She glared over her shoulder at him, but he carried on regardless.

Faye and Bertie took a couple of seats in the front row.

'You're not limping,' Faye whispered to Bertie. 'Have you got your lifts in?'

He nodded. 'Just the one, to even me out.'

'I thought they hurt your feet?'

Bertie shrugged. 'It's a special evening.'

'Bertie, poppet,' Faye said with a warm smile. 'It won't be special for you if you're in agony all night. You don't have to wear it if you don't want to.'

Bertie held his breath for a moment. 'It's killing me arches,' he admitted.

'Then take it out.'

'Now?'

'Now.'

Bertie untied the shoelaces of his right shoe and slipped it off, revealing a much-darned Argyle sock.

'That's better.' He wiggled his toes.

Mrs Birdwhistle, who worked at the Post Office, looked on aghast as Bertie plucked the cork lift out and tucked it in the inside pocket of his blazer. Both Faye and Bertie gave Mrs Birdwhistle a smile and she twisted back to watching the show.

Reverend Jones brought his song to a screeching conclusion and a smattering of polite applause.

Bertie put his shoe back on, feeling himself again, as Reverend Jacobs introduced the next act.

'Thank you, thank you, and how lovely to see so many of you suddenly arrive. Has the Green Man run out of beer?' This was received with a boozy cheer from some. 'Quite. And, without further ado, it is my great pleasure to introduce Betty Marshall on the spoons!'

Captain Marshall's daughter, a girl the same age as Faye, dragged a chair to the centre of the stage with all the enthusiasm of a woman condemned to be shot by firing squad.

Within moments she was slapping the spoons against her thighs, hands, arms, knees and even her forehead in an infectious rhythm. It wasn't long before the audience started clapping along.

Faye was relieved to be doing something with her hands. She wanted to hold Bertie's. Actually, she wanted to do a lot more than that, but that would have to wait till after the show. They had both been really looking forward to finally having some time alone, but first they had to sit in a hall full of their village neighbours who were all aware of the burgeoning relationship and had opinions and expectations for the pair of them.

Trouble was, Faye had no idea what those expectations were. All she knew was they kept getting knowing looks from the other villagers and it made her all squirmy.

Faye glanced at Bertie sitting next to her, a sweet smile on his face as he enjoyed the show, bobbing his head in time with the rhythm. Suddenly all those gawping faces meant nothing. Sitting here with Bertie felt right and proper. But she had to wonder how many more moments like this they would have together. Bellamy's cone of power ritual sounded like it was going to take over Faye's life for the foreseeable future. How would Bertie feel about her gallivanting off on secret missions? Would he have the patience to let her go without any explanation and wait for her return?

There was another round of applause as Betty finished her act on the spoons.

'Marvellous, simply marvellous.' The Reverend Jacobs led the applause. 'And now, ladies and gentlemen, the Morris Men of Woodville!'

'Oh, blimey. Really?' Faye said a little too loudly, getting a glare from the Morris Men, who took to the stage in their get-up of sashes, waistcoats, braces and straw hats. It was well known in the village that the bell-ringers and the Morris Men did not get on for reasons lost to time and gossip.

Mr Shackle – local butcher and squire of the Woodville Morris Men – moved stage front, his accordion wheezing with his every step, and wagged a finger at Faye.

'Have some respect, young lady.' Mr Shackle had a neat little tache like a pair of wings, and it did a little shuffle whenever he got cross. As the village butcher, he had gone a little mad with power since rationing started. 'This is an ancient tradition.'

'Ancient?' Mrs Pritchett cackled at the piano, then turned to Faye. 'They were formed in 1927, Faye. I've got socks more ancient than this lot.' She dropped the lid on the piano and the reverberation echoed around the hall. 'Get on with yer prancin' about, you great wallies,' she said, before shuffling off the stage.

Mr Shackle curled his lip, then started playing his accordion. As the Morris Men began hopping about and clacking their sticks together, Faye shrank into her seat, feeling the eyes of everyone behind them judging her.

Bertie's rough-skinned hand slipped into hers

suddenly and gave it a gentle squeeze. Her heart trembled and she squeezed back.

She leaned closer to Bertie, to whisper a thank you in his ear and to promise him that there was more to come than hand-holding, but instead she blurted out, 'What the blimmin' 'eck is he doing here?'

'Eh?' Bertie shook out of his reverie. Faye was looking over his shoulder at a man a few rows behind. He wore a tweed suit and had a neatly trimmed beard. He sat next to Mr Loaf, the funeral director, and smiled politely at the Morris Men's display. 'Who is he?'

Faye made a pained face. 'I'm not allowed to say. Sorry, Bertie.'

'Witchy stuff?'

'Witchy stuff. Top-secret witchy stuff.'

'Fair enough.' They turned back to the stage just as the Morris Men drew their ceremonial swords and formed a circle with them.

'He's a funny one,' Faye whispered. 'Bit full of himself and doesn't like people answering back.'

'And he's working with you three? I give him a week.'

Faye smiled and squeezed Bertie's hand tighter. She hated keeping secrets from anyone, especially Bertie, but since she was made to sign the Official Secrets Act a couple of months ago, it was all she seemed to do these days.

The Morris Men clattered to the end of their display and got a smattering of applause from the audience. Bertie's hand slipped from Faye's.

'Back in a mo',' he said.

'Where are you off to?'

'We're on after Mr Paine,' Bertie said, as if that explained everything.

'Who's on?' Faye asked, then saw Mr Hodgson through one of the village hall doors with the box of handbells from the tower. He was joined by Mrs Pritchett, Miss Burgess, Miss Gordon and the Roberts twins. She looked back at Bertie whose cheeks were ripe as fresh tomatoes.

'I . . . I thought you knew.' He was frozen in a crouch halfway between getting up and staying.

'You're ringing handbells and you didn't ask me?' The hurt started, of all places, behind her nose. She felt tears of betrayal welling.

'We reckoned you were busy with all your secret witchy stuff.' Bertie bit his lip. 'And you've always said that handbells ain't proper ringing.'

'That's not the point. At least ask me, so I can say no.'

'I'm sorry.' Bertie was still stuck in his half-crouch, his head darting between Faye and the other ringers gathered by the door to the stage. Mr Hodgson tapped at his wristwatch. 'What shall I do?'

'What songs are you playing?'

'"Amazing Grace", followed by "Sing as We Go".'

'The Gracie Fields song? You're doing "Sing as We Go" on handbells?'

'It's a bit of a mess, if I'm honest.'

Faye sat back, smiled and folded her arms. 'Go ring those bells, Bertie. "Sing as We Go", eh? I shall enjoy this.'

Bertie scurried away, joining the other ringers as they slipped through the stage door. All except Mrs Pritchett, who returned to the piano as Mr Paine, local newsagent and ARP man, strode onto the stage. Faye liked Mr Paine. He was tall and broad and thoughtful. She had no idea he could sing. He wore an impressive tuxedo with a white dickie bow, and he looked like Caruso as he bowed to the audience. Mrs Pritchett – whose playing up till now had been very much in the *you-hum-it-I'll-play-it-on-the-old-Joanna-pub-knees-up-style* – tickled the ivories with a lightness of touch that was warmly welcomed after the puffing and thumping of the Morris Men.

Faye recognised the opening melody of 'Sonny Boy', the weepy, sentimental ballad made famous by Jolson, and a favourite of amateur tenors the world over. Mr Paine's voice was sublime. He sang with passion and expression, and Faye heard sniffs from the audience as men and women reached for their hankies.

As Mr Paine once more urged the titular boy of the song to clamber onto his knee, the lights in the hall flickered, and somewhere in the distance an air raid siren wailed.

There were tuts of annoyance throughout the hall at such a beautiful song being interrupted. Faye heard someone mutter, 'Bloody Luftwaffe, ain't they got nothing better to do?'

Somewhere a baby's wailing created an eerie harmony with the siren. Chairs scraped as the audience got to their feet. Mr Paine had stopped singing immediately, and his training kicked in. He cupped his hands around his mouth and spoke in a loud, even voice. 'Air raid, ladies and gentlemen. Calmly make your way to the nearest available shelter, please. There's one under the stage, and a couple of Anderson shelters on the allotment. Air raid, ladies and gents. This way, thank you.'

AIR RAID

Air raids were an exercise in tedium and terror. There was the annoyance of stopping everything to get yourself and your family crammed into the little tin Anderson shelter in your garden, or the rabbit-hutch-like Morrison shelter under the dining table, or just squeezing under the stairs while the Luftwaffe roared overhead. That was when the dread seeped into your very bones. The thought that some fella, hunched over the controls in a Junkers, could make the difference between life and death with a twitch of his thumbs, weighed heavy. Just last week, a couple of bombs landed near Therfield Abbey during a raid. The abbey's ancient ruins were untouched, but Mr Hodgson took great delight in letting everyone know that, had those bombs been released just a couple of seconds later, they would have landed smack bang on top of the Green Man pub. Quite how Mr Hodgson figured this out, no one knew, but Terrence very nearly barred him for life for even mentioning it.

The worst bit was the waiting. Listening to the planes drone overhead, fading away, then returning, sometimes circling, and all you could do was sit there and hope that it wasn't your unlucky night.

As Mr Paine gave instructions from the stage, Faye felt that now-familiar combination of annoyance and panic. She wasn't one for curling up into a ball and praying for the best. She and Bertie marched up to the stage.

'Reporting for duty, Mr Paine, sir.' Faye gave a snappy salute.

'Me, too,' Bertie said with a little wave. 'I know I'm not ARP, but I do like to be helpful.'

Mr Paine was a tall chap anyway, but seeing him four feet up on the stage gave him the look of Gulliver in Lilliput.

'Ah, Faye, Bertie.' He looked down at them, hands on hips. 'Perfect timing. The shelter under the stage –' he glanced into the wings where people were lining up to squeeze into the large storage area beneath his feet '– looks full. I'll make sure those folks are all right. Can you two man the door and point people to the nearest shelters on the allotments? Though most of 'em should probably hurry home.'

'Wilco!' Faye saluted again and dashed to the big double doors at the back of the hall with Bertie hobbling after her.

The place was already half empty by the time they got there. The villagers had become used to the drill, especially since the raids had increased in regularity these past few weeks.

'Allotment shelters that way, ladies and gents, or pop off home if it's quicker,' she said as Bertie held the door open and the last few villagers hurried out into the summer twilight.

The evening was still warm and the scent of honeysuckle filled the air. The moon was in its first quarter, the sky fading from purple to black, and bats flapped around the bell tower. It would have been a perfect evening were it not for the wailing siren and the drone of the bombers.

Distant searchlights stabbed the night sky and started fanning back and forth.

'All clear,' Mr Paine said as he puffed towards Faye. They closed the door and made their way down the Wode Road. 'We'll go to the ARP post and fetch our helmets, then—'

A flash lit up the eastern horizon, leaving green dots dancing about on Faye's eyelids. A heartbeat later came the boom of impact.

'Mansfield Airbase,' Bertie whispered.

Two more impacts turned the sky white.

'I reckon you're right,' Mr Paine said, picking up the pace. 'Hurry.'

A barrage flickered night into day once more, and Faye felt the ground beneath her heels tremble.

'They're getting a proper thumping tonight,' Bertie said, thinking back to the raid just a few nights ago. 'They've had it bad before, but never like this.'

They rounded a bend by the antiques shop to find Mrs Teach, Miss Charlotte and Bellamy Dumonde standing facing one another.

'Make your way to the nearest shelter, please, folks.' Mr Paine waved his arms in a herding gesture.

Miss Charlotte and Bellamy remained where they were. Mrs Teach stepped before the big man.

'Mr Paine, what a splendid job you're doing on this frightful evening.'

'Mrs Teach, I must insist that you return home and take shelter immediately.'

'Have I shown you my engagement ring?' She extended her hand, flashing the ring under Mr Paine's nose.

'I, er ... no. What?' In the blink of an eye, he was staring helplessly at the twinkling diamond.

'My late, beloved Ernie got me this. Isn't it beautiful?'

'It ... yes ... I ... shelter.' Mr Paine was well and truly mesmerised.

'Mr Paine, I suggest that you get whatever you need from the ARP post and then take cover with all the other villagers. I think Faye can handle it from here. Can't you, Faye?'

'Er, yeah, if you say so, Mrs Teach,' Faye said with a shrug.

'Shelter, yes.' Mr Paine jogged over to the ARP post and put on his helmet. 'Right away,' he added before hurrying back around the bend and out of sight.

'Will he be all right?' Faye asked.

'He'll be safer in his shelter than out here.' Mrs Teach glanced up at the sky as anti-aircraft flak began to flash and bang. She then turned to Bertie. 'Bertie, have I shown you my engagement ring?' She held the ring before Bertie's wide eyes. Faye smacked it away.

'Don't be daft,' she told Mrs Teach. 'It's Bertie. He's seen more magic than most.'

'Regardless,' Mrs Teach said, 'you should get to shelter, my boy.'

'I reckon we all should.' Bertie jabbed a thumb back up the Wode Road towards the pub.

'Nonsense, lad,' Bellamy said firmly. 'Pop off home and leave this to us.'

'I ain't leaving.' Bertie shuffled to the ARP post and grabbed a pair of binoculars from where they sat on a shelf next to the tea caddy and biscuit barrel. 'But I can keep watch,' he said defiantly, standing on a park bench by the Post Office and scanning the night sky. Searchlights swept across the stars, occasionally revealing clusters of bombers.

'Don't say we didn't warn you,' Bellamy muttered as he strode over to Faye. 'Good evening, Faye. I thought this might be the perfect opportunity for a little demonstration of my cone of power ritual.' He took her by the shoulders and moved her into position. 'We stand at the cardinal points. North, south, east, west. You, Faye, are west, facing the east. Do not move until I say so. Is that clear?'

'Roger that.'

'If we're quite ready?' Miss Charlotte took her place, standing east, facing west. Mrs Teach stood south, facing north.

'We are.' Faye flexed her fingers.

'Good. We haven't much time, so please do exactly as I say.'

'Bellamy.' Faye raised a hand and the man grimaced with irritation.

'Yes?'

'We're not doing this in the nuddy, are we?'

'We convinced him otherwise.' Mrs Teach smiled sweetly.

'You convinced him,' Miss Charlotte said. 'I was up for it.'

'This is merely a demonstration,' Bellamy snapped. 'A rehearsal, if you like. There isn't time for the full ritual, and besides I don't have enough goose fat to keep us all warm. Now, please remain still and silent.'

He drew a dagger from within his tweed jacket. The handle was black, the blade looked like it could slice the very air.

Bellamy stood on his spot, north, and closed his eyes. 'Listen to my words. Four words. Listen to them and when I say so, recite them with me.' He said four words in a language that Faye had never heard before. The tip of the dagger glowed red, then orange, then white. 'Now,' Bellamy said, reciting the words over and over. Faye, Mrs Teach and Miss Charlotte joined in.

The words made Faye's tongue feel fat, her teeth seemed too big for her mouth. It was as if the words knew that their being uttered out loud was forbidden and they were doing whatever possible to prevent it. Out of the corner of her eye she could see Bertie lower his binoculars. He gave her a smile that was parts encouraging, loving and terrified. Faye winked and he resumed keeping watch.

Once the witches had the hang of it, Bellamy stopped singing and busied himself with the glowing dagger. He raised it before him and drew a pentangle in the air. The lines sizzled like fireworks, hovering before them. He moved to stand before Mrs Teach and did the same. Hers glowed white. He moved to Miss Charlotte. Her pentangle burned red. He stood before Faye, looking into her eyes as he made the shape. Her pentangle was golden as the rising sun.

A familiar sensation of power took root in Faye's feet and began rising.

Bellamy returned to his north spot and slipped the dagger back into his jacket. He extended his hands to Miss Charlotte and Faye. They took his and extended theirs to Mrs Teach. They formed a circle and the power in Faye surged. Her skin tingled like it was both hot and cold, and her breathing became deep and slow.

'And now we dance!' Bellamy cried. 'We move in a circle and do not stop reciting the words. Now, ladies, now!'

They began to move, slowly at first, chanting and dancing with a little skip. A flutter of magic stirring in their bellies.

'Bombers!' Bertie cried over the singing. Faye glanced to where he stood, the binoculars pressed to his eyes. 'They're on the run.'

Faye's head rocked from side to side as they danced faster and faster. Bertie and the world around became a blur, tilting and spinning. The flutter inside her bloomed.

The air within the circle crackled and bolts of energy whipped between the glowing pentagrams. A clouded veil manifested around them, forming a dome that drained the world of its colour. But inside the circle was a whirlwind of magical energy.

'This is the vertex of the cone,' Bellamy yelled over the noise. 'It protects us and channels the magical energy created by the dance. It won't be as powerful as our cone at Dover, but this village is positively dripping with magic and should give us plenty for demonstration purposes.'

Streaks of light scratched Faye's eyes and she snapped them shut.

Bombers. Bertie was right. She could see them in her mind's eye.

The magic inside her grew and grew.

A formation of twelve. Four groups of three. The air around them bursting with flak.

Faye couldn't resist as the power flushed through her veins.

One of the bombers shook, then fell apart, a wing spiralling to the sea. The others banked sharply, turning home.

Faye's mind felt weightless, her body clenched like a fist.

All bombers except one. It stayed on course and was heading directly towards Woodville.

'There's one coming this way,' Bertie said, sounding like he couldn't quite believe it. His voice was muffled by the protective cone. 'It's too low, I think it's been hit and—'

An explosion scorched the sky as a bomb landed somewhere on the coast road. It was followed by another, and another. They were getting closer and closer, each impact making the ground quake. Windows and letterboxes in nearby houses rattled.

'It's coming straight for the village!' Bertie cried. 'Faye! Everyone! Take cover!'

'No.' Faye opened her eyes. All around them, the energy from the glowing pentangles fizzed and snapped.

The strange sensation in Faye was overwhelming. Every part of her was trembling. There was a weird inevitability about its rising within her. Nothing she did would be able to stop it.

A searchlight waved across the night and Faye got a glimpse of the rogue bomber, the drone of its engines growing loud and louder.

'No. Not my village!' she cried, breaking the circle and moving to the centre. She was giddy with magical energy. Her thoughts were foggy and the only way she could clear her mind was to be rid of this thrumming inside her. She summoned the power of the moon without thinking. She grasped the light of the pentangle and took it without asking. She gathered it all in her hands, forming a ball of energy brighter than the sun. Gritting her teeth, she hurled it at the approaching bomber.

The power that burst from her hands split the air like lightning, whipping over the village and into the bomber's starboard engine.

The propeller housing burst into orange and red flames, the fire consuming the aircraft in moments.

Smoke belched from the cockpit as the plane lurched over. It chugged directly overhead, and Faye, Bertie and the others ducked as the Junkers only just missed the bell tower of Saint Irene's. With a final wail, it crashed into a field on Harry Newton's farm in a ball of raging flame.

Silence followed. The protective veil was gone. Faye stood, surrounded by the others, looking at the palms of her hands.

'What ...' She could barely speak. Her mind was her own again, but she had to force herself to breathe. 'What did I just do?'

CRASH

Faye's hands were clammy, her mouth was dry. She could only stand and stare at the pulsing red glow of flames that silhouetted Saint Irene's Church.

Bertie was the first to run to her. Mrs Teach and Miss Charlotte were close behind. Bertie took Faye by the elbow and steered her towards the bench by the Post Office.

'I just ... I just killed them all.' Faye could only stand and tremble. 'In that plane. They're all dead. 'Cos of me.'

Bertie held her a little tighter.

'They were going to bomb the village, Faye,' Miss Charlotte said in a soft voice. 'They were going to kill us. It's war.'

'You saved us,' Mrs Teach whispered in Faye's ear. 'I don't know how, but you did.'

Faye knew. She used Bellamy's cone of power to draw on the power of the moon. That's what had been building inside her since her encounter with Otto. And now she was rid of it. She felt guilt at the relief that flooded her. Her mind was back to something like normal. It was like the clouds clearing after a storm.

'No one should be able to do what she did,' Miss Charlotte whispered urgently to Mrs Teach. 'That was raw magical energy. She should be burned to a crisp.'

Bertie said nothing, simply wrapping his arms around her, and she loved him for it.

'Truly remarkable.' Bellamy looked at Faye the way one might at a juggling dog. 'Faye Bright, how did you do that?'

'Don't know,' she lied, sniffing a tear away. 'Just don't ask me to do it again.'

Bellamy twitched, desperate to interrogate her further, but deciding that perhaps now wasn't the right time. He turned and faced the church, hands on hips, looking at the red sky. Somewhere in one of Harry Newton's fields a plane was burning. 'Was that a success? I'd say it was, rather.'

'It took all four of us to send back twelve planes,' Miss Charlotte said. 'And who's to say they weren't headed back anyway?'

'They were heading south-east, except for that one.' Bertie nodded towards the flames. 'I reckon he was hit and wanted to go out with a bang.'

'I'd say he did that and then some, eh?' Bellamy raised his eyebrows.

'And we're utterly exhausted,' Mrs Teach added, then nodded to Faye. 'And this one will need all the tea in China before she recovers.'

'Yes, yes.' Bellamy puffed and flexed his lips in a display of concern. 'Poor lamb. But still ... imagine what more of us could do, hmm?'

Faye could hear their voices, but they sounded like they were in another room. The fog had gone from her mind, but it was still a jumble. She knew she would never be the same. Faye had known villagers who had died, of course. There had been a funeral for poor Herbert Finch only a few weeks ago. The poor lad was lost at sea with his ship, and he wasn't much older than Faye. But she had never imagined that she might have to kill someone herself.

'What have I done?' she muttered again, her head resting on Bertie's chest.

'What you had to do,' Mrs Teach told her.

'How many are in a bomber like that?' Faye asked.

'Looked like a Junkers JU88,' Bertie said, matter-of-factly. 'Crew of four.'

'Four.' Faye's voice cracked.

'Four crew trained to kill by the Luftwaffe,' Bellamy added hastily. 'Don't forget that.'

'I bet one of them lads didn't want to be there. I bet he'd rather be at home playing football, or drinking beer, or whatever they do in Germany.'

'Surely this isn't your first kill, Faye?' Bellamy sounded surprised. 'I read the reports. You were instrumental in vanquishing a demon.'

'He wasn't human.'

'He might've been once,' Bellamy said.

'Oh, what? Really?' Faye crumpled into Bertie who gently stroked her back.

'Yes,' Bellamy continued. 'And I'm sure Harry Aston perished after your encounter with him, so you should count that one as an assist.'

'I'm not sure you're helping.' Miss Charlotte put herself between Faye and Bellamy.

Mrs Teach and Bertie helped prop up Faye. 'Let's get you home, petal.'

☙

Faye slept. Faye dreamed. She played those moments over again and again, but it always ended the same. Faye knew she had no choice, though it gave her little solace. She had been scared and acted in fear to save herself, and now people were dead because of her.

And that power. It was gone. For now, at least. Though the feeling of it rushing through her was unlike anything she had experienced before. The sheer relief of unleashing it had been almost joyful, but now she felt a dark self-loathing, because a little part of her missed it.

She rose with the sun and found her father in the kitchen in his Home Guard uniform. He had just boiled the kettle and was pouring a cuppa. He offered her one and she gladly accepted.

'Didn't know you had a shift last night.' Faye thought about telling him what she had done, but she knew it would only worry him. She pasted on a weak smile.

'I didn't, but a bomber crashed on Larry Newton's farm, and they needed someone to stand guard, so I volunteered.' Terrence took a box from the shelf by the door and placed it on the table. 'Poor Larry's chickens were spooked. They won't be laying for a few days. Have we got enough powdered eggs?'

Faye gripped her teacup with two hands. 'You saw the bomber? What was it like?'

'Flat as a pancake.' Terrence popped on his reading glasses as he inspected the box. On the top was an illustration of a clipper ship at sea. 'Like someone had taken a bloody great hammer to it.'

Faye's heart turned cold. She sipped her tea, feeling the warmth trickle down her gullet. Miss Charlotte's words came back to her. It's war. They were going to bomb the village. Faye had saved lives.

The warmth of the tea reached her belly. She took another sip and started to feel herself again.

Terrence took the lid off the box, revealing dozens of slivers of wood.

'What's that?' Faye leaned closer to her father, desperate to change the subject.

'Mr Gilbert and Mr Brewer popped in for a quick drink last night and I told them of my hobby predicament. They got this in a house clearance and said, as it wasn't exactly the sort of thing they could sell in their antiques shop, that I could have it for free.'

'What is it?'

'A ship in a bottle.'

'Looks like a bunch of twigs.'

'Well, I have to *make* the ship first, don't I? I make it, then ... pop it in a bottle.'

'Where's the bottle?'

'I supply the bottle. Luckily for me, I'm the landlord of a pub and I've got a few goin' spare.'

'There's a war on, Dad. Glass is in short supply.'

'I doubt the country will fall to the Nazi jackboot due to bein' short of one bottle.' He unfolded the instructions that came in the box. It kept unfolding until it was the size of an Ordnance Survey map and completely hid Terrence from view. His muffled voice came from the other side. 'Blimey.'

Faye wanted to ask him about the ship and how it would fit in the bottle. She wanted to witter on about any old nonsense, but she kept seeing that bomber come crashing down in flames.

'Were there . . . bodies?'

Terrence lowered the instructions.

'Were there *what*?'

'At the bomber.' Faye's mouth was suddenly dry. 'Did you see any bodies?'

'You're a bit morbid this morning.'

'Was there?'

''Course there were. The thing didn't fly itself. The army's taken over now, so I reckon the bodies are gone, so you're too late if you want to see 'em.'

'No, Dad, I really don't.'

⌘

She went anyway. She couldn't help herself. She walked past the church and up towards Larry's farm. The crash site was cordoned off, but there was a crowd of people huddled in front of the bomber having their photo taken, including Larry.

The bomber was a sorry crumpled wreck, as flat as her dad had described. The tail end had broken away and the fuselage was riddled with bullet holes and blackened by flames and smoke. *That weren't me*, Faye thought. Bertie was right. It had been hit.

'Say cheese!' the photographer said, and those gathered duly obliged.

Faye turned back the way she came, remembering she'd promised Larry Dell to look in on his haunted barn, grateful for something to do.

⚡

Faye basked in the peace of a late-summer Sunday as she walked, though August was her least favourite month. It was hot, listless and the warm huff of manure from muck-spreading could sneak up on you at any moment. All the raspberries were past their best, and the apples and blackberries weren't quite ripe yet. Even the bees looked aimless as they scavenged for pollen. She passed a field of cows, who could only stand about, waving flies away with their tails.

Hurricanes flew high above. Twelve of them in tight formations of three. If Mansfield had been hit last night, then it hadn't stopped them from flying. Faye imagined the pilots sitting in those tight little cockpits. The growl of the engines, the smell of fuel, the wind buffeting them about and the lads wondering how many of them would make it back.

Faye wanted it all to stop. This war had made her a killer. Or was it magic that had done that? If it wasn't for magic, she wouldn't have been with the others. She would've been with Mr Paine, doing her bit in the ARP, and not crashing bombers with bolts of magical energy.

Faye felt something in her belly. The same familiar swirling feeling inside. It wasn't much, but it was back. Her fingers began to tingle as her heart sank. Was there no getting rid of this sensation? She made her hands into fists and kept walking.

When Faye arrived at the barn there was no birdsong. No creatures moved in the hedgerow. The bees stayed away.

Faye stepped inside, and the sweat on her back turned ice-cold. She dared to look into the dark corners, but the burned pilot could not be seen. Spoils of war lay about. Larry boasted that several planes had crashed in his fields, and he was gathering quite a collection. Propeller blades, a tail wing, a pilot's fur-lined flight jacket.

At the edge of her hearing came a crackle. A tinny hiss of white noise. Faye turned to find a pilot's helmet and goggles resting on an oily workbench among the nuts and bolts.

The hiss would occasionally break and a voice could be heard.

Faye stepped over to the workbench and picked up the helmet, turning it over to find headphones and a microphone built into it.

'Hallo?' the voice came from the headphones.

Faye slipped the helmet on.

'Hallo? Can you hear me?' It was a man's voice. His accent wasn't English. Czech, maybe? Or Polish? Faye had served a few in the pub.

She moved the microphone in the chin-strap closer to her lips. 'I can hear you. Where are you?'

'Behind you.'

Faye spun to find the burned pilot looking at her with a desperate smile, reaching out with both arms.

CZAROWNICA

Faye hissed through her teeth at the wretched man's appearance. For a ghost he looked all too real. His entire right side was burned. Half of his scalp was bloody and raw, dotted with little tufts of hair. One of his eyelids was melted shut, and the skin around his right cheek, jaw and neck was blistered and red. His right ear was completely gone, leaving only a hole. And it all glistened fresh, and the air was filled with the aroma of pork crackling. His trousers were blackened, but his left side was largely untouched. As he stepped forwards into a shaft of light he took on an ethereal glow, but Faye could better see the man he was. His angular cheekbones and sharp green eyes. He was older than most of the pilots she saw in the pub, maybe mid-thirties, and he wore RAF blues with a life vest that had recently been painted yellow. A patch with the word 'POLAND' was sewn under the wings on his left arm.

'Please.' He reached out to her, his hands trembling.

She could hear his voice both through the headphones on the helmet she wore, and in the barn. 'What am I doing here? Why can't I leave?'

He looked solid enough, but every now and then the light fell on him in such a way that Faye could see straight through him. How do you tell someone they're a ghost without upsetting them?

'What's your name?' Faye spoke into the flight helmet's microphone. 'I'm Faye. You're a pilot, yes?'

'Flight Officer Leopold Byk, 145 Squadron. I have to report back. I . . . I don't know . . . I think . . . I think I was shot down. I don't know how I got here.'

'Leopold, look at me.' Faye directed him towards her eyes. 'Look at me, Leo. Can I call you Leo?'

He nodded.

'Leo, what's the last thing you remember?'

He looked down, crow's feet forming around his good eye. 'I . . . don't know.'

'Were you in a plane? A Spitfire? A Hurricane?'

Leo looked at his burned hand, turning it over. He slowly reached up, touching his face. It didn't seem to hurt him, but he knew that something was wrong. He reached around the ear that wasn't there. His lips parted as he looked at Faye. 'What has happened to me?'

'Were you shot down, Leo? Did you bail out?'

He ignored her, rushing to the other side of the barn where the canopy from a Hurricane leaned against the wall. Most of the glass was broken, but a few shards remained in place. Leopold leaned over the glass, angling his head to catch his reflection.

'Leo, I don't think that's such a good—'

He wailed and staggered back, his head in his hands. He began cursing in Polish and raised a leg to kick the canopy over.

His leg passed straight through it.

He froze in place, wondering what had just happened.

'Leo.' Faye tried to keep her voice even. 'I think you're a ghost, matey.'

'No!' He turned on Faye, marching towards her, jabbing a finger. 'I don't believe in ghosts. I am a pilot. I want to fly. I want to fight!'

As he spoke, the barn's rafters began to rattle and dust drifted down. Planks in the walls shook as if there was a storm, and a hammer flew up from the workbench and smashed into the barn door.

Faye ducked under the workbench.

'Leo, please, listen to me! I can help!'

Leo stood in the centre of the barn, knees bent, teeth gritted, fists clenched. He let out an almighty cry and all the tools that hung above Larry's workbench took to the air. Saws, hammers and chisels whirled around Leo, getting faster and faster. He raised his arms and they hurtled away, stabbing into the barn's shuddering planks.

The aircraft scrap now rose. Propeller blades, wheels and bits of fuselage began to swirl about.

Faye thought back to when they banished the barn's other poltergeist. It was tricky even with three of them, but at least he seemed to know that he was dead and behaved as such. This chap would take a little more convincing.

Faye needed to dash to the barn doors, but one knock from a flying propeller and she was done for. A piece of Hurricane tail fin smashed into the workbench, and Faye ducked down.

'Sod this for a game of soldiers.' Faye closed her eyes and drew on a tiny ember of energy. There it was. A glimmer in the darkness. It grew and grew. Faye controlled her breathing, letting it bloom, waiting for the right moment.

Glass smashed, and something heavy crashed in the rafters, but she kept her eyes closed. Here it came. Nearly. Nearly.

Now.

Faye stepped out from the under the workbench, opened her eyes, raised her arms and cried, 'STOP!'

The air around them shimmered, the barn stopped shaking and anything airborne dropped to the ground immediately.

Outside, magpies could be heard chattering.

Leopold looked at her, backing away.

'Leo, listen to me.' Faye tried not to let the fear trembling in her belly affect her voice. She had done it again. She had unleashed more power than she was expecting and it scared her. 'I can help you.' She just hoped that he wouldn't ask how.

'How?' he said.

Faye winced. 'I'm not entirely sure, but I know a little something about the supernatural, and I have friends who can—'

'You were here before.' Leo backed away. 'You and

112

two others. Those women. You were with them, and there was another pilot.' He began pacing around the barn. 'Yes, he was a Nazi, he was angry, and you were chanting and you ...' He stopped. 'You sent him to the dark place.'

'Yeah, that was a bit of a kerfuffle.' Faye gave a cheeky smile in the hope they would start laughing about how scary it had been.

'You ...' Leo's voice dropped to a fearful whisper. 'You are *czarownica*!'

'Let me guess.' Faye folded her arms. 'That's Polish for witch?'

'*Tak!*' He scurried back. 'The air – there, by the doors – it broke apart, and there was a great ... nothing. A darkness. A cold, undead eternity. I can't explain.'

Faye followed his gaze to the barn doors. 'That's where the other pilot went.'

Leo nodded.

'But you didn't follow?'

He shook his head.

'I don't blame you.' Faye strode over to the barn doors and pushed them open, stirring up dust in the air as the summer sun beamed in. 'But it's not there now. Have you tried to leave?'

'You think I haven't?' Leo raised a finger. 'Observe.'

He marched towards the open doors, arms straight as if on parade. Bathed in sunlight, he vanished as he stepped over the threshold.

'Leopold?' Faye took a step back. 'Leo?'

'I'm here.'

Faye spun to find Leo standing behind her.

'Happens every time.' Leo's anger faded as a terrible realisation sank in. 'I'm ... I'm dead, aren't I?' His head dropped, his shoulders sagged. All the fight was gone from him. 'Please, I need to be alone for a while. I remember now. I remember what happened. Leave me.'

Faye had met enough pilots in the pub to know there were times not to ask any questions. Mostly, they just wanted time to think.

Faye crossed the threshold and felt the August sun on her face. 'I promise I'll come back. I'll find a way to help you, Leo. In the meantime, try not to spook Larry's dogs.' She looked back inside the barn, but he was gone.

⌀

Jennifer Gentle's morning had been fractious to say the least. Elsie's murder was fairly straightforward. She was no fool, but over the summer Jennifer had befriended her with cheerful smiles, listening to the old bat's boring stories with the patience of a saint. As far as Jennifer was concerned, trust was essential when it came to offing someone in a clean and efficient manner. It's astounding how effective a few shopping trips and afternoon teas are when it comes to lowering even the most suspicious person's defences.

Elsie now had enough faith in Jennifer to allow her to make the tea, effectively signing her own death warrant.

Jennifer was in a hurry and so tripled the strychnine

dose, hoping that would chivvy things along. Elsie took one sip of her Darjeeling, commented that it tasted peculiar, then fell face first onto the Portobello Road faux Persian rug in front of her fireplace. Nevertheless, it still took a good twenty minutes for her to stop twitching as Jennifer paced back and forth, checking the clock.

Ophelia was a different matter entirely. A tall and broad woman who would make a splendid full back that any rugger team would be proud to have, was already packing her clothes and scrying mirror. She boasted that she had received a telegram from Bellamy Dumonde just before Jennifer arrived. She refused to say any more – 'Loose lips sink ships and all that' – but she did let slip that she was catching a train to Dover and therefore wouldn't have time for tea as she began herding Jennifer from the house.

Jennifer took drastic action, smiling sweetly as she slid her knuckledusters into place. She punched Ophelia in the schnozz before wrestling her to the ground. There followed a clumsy and ugly fight that ended with Jennifer strangling Ophelia with a belt from her raincoat. Not ideal, but she would float down the Thames just like the others, with that same puzzled expression on her face. They were both lying stiff in the ambulance for the moment. Jennifer would dispose of them tonight.

For now, Jennifer sat exhausted in her scrying circle, Dolly's nameless cat in her lap, delivering a report to Otto.

'Jennifer Gentle, you do not disappoint,' he said when she was done. 'What an efficient and ruthless ally you are.'

'Ophelia was going to Dover,' Jennifer said. 'To meet Bellamy, one assumes.'

'You assume correctly,' Otto said. 'And you will be taking her place. You see, Bellamy will be desperately in need of scryers for his tedious little ritual and I have sent a telegram on behalf of the late Dolly Greengrass. She apologises for dropping out at such a late hour and recommends a young noviciate witch called Jennifer Gentle to take her place. She names you as one of the finest scryers she has ever known.'

Jennifer's skin tingled with excitement. 'Will he believe that?'

'He cannot allow his ritual to fail, Jennifer. There's too much at stake for him to be so choosy. I wouldn't be surprised if a telegram was already on its way, begging you to come to Dover.'

Jennifer bristled at the thought of being anyone's last, desperate choice, but she let it pass. 'And I'll be going?'

'Oh, you most certainly will. Everything has been leading to this, Jennifer Gentle. There's someone very special that I want you to meet. A very special young lady indeed. I want you to become her best friend. And then I want you to kill her.'

BERTIE'S GIFT

'I went for a walk. I'm fine.' Faye was flanked by Mrs Teach and Miss Charlotte in the snug of the Green Man, with only half a cider to defend herself. A walk was something of an understatement. After leaving the barn, she popped along to reassure Larry Dell that, yes, he still had a ghost in his barn, but it was all in hand. Then she decided to wander along the coast road. The gentle lapping of water on shingle helped soothe her mind, despite the ever-present barbed wire, barrage balloons and other invasion defences. As she walked, the tide retreated, revealing a sandy shore. She took her plimsolls and socks off and wriggled her toes in the water.

It was when she nearly ended up in Herne Bay that she decided to turn back. The sky was a duck-egg blue when she arrived at the Green Man, and the half-moon was high and bright. The pub was packed, and Bertie waved, trying to get her attention. Faye waved back, feeling a pang of guilt. She wanted to talk to him, especially after their special night had turned out to be such a disaster, but she somehow knew as soon as she stepped into the saloon that her sisters-in-magic would be waiting for her and they wouldn't accept being second in line. Faye gestured to Bertie that she would speak to him soon, then joined the others in the snug.

'Are you sure you're all right, petal?' Mrs Teach tipped her head to one side in concern. 'We were worried.'

'I'm tickety-boo. I just needed to sort me head out, is all. Let's not keep banging on about it.'

'I think it's good to talk things over,' Mrs Teach said. 'Get it all out, I say.'

'So I've heard,' muttered Miss Charlotte, before giving Faye a bit of side-eye. 'Where did it come from?'

'Where did what come from?' Faye tried giving a bit of side-eye back, but it made her eyeballs hurt.

'That power. It was extraordinary.'

'Was that a compliment from the mighty Miss Charlotte?'

'An observation. Have you ever channelled that kind of power before?'

Faye hadn't told them what happened in the darkness with Otto Kopp. The sensation of being all-powerful and feeling the ancient magnificence of the moon coursing through her veins. It just hadn't come up. Actually, that wasn't true. Faye had done all she could to avoid talking about it, because if she said it out loud then it was real. There was no running from it now.

'I dunno,' Faye said. 'Must've been the ritual.'

'Then why didn't we all have it?' Charlotte asked.

Mrs Teach placed a hand on Charlotte's wrist. 'Give it a rest.'

Faye caught a look that passed between them. Faye's power had clearly been the main topic of discussion all day. She had to tell them.

'I've had it once before,' Faye said, noticing that both of them sat a little more upright. 'When I was at the standing stones hiding with the German kiddies, and I stepped through to the darkness. Otto was there, and he was using the moon's power. And the only way I could stop him was to take it off him. I'm not sure how I did it, but I could feel the moon in my hand. Only it wasn't a tickle in me palm. It was like a punch, and I was able to keep it inside me.' She looked up into their astonished faces. 'And it's still there. I reckon that's where the power came from last night. But that's normal, right? You've got it, too?'

Mrs Teach took a sip of gin that turned into a gulp.

'No.' Miss Charlotte stuffed tobacco into her pipe. 'It is not.'

'Each of us has our own way into magic, Faye.' Mrs Teach ran a finger around the edge of her empty gin glass. Her voice was quiet and more thoughtful than Faye had ever heard it. 'Some will speak of the Goddess, or a power on this Earth, or the moon, that we all draw on. We use rituals and spells to reveal these mysteries to us. And, yes, it may be that those of us with the gift have something inside us that allows us to practise magic, but I've never seen anything like the display you put on last night.'

'I have.' Miss Charlotte started lighting her pipe. 'And it didn't end well.'

'When was this?' Faye asked.

'I don't like to talk about it.'

'Otto said you would be like this.' Faye watched as the two women pulled offended faces.

'Like what?' Mrs Teach said sulkily.

'He said something about you two fearing me, resentin' me. Turning on me.' Faye raised a finger before either of them could object. 'But I'll be jiggered if I'm going to let some stunted little Nazi stir up trouble between us. Agreed?'

'Agreed,' Mrs Teach replied immediately.

Miss Charlotte needed a nudge in her ribs from Mrs Teach but she finally repeated, 'Agreed.'

'I don't rightly know what happened last night,' Faye said. 'It scared me. But that doesn't mean you should be frightened of me. I ain't plannin' on becoming the next Otto Kopp any time soon.'

'We wouldn't let you,' Charlotte said, pipe clenched between her teeth in a rictus grin.

'Good, I wouldn't want you to.' Faye took a sip of her cider. 'What's next?'

Mrs Teach leaned forwards. 'Bellamy is very excited. He says he wants to escalate the stratagem.'

'Why don't he speak English?'

'He wants a bigger trial of the ritual,' Charlotte explained.

Fay nodded. 'Which'll mean more of us, I s'pose.'

'There are buses coming from the New Forest, London, Suffolk, Norfolk and Essex.'

'They're all comin' here? Blimey, it's going to be crowded.'

'Not here.' Charlotte nodded south. 'Dover. The cliffs. The closest point to occupied France. Bellamy claims to have created some kind of camp for us.'

'Don't like camping.' Faye grimaced. 'I like a proper lavvy nearby.'

'A camp?' Mrs Teach crinkled her lips. 'He never mentioned that to me.'

Charlotte grinned. 'He wants it to be a surprise.'

'Well, he can stuff it up his jumper. I will not be camping. He will put us up in a hotel. A bed and breakfast at the very least.'

'How long does he want us there for?' Faye asked. 'I've got ARP, and Dad will miss me if I'm not helping at the pub.'

'Probably till the full moon next week,' Miss Charlotte said.

'A week in a tent?' Mrs Teach quivered at the very idea. 'Not on your nelly. Myself and young Mr Bellamy Dumonde shall be having words.'

'You've got till seven in the morning,' Miss Charlotte said. 'That's when we leave. I have commandeered a vehicle and we'll meet at the war memorial.'

'What do I about my ghost?'

Mrs Teach patted Faye's wrist. 'We looked, petal. There is no—'

'I had a blimmin' conversation with him this afternoon. His name's Leo and he's a Polish Hurricane pilot and he's only just twigged that he's popped his clogs. I promised Larry that I'd sort it out.'

Miss Charlotte exhaled a cloud of pipe smoke. 'You know what to do.'

Faye shook her head. 'No. Not what we did to that other fella. That was proper 'orrible. There has to be a better way.'

'There may well be, but we simply don't have the time,' Charlotte said.

'But—'

'But nothing. Our mission is for the good of the nation. The good of the living. Larry and this Leo chap will understand. Seven sharp, ladies. Don't be late.'

Faye sat stewing where she was as the two witches left the pub, Mrs Teach furious and determined to find and harangue Bellamy, Miss Charlotte's jaw set and ready to do her bit.

After Faye calmed down, she collected the empties and started washing up in the little kitchen behind the bar. It wasn't long before Terrence popped his head in.

'You all tickety-boo?' he asked.

Faye wondered what her dad would think of her taking down a Luftwaffe bomber single-handedly last night. He would probably be proud, but Faye didn't much fancy telling him that his daughter had become a killer.

'Not exactly, Pa, truth be told,' she said, drying a pint glass till it squeaked. 'My boo is most certainly lacking in tickety, but it ain't nothing to worry about.'

'Witchy stuff?'

'Witchy stuff. Speaking of which, I'm going away for a few days. Can't say why.'

Terrence's face hardened. 'Is it ... dangerous?'

'No, but I will have to put up with Mrs Teach and

Miss Charlotte for longer than usual, so wish me luck as you wave me goodbye.'

'Are those two behaving themselves?'

'As much as they ever do. They might be a pair of odd fish, but they understand this magic malarkey better than anyone, so they're all I've got, I suppose.'

'I wish your mum was here.' Terrence rested a hand on her shoulder. 'She'd be able to help with what you're doing.'

'I wish she was here, too, Dad, but ...' Faye twisted the corners of her lips. 'I don't know if she would approve.'

Terrence frowned. 'Oh yeah?'

'For months and months now, we've all been sayin' there's a war on. Food's short, there's a war on. Petrol's short, there's a war on. Beer's gone up a penny, there's a war on. All it's been to us so far is a bit of an inconvenience. But y'know what, Pa? There really is a war on, and it's getting closer every day. It's going to make us do things we might regret.'

'Like what, exactly?'

'Thing's that'll change us. All of us. I worry this village might never be the same.'

'Nothing ever stays the same, Faye, much as we might like it to. But so long as we've all got each other, we'll be ...' Terrence smiled. 'Tickety-boo.'

Faye leaned into her father's arms and he gave her a squeeze.

'How's the ship in a bottle coming along?' she asked, speaking into his chest.

'It ain't exactly the HMS *Victory*, and it's more glue than wood, but it should be seaworthy in a few days. Well, bottle-worthy.'

The clock struck the hour and he patted her back.

'Bertie's due a break,' Terrence said. 'He's been funny all afternoon.'

'Funny how?'

'Like the cat who got the cream. He wants a word with you.'

§

'How are you, Faye?' Bertie was sitting on the two-seater in the living room. He'd made them both tea and opened a packet of biscuits.

Faye flumped down next to him and started talking and she didn't stop until her tea was cold. She told him about the power she felt, how it was strange and uncontrollable, and how she was sick at the thought of it all. Bertie, for his part, sat and listened, and never interrupted. The more Faye spoke, the more overwhelmed she was by a sense of relief to finally get it all off her chest. When she was done, Bertie calmly poured a fresh cuppa from the pot. They sat and said nothing as they drank. Faye felt his hand slip into hers.

'You know what this means, don't you, Faye?'

Faye shook her head.

'That you feel so bad about it? It means you're still a good person. It's folks that take pleasure in killin' that scare me. You just did what you had to do.'

'What did I ever do to get a friend as good as you,

124

Bertie?' Faye could feel her smile returning. 'Sorry I ruined our special night.'

'No, you didn't. And besides, there'll be other nights.'

'There will, though not for a little while.'

'What do you mean?'

'I'm off for a few days. Can't say where. Top secret and all that. But I'll be back before you know it and then we'll have another special night and ...' Faye trailed off as a thought occurred to her. She licked her lips. 'Or ... or there's now.'

Faye glanced at the living room door. Bertie followed her gaze. It was only slightly ajar. They both turned to one another and realised in the same moment that they were alone.

Without saying a word, both Faye and Bertie knew there would never be a better time. Parting her lips, Faye moved closer to Bertie, feeling his breath on her skin. Her heart began to quicken in anticipation as his hand brushed against her knee, sending a tingling sensation all the way up to her—

'Don't mind me!' Terrence crashed into the room, heading straight for the drinks cabinet.

Faye and Bertie jolted like they'd been jabbed with a cattle prod.

Bottles clinked as Terrence sorted through them. 'Mrs Pritchett asked if we had any absinthe,' he muttered. 'Can you believe that woman?'

'Do you have any?' Faye's voice was a little wobbly as she reached nonchalantly for her tea.

''Course I do.' Terrence stood triumphant, a

half-empty bottle of the mysterious green spirit in hands. He blew some dust off it.

'Where did you get that from?'

'Long story. Don't ask.' Terrence headed out of the door, then stopped and peered back around. 'And don't think I don't know what you two are up to. Bertie, have you shown her your big surprise yet?'

Terrence ducked out of the room, leaving the door ajar and the burble of chit-chat and laughter from the saloon bar came drifting in, reminding the red-faced lovers that they were far from alone.

'What big surprise?' Faye asked, wondering if she really wanted to know the answer.

Bertie's face lit up. 'Wait till you see this. It arrived this morning.' He hobbled over to where his coat hung by the back door, a big, silly grin on his face.

'What's arrived? Bertie, you look like you're about to have conniptions.'

Bertie took a parcel from his coat pocket. It was the size of a notebook and wrapped in paper and string. The string had been cut and retied in a knot. He handed it to her. 'I had to check if it was right before I gave it to you,' he said by way of explanation.

'What is it?' Faye undid the knot.

'I saw it advertised in the back of the *Daily Mirror*.' Bertie clasped his hands together. 'And I know it's no replacement for what you lost, but I reckoned what's the harm in getting you one? It might be useful, so—'

'Bertie, you're bletherin'.' Faye tore at the paper wrapping.

Two eyes stared at her from the cover of a paperback book. She slipped the book out to reveal the cover and title.

THE ANCIENT AND MYSTERIOUS
SECRETS OF MAGIC,
CONTAINING ARCANE RITUALS OF THE
OLD MASTERS AND ADEPTS,

BY ZADOC BROWN.

PRICE $5.

The pair of eyes loomed over the title, and in the corners were illustrations of a moon, candles, a skull and a pentangle.

'It's come all the way from America,' Bertie said. 'Actually, a warehouse in London, but before that it came all the way from America. It's been on order for weeks.'

'Thank you, Bertie.' Faye turned to the first page. There was a photograph of the author, sitting cross-legged and wearing a turban and a robe. He didn't look Hindi, so Faye wondered why he had that get-up on. Faye flicked through more pages. The magic and rituals written in here were unfamiliar to her. Words like 'mastery' and 'ascendancy' were used more than was possibly healthy. All the magicians in the illustrations were men with pointed beards and Devil's peaks, dressed in long, flowing robes. She suspected old Zadoc Brown was a bit of a huckster.

'Is it right? Is it any good?'

Faye looked up into Bertie's expectant face. Who would want to disappoint that happy mush?

'I reckon it might come in handy.' Faye made a point of nodding at a few of the illustrations as if they had some kind of magical significance. That made Bertie beam, so she continued turning pages. 'I mean, who knows? There might be something in here that changes the course of the war.'

'Now you're bein' funny.' Bertie nudged her playfully. 'I know it's not your mum's book, but it says it has all sorts of ancient rituals and stuff. I thought it might help.'

Faye was about to apologise when she turned one more page and froze.

'Actually, Bertie.' Faye's eyes fixed on the page. 'This might be exactly what I'm looking for.'

She had turned to a chapter halfway through the book. There was an illustration of a robed man standing in the centre of a pentangle. Above him were the words: HOW TO BRING PEACE TO RESTLESS SPIRITS.

LEO'S MISTAKE

After sunset, Faye hopped on her bike and cycled to Larry Dell's barn. She thought about calling on Mrs Teach and Miss Charlotte but didn't want a repeat of their previous agonising encounter with a ghost. And besides, the ritual in the book that Bertie gave her looked simple enough. A circle drawn on the ground, some candles and a few carefully chosen words would open a door to allow the stranded spirit to leave. Or so the wise and ancient author Zadoc Brown claimed. Faye wasn't entirely sure she could trust anyone whose book ended with ten pages of advertisements for more books promising to ward off the perils of the evil eye, to reveal the secrets of the missing eighteen years of the life of Jesus Christ, and a cure for baldness. But there was just enough in his writing to make her think it could work.

Faye didn't need the lamp on her bicycle. The moon was bright and gibbous. It hung over Larry's barn, a silent sentinel.

As usual, there was an odd stillness around the barn.

The creatures of the night knew to stay away. Faye carefully lowered her bike to the ground and opened the tall doors wide, letting the moonlight beam in.

'Leo?' she called, but the darkness did not respond. Then she remembered the flight helmet. She found it where she'd left it on the workbench. She wriggled it on her head and spoke into the mic on the chin-strap. 'You there, Leo?'

She heard the crackle and hiss of white noise, but no response.

The howl of air raid sirens drifted over the fields. Faye stood framed by the barn's entrance as searchlights swept across the sky. They were some distance away, so she was in no immediate danger. The horizon flashed and the delicate thunder of bombs rumbled moments later.

'Dover,' said a voice in her ear.

Faye jolted and turned to find the ghost of Leo standing next to her, watching the sky's distant display.

'They're bombing Dover. I should be in the sky. Doing something. Instead, I am stuck here.'

'You've done your bit, Leo. And you sacrificed everything. I think you're entitled to a rest.' Faye took a stick of chalk from the workbench, moved to the centre of the barn, and began to draw a circle on the floorboards. 'I have a ritual that I think will help.'

'Ritual? What sort of ritual?'

'One that will bring you peace.'

'Has it occurred to you that I might not want peace? I want to fight.'

'I hate to be the one to break it to you, Leo, but you're a blimmin' ghost.' Faye placed a candle at the north point of the circle, struck a match and lit it. 'You ain't in no state to be fighting no one.'

'I cannot give up!' Leo raged, throwing his arms wide. A gust whipped through the barn, snuffing out Faye's candle.

She stood, hands on hips. 'Then I dunno what to do for you, matey. If you won't let me help you, then Larry's going to ask my friends to sort you out, and you saw what they did to that other pilot. It didn't look like a barrel of laughs to me.'

'He had it coming,' Leo said with a growl.

'And why're you spoiling for a fight, anyway?' Faye's belly churned at the thought of the lads in the bomber she brought down. 'It ain't right.'

'You're a child,' Leo muttered. 'You don't know what you're saying.'

'I know that killing folks is wrong.'

'Those bastards took everything from me!' Leo rushed at her, his one good eye glistening with tears. His burns still looked as fresh as when they first blistered his skin. His lips trembled, but Faye stood her ground.

'Let's get on with it, shall we?'

Faye relit the candle, then stood in the centre of the circle facing it. She opened the book at the appropriate page and began reciting the ancient words as prescribed by Zadoc Brown.

Even as she spoke, she knew this was a damp squib.

131

There was no magical sensation, even in her heightened state of magical sensitivity.

A light breeze blew the candle out again.

'Is something supposed to happen?' Leo asked.

Faye flicked through the book and took another look at the illustration of the author. 'Sorry, Leo. I'm beginning to realise that Zadoc Brown was nothing more than a clever man with a second-hand turban and the gift of the gab.' She tossed the book away and leaned against the workbench, head down, hands tucked into her armpits.

Leo's head hung heavy, and he shuffled over to the barn door, looking out to the field. 'My father had a farm like this one,' he said. 'He kept cows. My sisters and I would milk them every morning. Mama, too, when she wasn't looking after her chickens. She loved them so much.'

'What did you do?'

'I was at the Polish Air Force Academy, but I helped whenever I came back.'

'Is that where you learned to fly?'

'I was an instructor. I'm older than most pilots. Slower, but more experienced. I was there on the first day of September. When the Stukas came with their bombs. I volunteered for combat. We flew P.11s. You ever see one?'

Faye shook her head.

'A good plane. The best we had, but a tin can compared to the Luftwaffe's fighters. You British promised us Hurricanes, but they never came. Our planes were old, underpowered, tired. Mine didn't even have a radio. But it was our homes, our families. We had to take to the skies, we had to fight.'

Guilt gave Faye a squeeze.

Leo continued with a satisfied smile. 'We gave them a bloody nose. I shot down a bomber.' His smile faded. 'On the second day I was hit. Had to bail out. Burned my hand. After getting treatment I was ordered to fly to Romania, then France, then here. Running. Always running.' He turned and moved towards Faye. Less aggressive than before, but no less passionate. 'But now we get to fight back. In a beautiful Hurricane. It's like being a bird. And the Luftwaffe ... now it's their turn to be afraid. My first flight in a Hurricane, I got my first kill. Second day, I got two kills!'

'All right, mate, no one likes a show-off.' Faye thought back to the pilots in the pub who spoke about their battles like they were a game.

Leo nodded. 'You're right. And that's what went wrong. I got greedy. I wanted three for three.' He looked up as clouds passed over the moon and darkened the barn. 'We were flying back to base, twelve of us, all in formation. I saw a Dornier bomber. All alone and heading back to France. I told my commander, who ordered me to stay in formation. I ignored him and attacked. I hadn't seen the Dornier's escort. Three Bf 110 fighters.' Leo glanced at Faye, twitching a smile. 'I tell myself now that I didn't stand a chance, but I should have turned back. I had time, but I was so ... so *furious*. The first shells hit my fuel tank. Petrol spilled

into the cockpit. I looked down and I was surprised –'
Leo gave a little chuckle '– to find that my legs were
on fire. I tried to open the canopy and bail out, but the
second round of shells took my starboard wing. The
sky spun around me. I hit one of the Bf 110s. I was
blinded by fire when I hit the ground.'

The clouds moved past the moon and its light filled
the barn once more.

'I remember all of it,' Leo said. 'The cold fear. The
pain. And then I found myself here with the other pilot.
I thought we had somehow survived. Strange how the
mind works.'

'Was he in the plane that you crashed into?'

'Yes. Angry man. We didn't talk much. I was glad
when he was gone.'

The sky lit up again and a distant boom rumbled
through the soles of Faye's plimsolls.

'That's Dover, you reckon?' Faye nodded in the direction of the fading light. 'I'm going there tomorrow.'

'It will be a mess.'

'Maybe. I don't know if we'll be anywhere near the
docks. It's a meeting of witches. We'll be doing our bit.'

'Other witches?' Leo perked up. 'Could they . . .
bring me back?'

'That's necromancy, Leo. I know a demon who tried
that recently and it ended very badly for all concerned.'

'If I am a ghost, perhaps I am still here to make
things right? How can I make things right?'

'I'm not sure we can, Leo.' Faye bit her lip and adjusted
her specs before saying, 'I took down a bomber, too.'

Leo snorted. 'Really?'

Faye looked at him over the rim of her glasses. 'Remember who you're talking to, Leo.'

He stiffened. 'How?'

Faye filled him in on the details. 'I was scared. Really scared. And now I feel awful for those lads.'

'You had no choice, Faye. I would have done the same.'

'You're trained to do that. You signed up to go to war. I don't want to have anything to do with any of this now.'

'Do you think my father did? My mother? My sisters?' Leo's voice was even, but Faye could sense the rage behind it. 'When my hand was healing, I got word that their farm was gone. Obliterated by the Blitzkrieg. I'm almost certain they are dead. Father might have surrendered, he was a practical man, but Mother ... She's where I get my anger from. She would have spat in the Nazis' faces. As would my sisters. And they would have paid the price. I wish I could see them all one more time.'

'I know that feeling.'

'War is here, Faye.' Leo pointed to the horizon and then the sky. 'Over there, and above us. Few of us want this, but when the enemy comes we must be prepared to fight. We've all run here to this little island. The Poles, the Czechs, the Belgians, the French. We need you and you need us. If you do not stand and fight with us, then our fate will be yours.'

The all-clear siren sounded off in the distance.

'We're all in it together, right?' Faye twitched a smile.

'We are.'

'I'll speak to my friends tomorrow.' Faye gathered up the candles. 'I'll explain that you don't want what we did to the other fella. We'll find a way to bring you peace.'

'Thank you, Faye.'

Faye took the candles to her bike and popped them back in the front basket. 'What do you do when you're alone here, Leo?'

He shrugged. 'I sleep.'

'Do you dream?'

'A little. There is only me and the moon.'

Faye tingled. 'You might not be dreaming, Leo. I think I've been to that place.'

'You might be right. I hear voices there. Some . . . are not good. Others are kind. Oh.' He raised a finger as if just remembering something trivial. 'I forgot to say. I have a message from your mother,' he said.

THE MESSAGE

Faye's feet felt like lead. Blood froze in her veins.

'This had better not be a joke, Leo.'

'I would not joke about such a thing. Her voice came to me. She said her name was Kathryn with a K, that she was your mother, and that she could not stay long. She asked me to pass on a message.'

'What message?'

'She said you need to learn to fly.'

Somewhere, an owl hooted.

'Wot?'

'That's all she said.' Leo gave a shrug. 'But she said it in a way that sounded like it would make sense to you.'

'Well, it don't.' Faye began pacing back and forth. 'What does she mean, learn to fly? In one of those?' She pointed to the tail fin of the Hurricane in the barn behind Leo.

'It's fairly straightforward. I could teach you. They have girls flying in the ATA now. Or ...' Now he started pacing as he got excited. 'Or you could steal a plane to fly in combat and we could avenge my—'

'Calm down, Leo. We're getting ahead of ourselves here. How am I supposed to learn to fly?'

'You are a witch. Can't you fly on a broomstick?'

'We don't fly on broomsticks. What else did she say? That can't have been it.'

'Her voice was fading as she spoke.' Leo frowned as he thought, and the still-fresh burns on his face made a moist, sponge-like sound. 'She said something about a book. Yes. It's all in her book. Does that make sense?'

Faye threw her hands to the night sky. 'I don't have her blimmin' book. They made me burn it!'

'The Nazis?'

'The witches.'

'They burn books?'

'It's a long story.' Faye kicked at the dirt. 'Buggeration.' Exhaustion dragged at her, and she wanted to curl up in her bed and put all of this out of her mind. 'I'm knackered, Leo. I've got a long day tomorrow and I need to get some kip. I have to go.'

'I understand. I'll be here.'

Faye picked up her bike and swung a leg over the saddle. 'If you hear from my mother again, see if you can't get her to hang around till I get back. And try not to—'

'Spook Larry's dogs. I promise. I will not.'

'See you soon, Leo.'

'Goodbye, Faye. Good luck in Dover.'

✠

'Treasure, Bertie, there's treasure in that there barn.'

Larry Dell's evening at the Green Man had been one of many refreshments. Perhaps a few too many. Larry could barely stand on his own two legs. Even when he tried the simplest movement – like heading for the loo – he began shuffling in circles. Larry's left leg remained firmly rooted to the spot as his right one staggered about. Terrence watched him do three complete circles before Bertie volunteered to take the old farmer home once he had finished the latest entry in his Battle of Britain diary.

'You're a good lad, Bertie Butterworth, a heart of gold, a heart of gold.' Larry patted Bertie on the back as they took the moonlit path to Larry's farmhouse. He had an arm slung over Bertie's shoulder.

'Tell me more about the treasure, Mr Dell,' Bertie said, feeling the tiniest tug of guilt in his belly. His offer to help Larry home hadn't been altogether altruistic. All night Larry had been quietly confessing to Bertie about the treasure in his barn, and it wasn't gold or jewels, but the kind of treasure that a lad like Bertie loved most.

'Bits of Hurricanes an' Spitfires, laddie,' Larry slurred as they turned onto the path to the cottage. 'Messerssshhh— Messer— Mess— German planes an' all. I've got the ... things ... whizzy things at the front.' Larry poked a finger into the air before him and twirled it around.

'Propellers?' Bertie's heart fluttered at the word.

''S'right, plopellerers, wheels and tails and bits of

wing and all sorts of paraphen— paraphenay—' Larry gave a little burp. 'Stuff.'

Bertie had already heard the rumours in the pub about Larry's collection, and it had been his secret desire to see it for himself, but there was a problem.

'Mr Dell.' Bertie lowered his voice to a whisper. 'You're supposed to report any wreckage, Mr Dell. It's needed for the war effort.'

Larry swung his free arm about like he was swatting a fly. 'Ah, what difference does a few scraps make, eh, Bertie? And if it lands in my field, it's mine. Finders keepers, losers weepers.'

'I'm not sure that will stand up in a court of law, Mr Dell,' Bertie joked.

Larry stiffened. He staggered back from Bertie, then lunged forwards, grabbing the lad's lapels. 'Court of law?' Spittle was forming on Larry's lower lip. This close, Bertie could smell the beer on the farmer's breath. He could also see the dent in Larry's head and was tempted to give it a little prod, something Bertie had wanted to do since he first saw it as a child, but Larry yanked Bertie closer. 'Court of law, Bertie? Court of law, you say? What's all this talk, eh? Courts, and judges, and rozzers?' The old man looked about, head darting from side to side as if expecting them to leap out of the bushes to nick him. 'You won't dob me in, will you, Bertie?' His eyes widened, the pupils drifting about as he recalled some terrible memory. 'I won't go back, I tells yer. I won't!'

Bertie shook his head vigorously. 'No, Mr Dell, I won't dob you in.'

'You promise?' Larry wrapped his arms around Bertie like a sailor clinging to a life raft.

'Scout's honour,' Bertie said, making the most solemn promise he knew.

Larry rested his head on Bertie's chest. 'You're a fine lad, Bertie. A fine lad.' He began breathing deeply and gave a little snore.

'Mr Dell?' Bertie whispered. 'Mr Dell, are you asleep?'

Bertie gripped Larry by the shoulder and stood him up. Larry snorted and opened his eyes.

'We there yet?'

'Almost.' Bertie took Larry's arm and slung it over his shoulder again, leading him home. 'Look, there's the cottage.'

Larry's whitewashed home was topped with an enormous thatched roof, giving it the look of a giant mushroom. Three Labradors came bounding over the garden gate, one black, two brown, each with the same look of disappointment and expectation.

'I reckon you're hungry,' Bertie said, and they all barked in unison. 'Let me sort Larry out first and then I'll get your grub.'

Bertie found Larry's door-key and took the old farmer into his living room. He helped him into an armchair, tucking a warm blanket around him.

'Bless you, Bertie.' Larry's voice was on the precipice of slumber. 'I'll tell you what, Bertie, I'll tell you what. Because you've been such a good lad, because of your kindness, I'll let you see me treasure.'

141

Bertie trembled with excitement. 'That's very kind, Mr Dell. When would be a good time to—'

'No time like the present, laddie. Go now. Ivy Barn. The big one on the coast path to the village. Have a good look. I know you'll appreciate this stuff more than most, just be careful ...' Larry yawned. 'There's a ... whotsit ... poultry ... geist ... thing ...' He surrendered to snores and fell into a deep sleep.

Bertie checked Larry was still breathing, then wondered why Larry would want to warn him about a chicken. Perhaps it was an aggressive cockerel? He would have to be cautious.

Bertie hurried to the kitchen where the trio of Labradors waited patiently. He filled their food bowls, gave them fresh water and asked if they could keep an eye on Larry. They all chuffed and nodded as if they were used to his inebriation, and Bertie, satisfied with Larry's safety, hurried to Ivy Barn.

Bertie wished Faye was with him, but he knew she had all kinds of top-secret things going on and was preparing to go away. Bertie had become used to her having secrets. Most people did these days, though Faye's came with more than a little danger, what with everything that happened at the Summer Fair last month and the whole village being in thrall to a Nazi occultist. That's the sort of palaver that can really ruin a day out.

But Faye had saved the day again and everyone went back to some sort of normality. Everyone but Faye, that is. She had to remain – what was the word? – *vigilant*.

And Bertie knew that even though he didn't have any kind of magic, he could be vigilant with her and support Faye in her time of need. Though she hadn't been the same since she brought down that bomber. He wanted to be helpful. That was what the Zadoc Brown book was about. But he was fooling himself if he thought that book would do any good. What was he thinking? Silly fool. What could he give her that would let her know she was ...

He almost said the word. The one beginning with 'L' that rhymes with 'gloved'. Was that what it was? Whenever he held Faye's hand he found a kind of peace and belonging that he'd never found anywhere else. But he also wanted to pepper her with kisses and whisper sweet nothings into her ear as he nibbled on her earlobes. And he wanted Faye to kiss his neck, and move her hands over his skin and grab him in all kinds of intimate places, and then they could fall onto the two-seater in the pub living room in a passionate frenzy of—

'Blimey.' Bertie shook his head clear. All thoughts of ardour and romance had clouded his mind and he had walked straight past Ivy Barn.

He turned back. The moon drifted over its roof. Bertie wished he had Faye's hand to hold now as another kind of desire overwhelmed him.

Voices in his head – not Otto Kopp's, but sensible voices – kept telling him to go straight back to the pub where Terrence was waiting for him to help clean up.

But, Bertie, another voice said, *think of all that treasure.*

That was Bertie's more adventurous side. He didn't come out very often, but when he did he could be very convincing. *It can't hurt to take a peek, can it?*

Bertie stood before the barn. It was dark and still, but the moon was bright as a street lamp. If there was any dangerous poultry around, then it was asleep.

'I'll just open the doors,' Bertie said aloud. 'I'll just open them, have a quick peek and be on my way. I won't even go inside.'

Bertie found himself opening the barn doors. He was surprised there was no lock, but this barn was far from prying eyes and only a fool would be sneaking around a creepy barn at night.

'Oh, my giddy aunt,' Bertie said with a gasp.

Propeller blades from a Hurricane, the canopy of a Bf 109 cockpit, the tail wing of a Spitfire, the wheels of a ... Well, Bertie couldn't tell what plane the wheels were from, so he dashed inside to get a closer look. But his eye was caught by an RAF pilot's helmet and goggles, and a leather jacket hanging on the wall. Dare he try them on?

Dare, Bertie, dare!

Bertie's lips were dry. He licked them as he reached out for the precious garment.

As he did, a gust of wind slammed the barn doors shut, casting him into darkness. Bertie spun on his heels, guiltily retracting his hands and clasping them together. His breath quickened and puffed in the air. The barn had become suddenly chill.

Out of the corner of Bertie's eye he could see it. The

man standing there. The dark, silent silhouette that wasn't there a moment before. Bertie wanted to run, but his feet were somehow made of lead. The man rushed towards Bertie, arms outstretched.

THE DOVER WITCHES

Miss Charlotte commandeered Mr Gilbert and Mr Brewer's motorcycle and sidecar combination for the trip to the station. Mrs Teach sat in the sidecar with the luggage. She had agreed to come after a long and loud telephone conversation with Bellamy late last night. He was already in a bunker somewhere in Dover and had to shout over the racket of anti-aircraft guns fending off another Luftwaffe air raid. After a short chat brimming with more threat than the falling bombs, he cracked and promised them a shared hotel room in Dover with a sea view.

Faye wrapped her arms around Charlotte's waist as they hurtled to Therfield Station. From there, they would take the train to Dover.

Buying tickets in the shadow of 'Is your journey really necessary?' posters, Faye wondered just what to expect at their final destination. Bellamy had promised them busloads of witches for his ritual, and Faye wasn't sure she was prepared for a cliff bustling with witches, especially if they were anything like Miss Charlotte and Mrs Teach.

Faye would usually be thrilled at the prospect of travel and adventure, but this was a bad time to leave the village. Not only was Faye already missing her father and Bertie, but there was Leo and that message from her mother and the small matter of learning to fly. Faye had to do her bit, though, and that meant sacrifices and rolling her sleeves up. She took a seat opposite Mrs Teach and Miss Charlotte, and watched the countryside roll by as the train plodded along.

Never let it be said that something like the Battle of Britain and incessant bombing raids would stop the trains from running. They didn't run on time, of course. The train took for ever, constantly slowing and stopping as dogfights took place overhead. The ticket collector passed through, advising passengers to lower the blinds on the windows to prevent injury from flying glass, or to lie on the floor of the carriage. Faye felt the sticky floor beneath her plimsolls.

'Fancy lying on the floor, Mrs Teach?' she said with a grin.

Mrs Teach's grimace told Faye all she needed to know.

They passed fields full of craters, and they stopped at one station that had been obliterated. Faye couldn't be sure which station it was as all the signs had been taken down as part of the anti-invasion measures. That didn't stop two women in summer dresses and hats tiptoeing around the rubble to board the train.

Miss Charlotte's pipe smoke soon filled the carriage and Faye opened a window.

'Do you mind?' Mrs Teach bristled. 'I'll catch a chill.'

'Anything's better than my lungs filling up with whatever she's puffing on.' Faye waved Miss Charlotte's smoke away.

'If you find it objectionable,' Miss Charlotte said, 'consider sitting on the roof.'

'I might.'

'Children, please.' Mrs Teach pulled the window halfway shut. 'We need to be on our best behaviour today. We can't have witches from foreign parts thinking we're a bickering rabble.'

'That's us stuffed then, isn't it?' Faye said. 'And what do you mean "foreign parts"? They're from London, aren't they?'

Mrs Teach made a disapproving noise at the back of her throat.

Miss Charlotte took the pipe from between her teeth. 'They do things differently there. Though Ophelia Babbage is an excellent scryer.'

'Not to mention Dolly Greengrass,' added Mrs Teach. 'She's a jolly old soul. I hope she's coming. And Elsie Nicholls, mad as a brush but knows her magic. Those two I can tolerate, fine witches, but as for the rest of those country bumpkins ...'

'Mrs Teach, we live in a village in the countryside. Surely that makes us all country bumpkins?'

'How dare you, Faye Bright. I am a worldly woman and have experienced much beyond the confines of

Woodville. For some of these witches, I dare say this is the first time they'll have seen a train or the sea. Be prepared to indulge their simple ways.'

'There's no need to be snooty, Mrs Teach. We're all on the same side, after all.'

'Of course.' Mrs Teach rested a reassuring hand on Faye's. 'But some of their methods can be somewhat erratic. Do not be led astray, young lady.'

Faye felt a tingle of excitement. She quite liked the idea of being led astray by other witches. She wondered if any of them knew how to deal with a reluctant poltergeist. Or how to fly.

Faye looked to the skies and tried to fathom how she might get up there without wings and a powerful engine. She leaned forwards, beckoning her fellow witches closer.

'Did witches ever really fly?'

Mrs Teach glanced around to ensure no one was listening. 'What's brought this on?'

'Just . . . curious.'

'Yes, they have,' Miss Charlotte said from behind her veil of pipe smoke. 'Though not for a very long time.'

'Why not?'

'It takes an incredible amount of power that very few witches possess. And you may have noticed that we have trains, motor cars and aircraft these days, so why bother?'

'And it draws the wrong kind of attention,' Mrs Teach added. 'No one's really flown since the days of the witchfinders. A sure way to get yourself strung up was to be seen floating through the air with your bloomers on display for all to see.'

'Flying only leads to trouble.' Miss Charlotte pointed the sticky end of her clay pipe at Faye. 'Keep your feet on the ground. Understand?'

※

They could smell Dover before they saw it. The air was still laced with cordite after last night's air raid. As they pulled into the station, Faye's eye was caught by the remains of a tall building. Two chimney stacks were standing amid a pile of smoking red brick rubble, the firemen still hosing it down.

The train doors clattered open and shut, echoing all around the vastness of the station as they disembarked. There were troops everywhere, many marching in line, vastly outnumbering the few civilians trying to go about their day amid the ever-present threat of destruction.

Bellamy was waiting for them at the end of the platform. Today he wore RAF blues.

'Is this the eye of the storm?' he asked by way of greeting them. 'I would rather say it is. This way, ladies, this way. Can I take those, Faye? Mrs Teach?'

He carried their travel bags as he shepherded them out of the station and into the rear of an army truck parked outside. He popped the bags in the back before hopping in with them, gripping the metal frame of the truck.

'Hold tight,' he announced as the truck lurched into traffic.

Faye craned her head to see more rubble in the streets.

'We took a bit of a pounding last night,' Bellamy said. 'Got quite hairy, I don't mind telling you. One can't help but feel that the Hun is building up to something, which makes our work more imperative than ever.'

The road rose up, and Faye got her first proper look at the docks. There were no warships, but she did see a refurbished pleasure cruiser with a red cross painted onto its white hull. Smoke billowed from the aft deck where it had been hit.

The truck veered away from the cliffs and onto a narrow, winding road that became increasingly bumpy. Before long, they left the road and found themselves bouncing across a field. They stopped at a gate guarded by soldiers. Their driver showed papers, and the guards peered into the back of the truck to find Bellamy saluting, Mrs Teach clutching her handbag, and white-haired Charlotte sucking on her pipe. Faye gave them a little wave, and one of them sneered before signalling to his fellow guard to raise the barrier.

The truck came to a stop on a rise above the cliffs. The sky was a bright blue, the English Channel glistening, and three Spitfires flew by at eye level, patrolling the coastline beyond the line of barrage balloons.

Faye took off her specs, giving them a quick clean with the cloth in her pocket. Putting them back on, she could see coils of barbed wire lining the cliff's edge. And beyond that, on the horizon, was a pale smudge of land. France. Faye shuddered. That's how close the Nazis were. If she could walk it, she would be there before teatime. She imagined the sea full of invading warships, the sky blackened by Luftwaffe fighters and bombers. No amount of magic could repel an invasion like that, surely?

'Nearly there!' Bellamy led them along a chalk path, where they found a pair of enormous guns poking out of camouflage netting towards France. They were flanked by searchlights, and somewhere a generator rattled, coughing out diesel fumes.

'Might I ask where we are?' Mrs Teach inspected the bunker beneath the guns and grimaced at what she saw.

'I would say ...' Faye sucked air through her teeth. 'Dover. Yeah. Definitely Dover. The big white cliffs are a bit of a giveaway, Mrs Teach.'

'Impudent child,' Mrs Teach muttered, then turned her attention back to Bellamy. 'By which I mean, of course, what is this facility?'

Bellamy smiled and shook his head. 'I'm afraid I cannot say, Mrs Teach.'

Mrs Teach made disappointed noises from behind a pouted mouth.

'Loose lips sink ships and all that, Mrs Teach,' Faye said. 'Now we're on a secret mission, I don't think we'll be getting answers to questions like that.'

'I wish I'd known we were going hiking.' Mrs Teach carefully negotiated the concrete steps that led down to a steel door beneath the guns. 'I would have worn more suitable shoes.'

Another guard checked their papers, saluted Bellamy and opened the door.

The summer sunshine and warmth were gone in an instant as they descended into the clammy atmosphere of a steep stairwell.

'Watch your step,' Bellamy advised. 'This place is primarily an air raid shelter for the crew of the battery above, but we have a room of our own down below. Use the handrails. Oh, and I would remind you that we are guests of the army, so best behaviour please.'

Both Miss Charlotte and Mrs Teach blanched at the very idea.

Corrugated steel lined the arch-shaped stairwell and electric lamps flickered yellow light, throwing long shadows and disorientating Faye who was struggling to tell up from down.

She was relieved when they came to a landing and another soldier checked their papers long enough for her to get her sense of direction back. He opened another door and Bellamy led them through a much bigger room. Well lit, with double bunks lining the walls, it could sleep two-dozen soldiers. There was only one today, resting on a top bunk and filling out his pools coupon. Faye gave him a smile, trying not to wince at the lingering odour of cigarettes and farts.

'Ah, you must be Bellamy.' A stout woman in a green ATS uniform marched towards them, a clipboard tucked under her arm.

'Yes, indeed. Bellamy Dumonde, reporting.' He handed her his papers. 'You have a meeting room for us, I believe.'

'Hmm.' The woman checked his papers carefully.

'We do indeed. The rest of your party has already arrived. I can't say I approve, but needs must and all that.' She handed Bellamy his papers. 'Follow me. Quick as you can.'

They marched down a long chalk-lined corridor. It looked freshly dug out. At the end was another steel door.

'This is you lot.' The woman pointed back the way they'd come. 'You can find tea and biscuits in the refectory. Lavatories are that way, too. Be sparing with the toilet paper.' She said this last bit with a voice that echoed up and down the corridor. 'Understand?'

They all nodded.

'Very good. I'll let you get on with it.' She marched away, leaving them facing the steel door.

'Shall we?' Bellamy asked, not waiting for an answer and swinging the door open.

Beyond was a room not much bigger than the truck they had come in. They found three witches sipping tea. It was like looking in a fairground mirror.

A slender woman with jet-black hair was leaning on a bunk, smoking a Gauloises. An elderly lady with wispy grey hair drank from a china cup with her pinkie finger pointing up. She was thin as a rake with skin like the bark of an oak tree and wore a long black dress buttoned up at the front. And a young woman, not much older than Faye, but with mousey blonde hair, sat wearing a khaki First Aid Nursing Yeomanry uniform, stroking a black cat in her lap.

'Is this everyone?' Mrs Teach sounded unimpressed.

'Where's Dolly, Elsie and Ophelia?' Miss Charlotte asked.

'Untraceable, sadly,' Bellamy said.

Charlotte arched a suspicious eyebrow. 'They can't have just vanished.'

'It seems that they can and they have. Dolly did the decent thing and sent me an apologetic telegram, but I've not had a peep out of the others. From Dolly's message I discerned the possibility that the three of them might have been reassigned to another top-secret operation. We shall continue to make enquiries, but in the meantime—'

'Hardly the "busloads" we were promised, Bellamy.' Mrs Teach curled her lip and raised her nose.

The woman with the Gauloises flicked ash from the tip and jerked back her head. She spoke fluent English with a Parisian accent heavy with ennui. 'Imagine our disappointment when you walked in.'

'Oh, you're French.' Miss Charlotte flared her nostrils. 'I would imagine you'd be used to disappointment by now.'

'Ladies.' Bellamy raised pacifying hands. 'Best behaviour, please.'

'Perish the thought.' Miss Charlotte smirked. 'A Frenchie putting up a fight.'

The air crackled with Gallic swearing as the two women squared off.

Bellamy threw himself between them like a boxing referee. 'That's enough, thank you very much. Silence, I will have silence! Stop fighting! What would the army think?'

Miss Charlotte and her French counterpart backed

away, chins raised, round two postponed until further notice.

Bellamy dabbed his forehead with a blue and white polka-dot handkerchief. 'Scrying, it seems, is something of a rare skill these days. I ... I may have overestimated the number of practitioners, but nevertheless we have a trio of the finest scryers in the country, which is ample, and of course you three.' He gestured to Faye, Mrs Teach and Miss Charlotte.

Faye reckoned now was as good a time as any to break the ice. 'How do,' she said to the new trio. 'I'm Faye.'

'Yes, Faye. Introductions.' Bellamy tucked his hankie away. 'These are the witches from Woodville Village that I was telling you about. Faye Bright, who just introduced herself so politely. Mrs Philomena Teach, and Miss Charlotte Southill.'

'Southill? Ah, that explains so *very* much.' The French woman smiled crookedly and looked Miss Charlotte up and down.

'Er, yes.' Bellamy then moved across the room to introduce the new trio. 'From Paris, this is Mademoiselle Martine de la Barre.'

'*Enchanté*,' Martine said, sounding anything but enchanted as she exhaled cigarette smoke.

'From Norfolk, this is Mrs Hilda Housego.'

'Are ye orrite?' Mrs Housego ducked her head in greeting.

'And from London, Miss Jennifer Gentle.'

Jennifer sat upright, startling her cat, which leapt off

her and darted into the shadows. 'Jolly lovely to meet you all.' Her voice strained with enthusiasm. 'How exciting to be here.'

Faye was delighted to see another witch who wasn't old enough to be her mother. Jennifer wore make-up and her hair was a proper do, not simply brushed back like hay. And Jennifer's uniform actually looked like it was made for her, whereas Faye's ARP kit hung off her like a sack. Faye wondered how Jennifer discovered she could do magic, if she had a mother who was a witch, and if she had any tips for making an ARP uniform look less sack-like.

'Please, take a seat.' Bellamy moved back to the door as if to prevent anyone from escaping.

Charlotte remained standing, as did Martine. They mirrored one another, like a pair of praying mantises, wondering which one would bite first. Mrs Teach found a chair and sat upright, clutching her handbag as if someone might steal it. Faye hopped onto a nearby bunk and sat cross-legged.

'My original point still stands,' Mrs Teach said, the hoity-toitiness of her voice raised several degrees from its usual sniffiness. She did this when she wanted to impress new people. 'Where are the promised busloads of witches, Mr Dumonde?'

'There's been a slight change of plan.' Bellamy flashed a nervous grin. 'This operation has been deemed so sensitive that the powers-that-be want to keep the numbers of personnel involved strictly limited. I had to fight to get you six.'

'Good, the smaller the better.' Martine tapped ash

from her cigarette into a tin cup. 'I have worked with groups like this before. Too many captains, all pulling in different directions. It always ends in disaster.'

'W-well, not always, Martine.' Bellamy raised a hopeful finger.

'Always,' she said, brooking no argument as she put another cigarette to her lips and struck a match. The phosphorus tickled Faye's nostrils.

'Putting aside the experiences of our French colleague, I am assured that I have before me the most powerful witches in the country.'

'That's not quite true, is it?' Faye rubbed her nose.

'Beg pardon?' Bellamy was developing a twitch in his right eye.

'Where's Vera Fivetrees? I know she's suspended an' all, but if this mission is so important, and we can't have busloads of witches, then why don't we have the most powerful witch there is?'

'I agree,' a voice said behind Faye. She turned to see Jennifer giving her a small smile. Faye felt a little glow of pride. Jennifer continued, sounding like the head girl at a posh school, 'Without Vera, we're seriously depleted.'

Bellamy tucked his hands into his armpits and rounded his shoulders. 'Yes, yes, I understand your concern. I have asked myself this question many times. Should we include Vera Fivetrees? Sadly, I think not. The truth is, Vera is being investigated. There have been allegations – ones that I sincerely hope are false – of espionage.'

'Cobblers,' Mrs Teach blurted out.

'Indeed, but until she is cleared, we simply cannot risk the details of my plan falling into enemy hands. You ladies have all been thoroughly vetted by the Secret Service and cleared for this top-secret operation.'

'Vetted?' Mrs Teach stiffened. 'No one has vetted me.'

Bellamy's voice became thin with strain. 'It's the Secret Service, Mrs Teach. You wouldn't know if they were vetting you. That's their job.'

Mrs Housego raised a hand.

'Yes?'

'I told my Malcolm that I was comin' to Dover.' She bit her lip. 'That's not breaking no secrets, is it?'

'And Malcolm is?'

'My eldest. He's seventy-two and don't say much on account of not havin' many teeth left and only one lung.'

'That's somewhat regrettable, Mrs Housego,' Bellamy said.

'The teeth or the lung?'

'That you told him you were coming here.' Bellamy ground his teeth before continuing. 'But no harm done. So long as you didn't tell him why.'

'Good,' Mrs Housego said. 'Truth is, I din't know why I was comin' till you told me just now.'

'Somewhere in Norfolk,' Mrs Teach said out of the corner of her mouth to Faye, 'a village is missing its idiot.'

Faye shushed her.

'Do you have something to add, Mrs Teach?' Bellamy asked.

'As you were.' Mrs Teach fluttered her eyelashes and ignored the glare she was receiving from Mrs Housego.

Bellamy puffed out his cheeks. 'Shall we get some fresh air? Yes, I think we shall.' Bellamy swung the door open. 'And as we do, let me reveal to you, ladies, the details of Operation Cone of Power.'

OPERATION CONE OF POWER

The daylight made Faye's eyes throb, but the air was sweet, and the summer breeze warmed her skin. They followed Bellamy up and down the rolling path that ran the length of the cliffs. Popular with ramblers and dog walkers, it was now dotted with soldiers on patrol, sentinels watching the horizon for invaders.

Faye found herself walking at the rear with Jennifer, who carried her cat as they negotiated the path. Even here, with a Channel wind whipping around them and the faint aroma of cow dung, Jennifer looked as excited as a child on Christmas morning. She had something of Bertie's enthusiasm about her. Faye felt her tum turn over. She missed Bertie and couldn't wait to see his big silly smile again, but having a fellow witch who could put a spring in her step without complaining about her back was a delight.

'I say, Faye, one hates to confess this, but I was secretly delighted when Mr Chamberlain got on the wireless last September.' The cat leapt out of Jennifer's arms and began sniffing the edge of the path. This allowed Jennifer to open up her little silver powder mirror, moving her head about as she surveyed her make-up as they walked. 'I know, I know. It's a ghastly thing to say, but when war marches into one's life, all the dull certainties and inevitabilities of a girl's existence are tossed into the air. It's jolly liberating. It gave me the perfect excuse to sign up for the FANYs.'

'I know what you mean,' Faye said. 'This bleedin' war might be the best thing that ever happened to me, but there are days when I reckon I'd like the quiet life of working in me dad's pub, without the air raids and all that. Must be bad in London.'

'Oh, ghastly.' Jennifer snapped her powder mirror shut. 'I'm not sure I want to go back. I was cock-a-hoop when I got the telegram from Belly. Scrying to save the country. Sign me up.'

They came to a stile. Jennifer's cat leapt over it, chasing something into the bushes. She called after it. 'Don't go too far, you wretched thing.'

'What's the cat's name?' Faye asked.

'Not sure,' Jennifer mused. 'She hasn't told me yet.'

Faye let that slide. 'Is she new, then?'

'A stray that wandered through my back door last week. She simply won't leave my side. I think the poor little blighter might have shell shock from all the bombing, so I had to bring her along.'

'Witches are supposed to have familiars, I s'pose.'

'Yes, though this one might be getting a little too familiar.'

The path ended at a checkpoint where Bellamy showed papers to a pair of Military Police. Barbed wire was in season, and squat concrete bunkers were dotted about, bustling with soldiers.

Once the papers were checked they were waved through and the group approached the South Foreland lighthouse. Faye had come here for a picnic once before and the tower had been painted a dazzling white. Now it was daubed in the greens and black stripes of camouflage and its famous light was dark.

'Here we are!' Bellamy's voice carried over the Channel breeze. He stood in a wide-open grassy space before the lighthouse, his arms thrown wide, a tiny figure against the bright blue sky. 'This is the spot. It took me years of study to find it. This is where the ritual will take place. Come closer, please.' He waved everyone towards him and soon all the ladies were gathered round. 'Can you feel it?' He lowered his voice, an excited smile on his face.

Faye couldn't feel—

Oh, no, there it was. An unsettling sensation. Like a flashbulb popped in her head. She felt like she rose an inch off the ground, then dropped again.

'What the blimmin' 'eck is that?' She looked around at the others who were all wide-eyed at the same feeling.

'A convergence,' Bellamy said. 'Ley lines – ancient and mystical lines of magical power, intersecting on this spot. One comes all the way from Wales down the ancient Roman road we call Watling Street, another from Stonehenge, and another . . .' he broke away from

the gathering and pointed out across the water '...
from France.'

'Very good,' Miss Charlotte murmured in a rare
display of appreciation.

Bellamy was just getting warmed up. 'We will generate the power of the cone here.' He pointed two fingers
at the ground by their feet, before thrusting his arms
seaward. 'And then our scryers – Jennifer, Martine and
Mrs Housego – will focus all that energy towards the
enemy. We will implant the idea that the Channel is
impossible to cross, and they will ... I don't know ...
invade Russia instead.' Bellamy slapped his hands
against his thighs. 'Is this the best chance we have of
repelling the invaders?' he asked. 'I rather think it is.'

Faye spotted a patrol of Spitfires on the horizon. She
reckoned *they* might be the best chance of repelling the
invaders, but she didn't want to burst Bellamy's balloon.

Martine had no such reservations. 'This is ridiculous.'
She gestured at the grass where the ley lines converged.

'Beg pardon?' Bellamy asked, baring his teeth in a
patient smile.

'A cone of power ritual requires a fire, Monsieur
Dumonde. A flaming bonfire twice as tall as me. You
want us to stand here, exposed on the edge of a cliff, at
night, at the height of the Battle of Britain, next to an
enormous pile of flaming wood? You must be ... 'ow
you say? Off your chump, matey!'

Faye nodded, appreciating both the point and
Martine's grasp of English vernacular. 'Yeah, you
might as well paint a target on our 'eads,' she added.

'I'm a little hurt that you assume I hadn't thought of something so simple,' Bellamy said, placing his hands on the small of his back. 'Faye, you recall that little protective glamour we concocted in the village the other night?'

Faye felt a stab of guilt to be reminded of that fateful evening, though she nodded all the same.

'We will do the same thing here. The vertex of the cone of power will be on this spot. A magical convergence of extraordinary potency used by Druids and witches for centuries. So long as the moon is in the sky, we will be protected. Invisible to all, existing on another plane. Why, a bomb could drop on our heads and we wouldn't be harmed.'

'There'd be a bloody great crater when we're done, though,' Miss Charlotte noted.

'Indeed, but we would remain unscathed.'

'Until the sun rises.' Mrs Teach folded her arms. 'After that the moon's power weakens considerably.'

'Yes, yes.' Bellamy's twitch returned. 'But if we start at midnight, we will be done long before dawn.'

'This kind of protection uses an enormous amount of magical energy.' Martine shook her head. 'Magical energy that we need for the ritual.' She waved a dismissive hand and began muttering in French as she lit another cigarette.

'I assure you that I have been over my calculations again and again and any loss of magical energy is more than compensated for by performing the ritual here.'

He's not wrong, Faye thought. The convergence of

energy was doing strange things to her. She could feel it through the soles of her feet, rising through her body. This was even stronger than when she brought down the bomber. The power was attracted to her like lightning finding a copper rod on a bell tower. Faye's hair stood on end and her fingertips crackled.

Mrs Teach raised an enquiring hand. 'Does this added power mean that there will be no need for nudity?'

'Oh no,' Jennifer said with a moan. 'Not skyclad, surely? I say, that's rather rum not to mention it till now, Belly.'

'He told *us*,' Faye said, trying to ignore the fizzing feeling behind her eyes, 'and we all threw a wobbly, so I reckon he thought it better to keep quiet.'

'You tell them, but do not tell us?' Martine folded her arms. 'What games are you playing, Monsieur Dumonde?'

'I promise you, I'm not playing—'

'I reckon it's a great idea,' Mrs Housego piped up. 'Nudity is well known to boost magical energy. Standing by to disrobe, Mr Dumonde.'

'Nonsense, woman,' Mrs Teach declared, sparking a rabble of angry overlapping voices as Bellamy tried to explain. Jennifer berated him for not telling them sooner, and Mrs Housego defended her right to bare her body in the name of magic. Martine and Miss Charlotte stood back from the row. Faye caught them glancing at one another as if wondering who might look better naked. Faye, for her part, stayed silent as the magical energy continued to balloon inside her. She started to see sparkles at the edge of her vision.

'Please, for the love of all that is good, will you bloody women be quiet!' Bellamy yelled.

A passing gull screeched.

'Well, there's no need for language like that,' said Mrs Teach.

'We are on the verge of a pivotal moment in our nation's history, and you barmy lot of witches are driving me up the bloody wall,' Bellamy cried.

'What did I say, uh?' Martine shrugged and pursed her lips. 'Too many captains.'

'There are not too many captains, Martine, because I – Bellamy Dumonde – am in command here and you would all do well to remember that!'

Faye felt sorry for poor Bellamy. He had been so polite up to now. All it took was a few witches to nudge him off his rocker. She could only sympathise. As he continued to rant, his voice became muffled as Faye's skull began to vibrate. That was new. And there was a burning sensation in her bone marrow.

'Well, I for one did not come all this way to be spoken to like this.' Mrs Teach gripped her handbag like the reins of a horse, turned and trotted back the way she'd come. Miss Charlotte, Martine and Jennifer all joined her. Mrs Housego stayed where she was.

'No, please, no, come back!' Bellamy pleaded, but they all had their backs to him and their heads held high. 'You can't leave now. We're so close. My plan . . . it . . . I'm sorry!'

169

'Witches!' Faye cried, her voice carrying over the wind. 'Something strange is happening to me.' Faye held her hands a foot apart. 'Sorry, ladies, I can't keep this in any longer. Watch yourselves!'

Bellamy took a step back as a ball of blue light sparked between Faye's outstretched fingers. As it grew, the other witches huddled together. Mrs Teach and Miss Charlotte shared a grimace of horror. Mrs Housego and Martine hid behind Bellamy. An astonished grin crept across Jennifer's face, which was lit by the expanding blue ball. Faye found herself chuckling as her whole body felt vibrant and alive in a way it never had before. It filled her to the brim and she had to let it out. With a gasp, Faye threw her hands to the sky and a beam of raw magical energy punched into the atmosphere.

Eyes Closed, Ears Open

As quick as it burst into life, the light vanished. Bellamy felt the hair on the back of his neck stand on end as thunder crackled high above and the air became heavy and damp.

Light shimmered around Faye. Mrs Teach and Miss Charlotte stood together, hands and feet apart, ready to leap into action. Jennifer's cat dived off her shoulders and ducked behind a bush. Mrs Housego squinted, her thin hair whipping about her. Martine's latest cigarette flared in a shower of embers then was quickly snuffed out.

Bellamy had never seen anything like it. No one, not himself, not Vera Fivetrees, not even Lady Sage, could manipulate raw magical energy like this. The girl should have been burned to cinders, but all she did was take a few puffs to get her breath back as she stepped away from the convergence. A blackened patch of grass marked the spot where she'd stood. If one squinted, it took on a familiar shape. A triskelion of swirling lines.

'What . . . what the blazes was that?' Bellamy asked, his voice thin.

'The power here is really strong,' Faye told the other witches.

Not that strong, Bellamy wanted to say, but he could see on the others' faces that they were all as stunned as he. 'It's the convergence of ley lines. It amplifies your power. That's why I chose this spot for the ritual, but—'

'Don't be looking at me like that,' Faye said.

Bellamy glanced around to find the witches in varying states of awe and fear.

Mrs Teach feigned innocence. 'Like what?'

'Like I'm an unexploded bomb about to go bang. I'm fine. I just had to . . . get that off me chest. I was a little giddy, but now I feel better than ever. Bellamy's right . . . We can do this, and I don't reckon we'll need to be in the nuddy.'

There was a whimper of disappointment from Mrs Housego.

Faye continued, 'But only if we work together as a team and with Mr Dumonde as captain.'

Bellamy felt a warm tingle of gratitude at her kind words. He was about to thank Faye when Martine made a noise that was not quite approval.

Faye ignored her. 'Let's see if we can end this war while the sun still shines, eh?'

Mrs Teach looked to Miss Charlotte. The pair of them came to a silent accord and began to walk back to join Faye, Bellamy and Mrs Housego. Jennifer was still calling for her cat. Martine stood her ground, apart from the others, but the look of astonishment on her face remained.

'Th-thank you, Faye,' Bellamy said, still somewhat awestruck. 'And yes, I heartily agree. We can only do this together. Oh, hello.' He looked down to find Jennifer's cat rubbing her back against his leg.

'Ah, there you are.' Jennifer picked the cat up and scratched its neck. 'Please, Belly, do continue. You were saying?'

Bellamy winced. 'Could you kindly refrain from calling me that?'

'I'm most frightfully sorry.' Jennifer pressed a hand to her chest. 'Though you do have the look of a Belly about you.'

'Do I indeed?'

''Fraid so,' she said, glancing at Faye as she suppressed a laugh with a snort.

Bellamy flexed his lips a few times, remaining otherwise still. 'This is no joke, ladies. We can make a real difference to the war. Our work here will save lives. You can call me whatever you wish. I don't care, so long as you give your all in this effort. Do you understand?'

'We do, Bellamy.' Faye was still smiling though all the mockery was gone. 'Don't mind us. We might need to blow off some steam now and then, but we're all with you. Right, ladies?'

'Oh, most certainly,' Jennifer said, leading the overlapping replies. 'Do forgive me, Bellamy. I tend to be a bit of a show-off around new people. You have my total support.'

'Very good. Regarding your concerns about the ritual, I can see that performing it skyclad seems somewhat unnecessary,' Bellamy said, though the truth was if Faye could produce that kind of power on the night then they could perform the ritual dressed like Cossacks and it would still succeed. He could barely contain his excitement. This was actually going to work. 'The next stage of the plan is to run a series of tests.'

'Never mind the tests.' Mrs Housego raised her chin. It was a proper witch's pointy chin with a hairy wart. 'When are we doing the real thing?'

'I'm afraid that must remain a secret, Mrs Housego, loose lips and all that. And, as we have just demonstrated, we all need to learn to trust and work with one another. A few test runs are vital. I thought we could start after a spot of lunch.'

'Is that here or back at the hotel?' Mrs Teach didn't look particularly thrilled at the promise of either.

'Ah.' Bellamy's nostrils flared.

Faye tensed. That sort of utterance from Bellamy was top-heavy with dread.

'There's a slight problem with your hotel.' Bellamy tried to make light of it with a smile.

Mrs Teach's eyelids went to half-mast. 'What sort of problem?'

'The problem, yes. Now, don't get angry. This wasn't my fault.' Bellamy took half a step back. 'But the Luftwaffe reduced your hotel to a pile of bricks last night. The good news is no one was hurt. And our deposit is refundable.'

'I assume you have found us alternative accommodation?' Mrs Teach's voice was light and sweet. Faye feared for Bellamy's life.

'Of course,' Bellamy said. 'They're being delivered this afternoon.'

No one liked the sound of that. The witches began to surround Bellamy again.

'What are?' Mrs Teach raised a finger of warning. 'And if the next word from your mouth is "tent" or "yurt" or "wigwam" or any such variant, I shall grab you firmly by the breeches to the edge of that cliff and shove you—'

'Ladies, Bellamy, please.' Faye dashed to place herself between the aggrieved parties. 'I have an idea,' she said. 'To be honest, Bellamy, I think it's a bit daft to practise up here on the cliffs anyway. Like Martine said, we're exposed here. Even with your protective magic, we'll still be moving back and forth in full view of that.' Faye looked out to France. 'All it would take is one curious Nazi with a good pair of binoculars and they'll know we're up to something.'

'Then where do you suggest?' Bellamy asked.

'A place far from prying eyes.' Faye smiled. 'A place dripping with magic. A little village I know called Woodville.'

℘

'Ophelia Babbage, Elsie Nichols, Dolly Greengrass—'

The names dragged Jennifer out of her nap. The sudden shift from sleep to waking was like having a bucket of cold water emptied over her and it took a moment to remember where she was. A cramped train compartment rocking from side to side, a warm and anonymous cat purring in her lap, and witches all around her.

The train was heading towards Woodville, the village Jennifer had heard so much about from Otto. Faye's home and a place reputedly magical to its core. Bellamy had initially objected to Faye's idea of changing all his plans and uprooting to the village, but as it became clear that the alternative was a witch's rebellion, he somehow convinced himself that it was his idea all along, and the witches calmed down.

The two opposite Jennifer – Mrs Teach and Miss Charlotte – were the only ones awake in the train carriage and they spoke in conspiratorial whispers. They hadn't noticed Jennifer rousing and so she closed her eyes again but kept her ears alert.

Mrs Teach was the one doing all the talking now, so no change there.

'What do they all have in common?' she asked, but rattled on before Charlotte could take a breath to answer. 'They're great scryers, that's what. The best. It makes no sense. There are few enough scryers as it is, so why aren't they with us?'

Because I killed them, thought Jennifer.

Otto had come to Jennifer weeks ago. He had intelligence that Bellamy was planning to usurp Vera Fivetrees and he knew that there was a plan involving scryers.

'A cone of power,' Otto had said with a weary sigh. 'British magicians try one every few hundred years to delay invasion. They're obsessed with them. It's the island mentality. So predictable.'

Otto told Jennifer this was an opportunity not only to humiliate Bellamy, but also to wipe him out along with the country's most powerful witches. He had to get Jennifer on Bellamy's team, but there were other more powerful scryers who would be at the top of any warlock's list. He tasked Jennifer with befriending the top scryers in London and making them permanently indisposed. Something she thoroughly enjoyed. Her only regret was it had to be done in such a rush.

'What has become apparent,' Miss Charlotte lowered her voice to a murmur though it made little difference to Jennifer who had excellent hearing, 'is that we may not need them.'

Even with her eyes closed, Jennifer sensed the two witches shifting in their seats to turn their gaze on Faye Bright who slumped snoozing next to her.

Jennifer had never witnessed such an incredible demonstration of magic before. There was no denying that the sensation of the converging ley lines on the Dover cliff was extraordinary – she had felt their energy tingling all around – but to see another witch, and one so young, capture that energy and channel it the way Faye had simply boggled the mind. Jennifer understood Otto's interest in the girl.

'She's her mother's daughter, that's for sure,' Mrs Teach said.

'If only her mother were here,' Miss Charlotte said with a wistful sigh.

'Not like you to get sentimental.'

'I'm not. If the girl's mother was still alive, then we wouldn't have to play nursemaid to her every day.'

'You can be truly heartless sometimes, Charlotte Southill.' Mrs Teach bristled. 'The poor girl's mother died when she was only four.'

'Then she should be used to it by now.'

'May the gods forgive you, woman.'

'Oh, shush.'

So, Faye's mother was dead. And died young, too. Faye surely clung to the few memories of her mother. That was ripe for exploitation. The girl's sentimentality and refusal to let go of the past could be her greatest weakness. All Jennifer had to do was play a twist on her own orphaned status and Faye's defences would fall like sand. Nothing could bring the two of them together more effectively than the shared woes of grief. Jennifer vowed to be Faye's greatest chum and cheerleader. Until Otto gave the word to get rid of her.

The train began to slow. How long had they been on this infernal thing? Surely they had to be close now.

'One more stop.' Miss Charlotte's sharp voice jolted everyone out of their slumber.

Mrs Teach joined in with a chortle. 'Wakey-wakey, eggs and bakey.'

That woman's ghastly irrepressible cheer made Jennifer's teeth ache. She could barely keep up her own charade of can-do optimism without wanting to scream at herself to be quiet, so quite how Mrs Teach sustained it for so long was baffling. Jennifer hoped that Otto would give the order to wring the old bat's neck, too.

Jennifer blinked her eyes open and yawned. Beside her, Faye did the same.

Mrs Housego, whose snoring had been masked by the chuffing of the steam engine, snorted herself awake. And Martine – who looked vampiric in sleep with her arms resting across her chest – simply opened her eyes and looked alert and ready for action. Jennifer noticed the French woman's eyes slide over to Charlotte who was pointedly ignoring her.

The Frenchie was right about one thing. This little group had too many captains. Everyone in this not-so-merry band – with perhaps the exception of Faye – was used to being in charge. Creating a little discord among this bunch of egomaniacs would be child's play.

Bellamy lifted his chin. His arms remained folded. The bags under his eyes looked like they could be inflated to the size of barrage balloons. A frown of deep creases never left his forehead. If Otto's plan didn't kill him, then another few days with these witches surely would. Jennifer almost felt sorry for the man.

'Ladies.' He smacked the dryness from his mouth. 'Please ensure you have all your belongings. Miss Gentle, Mademoiselle de la Barre and Mrs Housego – with some last-minute telephone calls and a great deal of money from the Council's coffers, I have arranged rooms for you at a place called Hayward Lodge just outside the village. It really is rather splendid. There should be transport waiting for us at the next stop. Get a good night's rest. We have our first rehearsal tomorrow.'

Jennifer had slept enough. She had important work to do this evening. As soon as she could, she would find a quiet spot for scrying. She had the exact location of Bellamy's silly ritual and she would send it to Otto immediately.

BERTIE IS IN KNOTS

No one spoke to Faye on the long train journey home. She caught glimpses of Mrs Teach and Miss Charlotte sharing whispered conversations. And the ride from the station to the village in the motorcycle-and-sidecar combination was also unusually quiet, with their usual cheery goodbyes reduced to a few mumbled words. She could have been imagining things – they were all tired from a long day – but she knew they weren't fond of this new-found energy that was brimming inside her.

Faye, for her part, was beginning to love it. And that's what worried her the most. When she first encountered the moon's power it scared her. Now it left her feeling giddy. Like a night on the cider, only without the hangover. There was a part of her that wanted more, and another part that knew that would be a very bad thing indeed. But that part of her could go hang, because the overwhelming sensation of delight was unlike anything she had encountered before.

The other witches were met by an army truck to

take them to Hayward Lodge. The grand old mansion had been fully requisitioned by the military after the strange events last month with Lord and Lady Aston, and the out-of-towner witches were excited at the thought of a bit of luxury.

Bellamy asked them all to meet at the standing stones the next morning at ten sharp.

Faye stood outside the Green Man under a gibbous moon. She thought about visiting Leo to see how he was, and if he'd heard any more messages from her mother, but her bones ached and it was drizzling. She creeped in and flopped onto her bed.

♀

She woke to find her father making far too much noise banging chairs and glasses as he prepared the pub for the day ahead. She came downstairs to find him with a familiar expression on his face. The one that looked like someone had turned his nose a hundred-and-eighty degrees and the rest of his face had twisted with it.

'Back so soon?' he said. 'I thought you was off doing witchy stuff.'

'We decided to do it here. You look miffed, dear Father.' Faye yawned as she helped him. 'Wassup?'

'That drip Bertie didn't come back to finish his shift Sunday night.' Terrence jabbed a thumb at the bar. 'Luckily, Mrs Pritchett stepped in, but I could swing for that lad, I really could. And he's supposed to be here this morning, too. I shall be havin' words.'

'That's not like Bertie. I thought he was doing well.'

'When he bothers to turn up. I don't care how good he is, he's no good to me if he ain't here.'

Faye squinted and adjusted her specs as she thought. 'When did you last see him?'

'The lad should be perfectly capable of making his own way here on time for his shift.'

'I know that, Dad, just answer the question.'

'Some time last night. I don't remember exactly.' Terrence's eyes slid up to one corner. 'Even then he was doin' more chattin' than workin'. Him and Larry Dell were whispering about something and Bertie was gettin' all excited.'

'Oh no.' A cold dread weighed in Faye's belly. She knew exactly where Bertie had gone. 'Wait there,' she said, and darted out of the pub.

As she jumped on her Pashley Model A and cycled down the Wode Road, she could hear her father calling after her. 'Who's gonna do the bloody lunch shift?'

✗

Faye arrived at Larry's barn, her lungs burning and legs aching. She let the bike clatter to the ground and ran to the barn doors, calling out Bertie's name over and over. There was no reply. She swung the barn doors open.

'Bertie, you in here?'

He was. Bertie Butterworth was tied to one of the supporting beams. Thick rope had been wound around him three times and tied in a knot that looked like a child's idea of how one should be tied. A rag had been stuffed in his mouth. The boy's chin rested on his chest and he was snoring.

'Bertie!' Faye ran to him, taking the rag from his mouth.

His eyes blinked open, taking a moment to align and focus. 'F-Faye?' His voice was dry as sandpaper. 'You're back! That was quick.'

'Change of plan. Wait there. Oh, silly thing to say.' Faye grinned as she dashed to the workbench, snatching up the first sharp thing she could find to cut through the rope.

'That hacksaw looks a bit rusty,' Bertie said.

'Better keep still then,' Faye advised him as she began to slice the blade over the rope. One of her eyes was half shut, and her tongue stuck out.

'What time is it?' He blinked into the morning sun outside the barn.

'Just gone half-nine,' she said, aware that she had an appointment at the standing stones that she might just make in time.

'In the morning? What day is it?'

'Tuesday.'

'Oh, blimey. Your dad will have a right go at me. I've missed two shifts.'

'Don't worry about that, you silly goon.' Faye finally cut through the rope. 'What happened?'

Bertie wriggled free of the rope and stretched his limbs.

As he did, a propeller blade flew across the room. Faye grabbed his hand and they both scrabbled behind a workbench.

'That happened,' Bertie said as a lightbulb smashed above their heads.

'What were you doing here in the first place?' Faye ducked as a boot thudded into the wall behind them, cracking one of the barn's wooden slats.

'Larry said to have a look.'

'And you couldn't help yourself, could you, Bertie?'

'Look at this place, Faye.' Bertie's tired face transformed into one of eager excitement as he gestured at all the scavenged parts from Spitfires, Hurricanes and Messerschmitts, some of which were swirling in the air. 'It's an Aladdin's cave.'

'I don't think Aladdin collected propeller blades, Bertie.'

'Anyway, I popped my head round and I couldn't believe it. A Dowty tail wheel from a Hurricane, the oil cooler from a Bf 109 and the bulletproof glass panel from a Spitfire. That was just for starters. So, I ran in and—'

The oil cooler tumbled across the barn like a boulder.

Bertie twisted his lips as he remembered. 'There was someone else here with me. A shadow, Faye, the shadow of a man. Out of nowhere I was thrown against that beam, and this rope whipped around me, pinning me tight, and I couldn't budge. It was all moving by itself, Faye, like this stuff is now.' They both flinched as a Hurricane's oxygen tank clanged into one of the beams.

'The ends of the rope were trying to tie themselves into knots,' Bertie said, 'but they didn't really know

185

how to do a knot, so I thought I'd do them a favour and tell them how, but a distant voice told me to shut up and mind me own business.'

'Bertie.' Faye removed her glasses and pinched the bridge of her nose. 'You mean to tell me that a shadowy spirit was trying to strap you to a beam, and there you was givin' it advice on how to tie better knots?'

Bertie shrugged. 'Whoever it was, I noticed they were throwing stuff at the walls. They weren't aiming at me. They weren't trying to hurt me. Look at me. Not a scratch. So I thought I would be helpful and let them have their little moment, then have a chat when they calmed down. It's something I've learned from working in the pub. But once they tied me up they vanished. I tried calling for help, but then it came back and shoved a rag in me gob, so I had a kip. Then you arrived.' He smiled.

'And now it stops.' Faye pushed her glasses back up her nose. 'Leo! Listen to me. If you don't pack this in right now I shall send you straight to the dark place.'

'That don't sound nice,' Bertie said.

'It ain't,' Faye replied.

'How do you know his name?'

'Larry asked me to help him out. He's a pilot. Stay down and leave this to me.'

The barn fell silent and she peered over the top of the workbench. It looked like the whole structure had been tipped on its side with farm tools and plane parts scattered to every corner. Motes of dust swirled in the air.

Faye made to stand, but Bertie took her hand.

'Are you sure it's safe?' he asked, biting his lip. 'Blimey, my heart's beating like a drum.'

'Mine, too.' Faye found herself entranced by Bertie's wide eyes. She guided his hand to her chest. 'Feel it,' she said, thrilled by the touch of his hand on her body. Faye knew this was completely the wrong time and place for hanky-panky, but it was the first time they had been alone since she got back. She leaned closer to him, parting her lips.

Her breath turned into chilly vapour. Bertie jerked back, breathing his own puffy little clouds.

'He's close.' Faye muttered a quiet curse at the timing of Leo's arrival.

Bertie nodded. 'I've seen this before. It got all cold before that shadow started shoving me about.' He rubbed his arms to warm them up.

'Bloody gooseberry.' Faye stood and moved to the centre of the barn, hands on hips. 'Leo! Show yourself. Make yourself known to me now, please.' No reply. 'Bertie is a friend.' Faye beckoned Bertie towards her. The lad looked doubtful, but heaved himself to his feet and shuffled to her side. 'Leo, come on, old chap. I want you to say sorry to Bertie and we'll all be right as rain.'

A gust of wind blasted through the barn and the doors blew wide open.

'I think he wants me to leave,' Bertie said.

Faye snatched up the pilot's helmet from the workbench and spoke into the mic. 'Leo!'

Bertie looked puzzled, but he had spent enough time around Faye to know magic when he saw it.

'Leo, show yourself!'

'He has to go,' Leo's voice crackled in Faye's ears.

Faye looked to Bertie.

'I heard him,' Bertie said. 'Will you be all right?'

'He won't hurt me, but he might hurt you. I've got to meet the other witches soon, so it's best you go home, Bertie. Actually, can you pop in and see me dad and let him know what happened?'

'Really? All of it?'

'He'll understand.'

They stood a little apart, Bertie framed in the barn doors with the morning sunshine glowing around him. Faye wanted to rush to Bertie and kiss him on the lips, but the barn started to rattle and dust drifted down from the rafters. Leo was impatient.

'Go, Bertie,' Faye told him. 'This might take some time, and I have a witchy thing after this, so I won't see you much today. Or for the next few days. Sorry.'

'There'll be other days,' Bertie said with a smile.

He chuckled and waved her goodbye, limping off towards the village, taking a little bit of Faye's heart with him.

Her anger with Leo, however, remained. 'Leo, I swear, I haven't got time for this,' she said into the mic.

'I didn't know he was your friend.'

Faye spun to find Leo standing in a dark corner of the barn, head slumped, arms folded.

'It doesn't matter if he's a complete stranger or the King of England, you don't go tying people up. And what sort of a knot was that, anyway?'

'I am not a sailor. What do I know about knots?'
Leo shrugged. 'And he was snooping around like a spy.'

'He's no spy. He's a lad who gets a bit giddy about
fighter planes. This place is like a sweet shop to him.'

'These are not his sweets.' Leo flung his arms about
and more pieces of scrap flew through the air. Faye
instinctively flinched, and when she looked up, Leo was
nowhere to be seen.

'Well, he knows that now, doesn't he?' She listened for
a reply through the crackle and whine from the helmet's
headphones, but none came. 'Leo, I met some other
witches in Dover. We have a job to do – which I'm late
for, by the way – but I'll try and find a moment to speak
to them and see if they can help me with you. And ... and
help in a way that won't hurt you. They seem like good
people. I just need you to be patient a little while longer.'

'Patient?' Leo's disembodied voice was so angry that
it was distorted in the headphones. 'I wait here all day
for you, while you go off on adventures with witches.
I have been patient, Faye Bright. I need to get back to
the fight. Why won't you help me do that?'

Faye puffed her cheeks. 'You're right to be cross,' she
said in a calm voice. She wanted to tell him that she
sort of half remembered something about poltergeists
from her mother's book, but a sort of half-memory was
no use to anyone.

'The thing is, Leo, I just don't know the right magic
to help you. I have some powers, and they're growing.
I can feel them getting stronger, but I need help. I'm
sorry. Can you wait a little while longer?'

'No, I cannot.' His voice was getting strained. 'If I stay in this barn one day more I swear I'll smash it to pieces.'

A section of a Hurricane's tail rudder whooshed out of the doors and tumbled across the field. The barn's doors slammed shut and the supporting beams juddered.

Faye half ducked, ready to leap for cover. 'I promise you, Leo. I'll do everything I can. You do believe me, don't you, Leo?'

There came only the hiss of white noise over the headphones. The barn doors swung open again. Daylight beamed in and the temperature rose. Leo was gone.

FLED ZEPPELINS

Bertie Butterworth's Battle of Britain Diary

Tuesday 13th August, 1940

*Found a treasure trove of plane wreckage in Larry
Dell's barn. Was accosted by a ghost. Faye came
to the rescue. Nearly did some canoodling again.
But didn't. All we want is a little time together.
Weather good. Some distant AA fire overnight.
This has been a very peculiar summer.*

Faye arrived at the standing stones a little late, and she
expected either to find scenes of chaos as the witches
harangued Bellamy, or to be told off for her tardiness.
To her surprise, what she discovered was a picnic scene,
with tartan blankets laid out inside the stone circle, and
the ladies enjoying tea from Thermos flasks.

In the centre of the clearing, by the flat slaughter
stone, was a small fire. From the white-hot glow of
the logs at its base, Faye reckoned it had been burning

for some time. It felt odd to have a fire on a summer's morning, but Faye recalled the ritual needed a bonfire and was grateful that it wasn't raining.

Martine, cigarette on her lip, was already practising her scrying. She sat cross-legged by one of the smaller stones with a crystal ball in her right palm. She raised her left hand above it and the ball began to glow with iridescent light. It wasn't smooth, like the crystal balls Faye had seen in the movies. This was like a giant marble, chipped and scuffed, its glass cloudy and inscrutable.

She was watched by Miss Charlotte who leaned against one of the standing stones, idly puffing on her pipe.

Next to her, Mrs Housego unpacked a silver dish for her scrying. She laid it flat on the grass, then took a small flask from a knapsack and poured water onto the dish.

Jennifer carefully placed clay tablets, a gold medallion and a flat obsidian mirror before her as if they were Tarot cards. Once in position, she made tiny, precise adjustments to their alignment. She glanced up and gave Faye a jolly wave. 'Faye, darling. Come and plant yourself here.' She patted the ground beside her and Faye felt compelled to obey. 'I don't suppose you've seen my wretched cat, have you? It's jolly hard to concentrate when the little monster goes hunting.'

'No, sorry.' Faye looked around, but the cat was nowhere to be seen. 'Couldn't you find someone to look after her? Your mum or dad?'

Jennifer took a breath. 'Daddy passed before I

was born, and Mummy died when I was six. Hardly knew her.'

Faye gasped a little, almost ready to blurt out, 'My mum's dead, too,' like it was some kind of boast. For some reason, she really wanted to impress this odd girl.

As Faye wondered how to say it without sounding like a loon, Jennifer's black cat came hurtling out of the bushes and into her arms and clambered onto her shoulders. 'Ah, there you are, you ghastly horror!'

'Sorry about yer mum,' Faye said, lowering her voice. She took a breath and decided to reveal all anyway. 'I'm the same. Mum died when I was four. Ain't a day goes by when I don't wish she was around to show me the way.'

'Oh, my darling.' Jennifer took Faye's hand and squeezed it tight. 'We shall be fast chums.'

'Er, all right then.'

'You must tell me all about her. We'll have tea and cake and cry our eyes out.'

'If you say so,' Faye said, thinking that might be a bit strong, but also amazed at how soft Jennifer's hands were. Silky and smooth. Not even Mrs Teach had hands that soft.

'Is this Faye Bright I see before me?' Bellamy was unpacking a tiny accordion from a case. He greeted Faye with a chuckle as his little instrument wheezed. 'Indeed it is, and just in time. We were about to put a protective veil around the stones. Wouldn't want anyone stumbling in on our top-secret gathering, now, would we?'

'That's a little accordion.'

'It's a concertina,' he said, with the weary resignation of someone forced to explain this more times than he cared to remember. 'Its design dates back to ancient China and the sound is far more pleasant to the ear than a bog-standard accordion.'

'If you say so.'

'I do. Shall we begin?'

'Mornin' all,' Faye said and got a bunch of cheery Good Mornings in reply, though Mrs Teach – who sat down right next to her – simply stared at the fire.

Faye raised her voice, 'I said, mornin', Mrs Teach!'

Nothing. Philomena Teach continued to gaze at the flames.

'I said—' Faye tapped Mrs Teach on the shoulder and the woman nearly jumped out of her skin.

'Good Lord, Faye, you'll give me a heart attack!'

'Sorry, but you—'

'Wait a moment, wait a moment.' Mrs Teach waved Faye into silence, then reached into her right ear, removing a lump of cotton wool. She winced. 'Scrying makes my ears whistle. I have to block them up, otherwise it's unbearable.'

'Oh, sorry. I was just saying good—'

'Yes, yes.' Mrs Teach rammed the cotton back into her ear, smiled and nodded.

Faye knew when she wasn't wanted and so turned back to Jennifer. She leaned closer and lowered her voice. 'What's with all the tea and picnic blankets? I thought the fate of the country was at stake and all that?'

'I think Belly has learned that if one is to inspire sisters-in-magic, then yelling and stamping one's feet is not the best strategy.'

'Righto.' Faye nodded in approval. 'And the little accordion-concertina-thingy?'

'Not the foggiest, darling. Though I fear the worst.'

'Could we form a circle, please?' Bellamy asked.

Martine and Mrs Housego stopped scrying, Mrs Teach removed the cotton wool from both her ears and they all took their places, holding hands. Bellamy drew the black dagger from his tweed jacket and repeated the ritual he performed at the village the night of the air raid. Bright pentangles hovered sizzling in the air before each of them and a protective veil descended over the stones. The air shimmered, the world beyond paled to grey and the sound of woodland birdsong became strangely muted.

'That should do it.' Bellamy looked around. 'Any passers-by will feel the uncontrollable urge to avoid us. We should remain undisturbed for the duration.'

Faye raised her hand.

'Yes, Faye?'

'I'm trying to help a ghost in Larry Dell's barn, a pilot, and he—'

'I'm sorry, Faye,' Bellamy interrupted, 'but does this have anything to do with the ritual?'

'Er, no.'

'Then could I kindly ask you to save any other business for the end, please?'

'But I thought, while we're all here—'

'Indeed, but we have a mission and very little time.' The jollity in Bellamy's tone was at breaking point. 'This isn't a coven.'

Faye saw Miss Charlotte wince at his use of the word.

'Fair enough,' Faye muttered.

'Splendid, thank you, Faye,' Bellamy said, getting back on track. 'Once again, I should like to thank you all for your efforts in this endeavour thus far, but I should, in fairness, warn you of the hardships to come.'

Faye wasn't sure she liked the sound of that, but no one else around her seemed the slightest bit put off, so she kept quiet.

'I thought I would begin today by inviting Mrs Housego to speak,' Bellamy continued. 'One of the reasons I invited Mrs Housego onto the team – aside from her spectacular strengths as a scryer – is she is the only living witch I know who has helped generate a cone of power, and I've asked her if she could kindly share her experiences with us. Mrs Housego ...' Bellamy started to applaud and the others joined in. Faye wondered if she'd wandered into a Women's Institute meeting by mistake.

'Thank you, Mr Dumonde.' Mrs Housego sat on her blanket, knobbly knees drawn together, as she addressed the witches who also took the opportunity to sit and rest. 'It was during The Great War. I still don't know why we call it that. Din't feel great back then and certainly don't feel like it today. The Germans din't have the kinds of fighters and bombers that they have now, but they did have bloody great airships. Zeppelins, they called 'em. I would see them come over my village, Wells-next-the-Sea in Norfolk, following the River Ouse to London to drop their bombs.'

Faye recalled her dad talking about seeing the Zeppelins bombing Margate when he was a lad. He made a joke about no one noticing any difference the next morning.

'The army took potshots at 'em, but they missed more than they hit,' Mrs Housego continued. 'They flew too high, out of the range of the guns. You have to imagine these things. Brighter and bigger than the moon, shining silver, with anti-aircraft fire flashing around them ... and there's you stuck on the ground, helpless as a lamb.' Mrs Housego leaned forwards. 'And that's what made it worse. Folks din't take shelter like they do now. They used to gather in the streets to watch 'em pass over like it was a May Day parade or something.' She lowered her eyes. 'That's when the bombs dropped. I was staying with my sister in Kings Lynn when it was first hit by a raid. I've never been so scared in my life. I don't need to tell you what it's like as we're goin' through worse now, but I din't know any better then and I don't mind tellin' you I was that close to widdlin' in me knickers.'

Faye tried to imagine Mrs Housego as a frightened younger woman, but she couldn't do it. The wise old matriarch sitting on the blanket before her was all skin and bones, but still looked like she wouldn't take any nonsense from the whole Nazi Blitzkrieg.

Mrs Housego continued, 'As the war went on, they got bigger – over six hundred feet long, they were – and they flew higher and faster. Something had to be done.' She took a moment to pluck a hankie from her sleeve and blow into it. Wrinkling her nose, she tucked the hankie away and continued. 'It was Lady Sage who had the idea to use a cone of power.' Mrs Housego looked again to Faye and Jennifer. 'You young 'uns might not know Lady Sage, but she was a hell of a witch, and one of the best High Witches of the British Empire we've ever had – even our Vera Fivetrees will tell you that – and she came to us witches in Norfolk and told us what she had planned. We didn't wait on no highfalutin officers in the army to give us the go-ahead.' Mrs Housego gestured to Martine. 'Like you, young lady, Lady Sage hated anything with too many captains. We just went ahead and did it. She gathered us up, much like we are now, and practised the same ritual, and one wet day in March 1917 we built a bonfire on the sands, gathered our scryers, danced and created a cone of power.' Mrs Housego looked around the circle of witches. 'We imagined the pilots in the airships. We clouded their minds, and we saw them off. Five of them. One of them blew up!'

Faye shivered, the image of the bomber she'd brought down flashing in her mind's eye. She shook it away.

'We did it again in May. Six Zeppelins this time, all on their way to London, all turned their tails and fled. Official reports will tell you it was the weather, but that's a load of old squit. I know it was us.' She took a sip of her tea. 'That last night did Lady Sage in, though. Poor old Peggy was wobbly on her pins at the best of times, but her ticker had enough that night and as those airships turned and disappeared into the clouds, she fell to the sand, shaking like a newborn bird.' Mrs Housego's eyes glistened. 'Of course, her bein' in the nuddy din't help none.'

'You were skyclad?' Faye asked.

Mrs Housego nodded. 'I had a bit more meat on me bones back then, and we was covered in goose fat to ward off the chill, but nothing else. We tried to keep her warm, but all of us was cold as stone and even as we huddled around her she passed away. I ain't ever forgiven meself.'

'That weren't your fault.' Faye rested a hand on the old woman's arm.

'That's kind of you to say, Faye, but I was prone to vanity back then. I had bought a new coat that winter and didn't want to get any seawater or sand on it, so we left all our clothes on a cart some half a mile from the shoreline. If I'd only had my coat, she might've lived.'

A brief and solemn silence fell, broken by Miss Charlotte. 'Did it work? Being skyclad? Did it intensify your power?'

'Oh, most certainly.' Mrs Housego sniffed her tears away and nodded firmly. 'We needed every bit of magical energy we could muster to turn those airborne devils away and bein' skyclad did the job.'

Bellamy said nothing, but slowly and deliberately folded his arms with an infuriating *I-told-you-so* expression on his face.

'With all due to respect to Mrs Housego,' Mrs Teach began, in a way that implied that her entire life's supply of due respect to Mrs Housego could be contained in a thimble, 'magic isn't something you can measure on a barometer.'

'A *bare*-ometer,' Faye joked. Her smile vanished as Mrs Teach glared at her. 'Sorry.'

'It will take more than a decades-old anecdote of an event to convince me, I'm afraid,' Mrs Teach concluded.

'*Excusez moi*, Madame Housego.' Martine exhaled cigarette smoke. 'We are not talking about a few Zeppelins. I have seen the Nazi Blitzkrieg and ... it's unstoppable.' Martine's eyes gazed into the cloud of smoke drifting around her. 'Thousands of tanks, aircraft, men. They won't be so simple to turn away as a few balloons.'

Faye nodded. 'And there's only six of us.'

'Indeed,' Jennifer agreed. 'And with all due respect to the witches gathered here, I doubt any of us have the skills of an esteemed practitioner like Lady Sage. How on earth are we supposed to turn back the might of the Nazi forces?'

'I'm glad you asked.' Bellamy slapped his thighs and got to his feet. 'And thank you, Mrs Housego, for that scintillating and deeply moving account. And I shall indeed be looking to replicate Lady Sage's cone of power, enhancing its strength with my own research into the writings of the Celts, and adding one slight change that will tip the odds of success in our favour. Ladies, if you could kindly be upstanding.'

Bellamy raised his hands, and the six witches stood with varying levels of groans and popping joints. They formed a circle around the small fire.

'A cone of power is about generating huge amounts of magical energy,' Bellamy said. 'It requires a great physical effort, and, if all goes well, will take anywhere between four and six hours.'

Faye heard a whine of complaint that she thought came from Mrs Teach.

'One of our scryers will begin, er, scrying, and the rest of us will hold hands,' Bellamy continued, 'and dance in a circle around the fire. Of course, our bonfire on the day will be much bigger than this one, which is for practice purposes only. And we will be on that convergence of ley lines on the cliffs in Dover, which will boost our power considerably. Hands joined, we'll dance faster and faster, reciting the words I have given you. Then, on my word, we will stop and you, Faye Bright and Mrs Housego, will break hands with the circle and dance in the opposite direction, inside the circle. One by one, the others will join your new circle until we have created enough magical energy for the task at hand. Every half an hour, we'll switch scryers to keep the energy fresh. This brings me to the little twist in the recipe.' Bellamy hurried to a rucksack leaning against one of the standing stones. He fiddled with the buckle and rummaged inside. 'Mrs Housego told us that she and her fellow witches tried to imagine the pilots in their Zeppelins. And, as Martine and Faye rightly pointed out, to do so with the might of the Luftwaffe bearing down upon us would be folly. However ...' Bellamy hurried back to the head of the slaughter stone and placed three photographs on the stone. 'I would ask you to imagine these three ghastly men.'

'Ugh. Really?' Faye grimaced.

'Oh, I say, how awful,' Jennifer agreed, inching closer to Faye.

The first photograph was unmistakably Adolf Hitler. Faye vaguely recognised the other two from the newspapers and newsreels.

'This one you'll know.' Bellamy tapped the photo of Hitler. 'This portly chap is Reichsmarschall Hermann Göring, and this stern fellow is Grand Admiral Erich Raeder. All three would be the architects of any invasion of our shores. Rather than try and repel the countless minds of the invaders, we need to focus our energy on these men and make them think that crossing the Channel is a very bad idea indeed. That it simply cannot be done. To do this, we will repeat these words over and over: "You cannot cross the sea, you cannot cross the sea, you cannot cross the sea."' Bellamy stood upright from the photos, clearly delighted with his plan.

'In English?' Faye asked.

Bellamy twitched and cocked an ear. 'Beg pardon?'

'If we're trying to convince these Germans that invasion is a bad idea, shouldn't we be speaking in German? Otherwise how will they understand us?'

The twitching in Bellamy's eyes had expanded to his cheeks. 'It ... er ... So long as they get the gist.'

'*Sie können das Meer nicht überqueren,*' Martine said in a very good Berlin accent. 'I'll write it down for you.'

'That's very kind, Martine. Yes, in German, Faye. Very good.'

'And that will do it, will it?' Faye asked, trying not to sound too despondent. 'Just saying that over and over?'

'Oh, yes. We cloud the minds of their leaders. Cut off the heads.' Bellamy drew a finger across his throat. 'Or at least convince the heads that invading Russia is a better use of their resources.'

'It's a good plan.' Mrs Housego nodded. 'We've done it before and we can do it again. Just bigger this time. I reckon it'll work.'

Bellamy clapped his hands together. 'Splendid! Shall we give it a go?'

'I have one question.' Mrs Teach raised a finger.

Bellamy blinked rapidly. 'Indeed, Mrs Teach?'

'Do you consider yourself a gentleman, Mr Dumonde?'

'I certainly like to think so.'

'Are you aware of the definition of a gentleman?'

Bellamy tapped a foot impatiently and plastered on a smile. 'Do please enlighten me.'

'A gentleman, Mr Dumonde, is a chap in possession of an accordion, but who chooses not to play it.'

Bellamy's smile vanished. 'It's a concertina.'

'The same principle applies.'

'I'll have you know, Mrs Teach, I am quite accomplished. We shall need to dance, and to dance we shall need music.'

'I fear that the racket that emanates from that thing could scarcely be described as music, Mr Dumonde,' she said, popping cotton wool back into her ears. 'It is a tool of Morris Men and I'm not sure I approve.'

Bellamy jutted his jaw. 'Form a circle, ladies!'

⅌

What followed reminded Faye of when she was once press-ganged into country dancing at the harvest festival a few years ago. A lot of uncertain shuffling, bumping and foot-treading as they danced in circles. All while Martine was scrying through her cloudy crystal ball and Bellamy played his concertina. Yes, he was by concertina standards accomplished, but it still sounded like the air from a bellows being pumped through a mouth organ.

As Faye and Mrs Housego broke the circle and started dancing anticlockwise, she felt a little spark of magical energy surging within her. Nothing like what she had experienced on the cliffs at Dover, and not nearly enough for the ritual to work. Faye wondered if her power had gone again and she wished it would make up its bloody mind. Truthfully, she missed it. She wanted it back.

They continued to dance, faster and with more fluidity. After the first hour there came a point where muscle memory took over and they stopped thinking about the moves. The air around them began to crackle with magical energy ricocheting off the protective veil. The witches were sweaty and their feet grew heavy, but their minds were clear and blissful as they felt a unity in thought and motion that belonged only to them. And for the first time since Bellamy arrived, Faye thought that this mad plan might just work.

204

MRS HOUSEGO'S
MUSHROOM SOUP

'That was an amazing story, Mrs Aitch.' Faye and the other witches were in the snug of the Green Man. Bellamy had offered to buy them all a round after a splendid morning's work, and that had turned into three and now they were all rather jolly. The conversation bounced around the table as the witches discovered they had more in common than not, although most of them were cooing over Jennifer's cat. Faye found herself squeezed between Jennifer and the bony Mrs Housego. 'It must've been terrifying,' Faye continued. 'Just the six of you on a beach with those bloomin' great airships bearing down on yer, while you was all naked as the day you was born.'

'Apart from the goose fat,' Mrs Housego said with a chuckle. 'We were scared, yes, but we had each other. Nothing could have broken us. Even as the ships got so close, we stood our ground. I could see the numbers on the side. LZ45 was the first, followed by LZ50, then LZ53—'

'Blimey, how do you remember the numbers?'

'If you can guess how, I'll give you the how-to.' Mrs Housego winked.

'Magic tea?' Faye guessed.

Mrs Housego shook her head.

'Magic coffee?'

Another shake.

'Magic soup?'

Mrs Housego narrowed her eyes. 'How did you get that so quick?'

Faye gave Mrs Housego a playful nudge. 'There's a Thermos flask poking out of your handbag, Mrs Aitch, so I took a punt.'

Mrs Housego looked down to find her handbag was indeed open, revealing a tartan flask. 'Well, aren't you the clever one?'

For a moment, Faye thought that the old woman might be cross, but she flashed a gap-toothed grin and cackled.

'Am I right?' Faye asked. 'What is it?'

'A little bit of goblin meat.'

'Eh?'

Mrs Housego glanced over at the other witches who were still entranced by Jennifer's unnamed cat. She lowered her voice. 'Mushroom soup, pet. A recipe handed down from one mother to another. Helps with memory.' She tapped the side of her head. 'Young Master Bellamy drove up to see me a few weeks ago. He knew I was there when Lady Sage died and he wanted me to tell her story for you young 'uns. I told him I could barely remember what day of the week it was, then he says he knows about my mushroom soup, and how it helps a person remember everything. I told him that's not how it works, but he asked me all the same.'

Faye felt a flutter of excitement in her belly. 'It helps people remember things?'

'You need a token,' Mrs Housego said. 'I had a letter that Peggy Sage once wrote to me. That, combined with the soup, unlocked the memory like it happened yesterday. That's how I remember things like the numbers on the Zeppelins.'

Faye immediately thought of the page from her mother's book. The one with the recipe for jam roly-poly. She wanted to ask Mrs Housego more, but the novelty of Jennifer's cat was wearing off and the witches were less distracted. Faye had to get Mrs Housego to herself.

'Right, my round, I reckon. Same again, everyone?' This got a cheery reception from the witches, and Faye wriggled out from behind the table. 'Mrs Aitch? Want to give us a hand?'

Mrs Housego understood and smiled. 'Happy to, my pet.'

Terrence and Bertie were run off their feet tonight as the place was packed with more pilots than Faye had ever seen in the pub. Most were new faces, no doubt sent here to fight on the aerial front lines of the Battle of Britain. There were half-a-dozen of them waiting to be served before Faye and Mrs Housego, so they had plenty of time to chat.

Bellamy and Martine had moved to a seat by the fireplace. Bellamy began gently squeezing his concertina and Martine began singing a sad ballad in French. Faye couldn't be sure what Martine was singing about, but it was a seductive tune and all in the pub were enraptured.

Faye glanced over to Mrs Teach and Miss Charlotte. They were also momentarily distracted by the new musical turn, so this was Faye's chance. She asked Mrs Housego in an urgent whisper, 'What if there was something I wanted to remember? Would the soup work for me?'

Mrs Housego gave a nod. 'A girl with your magical powers? I reckon it would work wonders.'

'I just want to remember a specific thing, though,' Faye added. 'I don't want to be remembering everything that ever happened since I was born. That would drive me loopy.'

'It don't work like that, dear.' Mrs Housego tapped a reassuring hand on Faye's wrist. 'The soup fires up your noggin and opens doors. It's up to you to decide if you want to step through.'

'And if I have the right token, then I can choose the memory?'

Mrs Housego gave Faye's hand a little squeeze. 'What troubles you, dear? Is it that ghost you mentioned?'

Faye had asked for advice on Leo on the walk back from the rehearsal. Jennifer and Martine both suggested banishment rituals similar to the one that Faye, Mrs Teach and Miss Charlotte had inflicted on the Luftwaffe pilot. Bellamy advised Faye not to get involved, which was no help whatsoever, and Mrs Housego wondered if getting an exorcist in might do the trick. Everyone had torturous ideas on how to be rid of Leo, but not how to help him.

'Sort of. My mum . . .' Faye looked around again as Martine and Bellamy ended their song and the pub's patrons applauded. Mrs Teach and Miss Charlotte were now deep in conversation. Jennifer sat nearby, tickling her cat's chin. She was looking in Faye's direction and raised the cat's paw to give a little wave. Faye waved back and Jennifer resumed with the tickling. 'My mum wrote a book,' Faye continued, satisfied that no one was eavesdropping. 'A book of magic, and we had to burn it. I saw every page before we did, but I hardly remember any of it, and now I need it to help this pilot . . .'

'Oh yes, I heard about the burning. Very sad, but those are the rules.' Mrs Housego raised a thin white eyebrow as Martine and Bellamy performed an uptempo and jolly number. Two of the airmen began to dance, linked at the elbows, spinning in circles. The others clapped in time. Mrs Housego smiled and joined in with the clapping. She leaned closer to Faye. 'And now you want to read it again? Well, that's perfectly understandable, pet.'

'And the soup will do that?'

'What token do you have?'

'I still have a page. A recipe for jam roly-poly,' Faye said, causing Mrs Housego's face to wrinkle in confusion. 'Doesn't matter, but yes, I have a page from the book. Now, how do I make this soup?'

'Oh no, poppet, you couldn't possibly.'

'Why . . . why not?'

'These are very special mushrooms.'

'What sort? I'll find them.'

'I get them sent in the post from a man in Wales. They have an uncommon selection there. You have to be ever so careful. Pick the wrong ones, you'll turn your toes up, my pickle.'

'Can you give me his address? I can make the soup myself. I'll—'

'Here.' Mrs Housego handed the tartan flask to Faye. 'You have the rest of mine.'

'No, I couldn't possibly—'

'Take it. You're clearly in a hurry. It must be important.'

'It is,' Faye said. 'It really is. So what do I do? Just heat it up and drink it?'

'Heat the soup till it simmers, don't let it boil over, or it won't work. No salt or pepper. Hold the page with the jam roly-poly recipe in one hand and drink it all as the clock strikes midnight, and you'll need to have finished it by the twelfth stroke. Wolf it down if you have to.'

'Then what?'

'Sleep for one hour and one hour only,' Mrs Housego said. 'And when you wake, it'll all be there, like reading a book.'

Faye looked at the flask, hope swelling within her.

Martine and Bellamy's song came to a thundering con-clusion and the pub rattled with applause and cheers. Faye noticed Terrence waiting for their order. She handed him the flask, whispering, 'Stick that behind the bar. Don't touch it, definitely don't drink it. I'll pick it up later. Oh, and same again please, Dad.'

Terrence nodded wearily – resigned to Faye's magic strangeness – and started pulling pints.

Mrs Housego gently squeezed Faye's hand. 'A word of warning,' she said.

'Warning?' Faye's hope began to fizzle. 'What warning?'

'It can go wrong. And it can do more harm than good.'

'What sort of harm?'

'It can make you go a little doolally,' Mrs Housego said. 'Nothing permanent, but I've had days where I don't know left from right and can barely remem-ber my name.'

'Oh, blinkin' flip. Why does that happen?'

Mrs Housego shrugged her bony shoulders. 'Recipe could be wrong, mushrooms might be off. All sorts of reasons. But it don't happen often. Much.'

Faye wasn't particularly reassured by this, but she had survived all the strange stuff that witchery had thrown at her so far. How bad could it be?

Mrs Housego raised an emphatic finger. 'Oh, and this is important: the effect will only last till sunrise.'

'What do you mean?'

'The soup opens doors in your memory, Faye.' Mrs

211

Housego mimed a double-door opening. 'Once you wake you can wander around those memories to your heart's content. Then as soon as the sun pops over the horizon—' She snapped her hands shut. 'No more.'

'But I'll still remember what I've seen, right?'

'I find it helps to take notes. Lots of them. There's something about writing it down that helps make it stick.'

'Surely, if I forget stuff I can just take more of the soup the next night and—'

Mrs Housego wagged a finger, silencing Faye. 'Trust me, girly. Witches with powers greater than ours have tried and gone mad. Every time. My poor mother got like that. She wasn't much for witchin'. She wanted to be an actress. Loved her Shakespeare, she did, but she could never remember all them words. So she took the soup. Again and again. Made her proper off her rocker, it did. At the end, she could only speak in iambic pentameter.'

'Oh, Mrs Housego, I'm so sorry.'

'We warned her, but she wouldn't listen. She made a fair few quid standing outside the Norwich Theatre Royal reciting Shakespeare for tourists. It helped keep her comfortable in her dotage.' The old woman rested a hand on Faye's shoulder. 'But don't listen to me bein' all melodramatic. If you want to unlock those memories and read your mother's book, follow my instructions, drink the soup, take lots of notes and you'll be fine.'

✄

Faye sat alone in her room waiting for the longcase clock downstairs to strike midnight. She alternated between bouncing her knee impatiently and tapping her foot on the floor like a rabbit in springtime. How much of her mother's magic would be revealed to her by Mrs Housego's soup? Faye had to sleep for one hour as instructed, and then she'd have quite a few hours to jot down as much as possible. Faye thought about getting a pencil and pad ready, but she reasoned she had oodles of time for stuff like that. There was no reason why she couldn't recall *all* of the book before sunrise. Faye wondered if it would be like meeting her mother again. Or perhaps it would be like having a very one-sided conversation where Faye did all the listening? She chastised herself for being silly. It would only be words. Memories of words on a page. But Faye reminded herself that when she read her mother's book for the first time, she could almost hear her voice again. Clear as day.

The longcase clock chimed. It was midnight.

Faye downed the soup, having prepared it as per Mrs Housego's instructions. It was thick and nutty and stuck to the roof of her mouth. It had a peppery after-taste and made her burp. It felt warm in her belly and she immediately felt drowsy. *One hour*, she reminded herself. *Sleep for one hour only. Set . . . set the alarm.* Faye wanted to reach for her bedside alarm clock, but it was so much easier to close . . . her . . . eyes . . .

The next thing she knew the longcase clock struck five.

FAYE GOES DOOLALLY

Bertie Butterworth's Battle of Britain Diary

Wednesday 14th August, 1940

Raids on and off all day. Heavy battle overhead from 4.30–6pm. At least 50 Nazi planes destroyed. 20 RAF. Haven't spoken to Faye all day, and in between cleaning the pub and helping Dad with his tractor I couldn't help but wonder how she was after all that scary stuff with the ghost. I wish I could help her. Whatever she's doing, I hope she's fine and dandy.

Faye was not fine and dandy.

It was five in the morning. The sun was due to rise in just over half an hour and her mind was flooded with new and baffling memories.

Faye bolted upright before the fifth chime's echo died away, cursing herself for not setting the alarm *before* she took the soup.

But it had worked. Her mother's book was there, in her mind's eye, as vivid as if it was open in her lap. Words and images came to her in a rush. What now? What should she do?

Notes. Mrs Housego had told her to take notes.

Faye scrabbled off the bed and dashed to her sideboard, pulling open drawers and rummaging through the various books and bits of stationery.

She found a fresh notebook and a pencil and tumbled back onto the bed. As she pressed the pencil to paper the lead point snapped.

'Oh, for—'

Cursing herself for not preparing this earlier, Faye hurried back to the sideboard and found another pencil. Blunt. She tossed it over her shoulder and found a third. A good HB pencil. She started to write.

At first, she scribbled down whatever popped into her mind. Recipes, rituals, warnings about poisonous mushrooms, cures for headaches, and a forbidden ritual that could make your plants and vegetables grow by talking to them.

'This isn't what you need, Faye,' she told herself. 'Concentrate. Poltergeists. How to help poltergeists or ghosts.'

She clenched her eyes shut. A few notes came. How to tell when you were in the presence of a ghost, where you might find one, how to communicate with one. There were two pages on poltergeists, one describing what they were and the other describing a case in London where one had smashed all the cutlery in a hotel kitchen, but nothing else.

'That can't be it, Mum, surely?' Faye closed her eyes tighter and made fists. She thought about ghosts, ghouls, spirits . . .

And there it was. A ritual for helping spirits lost in the earthly realm. It was a long one. More than four pages of detailed instructions. Faye's wrist hurt, but she didn't stop.

The longcase clock chimed the half-hour.

'No, no, I need more time.' Faye's mind was a desperate flurry as she jotted down the last few notes. As she finished, she sat back and took a breath. She closed her eyes again and one phrase flashed before her.

How to fly.

Faye recalled the message Leo passed on from her mother. *You need to learn to fly.* The pencil's tip was a blur as she wrote down the ritual. She had cramp in her fingers, the lead was worn down to almost nothing and her handwriting had become a childish scrawl. Somewhere a cockerel crowed. Beams of sunlight slipped through the curtains and Faye's mind began to empty. She was still writing when she fell back into a slumber.

⅌

Faye woke some time later, though she couldn't be sure when. Her mind was foggy. She tried to recall what she had planned for the day, but it wouldn't come. Breakfast was usually first, wasn't it? She shuffled down to the kitchen to greet the man who was always there. He was important, for sure, but she couldn't quite place him. He had a wrinkled face, and hair like clouds, and she knew they had met before. But why was he in the kitchen? He said something cheery and offered her tea from the pot. Bleary-eyed, she accepted it. Tea was something she liked, she was fairly certain of that.

She wondered what to do today. She had a nagging thought at the edge of her mind. It was just past seven in the morning. There was something really important she had to—

She blinked. The man in the kitchen was asking her if she was 'tickety-boo'. Faye glanced at the clock. It was a quarter-past and the tea was cold. Had she been staring into space for that long? He clapped his hands together and suggested she help out around the pub. Faye wondered why a house would have a pub in it, or why a pub would have a house, and that's when she realised something was definitely wrong. She knew this place. Sort of. Did she work here?

The man was looking at her funny. He was asking her to do things, but she kept getting them wrong. She broke pint glasses, dropped a beer barrel and broke a broomstick.

'How did you do that?' the man asked, holding the two bits of the broomstick handle and inspecting them in disbelief.

How did she do it? Faye could barely remember the time of day, let alone what happened ten minutes ago.

'Dunno,' she said with a shrug.

'You don't know? How can you not know? Faye, what's going on?'

'Faye!' she cried. 'That's it.'

'What's it?'

Faye started to reply, *'That's my name!'* because she had quite forgotten it, but from the look on this man's face, she was sure that telling him this would only create more confusion.

'I ... trod on it,' she said. 'The broomstick. Sorry, sir.'

'Sir?' The man's already wrinkled face now creased like a bulldog's. 'Are you sure you're all right?'

Faye nodded. 'Tickety ... er ...'

'Boo?'

'Yes. That.'

The man pressed fingers against his forehead. 'Faye, I haven't got time for this today. I've woken up with an 'eadache that would floor Goliath and I need you to help—'

'Headache? Drink lots of water, get some rest and try to have more spinach and carrots in your meals,' Faye blurted, wondering where it came from.

The man looked at her like a dog that had just pulled its own pint.

Something started happening at the back of Faye's mind. Her eyes felt bigger. Her brain was light and floaty.

The saloon door opened and a young chap with a smiley, freckled face shuffled into the pub. He walked with a limp and carried a trug full of small dark fruits whose name eluded Faye for the moment.

Just the sight of him made Faye feel all hot inside and she fought the overwhelming urge to jump on him and unbutton his shirt while kissing his bare chest.

'Sorry I'm late, Mr Bright, but I saw the first ripe blackberries by the side of the road and I thought I'd harvest a few to—'

'Blackberries, yes!' Faye pointed directly at the lad. 'Good, good! Eat them before Michaelmas, 'cos the Devil pees on blackberries on Michaelmas, and they're no good after that.'

The man and the lad shared a concerned look. Faye wanted to share it with them. What was happening to her?

'What the bloody hell is wrong with you, Faye?' the man asked.

'I can't ... what's the word? Me-member? *R*emember! I can't remember things, but they're coming back. Oh yes. Give me ... give me a mo'.' She took a few steps back as a million thoughts rushed at her at once, all in neat, cursive handwriting – her mother's handwriting! – then they faded away to nothing. It was like someone had stuck a tap on the side of her head and drained it.

Faye put her hands in her hair, and the lad hurried to fetch a chair for her to sit on. The older man brought her a glass of water.

'You dropped this.' The lad handed her a notebook.

Faye opened the notebook and read the first line out loud, 'Dear Faye, just in case you go doolally ...'

'What is it, Faye?' the lad asked.

'Soup!' she cried.

'Soup?' The old man frowned.

'I wrote myself a note before taking Mrs Housego's soup.' Her mind was filling like a bathtub. 'Yes, her mushroom soup. I did just as she told me. I heated the soup in the pan, and wolfed it down at the stroke of midnight, then I felt all sleepy. Oh, Dad, it was . . . Dad!' She jumped to her feet and pointed at Terrence. 'You're my dad! Yes, I knew you were someone important.'

'Oh, ta very much,' he said.

'And Bertie, dear Bertie.' She gave the lad's hand a squeeze and drew him closer, whispering in his ear. 'We will find time for canoodling, I promise.' Faye enjoyed the look of surprise on his face as she walked in little circles. 'Mrs Housego was right. It was the best sleep I ever had. No dreaming. Me brain switched off for the night, and then it came back on again, but I overslept. I didn't have enough time to do it all, so I wrote down what I could and . . .' She gasped and looked up at them both. 'I know how to control it.'

Terrence's head trembled in puzzlement. 'Control what?'

Faye made her hands into fists. 'The power. It's back. The power of the moon. It came by accident before, but now I want it to come. And yes, yes, I know how to control it. I think. I can stoke it like a fire. Yes, yes, and . . . Oh blimey! Mum's book. I could see every page, every word. It's gone now, but I wrote some of it down. I know all sorts now. I . . .' She stopped at one page of hastily scribbled notes and tapped the paper. 'Bloody hell, I think I know how to fly.'

She got to her feet and rushed to the door.

'Where are you going?' Terrence called after her. 'Your mother never flew, I can tell you that.'

'No. She knew how, but never tried it. She did little things to help her neighbours. She never had to do the big things and that's why she was so happy, and she loved us, Dad, more than anything, but she had her secrets and one of them was she knew how to fly!' Faye hurried outside to find her bike, and Terrence ran after her with Bertie hobbling not far behind.

'Don't go flying, Faye,' Terrence cried. 'Not in these skies. It's dangerous!'

'You'll catch a chill,' Bertie added.

'I was thinking more of the hordes of fighter aircraft having dogfights, actually, Bertie,' Terrence said quietly as he watched Faye cycle away, trailing a cloud of dust.

MEMORY MAGIC

Faye's mind was blooming like the petals of a flower as it rearranged itself, making room for the few new memories she had jotted down.

Not least that she knew how to fly.

Which made it very difficult to concentrate on her cycling.

She almost came off at the bottom of Gibbet Lane, but managed to keep going till she got to Larry Dell's haunted barn.

She dropped her bike, swung the barn doors open and rushed inside, ready to call Leo's name, but he was already visible, lying on his back, staring at the ceiling.

'Leo, it's true! I can fly!' she said, and he sat up and spoke, but she couldn't hear him.

'Hang on a mo'.' She snatched up the pilot's helmet with the mic and headphones and wriggled it on her head.

'Why is that important?' he asked.

'It means you were telling the truth about my mother and her message.'

'You doubted me?'

'Don't take this the wrong way, Leo, but when an angry ghost tells you your long-dead mother has a message and that it's that you need to learn to fly, you take it with a pinch of salt, mate.'

Leo shrugged. 'And how have you acquired this knowledge?'

'It was in her book. I could see it in my mind and I wrote it down and it stuck. Well, my mind is still shifting about so much, it's like someone is rearranging the furniture, but it's all there. Just don't ask how,' she told him, though from the look on his face he wasn't about to.

'Her book? She was a pilot?'

'No, she was a witch like me.'

Leo got to his feet. 'A witch? I was right. You'll fly on a broomstick.'

'I told you, we don't fly on broomsticks ... At least, I don't think we do. But that's not what I'm here for.' Faye took a moment to catch her breath. 'I remember it all, Leo. Everything in Mum's book. All the magic. And now I know how to let you go peacefully.'

Leo edged closer. 'Really?'

'Yes, though ...' Faye bit her lip. 'It ain't quick. Y'see, what we did to the other pilot before – the three of us – was the quick way. It was forceful, violent. Like booting someone out of a pub. Mum's method is gentle. She explains it like this: There's our world. There's the underworld—'

'I'm not going there.'

'No. And there's the place you go when you die.'

'Heaven?' Leo asked.

'She never calls it that, but you can if it makes you feel happy.'

Leo shrugged again.

'The problem we have,' Faye continued, 'is it's tricky to move from one place to another. We did it forcefully with that other pilot.'

'I don't want that.'

'Neither do I,' Faye agreed. 'It says in Mum's book that all ghosts slowly fade to the other side over time. I have no idea how long you would take to cross over if you were left alone. Some take days, others years, or even centuries.'

'Centuries? In this place? Kill me now!' Leo's eyes boggled as he realised what he said. 'Oh.'

'What Mum's ritual does is speed things up a little in a way that's not painful to you. The only downside is it takes longer.'

'How much longer?'

'Couple of days, p'raps?' Faye waited for Leo to spit and curse, but his eyes drifted about as he nodded.

'Two more days and I will be at peace?' he said.

'Yes.'

'Let us begin.'

Faye clapped her hands. 'Righty-ho. I have a meeting at ten this morning,' she said, remembering today's cone of power rehearsal. 'But I might have enough time to do both. Wait there!' Faye winced, regretting the stupidity of that statement as she got on her Pashley Model A and cycled into the wood.

ℬ

The ritual required her to make a bowl of special ash from different kinds of wood. She needed a branch from an oak in the north of the wood, a branch from a horse chestnut in the east, a branch from an English elm in the south, and a sliver of bark from a silver birch in the west.

With each tree she had to ask permission first. She would stand before the tree, make the request and wait.

If a magpie landed in the tree and chuckled at her, then permission was granted. If a magpie circled above three times without landing, permission was not given.

Twice she was denied and had to find another tree.

She also had to gather up enough red dogwood twigs to make a broom-head. She arranged the branches and twigs in her bicycle's basket and headed back to the barn.

ℬ

Leo was waiting for her, pacing back and forth. All his previous excitement was gone, and his brow was furrowed.

'Why me?' he asked her. 'Why am I the one stuck here?'

There was an edge in his voice that made Faye wary. She carried the branches and twigs into the barn but stayed back, giving him space to rage.

'I honestly don't know, Leo.' She placed the branches

226

and twigs on the workbench. 'Who knows why anything happens?'

'Up there.' He looked to the sky. 'It was the only place where I belonged. I hated school. I hated church. I did not enjoy the company of others, but up there ... Those voices on the radio. We had a code. An understanding. When we flew together it was as if we were one. We looked out for one another. No one ...' Leo faltered, flexing his lips. 'No one was alone.'

Faye stayed silent. She clasped her hands together as Leo stopped pacing.

'Except me,' he said. 'I went after that Dornier alone.'

'Don't be hard on yourself, Leo,' Faye said gently. 'I hear pilots talk about this stuff in the pub all the time. They all do it and—'

'No. Not me. I should have known better. I was a fool and I paid the price.' He turned to her, jabbing a finger. 'That's why I'm here. I'm being punished.'

'I don't think that's how it works, Leo.'

'Ach. How would you know? You're just a girl.'

Faye would normally have given him an earful, but she busied herself looking for a suitable container for the fire.

'And now you tell me you can fly. Ha! Were you serious?'

'Of course.'

'And have you?'

'Have I what?'

'Flown? Like a bird?' Leo flapped his hands like wings, and Faye didn't like his mocking tone.

'Listen, mush, do you want me to help you or not?' she said, hands on hips. 'What's with the lip all of a sudden?'

'Have you flown?'

'No.'

'Then why say you can?'

'Look, I just ... *know*.' Faye tapped a finger on the side of her head. 'As me dad says, it's all up here for knowin', and down here for dancin'.' She pointed at her feet. The expression merely confused Leo all the more. 'What I mean is, I have the knowledge.'

'I was a tutor at the academy in Poland,' Leo said. 'It took months of training to learn how to fly. Years to master it. And yet you, a girl, claim to have the same knowledge from reading a book? No. No, this is not right.'

'We're not learning to fly, Leo. We're doing a basic ritual.'

'One you learned from this book?' He threw his hands up. 'What if your mother was wrong? How does she even know this? What if it's a cruel trick?'

'My mother was not cruel.'

'She was a witch.'

'I'm a witch. Am I cruel?'

'You showed little mercy to the other pilot,' Leo said, his voice trembling.

Faye's cheeks warmed with shame. She wasn't proud of what they had done to the other ghost. She wasn't proud of what she'd done to that bomber. 'I just want to make things right.'

'Then fly.' Leo pointed to the sky filtering through the gaps in the corrugated roof of the barn. 'Fly here and now. Show me.'

Faye knew what to do. Exactly what to do. Every step of the flying ritual was right there in her mind. But, for a heartbeat, she let her doubt show.

'You cannot do it.' Leo pointed an accusing finger at her. 'I see it, I see you, child. I cannot trust you with this. I am sorry. Please leave.'

'Leo, I—'

Leo roared and the whole barn shook. The branches and twigs that Faye had so carefully gathered flew around the room and she ducked for cover, dashing for the barn doors. She leapt to safety just as they slammed shut.

*

'There's no pleasing some people,' Faye told Larry Dell. 'Livin' or dead.' She had bumped into the farmer as she began to cycle to ritual rehearsal, leaving Leo and his anger in the barn.

Larry scratched at the dent in his head. 'Is it safe to go back in there yet?' he asked. 'There's quite a few tools I need. A scythe, in particular.'

'Larry, take it from me, the last thing you want to do is be in that barn with scythes and such flying all over the shop.'

Larry gripped his cap in his hand. 'Why is it taking so long? If you don't mind me asking?'

'One minute he's keen to buzz off, and the next

he's ...' Faye thought about Leo and his rage. 'The thing is, Larry, the chap in there, he's a Polish fighter pilot.'

'Oh, really?' Larry brightened up, like a collector of cigarette cards who had just discovered a rare one.

'Our lads up there now, they're fighting for King and country and all that, and at the end of a hard day's flying they go to the pub with their mates, and they step out with their girls, or go home when they have leave to see their dear old mothers. They've all got something to lose. Poor old Leo, he's lost it all already. All he wants to do is fly and fight and that's it. And he's blimmin' good at it, too, from what he told me, anyway.'

'He's called Leo, is he?'

'He is, and he's right miffed an' all. Can't say I blame him, either.' Faye looked back towards the barn. 'I've found a way to help him, Larry, but he's made it clear that he don't want helping quite yet.'

Larry put his cap back on and wrung his hands. 'Miss Faye, and I don't mean to be disrespectful, but when I struggle to do something on my own I'll always ask for a bit of help. I know there are others ...' Larry gulped, perhaps not wanting to name other witches out loud for fear of drawing their attention.

'I have asked,' Faye said, 'but they're all busy with something. I know that sounds a bit feeble, but it's something to do with the war effort. That's all I can say.'

Larry gave an understanding nod, but she had to admit he had a point. Maybe she had bitten off more than she could chew. Perhaps Leo would be a little less bolshie with three witches, or even six.

'Your suggestion's a good one, Larry. I'll give it some thought.' She patted him on the shoulder and swung a leg over her bike. 'We'll get it sorted soon enough. But until then, don't go in the barn.'

'But, my tools—'

'Tell you what, write me a list, pin it to the barn door and I'll get them out for you. I'll be back later tonight. Can't do it now, though.' Faye started to pedal away. What she couldn't tell Larry was that she had a ritual to rehearse. One that might save the whole country from invasion.

HELP

Jennifer followed Bellamy along the narrow path to the standing stones, each footstep heavier than the last. She had endured another long night at Hayward Lodge. The mansion was indeed as splendid as Bellamy had boasted. What he failed to mention was the place was packed to the rafters with ghastly wounded soldiers. Every room reeked of liniment, and the nights were punctuated by nightmarish screams and pathetic cries for Mother.

Martine found a grand piano in one of the rooms and had it wheeled from hall to hall so that she could sing torch songs to the traumatised men in their beds. Hadn't the poor blighters suffered enough? She played slow and turgid, with that ever-present cigarette stuck to her lip, and sang with a voice that sounded like she was gargling whiskey and shingle. Jennifer had half a mind to ask if any of them wanted poison to end their suffering there and then. Yet, bizarrely, they met the end of each song with wild applause. Jennifer supposed they had been starved of real entertainment for so long they no longer knew the difference between good and bad.

She did have her own room, which was a blessing. One with a lock that allowed her to practise her scrying in peace, and to inform Otto of the location of the cone of power ritual. They took a different route through the wood this morning and she found it impossible to note any significant landmarks. It was almost as if the wood was shifting around Jennifer in order to baffle her. Nonsense, of course, but she had this nagging feeling that if she lost sight of Bellamy or the other witches, she would be disorientated in moments. Not that there was much chance of losing track of this bunch. Bellamy's concertina wheezed in its case as he trudged ahead of her, Martine left smoke signals wherever she went, Mrs Housego's bones creaked like branches in a storm, and Mrs Teach and Miss Charlotte's conspiratorial muttering was an incessant drone.

Faye had already arrived at the standing stones and was stoking the ritual fire.

'Mornin' all!' she greeted them.

Jennifer plastered on a smile, gave Faye a wave and got into character.

Faye was an oddity. Very different from the other witches. None of that mightier-than-thou attitude so common in witchery. Though it had to be an act, surely? No one could be that chirpy all the time. Even if she was the genuine article, then it was a weakness to be exploited.

Playing the dead mother card had been a calculated

risk – it would be easy enough for anyone to check that Jennifer's mother had died only recently – but one worth taking. Faye's trusting nature made it very easy for strangers to get close to her. Close enough to use the knuckledusters, dagger or poison in Jennifer's bag. She was just waiting for Otto's command to kill her. Until then, they would continue to be fast friends.

Jennifer hurried to greet her. She genuinely wanted to know if Faye had taken any of Mrs Housego's godforsaken soup and what effect it'd had. Jennifer was just wondering how to broach the subject without giving away that she had been lip-reading their conversation, when the skeletal Mrs Housego barged past her.

'How did it go?' Mrs Housego asked Faye eagerly.

Jennifer noticed that both Mrs Teach's and Miss Charlotte's heads darted up at once to hear her answer.

Faye handed the flask back to Mrs Housego. 'I thought I'd lost my marbles for a few minutes, but it definitely works. Thanks, Mrs Aitch.'

Mrs Teach took a step forwards. 'You had some of Mrs Housego's soup?'

'Downed the lot.'

Martine took the cigarette away from her red lips. 'And it worked?'

Faye grinned. 'I found the ritual I needed, plus a few more. I made notes on everything. My poor brain is a bit all over the place this morning, so I'm sorry if I'm a sandwich short of a picnic today. There's still quite a bit of information squirrelling about looking for somewhere to settle down.'

'Does it *work* work?' Miss Charlotte asked, and for the first time Jennifer saw some genuine zeal from the woman. She wondered what Charlotte might want with a soup that restored one's memory. 'Have you ... tried out any of the rituals from your mother's book?'

'Not really. I'm trying to help my ghost first, and thank you for all your ideas on that, but I think I know how to get him where he needs to go once he calms down. But as for the other nuggets of knowledge that are now jammed into my noggin ... Knowing when and how to use all these new bits and bobs is another matter altogether. So ...' Faye clasped her hands together. Jennifer dreaded what was coming next. Another skin-crawling request to do something as a *team*. What was it with this lot and their inability to work alone?

'I'd be grateful if you ladies – oh, and you, too, Mr Dumonde – if you could give me the benefit of your own wisdom.' Faye tapped the side of her head. 'See, you can memorise a recipe for a cake, but I don't reckon that makes you a baker. So I hope you'll be all tickety-boo if I ask for your experience when I need it.'

Was that it? Jennifer thought to herself. At least it was mercifully short.

Martine gave a curt nod, the cigarette bobbing on her lip as she spoke. 'I am happy to help, Faye Bright.'

Jennifer had to stop herself from snorting. Had the Frenchie *ever* been happy?

'And me, my lovely.' Mrs Housego gave Faye a squeeze.

236

Mrs Teach and Miss Charlotte shared a look before both giving her a smile.

'As always,' Mrs Teach began, 'you can trust us to be by your side in times of difficulty, Faye.'

'Gosh, yes.' Jennifer hoisted her smile back into place, hurrying to Faye's side and taking her hand. 'Me, too.' *What rot*, she thought. *The only person you can trust is yourself and that's that.*

'Good, because, as a matter of fact, I'm still having problems with this ghost—'

'Perhaps later, hmm?' Bellamy tucked his hands into his armpits. 'This is all jolly good, but I don't suppose there was anything in that book about repelling an invasion, was there?'

Faye adjusted her specs as she thought. 'If there was, I didn't see it.'

'What rotten luck,' he said. 'Then we have work to do. Faye, perhaps we can discuss this further after today's rehearsal? Ladies, time is of the essence. Please take your positions and we shall begin.'

ß

The first hour or so of the ritual rehearsal went surprisingly well. They resembled, if not a team, then something slightly less shambolic than yesterday. Mostly because they all delighted in ignoring Bellamy and the instructions he hollered over the wheezing of his concertina. Instead, they found their own rhythm and took cues to change and move from the smallest of gestures. For some reason, this made the magical energy they created for the cone even stronger. Jennifer could feel it in the air.

Sadly, that same air was soon polluted by what sounded like a wounded farm animal wailing in agony.

All eyes turned to Bellamy and his concertina. It was playing the same droning note whatever buttons he pressed.

'Ah.' He turned the thing over and inspected it, then raised his voice to be heard over the racket. 'A key is stuck. I suspect a broken spring. Does . . . does anyone happen to have a Phillips screwdriver?'

'Belly, will you put that blasted thing out of its misery?' Jennifer cried.

'Yes, I'm not sure why it's . . .' Bellamy held the device to his ear. 'Hmm. This reed shouldn't be speaking.'

'If it is, it's saying, "Kill me now",' Miss Charlotte added.

'Shall we have a break?' Mrs Teach suggested at the top of her voice. 'Tea, anyone?'

'Yes, yes, jolly good idea.' Bellamy put the concertina down, silencing it. 'Everyone take a short break for refreshments.' He removed the protective veil from the circle of stones and daylight streamed in.

Charlotte struck a match and lit Martine's cigarette before filling her own pipe.

'Sterling work, ladies.' Bellamy clapped his hands together. 'Just a few more sessions like this and I think we'll be ready.'

As Mrs Teach produced a flask of tea and placed cups for all on the slaughter stone, Jennifer took some comfort that Bellamy hadn't said the word 'skyclad' or mentioned nudity at all today. She thought about bringing it up just to see how he would react, or to rile up the others, but she was too exhausted to enjoy any discord. Besides, she needed more subtle ways to antagonise the other witches without drawing any suspicion on herself. And, for once, she was in complete agreement with them. Skyclad rituals were just another perverted notion invented by men of magic, and she had no desire to see anyone's bits, especially this lot's.

Mrs Teach poured a cuppa for Mrs Housego who looked fit to drop. She sat against one of the bigger stones, sipping her tea while reading the latest issue of *Health & Efficiency*. Faye was the only one of them who didn't look utterly exhausted. Jennifer was beginning to appreciate Otto's fascination with the girl.

'Aha! A screwdriver,' Bellamy announced, taking one from his concertina case as if he had just pulled Excalibur from a stone. 'Oh no, hang it all. It's the wrong size.'

Jennifer watched as Faye made her way over to speak to Mrs Teach and Miss Charlotte. They were thick as thieves, muttering to one another, furtive eyes darting about, when she interrupted them. Faye's back was to Jennifer, so she didn't know what Faye was asking, but she got a patronising, 'Perhaps later, dear?' from Mrs Teach.

Faye nodded, stuffed her hands in her pockets and chewed her lip as she let the two witches resume their chat. Jennifer saw an opportunity. She scooped up her cat, wrapped the creature around her neck like a fur stole and skipped over to Faye, slipping her arm into the crook of her elbow. 'Stretch your legs?'

'Why not?' Faye smiled, and the pair sauntered out of the stones and into the wood.

'Don't wander off too far,' Bellamy called after them. 'I should have this fixed in a jiffy.'

'Jolly good!' Jennifer didn't bother looking back. 'That was a thrill, wasn't it?' She squeezed Faye closer to her.

'The ritual?' Faye blinked out of her stupor. 'Yes, at least, I think it was. I'm still a bit dazed from all that prancing about. The dancing stirs up a lot of . . .' Faye trailed off, looking back at Mrs Teach and Miss Charlotte. She lowered her voice. 'That thing that happened on the cliffs at Dover. I worry that it'll happen again and I won't be able to control it.'

'Oh, me too. All of us working together to generate that power. I've never known anything like it.' Jennifer didn't have to drum up too much fake enthusiasm. The ritual gave her a rather enjoyable tingle as the magical energy coursed through them. She could almost get used to it. 'I think we might actually pull this off.'

'I blimmin' hope so. For all our sakes.' Faye looked back again, but the stones were out of sight.

'Everything all right?' Jennifer tilted her head and pouted a little. 'I noticed Mrs Teach and Miss Charlotte giving you the brush-off.'

Faye let her shoulders drop. 'They've been acting funny and I don't know why. Have I done something wrong?'

'I hate to say it, Faye, but they might be jealous.' Jennifer bit her lip as she prepared to stir up trouble. It was almost too easy.

'Jealous? What've they got to be jealous about?'

'Your powers, Faye. You have to know that you're the most powerful witch here. Possibly the most powerful in the country.'

'Don't be daft.' Faye twisted her lip as she thought a little more. Jennifer knew to remain silent as Faye's simmering doubts came to the boil. 'Mind you, Bellamy said something silly about me bein' powerful and they've been a bit off since then. They might even be frightened of me since that night with the bomber. I've seen them whispering on the train home, between rehearsals and down the pub.'

'There you are, then. Faye Bright, you have an extraordinary power. One can either fear it or celebrate it. I was there on the cliff at Dover, I saw the magical energy that was bursting out of you and it was ... Well, I don't quite know where to start, but I can tell you that I've never seen anything like it, so—'

'And what use are funny balls of blue light?' Faye tutted and shook her head. 'Nah, it was building up inside me and I was like a balloon. Either I let it out, or I burst. I just did what I had to.'

Dear God, this girl's modesty was grating. Try a different tack, Jennifer.

'Regardless, I bet they wished they could have all that knowledge you have now, just like that.' Jennifer snapped her fingers.

'I'm not sure that's how it works. It's all there, but I don't know how to use it. Not yet, anyway. For a start . . .' Faye twisted her lips, hesitant. As if she wanted to tell Jennifer something, but didn't know if she should.

Jennifer opened her lips oh-so-slightly and widened her eyes. Bizarrely, the cat did the same. The pair were all but pleading to know.

'Oh, bugger it,' Faye said. 'I think I know how to fly.'

Jennifer wondered if she'd heard Faye correctly. She ran the words through her mind again, then put on a schoolgirl gasp.

'You had better not be fibbing.'

'Don't think I am.' Faye grinned. 'I know the theory, I just ain't put it into practice. And it might be a good way to let the magical air out of my balloon, if you get my meaning?'

'I . . . think I do.'

'S'pose there's only one way to find out. Jennifer Gentle. Do you want to learn how to fly?'

Jennifer tingled with joy. Maybe she wouldn't have to kill Faye Bright. Maybe the silly girl would do it to herself.

LEARNING TO FLY

'Do you need ointment?' Jennifer's question was unexpected. They had found a clearing in the wood that was ideal for secret flying tests. Almost perfectly circular, it was surrounded with dense foliage so that no one could sneak up on them without making a racket. The grass in the clearing was ankle high, and Faye found them a spot without anything prickly.

'No ointment,' Faye said, recalling the instructions from her mother's book. 'But we'll need to lie down.'

'I recall my mother mentioning flying ointment.' Jennifer stroked her cat as she recalled the ingredients. 'Belladonna, henbane, jimson weed, mandrake, hemlock and wolfsbane. Two drops would knock out an elephant, but it made witches *think* they were flying, even if they were not.'

'It's funny what you remember about your mother, isn't it?' Faye said. 'The way old memories come and go.'

'Cling to them, Faye.' Jennifer hugged her cat a little tighter. 'Treasure them like jewels.'

'Oh, don't worry, I do.' Faye lay on her back and clasped her hands across her belly. 'Lie like this.'

Jennifer did so, her cat sitting on her head.

'I don't think she's helping.' Faye nodded at the puss.

'Indeed. Bally thing, simply won't let me be.' Jennifer sat up, placing her cat on the ground. She looked the moggy directly in the eyes. 'Go hunting, little one. Enjoy.' The cat gave a little nod and dashed into the long grass.

The two girls lay side by side again.

'Righto,' Jennifer said. 'How do we do this?'

'If you're like me, you've probably been told that witches do not fly on broomsticks.'

'Very true.'

'According to my mum, she had a conversation with Lady Sage—'

'Your mother knew Lady Sage?' Jennifer was genuinely impressed.

'She mentions her once in the book and never again, so I don't think they were best friends, but I reckon she definitely had one good chinwag with her. Anyway, she said Lady Sage told her that witches had to stop flying centuries ago because, well, ordinary folk didn't like it and witches ended up getting burned alive and all that, so it seemed like a good idea to give it a rest.'

'Understandable.'

'Also, there's a knack to flying. And very few witches get the hang of it. And that's because it requires an understanding of the greater universe and, generally, witches ain't much cop at that. We tend to be a bit more grounded. We understand the natural world around us, herbs and such—'

'But beyond that we can get a bit dismissive,' Jennifer finished.

'Exactly,' Faye said. 'So the first magical folk to fly weren't from around here. They was out in Arabia and the Orient, where they were a bit more savvy about science and the like. This was back in the Dark Ages, so things here were pretty grotty anyway, but out there they studied the stars and planets. They discovered that our world is one of countless planets in space. And they sat down and did their sums and reckoned that we were moving in space, and not only were we moving, but we were whizzing through it. Earth is flying through space at tens of thousands of miles an hour.'

'Doesn't feel like it,' Jennifer said.

'Ah, but what if you could?' Faye asked, getting excited. ''Cos that's the key to learning to fly. You have to have to feel the Earth moving through space,' Faye said, sounding a lot more certain of herself than she felt. The words were all there in her head, unlocked by Mrs Housego's mushroom soup, and they all made sense in her mind, but now she said them out loud she began to realise how ludicrous it all sounded.

'I'm not sure I follow you, Faye,' Jennifer said.

Faye persevered. 'We've all been trying to learn to fly for centuries, and we look at the dicky birds and reckon we need wings like them. Or we stick wings on big engines and shoot ourselves into the sky. Well, Lady Sage and Mum tell me we've been doing it wrong.

All we need is a little understanding of our place in the universe.'

'And how does one acquire that?'

'Close your eyes. Let's give it a go.' She glanced over to see Jennifer squeeze her eyes shut. Faye did the same. 'Try to imagine the planet Earth in space, and it's moving, like a big old blue and green marble whizzing through the stars. Got it?'

'Got it,' Jennifer replied.

'You and me, we're attached to that marble, but we can choose to detach ourselves from it. Oh, there it is!'

'There what is?' Jennifer asked.

'Are you getting a weird feeling like magic is rising up inside you?'

'I'm getting a damp bottom,' Jennifer said. 'And not much else.'

'It starts in your belly, then spreads out and ... Blimey.' Faye's cheeks flushed red, and she began to puff, eyes still closed. 'Here we go. I'm beginning to think this was a bad idea. For all I know we could be catapulted into the moon.'

'Not bally likely.'

'Can't you feel it? We're like little planets, flying through space, just very, very close to planet Earth. We've stepped aside from our world, and we're flying alongside it.'

'How ...' Jennifer's voice came from an odd place, like she had moved to the other side of the clearing. 'How are you doing that?'

An odd sinking sensation made Faye feel light.

'Ooh, I've come over all peculiar. So maybe we should stop and ... Oh.' Faye opened her eyes.

She was rising above the trees.

Faye looked down to see her own feet dangling in the air below her, and below them were Jennifer and her cat standing in the clearing, looking up at her with panic in their eyes.

'Faye, please come down now.'

'I ... don't think I can.' The sky and the ground continued to swirl around Faye. There was no way to steer, and she kept rising oh-so-slowly.

'Hang on,' Jennifer cried, haring towards one of the taller trees. Jennifer clambered up with great agility, reaching the highest branches of a tall oak in just a few seconds. She snapped off a large branch and held it at the limit of her arm's reach. 'Grab it!'

Faye stretched as far as she could, but the branch was tantalisingly just beyond her fingertips.

'Nope.' Faye's voice was straining. 'Can't do it.'

'Then catch!' Jennifer took the branch in both hands and hurled it at Faye. It spun through the air, but Faye was already too far away to grab it and it fell to the ground.

'Blast.' Jennifer balled her fists.

'Never mind,' Faye said, still turning over and over. 'What was the plan with the branch, anyway?'

'I don't know. I thought you could use it to steer like a broomstick.' Jennifer shrugged. 'It would be a little extra weight, if nothing else.'

'Ah, well. It was a nice thought.'

'Try flapping your arms or something,' Jennifer called, but her voice was getting distant.

Faye slowly turned over like a balloon and her specs slid off her nose and tumbled to the ground.

'My specs! Jennifer! Catch them, please!'

Jennifer scrambled down the tree, reaching out for Faye's glasses, but the wind buffeted Faye and she was swept up high.

From here she could see the wood spread out beneath her. If she held a hand up to shade her eyes, she could blot out the clearing from where Jennifer's cat was still staring at her. At least, she thought that's what the little black dot was. Without her specs it was all a bit of a blur.

'I don't know what to do.' Jennifer's voice was almost lost to the wind.

Faye knew that flapping her arms wouldn't help, but she had to try the next-best thing. She needed to stop floating and actually fly.

She threw her arms and legs wide to see what that did.

Not much, apart from making her look like a giant floating starfish.

She continued to rise, buoyed by the magical energy fizzing inside her.

Despite the summer sun, the air was chilly up here, and she knew from chatting to pilots in the pub that the air got thinner the higher you flew. If she didn't stop rising soon, she would run out of breathable air, and then be the first dead person in space.

She was floating, but slowly. Faye thought of her

bicycle, and how when she first learned to ride a bike, she was slow and wobbly. Once she got to a certain speed, she had more control. How could she generate more speed? Annoyingly, there was nothing about this in her mum's book.

A memory flashed through Faye's mind. The last summer with her mother. All three of them had gone on a day trip to Margate. To Dreamland and its scenic railway. Dad kept calling it a rollercoaster, but Mum told him all the signs said it was a scenic railway. A railway that goes up and down like that *is* a rollercoaster, Dad had insisted. Whatever it was, they all got on, and the rattling train rose and fell on its tracks and the passengers all screamed in delight. Mum had kept her eyes closed for much of the ride, clinging onto Dad. Faye was in the car in front of them – she had insisted that she was a big girl and would ride alone – and she watched the train's brakeman. He rode between the first and second cars, standing on the bogie, using a large lever to operate the brakes. He would anticipate the bends and slow them down, then release the brake as they dropped.

Faye recalled the thrilling feeling of weightlessness before her whole body was thrown forwards. That's what she needed to do.

Taking a deep breath, Faye fought every instinct in her mind telling her not to do it and leaned forwards. Her head felt heavy, and her body tipped over as she plummeted back to the woods.

LEARNING TO LAND

Faye was flying.

The air roared around her ears, her eyes were streaming – not that she could see much without her specs, anyway – and her hair whipped all over the place. She spread her arms wide and raised her head, which helped her stay level as the trees rushed below. Leaning left and right gave her some steering ability, and arching her back had her rising again. This made her feel a little giddy, but it also came with a flood of excitement and she wanted more. Faye arched her back again and there was blue sky, then the wood. She had looped-the-loop, and she whooped like a cowboy as she did it.

She rose and fell and swayed like this for some time and was actually getting the hang of it. Yes, Faye was flying. Her body began to ache, her eyes stung, her ears were ringing from the pounding wind, and her skin was tight and stinging, but she had never felt so alive.

It began to dawn on Faye that Bellamy would want

to resume the ritual rehearsal any minute now and she should probably try to land.

As Faye's mother had never actually flown, there was nothing in her book about landing.

Faye perhaps should have given that more thought before taking off, but regrets were for the past, and it had her full attention now. First of all, she got her bearings. The green fuzzy thing was the wood, the blue fuzzy thing was the sky. The fuzzy thing that was an undulating mix of green and blue was the Thames Estuary, the coastline dotted with barrage balloons.

The wood was not terribly inviting. The idea of trying to land in that mass of pointy branches made Faye wince. To her left, she could make out farmers' fields. Larry Dell's farm wasn't too far away. She had a fancy to crash-land in his barn and give Leo the shock of his afterlife, but that was an encounter that would surely end in broken bones, and she was certain that her dad, Bellamy and Bertie would all be cross with her for that.

She was drifting closer to the Thames Estuary. If she didn't land soon she would end up flying all the way to Essex, and how on earth would she explain that to Bellamy and the others?

A familiar smudge appeared beyond the fields. The two towers of St Mary's Church at Reculver, an old ruin that dated back to the seventh century. She didn't much fancy slamming into the towers, but beyond them was a bigger, floaty smudge.

A barrage balloon.

Perfect. Not only was it high enough for her land on, but it was tethered to the ground. She lowered her head and made straight for it.

Faye was aware that she wasn't the only thing in the air. Curious birds darted about her, wondering who this interloper was. And in the distance, there came the buzz of fighters on patrol. She glanced up to see three Spitfires in formation, flying along the coast. They were just dots now, but they were getting closer. She tried not to think of the rollicking she would get from Mrs Teach and Miss Charlotte if she were seen. She tucked her hands tight against her body like a dart and accelerated towards the balloon.

She dared to glance over at the patrolling aircraft. There was no sign that they had seen her. When she turned back, she realised she had gone off-course and was now heading directly for the Reculver towers, where her chances of surviving the impact were about the same as a jar of strawberry jam's – which was, incidentally, what she would look like, too.

She tilted her body, veering between the towers, missing one by inches and startling a couple of pigeons, which flapped away in panic. One of them attacked Faye, its wings beating at her eyes as its beak pecked at her face. She smacked it away, and the bird circled back to the tower where its partner was sat. Both cooed at her angrily.

Faye looked up to find the barrage balloon filling her field of vision.

She had just enough time to raise her head and

stretch her arms and legs into a starfish shape before slapping into the side of the barrage balloon.

Made of rubber-proofed cotton fabric, it was surprisingly soft, and Faye felt the material embrace her as she plunged into it.

The sudden deceleration made her vision all the more blurry as the familiar pull of the Earth's gravity took hold. As the balloon began to expand again, Faye had visions of being pinged across the Thames Estuary like she was in a giant game of tiddlywinks.

She flailed about as she grasped for any kind of handhold. She found one of the rigging ropes and clung onto it, catching her breath and glad for the simple things in life, like being alive and not being strawberry jam on the side of an ancient church tower.

The balloon swayed back and forth like an enormous rocking chair, and Faye considered staying here for the rest of the day. Her body was tense, every muscle ached, her ears had popped, her nose was freezing, her eyes were streaming, she was giddy and she felt a little bit sick, but there was a tiny fizz at the back of her brain that wanted to let go and do it all over again.

'Faye? Faye Bright, is that you?'

The voice – a young woman's – came from below. Faye peeked down to see the barrage balloon's truck. It was a flatbed with a winch on the back that controlled the height of the balloon. It was tended to by a pair of the Women's Auxiliary Air Force's finest.

'It is her,' said another girl's voice. 'How the blazes did she get up there?'

With a cold dread, Faye realised who the voices belonged to. Milly Baxter and Betty Marshall. The terrible twosome.

'Morning, ladies,' she called down. 'Lovely weather, in't it?'

'I say, Faye Bright,' Betty Marshall cried, with all the authority of the daughter of the captain of the village Home Guard, 'this is our balloon, and I won't have you tampering with it. My father shall hear of this.' Betty punctuated most of her conversations with that phrase these days, but for once Faye took the threat seriously.

'Yes, Faye Bright,' Milly Baxter chipped in. 'Explain yourself, or shall we call the constable?'

'Call whoever you want.' Faye began negotiating the many guy ropes of the balloon's rigging as she clambered to get to the main flying cable. 'I'm here on official ARP business,' she said with so much confidence she almost believed it herself. 'Surprise barrage balloon inspection. There's been reports of leaks.'

'No one told us.' Betty folded her arms.

'Then it wouldn't be a surprise, would it?' Faye finally reached the flying cable. It was attached to the truck's winch and covered in grease. She realised that climbing down would surely mean the end of her favourite dungarees.

'I'm not convinced.' Milly sneered. 'I'm going to report this.'

'Fine.' Faye's voice strained as she shimmied down the cable. 'Report it. But when you do, make sure to include one important detail.'

'What's that?' Milly asked.

Faye jumped the last few feet from the cable to the bed of the truck. Her dungarees were smeared with grease, as were her hands and plimsolls. She wiped her palms on the back of the dungarees as she looked down at the girls. Without her specs their faces were blurred, but Faye could tell they were both a little spooked. As always when it came to anything magical, Faye decided it might be better just to tell the truth.

'Tell them I flew into it.' She hopped down from the truck and approached the girls, who both instinctively took a step back. 'Tell them you saw me hurtling through the sky like a bird, because I'm a witch and I can fly.'

Milly and Betty looked at one another, scrunched their faces and snorted.

'If you're a witch,' Betty said, 'where's your broomstick?'

'You're right.' Faye squinted up at the bright blue yonder. 'I should probably get one. Thank you, both. You'll be delighted to hear that the balloon has passed the inspection. Have a lovely day.'

THE OFFSIDE RULE

It was a bit of a walk back from the coast to the stones, but Faye needed not only the time to think, but also to enjoy the feel of the world under her feet. She hadn't realised quite how much she'd missed it. Being on the ground felt especially good, though she was sure she could still feel the planet turning beneath her. Completely awake and refreshed, her skin tingled all over like she'd just had a cold shower. Her cheeks were tender and pink, and her ears were hot, and that overwhelming magical sensation was gone. Burned off by the flight. She was idly wondering if that sensation would ever come back when she heard the familiar rattle of her Pashley Model A bicycle.

'Faye!'

She turned and shielded her eyes from the sun to see Jennifer cycling towards her, the cat sitting in the Pashley's basket like a tiny navigator. Faye gave a wave and Jennifer soon brought the cycle to a stop.

'I say ... how ... you ... what ...' Jennifer's head

was shaking and she could barely form words, let alone a sentence. The cat was less impressed. It hopped out of the basket and started scouting for mice.

'Take a breath, Jennifer, before you have a turn.'

'I saw you go up and up, and then loop-the-loop, and whoosh, you were off!'

'Never mind that. Shouldn't you be at the rehearsal?'

'Belly called it off. Got into a bit of a tizzy over his cursed concertina and sent us all home for the day. We're back on tomorrow.'

'Did anyone ask where I was?'

'I hope you don't mind, but I said you were answering the call of nature. That seemed to do the trick.'

'As good an excuse as any.' Faye grinned. 'I don't suppose you brought my specs, did you?'

'Oh? Yes. Of course.' Jennifer reached into one of her uniform's pockets. 'Bad news on that front, I'm afraid.'

Faye felt an old and familiar pang of regret. She had broken glasses before and it was always because of some silly accident that could easily have been avoided. There was that time at the beach when the wind whipped them away, dashing them on the rocks, and then on New Year's Eve someone bumped into her in the pub and they went skittering across the floor to be crushed by a conga line. This time, she only had herself to blame.

'Oh, buggeration,' Faye muttered as Jennifer handed over the broken remnants of her glasses. The lenses were cracked beyond repair and a couple of shards were missing. Even the frames were twisted. 'Blimey, these took a right old battering.'

'The cat found them,' Jennifer said with an apologetic grimace. 'So sorry, Faye. Do you have spares?'

'I've got another pair at home.' Faye pocketed the remnants in her dungarees. 'An old prescription, but at least I'll be able to see. Even if they do make me look like an old maid.'

'An old maid who can fly, Faye.' Jennifer pointed to the sky.

Faye looked to the clouds, not quite believing that she was up there just a moment ago.

'It was all I could do to follow you,' Jennifer said. 'How did you get down?'

Faye gestured at the grease on her dungarees. 'Me and a gasbag came to an understanding.'

'Are you all right? Are you hurt?'

'I'm fine. Thanks for coming after me.'

'How ...' Jennifer was still agog. 'How did you do that?'

'I dunno.' Faye shrugged. 'It just worked. Didn't you get a squirly-whirly feeling in your belly?'

'Can't say I did, no.' Jennifer looked around. 'Faye, this is all rather spectacular. We have to tell Bellamy.'

'I ain't sure about that.' Faye curled her lip. 'I almost bought it up there. I think there's a very good reason we witches don't fly much these days.'

'What's that?'

'It's bloody dangerous. And it's really nippy. And look at my barnet.' She pointed to her messy hair. 'But it's all good experience.'

'If you say so.'

'I do.' Faye couldn't wait to prove to Leo that she could fly. And she now knew what to do if she ever needed to burn off any excess magical energy. 'I can imagine what Bellamy will be like – all excited and he'll probably get his bloody concertina out again, and no one wants that. And I definitely don't want Mrs Teach and Miss Charlotte to know. They've made it very clear what they think of flying.' Faye extended her hand. 'Just you and me will keep this to ourselves.'

Jennifer shook Faye's hand. 'Agreed,' she said, then added with more than a little venom, 'I mean, why should we tell Bellamy and those dotty old bats anyway? What have they ever done for us, eh?'

'Quite a bit, actually.' Faye tilted her head to one side. 'You don't like other witches much, do you?'

Jennifer's head twitched down and she bit her lip. 'It's not that I don't like them,' she said eventually. 'I never had a Mrs Teach or a Miss Charlotte. I wrote letters to more witches than I can remember asking for help and never got a single reply.'

'That don't sound right. Not a one?'

'Not a sausage. I've had to get where I am today on my own.' Jennifer's voice was tinged with pain. 'My apologies, Faye. I don't wish to pour scorn, but we've had very different educations in magic.'

'I'm sorry, too,' Faye said. 'I don't know many witches, and the ones I know drive me up the wall a lot of the time and make me want to scream, but I can trust them with my life. And you can, too. They're good people, Jennifer.' Faye stepped forwards and wrapped her arms around Jennifer in a tight hug. 'Consider me a friend. If you ever need a cuppa and a chinwag, just let me know.'

They hugged a while longer until Jennifer let go of the Pashley and it clattered to the ground.

'Oh my goodness, I'm so sorry.' Jennifer broke away, hurrying to pick it up.

'Don't worry, that thing's been through a lot.'

Jennifer nudged the bicycle forwards. 'A more preferable mode of transport to floating through the air?'

'Definitely.' Faye took her precious bike back. 'I can get anywhere with this. Though not without my specs. Tell you what: you steer, I'll hang on for dear life.'

⌇

Faye dropped Jennifer off at the end of Edge Road and watched as she walked with only her cat for company towards Hayward Lodge. In Faye's blurred vision, she became little more than an unfocused smudge that eventually blended into the trees. Jennifer always had an eager smile, accompanied by a quick wit and a cunning eye, but she never spoke of any friends or a chap, and her family were long-gone. The girl was lonely. Why hadn't any witches replied to her letters? Another question for Mrs Teach and Miss Charlotte. The best Faye could do was be a good friend.

First thing Faye did when she got back to the Green Man was dig out her old specs. The lenses were smaller and everything was still a little fuzzy, but at least she wasn't bumping into the furniture. After lunch, Faye used a hot iron and white blotting paper to get rid of the grease stains on her dungarees. They didn't completely vanish, but the dungarees were old and scruffy enough that the stains looked like part of the general wear and tear. She sat in the kitchen in her dressing gown and slippers as she sewed a patch on one of the dungarees' knees, something she had been meaning to do for ages.

Bertie sidled in with a cup and saucer and spoke in a raised voice, 'Hello, Faye. I'm Bertie and this is a cup of tea. You *like* tea.'

'Bertie, I had a funny turn earlier but I'm fine now. Honestly. Ta for the tea.'

The lad puffed in relief, placing the tea on the table before Faye. 'Thank goodness for that. All that talk about flying and mushrooms. I was worried you'd gone doolally. I do worry about you, Faye.'

Faye was on the verge of telling him about her little patrol over the skies of Kent, but the words got lodged in her throat. Bertie did indeed worry about her, and she didn't think giving him something else to worry about was entirely fair.

'New specs?'

'Old ones.' Faye adjusted them self-consciously. 'They make me look old.'

'Not at all,' Bertie protested. 'You look like an owl.' There was an awkward moment as Bertie realised what he had said. 'I mean ... you look wise.'

'I know what you mean.' Faye patted the seat beside her.

'A bit of make do and mend?' He sat close to Faye,

nodding at her sewing. 'I didn't think those dungarees ever came off.'

Faye, glad for the change of subject, looked at him over the rim of her specs and grinned. 'Are you trying to get me out of my clothes, Bertie Butterworth?'

Bertie turned a shade of beetroot and didn't know where to look, so slurped his own tea noisily. For a moment, the air between them was heavy with lust, and they knew it wouldn't be long before they would surrender to desire and—

'Blimey, Bertie, you sound like a blocked drain.' Terrence wandered in and poured himself a cuppa. Bertie stopped slurping and started choking. Terrence patted the lad on the back as he spoke to Faye. 'How's the noggin?'

Faye rapped the side of her head and listened for a moment. 'Yup. All back to normal.'

'That's a shame, I was hoping you would give me a ride on your broomstick.' He cackled to himself. 'Flying. Honestly, Faye. The ideas you get sometimes. Oh! Larry Dell left a note for you while you was out.' He rummaged in his back pocket, producing a neatly folded piece of paper which he handed to Faye. 'Looks like a list of tools.'

'You're reading my notes now?' Faye snatched it off him.

'I thought he was a secret admirer.' Terrence shrugged. 'Thought it only fair to let Bertie know so he could prepare for the duel at dawn for your honour.' Terrence chuckled and Bertie went even redder.

'Don't listen to him, Bertie.' Faye unfolded the note.

It was indeed a list of the tools that Larry needed from the barn.

Bertie cleared his throat. 'Has he still got that ... thing in his barn?'

'That thing is a person, Bertie. Well, sort of. And he's a stubborn old sod who doesn't know what he wants.'

'Ghosts,' Terrence mused as he sat at the kitchen table. 'They're all about unfinished business, aren't they? That's what your mother used to say. Why don't you figure out what it is and help him with that?'

'This one has unfinished business with the entire bloody Luftwaffe, Dad,' Faye said. 'How am I supposed to do that?'

'Ah.' Terrence raised his china cup as he thought, his head wreathed in the steam of freshly brewed tea.

Faye knew the tone of that 'Ah'. She was about to get the latest deep thoughts from noted local philosopher Mr Terrence Bright, esquire.

'His need for revenge is a symptom, Faye, not the cause.'

'Here we go,' Faye muttered.

'What?'

'Nothing. Carry on.'

'See, when a fella gets angry at others, he's often just as angry – if not more so – at himself. I've seen it a million times in the pub. I will also admit to having experienced such feelings meself, though I am now at an age where I couldn't give a tinker's cuss for anger.'

'You lost your rag over a jigsaw puzzle just the other day,' Faye said.

'That's completely different.'

'How so? And where's that ship in a bottle you was working on?'

Terrence grimaced, glancing at the mantle. Faye followed his look to find a gin bottle on a little wooden plinth. Inside was what could only be described as a shipwreck. The clipper ship was on its side, masts broken, sails askew, splinters of wood scattered about.

'It, er ... ran aground,' Terrence said. 'And the bloody strings came unstuck when I tried to raise the sails.'

Faye peered closer at the wreckage, then turned to her father. 'Get angry, did we?'

'He was shaking it like maracas,' Bertie blurted.

'Yes, thank you, Bertie.' Terrence took a moment to inhale the tea's calming aroma. 'I must confess I very nearly succumbed to a spot of anger, but I took a breath and simmered down. Like I said, I don't get angry. I much prefer a good brew.'

'Anger doesn't fix anything,' Bertie said. 'It's why I never get a game with the Woodville Wanderers.'

Faye and Terrence blinked at Bertie.

'Woodville Wanderers?' Faye asked. 'The football team?'

Bertie nodded. 'It weren't my fault. I used to run forward and hang around the other team's goal. There weren't no defenders about or nothin'. I thought I was dead clever. I thought, *Why has no one ever done this before?* All my team had to do was pass me the ball, and I would knock it in past the goalie. But every time my team kicked the ball to me, the ref blew his whistle and the other side got a free kick. I did it so many times that I was sent off. Everyone was angry at me. My team. Their team. The ref. Me dad. And do you know what it was?'

'You were offside,' Faye and Terrence said in unison.

'I was offs— Wait, you know about that?'

Terrence pinched the bridge of his nose. 'Everyone who knows football knows about the offside rule, Bertie.'

'Well, I didn't,' the lad said. 'I couldn't understand why everyone was so cross, and then I got all cross. And then when it was explained to me I got angry and all hot and bothered, but I was angry with myself and that's why I'll never play professional football.'

'That's the only reason, is it?' Terrence asked. 'Was there a point to this little reminiscence, Bertie?'

The boy frowned. 'I'm sure there was when I started. Something about being a team player, or listening to others. Either way, I had to wash the team kit for a month after that.'

'Speaking of kit.' Faye shook her dungarees into shape. 'I need to get mine on, so if you gents wouldn't mind leaving the room, I have to pop out and rescue Larry's tools for him.'

෴

When Faye returned to Larry's barn, Leo was nowhere to be seen. Faye took the items from Larry's list and placed them outside where he could find them later. By the time she was done, the sun was low and the light dusky. She stepped back inside the barn and put on the flight helmet.

'Leo?'

No answer.

'Leo, I hope you're watching, 'cos I want to show you something.' She moved to the centre of the barn and lay on her back. 'This might make me come over all peculiar, but I want you to see it.'

She closed her eyes and – getting a pang of anxiety and hoping that what happened earlier wasn't just a fluke – Faye imagined the Earth moving through space. She began to rise.

If anything, this time was easier than before. She knew what to expect, and she could control the magical energy. She summoned it, rather than letting it spill over her. It felt as exhilarating as it always did, her skin tingling.

She found herself slowly moving up to the barn's supporting beams. There was a hole in the roof, and she could see the wood beyond.

'I learned this from my mother's book,' Faye said, gliding from one end of the barn to the other. She decided to leave out all the near-death stuff from this morning's adventure. 'I won't be making a habit of this, so enjoy it while you can. And I hope this proves that me mum weren't cruel, and she weren't a liar.'

The air in the barn chilled. He was here.

'I know you're angry about something. And I don't think I can help you till you tell me why.'

Still no answer.

'Suit yourself. But until you're ready to talk to me, there ain't nothing I can do.' As Faye drifted to the back of the barn, something caught her eye through the hole in the roof. Chimney smoke rose from the heart of the wood. Miss Charlotte's cottage. The smoke flashed green, then yellow, then a colour that Faye couldn't recall ever seeing before, but it left a purple and green streak on her retina. 'What the blinkin' flip?'

Faye gripped one of the barn's timbers and gently shoved herself towards the ground, landing gently and wishing she had known how to do this earlier.

'I'm off now, Leo,' she said, taking off the flight helmet and putting it back on the workbench. 'I hope this means you can trust me. I'll be back tomorrow, and we'll talk then, eh?'

The barn remained silent.

'Fine.' Faye marched outside where she righted her bicycle and headed towards Miss Charlotte's cobwood cottage in the middle of the wood.

RETURN OF THE GOAT

As Faye cycled through the wood, she breathed through her nose – mouth closed – grateful for the specs that shielded her eyes against the countless midges that swarmed along the path.

Miss Charlotte's cottage was designed to be unwelcoming to visitors. There were no clear paths, and certainly anyone on wheels would have to abandon them some way from the cottage. Faye hopped off her Pashley when she reached the hollow oak and leaned the bicycle against the tree, continuing on foot. Soon she came to a point where the path dwindled to little more than a line between waist-high ferns.

Faye waded through the ferns, getting close enough to the cottage to see lights flashing between the trees, sending shadows on a brief dance before vanishing.

That's when she heard voices.

No one came this deep into the wood without knowing where they were going. It was said that the wood itself would take lost ramblers and sort of steer them around Miss Charlotte's cottage for their own safety.

Faye ducked down, wondering who the voices belonged to.

'I swear, if he gets that concertina out one more time I shall not be responsible for my actions.' It was unmistakably Mrs Teach.

'Take a ticket and wait in line,' Miss Charlotte replied. 'That man's enthusiasm should come with some kind of warning.'

Faye's first instinct was to stand and greet her fellow witches, but a nagging thought stopped her. If Miss Charlotte and Mrs Teach were both out and about, then who was in the cottage?

'Wait.' Miss Charlotte stopped, and it felt like the whole wood fell silent with her. She turned her head, slowly scrutinising the trees.

Faye tried to curl into a smaller ball, but she knew that merely ducking down in the undergrowth wouldn't be enough to hide from these two.

A glamour. She needed a glamour. There were two kinds described in her mother's book. One that made you look like someone else, which was rather tricky and often required a token from the person you were impersonating. And the other helped you blend into your surroundings to the point where it looked like you weren't there. Faye needed the latter. And quick. She recalled the technique, slowing her breathing, remaining completely still and ... Faye wasn't exactly sure how it happened, but she was able to step outside of herself, drawing the dappled light from the dusky wood to cloak her from sight.

'What's wrong?' Mrs Teach asked.

Charlotte raised her head, almost sniffing the air. 'It's nothing,' she said eventually. 'We should hurry.'

Faye waited until they were out of sight. She knew where they were going. All their whispering and conspiring over the last few days must have something to do with the strange lights in Miss Charlotte's cottage.

Faye retained her glamour as she inched her way out of the ferns, the scent of aniseed drawing her closer to the cottage and its magical light show. Normally the cottage was a modest residence, but tonight it had become a multicoloured lighthouse as vivid reds, yellows, blues and pinks silently burst from its tiny windows.

Faye looked on in astonishment as she reached the clearing where Miss Charlotte's cobwood cottage sat. She planned to sneak around the back and peek through a window before daring to knock on the—

'Me-eh!'

The noise came from behind Faye. She slowly looked over her shoulder to see a creature that would not so easily be fooled by a mere glamour.

'ME-EH!'

Miss Charlotte's goat.

Faye recalled that Miss Charlotte denied ever actually owning the goat, but it patrolled the perimeter of the cottage with all the diligence of a prison guard. And now it had her.

'Evenin',' Faye said with a winning smile.

'*ME-EH!*'

'Yes, you said that already.' Faye pressed a hand to her chest. 'We've met before. I'm a friend of Miss Charlotte's.'

'*Meh?*'

'Why am I skulking about if I'm a friend? That's a good question. I should just stroll up to the door and knock, shouldn't I? Righto, I'll do that. I'll tell you what ...' Faye looked around, spotting a bale of hay and a bucket of water nearby. 'Let's get you something to eat, shall we?'

She nodded towards the hay and the goat appeared to assent and the two of them strolled over, the woodland floor lighting up around them.

Faye took a handful of hay and fed it to the goat, which munched it up. It then ducked its head as if granting permission to pass, and Faye stroked its back.

She took a few steps in the direction of the door and the goat let out a bleat of alarm so loud it could probably be heard in the village.

Faye froze, scowling at the beast.

The cottage fell dark, and from inside came three distinct voices, speaking in hurried whispers. A door was suddenly slammed shut and footsteps scurried about. Miss Charlotte and Mrs Teach must be inside.

Faye could have made a run for it, but why would she run away from friends? She stood her ground as a bolt slid back and the front door creaked open.

'Faye Bright.' Miss Charlotte glided into the moonlight. Night always came early to the cottage. 'To what do I owe the pleasure?'

Mrs Teach appeared behind her. 'You can remove your glamour, young missy. We know it's you.'

Faye stepped back into herself, and the night air shifted around her as she became visible again.

'I was on my way home.' Faye stuffed her hands into her dungarees' patchwork pockets. 'And I heard your goat—'

'He's not my goat,' Miss Charlotte snapped.

'And it sounded like . . . he . . . was . . . hungry.'

'Really?' Mrs Teach asked.

Faye sagged and kicked at the dry earth. ''Course not. I've been following you pair, 'cos you've done nothin' but act peculiar these last few days, and I reckon you're up to something. I don't know what it is, but I'm cross you won't tell me about it. There. Happy now?'

'I'm always happy.' Miss Charlotte's face was like granite.

Mrs Teach gestured to the cottage. 'As you can see, we're merely having a cup of tea before bedtime. You're welcome to join us if you like?' This last was said in a way that suggested Hitler would be a more welcome guest than Faye.

'Maybe I will.' Faye enjoyed seeing Mrs Teach stiffen.

'Or maybe you won't.' Miss Charlotte turned and strode back to the cottage. 'In fact, you can both bugger off. I'm tired. See you at rehearsal tomorrow.'

'I heard another voice in there,' Faye said, and Miss Charlotte stopped in her tracks. 'Who's in there? Martine? Mrs Housego?'

'It's none of your business.' Mrs Teach waved Faye away. 'Now why don't you—'

'No,' said another voice. A figure stood in the shadow of the cottage door. 'I think she needs to be a part of this, too. Good evening, Faye.'

Vera Fivetrees stepped into the moonlight.

TEA AND SECRETS

'I thought you was under – whatsit? – house arrest?'

'Good, that's exactly what I wanted you and every-one else to think.' Vera took a sip of Earl Grey. She was sitting beside Charlotte's fireplace where an old black kettle hung over the embers.

Far from being a cosy woodland retreat, Miss Charlotte's cottage had a cave-like ambience. The runes and pentagrams painted on the whitewashed walls weren't exactly welcoming, and the air itself hummed with supernatural unease. Miss Charlotte wasn't used to having visitors. Vera got the only chair in the room, Mrs Teach perched herself on the end of Charlotte's bed, Charlotte leaned against a timber beam, smoking her pipe, and Faye sat on a milking stool. They all drank Earl Grey tea, though Faye wasn't sure it deserved to be called tea. It was more like the stuff she was left with in a bucket after washing the pub's windows.

'I don't mean to be rude, Miss Charlotte,' Faye began,

'but there's something strange in the air in your cottage, and it ain't the pong of goats. Something magical.'

The other witches all feigned innocence with a combination of pursed lips, heightened eyebrows and minuscule shrugs.

'I saw all them flashing lights,' Faye said. 'What were you lot up to?'

'I am experimenting with something.' Vera looked Faye in the eye as she sipped her tea. Behind her, Miss Charlotte and Mrs Teach shared a conspiratorial look. 'That is all I can say regarding the lights for the moment.'

'Fair enough.' Faye had become used to folk having secrets in wartime. It annoyed her, but she knew there was no point in pressing further.

'Shall we get down to business?' Vera continued. 'What I'm about to tell you is top secret, and I would remind you, Faye, that you have signed the Official Secrets Act.'

'Righto.' Faye folded her arms, wondering where this was going.

'My arrest was stage-managed,' Vera said. 'Miss Charlotte's idea, in fact.'

Faye glanced over to Charlotte who sported a self-satisfied smirk.

'The Council of Witches has reason to believe that we have a spy in our organisation,' Vera continued. 'To draw them out, I arranged for my little sabbatical in order for Bellamy to think he's in charge and to begin his pet project.'

Faye gasped, then asked what she was sure everyone else was thinking. 'Is Bellamy the spy?'

Vera chortled. 'Oh, goodness, no. He's mostly harmless. An ambitious fellow with some rather interesting ideas of how to do things.'

Mrs Teach and Miss Charlotte murmured their disapproval.

'Not least the nudity,' Vera added.

'Oh, the nudity.' Mrs Teach shuddered.

'He's been badgering the Council to implement the cone of power ritual since the start of the war,' Vera said. 'He got particularly cross after Dunkirk, which he claims he could have prevented.'

'Could he?' Faye asked.

Vera lowered her teacup. 'Child, our magic is powerful, but the idea that we could stop the might of the Nazi Blitzkrieg is the stuff of fairy tales.'

'So why are you letting him do it?' Faye asked.

Vera, Mrs Teach and Miss Charlotte shared a look.

Vera's voice became subdued as she stared into the embers in the fireplace. 'What happened last month with Otto Kopp was a disaster. If it were not for you, Faye, things would have been much worse, and for that I shall always be grateful.'

Faye glowed with pride. She had always been iffy about Vera Fivetrees – you get like that when someone insists you burn the last vestige of the memories of your mother – but Faye couldn't help but admire the woman, and praise from her was a rare and special thing.

''Salright.' Faye shrugged. 'Just did what I had to.'

'You should never have been put in that position in the first place.' Vera raised her voice, angry at herself. 'There was an inquiry. How could he have fooled us – fooled me – so thoroughly? As we dug deeper, we discovered that someone had been communicating with Otto. And they continue to do so.'

Faye's belly churned at the mention of the Bavarian Druid's name. 'Otto's still alive, is he? Last time I saw him, he was about to be eaten by a demonic dog.' She thought back to only last month when Harry Aston, heir to Hayward Lodge, had been rewarded for his collusion with Otto by being turned into a Jäger, a ravenous and hellish hound.

'We had a credible sighting of him a couple of weeks ago by one of our operatives in Berchtesgaden.'

'On his holidays, was he?'

'We suspect he was meeting with top Nazi officials. Perhaps even Hitler himself.'

'And one of us witches has been pen pals with him?' Faye asked, appalled at the idea.

'Not pen pals,' Mrs Teach said before giving Faye a hint. 'They use a more magical form of communication.'

'Oh! Scrying.' Faye frowned. 'That's a right palaver. Why would they use that instead of a radio? Or pigeons?'

'Pigeons?' Mrs Teach crinkled her mouth.

'Very clever, pigeons,' Faye said. 'Reliable, too. If I was going to be sending secret messages, I'd use a pigeon.'

'Pigeons can be shot.' Charlotte removed the pipe from her red lips and grinned. 'Then eaten. But if you combine scrying with a blood ritual, you can send a message completely undetected.' She nodded to Mrs Teach. 'Except when she's around.'

Faye snapped her fingers and pointed to Mrs Teach. 'It makes your ears whistle.'

'I can tell when someone is scrying as far as ten miles away,' Mrs Teach said with more than a hint of pride.

'Oh!' Faye blurted as the penny dropped. 'Mrs Housego, Martine, Jennifer. They're all scryers.'

'Very good.' Vera smiled.

'And so you've duped Bellamy into organising the cone of power ritual – which needs scrying, a thing that very few witches can do – to bring the main suspects together to expose the spy.'

'That's the idea,' Charlotte said.

'Hang on.' Faye frowned. 'If Bellamy doesn't know the plan ... I thought he hand-picked all the witches for this ritual.'

'He was given a shortlist by the Council of Witches.' Vera gestured to Miss Charlotte and Mrs Teach. 'We created that list.'

'So that's why you've been all secretive,' Faye said to Mrs Teach and Miss Charlotte before turning on Vera. 'Why didn't you ask me? I could've helped.'

'Darling, Faye,' Mrs Teach's voice lilted until it was at its most patronising, 'don't take this with any offence ...'

Faye braced herself for something offensive.

'But you do wear your heart on your sleeve somewhat.'

'What does that mean?' Faye asked.

'You've got a big gob,' Miss Charlotte clarified, providing the offence that Mrs Teach hadn't.

'To put it more politely,' Mrs Teach added hurriedly as she glared at Charlotte, 'we were unsure of your abilities in the arena of *espionage*.' She pronounced this last word with an odd French emphasis.

'I'm sorry to have kept you out, Faye,' Vera said, 'but we could not risk jeopardising the mission with an inexperienced element. Once again, it appears I have underestimated you and I apologise.'

'No apology necessary, but it's come to something when you lot think I have a bigger gob than Mrs Teach.' Faye turned to Mrs Teach. 'Please don't take that with any offence.'

'I think I might,' the woman replied.

Vera leaned forwards. 'Please understand, Faye, that the stakes have never been higher. We believe Otto Kopp has been tasked by Hitler himself with destroying the Council of Witches, to throw us into disarray ahead of the planned invasion.'

'Is that . . .' Faye's mouth went dry. 'Is that why those other witches didn't show up?'

'Oh, they showed up.' Miss Charlotte puffed pipe smoke. 'A couple of them, anyway. Face down in the Thames.'

'They're dead?'

'Elsie was poisoned,' Charlotte confirmed. 'Ophelia strangled. Dolly's still missing.'

Vera's face hardened. 'Someone is trying to wipe us

out, Faye. And I strongly believe that one of Bellamy's recruits is the assassin.'

Assassin was a word Faye had read in books and heard in films and radio plays, but she had never heard anyone say it in real life before. It wasn't a word she particularly liked.

'You've come to know these witches over the past few days, Faye,' Vera said. 'What do you think?'

Faye was flummoxed. 'It can't be Mrs Housego. She's just so lovely and jolly.'

'She killed a man in 1922,' Charlotte said, then added a little too gleefully, 'at a nudist colony.'

Faye's face contorted in puzzlement. 'Because . . . he was a nudist?'

Vera shook her head. 'Mrs Housego has been a member of both The Sunbathing Society and The National Sun and Air Association since they were formed. She's a committed nudist. She killed the man because he was preying on children at one of the camps. The authorities looked the other way.'

Charlotte jabbed the air with her pipe. 'But that doesn't *not* make her a spy.'

'What do you think about Jennifer?' Vera asked Faye.

Faye thought back to her flight earlier today. If Jennifer was the one intent on wiping out witches, she had the perfect opportunity to let Faye do the job herself. She didn't want the others to know of her little airborne indiscretion, so she shrugged and said, 'Nice enough. Works hard at the rehearsals. Pleasant and posh, but as we all discovered not so long ago, that don't mean you're not a Nazi.'

'Indeed,' Miss Charlotte said. 'Jennifer was also a last-minute replacement.'

'One recommended by Dolly,' Mrs Teach was quick to add.

'Who's still missing.' Miss Charlotte arched an eyebrow.

'It's possible that Dolly is working on a secret mission,' Vera noted. 'There are some projects that even I don't hear of until after the fact, but I do know she was working with a group of code breakers recently. And Jennifer was thoroughly vetted by the Secret Service. I read the report. Nothing unusual was found. Just an orphan who was quick to volunteer for the FANYs to do her bit. Her association with Dolly makes her worth keeping an eye on, however.'

'What about Martine?' Faye asked. 'Every time she mentions the Nazis or the Blitzkrieg she looks like she's ready to fight them all over again.'

'Martine.' There was something about the way that Mrs Teach said the French woman's name that reeked of disapproval.

'I'm sensing mixed opinions,' Vera said. 'How is she?'

Faye pursed her lips and bobbed her head from side to side. 'She's always saying the operation is going to be a disaster, but she's a grafter, does her bit.'

'She speaks German,' Mrs Teach added in a way that suggested this was enough to condemn the woman.

Faye tutted. 'That don't make her Hitler. She's a good scryer and dancer. Always gives it her all, but apart from that I can't say I really know her, to be honest.'

'Neither do we,' Vera confessed. 'Martine escaped

France just as the Nazis invaded. We've been told that she worked with saboteurs, destroying bridges and train lines in order to slow the German advance, but the truth is she is a stranger to us. I've already tasked Miss Charlotte to get close to her, but so far her efforts have been rebuffed.'

'She's almost as standoffish as me.' Charlotte looked mildly miffed at being rejected.

'Let me try,' Faye said. 'I make friends easily enough.'

Vera glanced over at Mrs Teach and Charlotte. The two women oh-so-slightly shook their heads.

'You're still a child, Faye.' Vera rested a hand on Faye's shoulder. 'I don't want you to do anything that might put you in danger.'

Faye definitely was not going to tell Vera or the others about her little flight earlier today, in that case.

She counted off the names on her fingers. 'We've got a French Resistance witch we hardly know, a perfectly nice posh FANY and the oldest nudist in town.' A thought occurred to Faye. 'Does Bellamy know that Mrs Housego is a nudist?'

'Why is that important?' Vera asked.

'It's just, she's the only one keen on going skyclad. He thinks it's because of the added magical power, but if it's really because she just likes running around in the altogether—'

'It might break the poor man.' Vera nodded. 'Let's agree to keep that to ourselves.'

'So bein' skyclad really doesn't make any difference to magical power?' Faye asked.

Vera shook her head. 'Not in my experience. If anything, you should wrap up warm with as many layers as possible.'

'If I may bring the conversation back to the subject at hand?' Mrs Teach said. 'We still have no clue who the spy is. Though Martine seems to me to be the main suspect.'

Vera thought for a moment. 'Keep a close eye on her. If you see any unusual behaviour, report it immediately. Do not attempt anything on your own. Do you understand?'

Faye squinted one eye as a plan formed in her head. 'How about we try something together?'

'What do you mean?' Vera asked.

'I have an idea.'

Mrs Teach's Whistling Ears

'When was the last time your ears whistled?' Faye asked Mrs Teach. 'Outside of the ritual rehearsals, that is.'

The woman bristled a little at such a direct and personal question. 'If you must know, the day we went to Dover. No,' Mrs Teach corrected herself and raised a finger. 'Specifically, the evening after we returned from Dover.'

'Dover was big news, wasn't it?' Faye started to pace around Miss Charlotte's cottage. 'The location of the ritual. That's big enough news to break cover and risk contacting Otto. We need them to do the same again. We need to give them something to scry about.'

'Such as?' Miss Charlotte asked.

Faye turned to Vera. 'Bellamy can't know anything about this, can he?'

'The less he knows the better,' Vera said. 'If he discovers his pride and joy is little more than a ruse to expose a spy, he will get very upset.'

'I anticipate a tantrum,' Mrs Teach said.

'Or worse. Aggressive playing of the concertina,' added Charlotte.

'Aw, leave the fella be.' Faye felt a pang of sadness for the man. 'He means well. So we need to do this without his knowledge, and somehow also draw the attention of our number-one suspect, Martine. Righto. Here's what we do . . .'

✄

Bertie Butterworth's Battle of Britain Diary

Thursday 15th August, 1940

Air battle at 5pm. Sharp AA all evening. Faye briefly went doolally, then went back to normal, apologised and promised to make time for canoodling soon. Never a dull moment when Faye's around. Made some carrot and ginger buns. Very nice.

Faye, Miss Charlotte and Mrs Teach all arrived at the next morning's ritual rehearsal looking, in Faye's words, 'shifty'. Faye instructed them to arrive in silence, yet share the smallest looks and nods. Just enough for Martine to notice.

'Faye, darling, how's the noggin?' Jennifer was at Faye's side, leaning close with a red-lipped smile and speaking low. She was more than a little shifty herself.

'Oh, er, fine. Should we—'

'And have you been, you know, *up-diddly-up* recently? I do so worry about you.'

Faye glanced around. 'I've not told anyone else, so—'

'Completely understand, darling. You can trust me. Our little secret,' Jennifer whispered in her ear. 'Let's have a girls' night in tonight. Just you and me. I can show you scrying and you can show me flying. Gosh, that rhymes.'

Faye was wondering how to reply when Bellamy clapped his hands for attention.

'Good morning all.' Bellamy greeted them with a beaming smile. 'I have some very good news. First, though, I should like to thank every one of you for your sterling work these past few days. It's clear that we can generate incredible power when we work together as a team, and I have no doubt that we few, we happy few, we band of . . . siblings, for those who hath shed blood with me shall be my, er—'

'Bellamy, dear,' Mrs Housego said in a voice designed to calm toddlers, 'what's the news?'

'Oh, er, our orders have come through,' he said. 'We have the go-ahead.'

A silence fell around the standing stones. Finally, after days of rehearsal, Bellamy had found a way to shut them up. They all angled their ears towards him in anticipation.

'We journey to Dover on Friday at noon,' he said, then added for clarity, 'that's tomorrow.'

Everyone took a breath and stood a little taller. Even though Faye had her doubts that the ritual would actually work, it was a thrill to think they were going to use magic against the enemy.

'Golly,' Jennifer said, speaking for all of them.

Bellamy clasped his hands behind his back. 'We begin at midnight that evening and we *must* finish at dawn on Saturday morning. If we're not done by sunrise, we won't be protected by the moon's power. We'll be visible and vulnerable, but ... if this is a success it could open the door for more magical strategies. We could end this war and save countless lives. So.' He threw his arms wide. 'Shall we begin?'

The ritual went well. They started with Martine scrying, and the other witches dancing in perfect time. Jennifer insisted on being close to Faye and holding her hand. The energy they all commanded was stronger than ever. It had become routine for them to take a break for refreshments every hour or so. Bellamy had brought a picnic hamper to the rehearsals today and, in addition to the usual tea and biscuits, there was cheese and wine.

'A special treat before our mission,' he told them, and the ladies tucked in, though Martine complained about the quality of both.

Jennifer stuck to Faye like a limpet throughout, her arm tucked into Faye's. After yesterday's shenanigans in the sky they shared a secret and the bond that came with it was a strong one. It warmed Faye's heart to see Jennifer looking so happy, and she desperately wanted to return the friendship she was offering, but Faye had her own secrets.

'Jennifer, can you excuse me a mo'?' Faye wriggled out of the other woman's grip.

'Of course, darling.' Jennifer smiled, though Faye was aware of being watched as she made her way over to Mrs Teach and Miss Charlotte.

The two elder witches had resumed their shifty act and were sitting together at the head of the slaughter stone.

Part two of Faye's plan was to use what she called the 'Milly Baxter method of winding someone up'.

'And what, pray, does that entail?' Mrs Teach asked.

'As we speak,' Faye lowered her voice as she leaned closer to Mrs Teach, 'we need to glance over at Martine.' And Faye did exactly that. 'If we do it enough times, she'll get suspicious, but she won't say nothing here 'cos she won't want to make a scene. Then, after the ritual, she'll want to know what we're up to. If she's the spy we think she is, she'll follow us to the hollow oak, where we'll give her ...' Faye left the sentence to hang.

'Something to scry about,' Miss Charlotte finished, pursing her lips in approval, then slowly turning her head towards Martine.

'Milly Baxter does this all the time in church,' Faye said. 'She can make you feel completely irregular with-out saying a word. The girl's a genius.'

'Oh, please, the girl is an amateur.' Mrs Teach turned to Martine and smiled. 'I perfected this back in the twenties.'

Martine, who was sitting with Bellamy and grimac-ing at English cheese, caught Mrs Teach's gaze and narrowed her eyes.

'Oh dear,' Miss Charlotte said.

'Oh dear, what?' Faye asked.

'There's one flaw in your plan.' Charlotte kept her eyes on Martine as she spoke. 'Martine, need I remind you, is French.'

Faye shrugged. 'So?'

'This kind of cattiness works perfectly on the English,' Charlotte continued, still looking at Martine, 'because we're horribly repressed. That's why we wouldn't dream of making a scene. However, I fear that our cousins across *La Manche* have what might be called Gallic Affront.'

'What's that?' Faye asked.

Right on cue, Martine threw her cheese to the ground. 'What are you three gossiping about, huh?' She stood, hands on hips. 'Like silly children. If you have something to say, let's hear it.'

Bellamy's head darted about. 'What's, er, what's the hullaballoo?'

Martine gestured at the Woodville trio. 'All day, these three have been staring at me and muttering, *nip-nip-nip-nip*!' She rapidly tapped her two middle fingers on her thumb to make a chattering mouth. Then Martine added something deeply insulting in French.

'No, no, honest.' Faye got to her feet. 'We weren't sayin' nothing rude.'

'Then tell me.' Martine jutted her chin forwards. 'And be quick. No lies.'

'Ladies, please.' Bellamy tried to step between them, but Martine put her hand in the centre of his chest and nudged him away.

The others were all standing, too. Jennifer and Mrs Housego peered over Bellamy's shoulder as Martine awaited a response.

For once in her life, Mrs Teach was genuinely lost for words. Faye opened her mouth to speak, completely unsure what was going to come out.

'I think you're rather attractive.' The words came from Miss Charlotte.

There was a gasp from Jennifer, accompanied by a little chuckle from Mrs Housego.

'I know we're not supposed to do that sort of thing in this ridiculously uptight society,' Miss Charlotte added with a bob of her head, 'but I was discussing my dilemma with my close friends here.'

'D-dilemma?' Bellamy's voice was a wheeze.

'Whether or not I should tell Martine that she's one of the most intriguing women I've known, and ask her if she would like to come over for dinner one evening.'

'This, no, er, I cannot . . . it's not allowed, uhm.' Bellamy continued to splutter as Martine looked from Charlotte to Mrs Teach and Faye, scrutinising them for any sign of mockery. Eventually, Martine's face melted from hardened suspicion to an intrigued smile.

'*Oui*. Why not?'

'Not allowed.' Bellamy wagged a finger and shook his head. 'Such . . . *fraternisation* in the ranks is out of order. I will have to—'

Mrs Teach rested a hand on his forearm. 'Bellamy, dear, you will do precisely nothing. Not if you want this little ritual to go ahead.'

'Won't I, indeed?' Bellamy's cheeks were turning the colour of salmon.

'Hush now,' Mrs Teach continued. 'Ladies, I think we're all rather exhausted by today's excitement. Shall we finish early and call it a day?'

Before Bellamy could object, the others all cheered and began gathering their things.

Faye caught a glimpse of Charlotte whispering in Martine's ear. The two of them looked at Faye.

'What did you say to her?' Faye asked later, when they were trudging through the tall ferns. She glanced back, half expecting to find Jennifer trailing after her, but she had been quite keen to get away for some reason, hitching a ride with Bellamy back to Hayward Lodge.

'I told her to meet us at the hollow oak in the middle of the wood,' Miss Charlotte said with a knowing smile. 'I said we had a surprise for her.'

'And do we?' Mrs Teach asked as they arrived at the clearing with the hollow oak. 'You've been rather vague on this part of the plan.'

'I've been thinking about that.' Faye bunched her lips and stuck her hands in her pockets. ''Cos there's something I need to tell you two. Actually, I reckon I should just show it to you.'

'Whatever it is, you had better hurry.' Miss Charlotte was looking back the way they came. 'I can see her. She's nearly here.'

Faye puffed her cheeks out and lay flat on the ground.

'What are you doing, girl?' Mrs Teach asked.

'Stand back.' Faye waved them away. 'I need a bit of room for this.'

Miss Charlotte looked to Mrs Teach. 'She's not . . . ?'

'She can't be,' Mrs Teach replied.

Faye, eyes closed, rose from the ground into the air silently and without fuss.

'She bloody is,' Miss Charlotte said.

Faye arched her back and opened her eyes as she floated above the witches. The afternoon sun caught her in a beam that shone through the canopy.

'*Mon Dieu*,' said a voice, and they all turned to find Martine looking on in astonishment.

'Wotcha.' Faye gave her a wave.

'My ears!' Mrs Teach cried, clapping her hands to the sides of her head. 'My ears are whistling!'

WE'RE STUFFED

Faye brought herself down by the hollow oak, landing heavily and tumbling onto her bottom. She shook her head clear, her skin colour changing from flushed pink to her usual freckly eggshell.

'Now,' she said to Martine, 'I know what this looks like.'

'I'm not sure you do, Faye,' Charlotte said.

'You ... you can fly?' Martine took a step back.

'A bit.' Faye got to her feet and rubbed some life into her numb backside. 'Though it makes me belly go funny, and me head gets all woozy. Even a little trip like that can—'

'You can fly?' Martine's voice went up an octave.

Mrs Teach spoke out of the side of her mouth. 'I think she's about to throw a wobbly.'

'How are your ears?' Charlotte asked.

'Still whistling,' Mrs Teach replied.

'That means someone else is scrying,' Faye said quietly. 'So Martine is not the ... y'know.'

'Not the what?' Martine asked.

'Not the nothing.' Faye bared her teeth in what she hoped was an innocent-looking grin. 'Not the nothing at all. So, er, pub? Anyone?'

Martine was no fool. She jerked her chin at Charlotte. 'You think I am a spy?'

'Er. No . . . not now we don't,' Faye said.

'Martine, it's not what you think, dear.' Mrs Teach reached out, but Martine took another step back.

'And you.' Martine turned on Charlotte. 'You tried to seduce me, huh? What sort of people are you, you . . .' Her words blended into a tirade of very angry French.

'Martine, please.' Faye raised her hands to try and calm things down. 'Miss Charlotte was only saying those things so that Bellamy wouldn't suspect—'

'Oh no, I meant it,' Charlotte said. 'I was involved with someone else. A long time ago. A very long time ago, in fact. But I've come to terms with the fact that it's over, and I think I might be ready to move on.' Charlotte turned to Martine. 'If you're interested?'

Martine slapped her across the face and stormed off into the wood.

Charlotte dabbed at the tender skin on her cheek. 'I've not been courting for some time, but that's not normal, is it?'

'No, dear,' Mrs Teach said.

'We're stuffed,' Faye said. 'If she tells anyone that we think there's a spy, we are well and truly stuffed. We have to stop her.' Faye hurried through the ferns after Martine. 'Come back, please, Martine!'

There was more cursing in French and a dismissive wave of a hand from Martine.

'Martine, can you please just—'

Martine glanced over her shoulder, saw how close Faye was and started running.

'Please, *stop*!' Faye reached out, splaying her fingers wide, and something happened. The air around her pulsed, every tree in the wood shook. Startled birds and squirrels fled, leaves spiralled to the ground.

And Martine rose twenty feet in the air.

'Oh.' Faye stopped in her tracks and looked at her hand for some kind of explanation. None was forthcoming.

Martine was screeching in French. Faye didn't know the words, but she got the gist. The lady wanted to be let down. Both quickly and gently.

'What did you do?' Miss Charlotte was first to reach Faye.

'I ... er ... ooh.' Faye cupped her hands and called up to Martine. 'I'm so sorry.'

She got an angry fist waving in reply.

'I'm not sure what's happening, but I'll have you back on the ground in a jiffy.'

Mrs Teach tiptoed through the ferns. 'Get her down, Faye. At once.'

'This ... this wasn't in me mum's book. I don't know how I did it. Which means I ain't exactly sure how to get her down again.'

'Oh, spiffing, absolutely spiffing,' Charlotte said. 'You're a danger to yourself and others. Do you know that?'

'I didn't mean to do it,' Faye protested.

'And that's what scares us,' Mrs Teach said.

'Scared?' Faye noticed she was flanked by the two witches. 'Why're you scared?'

'You have all this power,' Charlotte said. 'All this knowledge. And you don't know how to use it. You're like a child with a tommy gun.'

'I think we have a rather more worrisome problem,' Mrs Teach said.

'What's that?' Faye asked.

'That someone we are supposed to trust has kept such a significant secret from us.' Mrs Teach turned on Faye. 'When did you learn to fly, young lady?'

'Oh, that?' Faye waved a hand vaguely. 'Er, yesterday, I think. Don't worry. I won't be making a habit of it.'

'I thought we had made it clear that flying was forbidden,' Mrs Teach said.

'No, you said it wasn't done much these days. Well, maybe we should. And I reckon we should bring back broomsticks, too, 'cos if you try and fly by just flapping your arms you end up going all topsy-turvy.'

Charlotte stood by Faye. 'Do you know how many witches I've known who can fly? Three. Including you. It's incredibly difficult and requires an extraordinary amount of magical energy. You should be exhausted.'

'I am a bit giddy.'

'No, you should be in a heap on the ground,' Charlotte said. 'How much flying did you do yesterday?'

Faye hesitated.

'Come on,' Charlotte snapped.

'I dunno. I flew a few miles. I wasn't exactly using a map.'

'And what did you do after that?'

'Cycled home and did the ironing.'

Now Mrs Teach's voice went up an octave. 'What?'

'I had grease on me dungarees. I had to use blotting paper to—'

'Faye.' Miss Charlotte's voice had an icy edge to it. 'What has happened to you?'

'Allo?' Martine's voice came from high above. 'I would very much like to come down now, *s'il vous plaît*.'

'Er, righto. Not sure how to get you down, exactly, Martine, but bear with me.' Faye bit her lip, then raised her hands, palms facing Martine. She closed her eyes, channelling power through her body.

Mrs Teach's voice came to her in the dark. 'Oh dear.'

'Oh dear, what?' Faye opened her eyes.

Martine was even higher. Almost up to the canopy.

Faye scrunched her nose. 'Buggeration.'

'What are you doing, child?' Mrs Teach's voice was an irritant, scratching at Faye's ears.

'Just stop, Faye, stop,' Charlotte joined in.

The two of them began babbling advice at Faye like a pair of backseat drivers.

'Fly her to a tree.'

'Throw her a rope.'

'Fetch some sandbags.'

'Zip up there after her.'

'Oh, will you two just be quiet!' Faye screeched,

making fists, pressing them to her temples, and then quickly bringing them down by her sides.

There was a scream and a thud as Martine dropped like a stone.

Faye looked at her hands, unclenching them. 'Oh no.' She dashed through the ferns to where Martine was writhing about, clutching her ankle. 'Martine, oh no, I'm so sorry.'

Martine was still cursing Faye's name in her native French, but there was now added fear in her eyes, and she tried to back away as Faye approached.

'Where does it hurt?' Mrs Teach barged past Faye and kneeled by Martine.

'*Ma cheville.*' Martine hissed in pain, pointing to her right ankle. '*Est tordue.*'

'Try not to move it.' Mrs Teach inspected the swelling.

'See what we mean?' Charlotte reached into a pocket inside her coat.

'She would be all right if you two hadn't been going on at me,' Faye protested, but she couldn't shift the sick feeling of guilt in her belly. Shame burned her cheeks.

'It's not just Faye, it's all of you!' Martine managed to sputter between agonised hisses of breath. 'I always said this would be a disaster and I was right, huh? I thought it was because we would have too many captains, but I realise it's because we have too many crazy witches. You three! All of you! Completely mad!'

'Well, there's no need for rudeness,' Mrs Teach said, crinkling her lips.

Charlotte crouched by Martine and gently cradled her head. 'This is for the pain,' she said and sprinkled dust over Martine's face. The French witch's eyes rolled back. She smiled and began snoring. Charlotte carefully lowered her head to the ground.

'There are nurses at Hayward Lodge,' Faye said. 'We need to get her there.'

'And how do you suggest we do that, hmm?' Mrs Teach stood, brushing woodland dirt from her knees. 'We're in the middle of the wood.'

Faye stuck her hands in her pockets. 'I could ... fly her there.'

'Certainly not,' Mrs Teach spluttered.

Charlotte bunched her red lips as she thought. 'Actually, I think in this case we can make an exception. Just this once. Faye, take Martine to Hayward Lodge. We'll report to Vera.'

Faye shivered a little at the mention of the High Witch. 'And then what do I do? We have a spy to catch, don't forget. They're scrying right now.'

'Do nothing,' Mrs Teach blurted.

'Await orders.' Charlotte's voice was calm. 'This complicates everything and we'll need to regroup.'

'Regroup where?' Faye asked.

'Help Martine, then go home,' Charlotte said. 'Understand?'

Faye nodded and lowered her eyes. She felt a sudden weight of shame for hurting Martine with her ham-fisted magic, and the righteous looks she was getting from Mrs Teach and Miss Charlotte made her feel like a silly schoolgirl. Humiliated, she lay down in the ferns next to Martine and took her hand.

'I'm sorry for being so stupid and clumsy, but you should know that Otto said this would happen.' Faye closed her eyes, imaging herself and Martine lying on the planet as it hurtled through the universe. 'He said you would be frightened of me and turn on me.' Faye felt the Earth fall away from her. 'Don't make him right.' Faye opened her eyes. They were rising up through the trees, hand-in-hand, Martine defying gravity as much as Faye. They turned in the air like dancers. As they flew away, Faye glanced down to see Mrs Teach and Miss Charlotte staring at her in silent judgement.

THE TWIST OF THE
TWISTED ANKLE

Jennifer had found the perfect spot for scrying. It wasn't in Hayward Lodge. Goodness, no. Yesterday, some oaf in a uniform burst into her room and declared that she would have to share with three nurses. They came waddling in like ducks soon after, giggling as they unpacked. Jennifer would have to find another quiet spot to commune with Otto.

She thought she might find a secluded niche in the wood, but there was something about the place that unsettled her. Even in the darkest nook, farthest from the house or any ramblers, she could still feel countless eyes on her at all times.

She then discovered a recently built pillbox on the cliffs overlooking where the North Sea met the Thames Estuary, though the squat hexagonal blockhouse had a large crack in the concrete running from the base to its roof. A hand-painted sign by the door warned of subsidence and promised that someone called Captain

Marshall of the Home Guard was looking into it. In the meantime, no one was to enter without permission.

It was perfect. Jennifer swanned in and made herself at home.

The evening sun shone through the loopholes, revealing an empty tin of beans and copy of the *Daily Mirror* left by the previous occupants from the Home Guard. There was a deckchair and a dusty old rug which she assumed was supposed to give this ghastly edifice some kind of home comfort.

Jennifer moved the rug to the centre of the pillbox. She drew a circle around it on the ground with chalk, lined it with black ash and sat in the centre, using the newspaper as a rudimentary cushion between herself and the rug. She placed her scrying implements around her, dropped a few spots of Otto's blood on the gold disc, and closed her eyes.

Otto was already waiting for her and didn't bother with any of the usual pleasantries. 'When?' he asked expectantly.

'We travel to Dover tomorrow and the ritual starts at midnight,' she replied. 'It promises to be bloody exhausting. We perform all evening and Bellamy is quite adamant that it ends at sunrise.'

'Hmm. You know why?'

'He said something about being protected by the moon.'

'He's right. The ritual transports you all to another plane as you generate power with your dancing. You will be unseen, untouchable and protected by the power of the moon. But as the sun rises, that protection fades to nothing. Jennifer Gentle, here are your orders.' Otto's voice took a turn for the terse. 'First, I need you to inform me as soon as the ritual is about to commence. I will depart as soon as I have that confirmation from you.'

'I just told you.' Jennifer tried not to sound too brusque. Good grief, the man could be dense sometimes. 'Midnight, tomorrow.'

'Bellamy is a puppet of the Council of Witches and the War Cabinet. They are no fools and often feed false information to spies to dupe the enemy.'

'I'm no fool, Otto—'

'I never said you were. It is simply a fact of war that one does not act until completely sure.'

That didn't ring true to Jennifer. Certainly not when based on her experience with the FANYs. All sorts of decisions were based on the most flimsy guesswork. But then she'd never flown a fully laden bomber across the English Channel, so she took his point. Besides, she had a more pressing question.

'How am I supposed to contact you? I'll be stuck on a cliff in Dover.'

'Do what you're doing now,' he said. 'Make an excuse and find a quiet spot.'

That's easier said than done, she thought. 'I'm running out of your blood. I have enough for one more conversation. Perhaps two.'

'After tomorrow I shall send more. After tomorrow we plan for invasion, and you will help me. Until then, obey your orders and confirm when the ritual has begun.'

Jennifer thought about arguing that it would be nigh-on impossible to find anywhere that wasn't teeming with witches and soldiers, but she knew Otto had little tolerance for excuses. She would have to think of something.

'Here is your second order,' Otto said. 'Keep Bellamy and his witches there till sunrise. Whatever it takes. Stall them, hide his concertina, ask impertinent questions. I know you have a particular talent for that.'

Jennifer was about to blurt, *How dare you?* but she knew better than to interrupt Otto when he was dispensing orders.

Otto switched to a more staccato rhythm to ram the point home. 'It is imperative that they must not complete the ritual before sunrise. Once the sun is up they will vulnerable and only then can I attack and destroy them.'

I wonder if that includes me, too? Jennifer thought. 'There's something else,' Jennifer began tentatively. She had wondered on the walk over if there was a delicate way to reveal this, but decided that she would simply come right out and say it. 'Faye Bright can fly.'

There was a long pause at the other end. Not a silence, exactly. Scrying took place in the aether where faint crackles from the birth of the universe could still be heard. 'Hello? Are you still—'

'Yes, I'm here.' Otto's voice was even, if ruffled. 'Fly, you say?'

'Like a bird. Actually, more like an untethered balloon, but she can make herself airborne as easily as popping upstairs. She's incredibly powerful.' More crackling from the dawn of time. 'I say, are you there—'

'I'm thinking!' Otto snapped. It was the first time he had raised his voice at her. Jennifer's shoulders tensed. She found herself hunching. 'She cannot be allowed to take part in the ritual.' Some of the calm returned to Otto's voice. 'If she can really fly, then she might even have enough power to perform the ritual alone.' He said it almost as if he couldn't believe it himself.

'Shall I, you know, send her down the Thames as originally planned?' Jennifer was surprised to find that she wasn't as keen on the idea of killing Faye as she had been a couple of days ago. Faye certainly wasn't an old bat like Elsie, Dolly or Ophelia. Sometimes Jennifer didn't even have to act when she was pretending to be her friend. 'I will if you order it, of course, but if she has this extraordinary power, then it might make sense to – I don't know – lock her up for the duration of the ritual, and then you can ... do what needs to be done.'

'You're quite taken with her, aren't you, Jennifer?' Otto said, and she could sense his patronising smile all the way through the aether.

What could Jennifer tell him? That Faye had hugged her? That Faye was the first person to show her any real kindness or trust in her life? Don't be silly, girl. It was merely a hug. How ridiculous that Jennifer should find herself swayed by such a pointless gesture.

It had been nice, though. And it prompted a

disturbing thought. Apart from holding hands in the ritual dance and murdering Dolly, Elsie and Ophelia, Jennifer hadn't enjoyed any significant physical contact with anyone since Mummy died. Even before that, Jennifer couldn't recall a hug that held any meaning for her. That absurd embrace in the woods had been warm and real and made her heart flutter. It was an appalling thing for Faye to do. For a moment, Jennifer realised that if other witches had been just a little more like Faye then she might have been less inclined to murder them.

'Is she your little friend?' Otto mocked.

'No,' she blurted defensively. 'It's just that if we kill her, we'll have no idea where she got this power from.'

'Jennifer, I know exactly where she got this power from. I was there when she got it,' he said, not elaborating any further. 'But you're right. If she's this powerful, then killing her might be beyond even your skills as an assassin. Besides, I should very much like to have a conversation with Faye. We have lots to catch up on.' Otto, with his breathy, Bavarian, tomb-like voice, was hardly the most uplifting speaker, but his words were oozing with a kind of desire that Jennifer had never heard from him before. Not lustful in the usual sense, but Jennifer got the feeling that Otto wanted Faye on their side. He wanted to turn her. 'She cannot interfere,' Otto said. 'She must be ... waylaid. Listen very carefully, Jennifer Gentle. I have a plan.'

ß

There was no summer heat at this height. Faye's eyes streamed and her skin prickled. The sun was getting low and the sky was a dusky blend of orange and purple.

Hayward Lodge, that sprawling manse on the edge of the village, was easy to find. Even now, as evening took hold, there were wounded servicemen resting on beds in the grounds.

Faye cast a glamour. Anyone who saw her moving would assume she and Martine were a rather large bird and nothing else.

Martine began to stir. Whatever Charlotte had given her was wearing off and her hand flexed in Faye's grip. The last thing Faye needed was to drop her again, so she drew Martine in and embraced her tight.

Faye closed her eyes, seeing herself and the planet drifting closer in her mind's eye. Resisting the pull of gravity just enough to bring them down in a clumsy stagger on the gravel drive just by the fountain.

A chap in RAF blues with a bandage around his head was having a sneaky fag by the main entrance and nearly coughed his lungs up when, seemingly out of nowhere, two young ladies were lying by the fountain.

'Blimey, girls,' he managed between hacks, 'where'd you come from?'

'Fetch a nurse, please,' Faye ordered, but the chap just gawped at her. 'Now!' she snapped, and he dashed inside.

Martine's eyes fluttered open and she began muttering, then hissed in pain.

'Martine, it's me, it's Faye.'

Martine tensed at the sound of Faye's voice.

'You've twisted your ankle,' Faye said, then corrected herself. 'No. *I've* twisted your ankle. I'm so sorry, Martine. But I've brought you back to your lodgings. You'll get help. There are doctors and nurses here. Please don't tell anyone about my flying. You—'

'What the blazes?'

Faye winced. She knew that voice, and it belonged to the last person she wanted to see, but the one she knew she wouldn't be able to avoid for long.

'Is this a disaster? I rather think it is.' Bellamy Dumonde came rushing from the mansion, hands pressed to the side of his head in an unwitting imitation of Munch's Scream.

Martine tried to stand. She put a tiny bit of weight on her right foot and cried in pain.

'Martine, what happened?' Bellamy rushed to her side, but the woman was still groggy, her eyes drifting about. 'Faye Bright, explain yourself.'

Faye hesitated. Would could she say?

'It was an accident.' Martine gasped in pain. 'I tripped. *C'est la guerre.*'

Faye gently squeezed Martine's hand in gratitude, then added with more hope than medical knowledge, 'It might just be twisted.'

'How can Martine dance in the ritual with a twisted ankle?' Bellamy asked.

'She can't. She'll just have to stick to scrying, I s'pose.'

'It's exhausting. Non-stop scrying will wear her out more than the dancing, Faye. And besides, we cannot afford to lose a single ounce of magical energy, or the whole thing collapses and—'

'Stand aside, please.' Matron's Edinburgh brogue burst out of the great house's doors before she did. 'Make room, that's it, away ye go. Now, lassie, where does it hurt? I'm guessing, by the way you're holding it, the problem might be with your ankle, yes? Oh, nothing gets by me. Just lie down, that's it.'

Faye and Bellamy stepped back as Matron attended to Martine.

Faye whispered in his ear. 'It was my fault. I'm so sorry.'

Bellamy looked at her with a mix of pity and confusion. 'What did you do?'

'I let you down. I've let you all down.'

Faye ran back along the drive, unable to bear Martine's hisses of pain or Bellamy's hurt expression any longer. Faye kept running and didn't look back.

Rudders, Ailerons and Flaps

Faye found herself at Larry Dell's barn. She had thought about running to the pub, but the sun was down and Dad and Bertie would have been busier than ever with no time for her shame or guilt. And so she ran. And then she was short of breath, so she walked. She'd considered flying here, but the very thought of it made her belly do flips. The barn was the only place where she could be alone. Or as alone as you ever could be with a poltergeist.

And besides, she had questions.

Larry had taken his tools from where Faye had left them. The barn door was ajar. Faye found the pilot's helmet on the workbench and put it on, speaking into the microphone.

'Leo? Are you there?' She stepped inside, and the sudden drop in temperature made her spine tingle.

Leo was lying on his back, hands clasped on his chest. 'I can see the stars.' He pointed up. Faye followed his finger and found a hole in the roof.

'Very nice.' Faye sat cross-legged close by.

'I saw a dogfight earlier. Too high up to make any sense, but the vapour trails swirled white against the blue sky. One of them turned black and fell away.' Leo shifted his gaze to Faye, his burns as fresh as the day he died. 'I wish I were fighting.'

'I wish I could help you.' Faye picked at the rubber sole of her plimsolls.

'I belong here.' Leo crossed his ankles and took a breath. 'I accept it now. It's not so bad. You get used to doing nothing. How was your day?'

'I've hurt someone,' Faye said.

'A Nazi?'

'No.'

'Shame.'

'Someone who's supposed to be on my side. I threw her up in the air and she twisted her ankle.'

'Oh. Very clumsy.'

'I don't make a habit of hurting people, Leo. You could at least show a smidge more sympathy.'

Leo made a grunting noise that was neither comforting nor sympathetic.

'Why did Mum tell me to fly?' Faye picked up a bolt she found on the barn floor and tossed it into a corner where it landed with a clang. 'It's brought nothing but trouble.'

'That's not what she told you,' Leo said.

'You said she said I should fly.'

'She told you to *learn* to fly.' Leo leaned up on one elbow. 'You think you flap your arms and that's all there is to it? It's difficult. Dangerous. People get hurt. A twisted ankle? Pah! Douglas Bader can fly and he doesn't have any bloody legs! That's the problem with children today. You're all wrapped in cotton wool and—'

'Oh, will you stick a sock in it?' Faye snapped. 'Because of that twisted ankle, we won't be able to do a ritual that could have stopped the invasion of Britain by the Nazis.'

'You think you can stop them with magic?'

'This fella Bellamy does. I ain't so sure.'

'The only thing that will stop them are pilots. Spitfire pilots, Hurricane pilots. The ATA pilots who move the planes, the engineers on the ground, the anti-aircraft units, the men and women in the operations rooms and on the radio. Not any of your silly hocus-pocus.'

'It's not silly. Not all of it. We do our bit in our own way.' Faye looked up through the hole in the roof. A silver cloud moved across the night sky. 'Could you teach me to fly?'

'Me?'

'You're a pilot and a flight instructor. You must know it all. What are the basics?'

'Don't hit the ground.'

'Very funny.'

'It's true. You'll be astonished how few pilots remember that.'

'What about maps and navigating and all that?'

'It takes thirty-six weeks to train a fighter pilot. Longer for bomber crew. You need hundreds of hours in the air. Why do you want to be a pilot, anyway?'

'I don't, but I need to learn to fly. You just said so yourself. I can't hurt any more people. No more accidents.'

Leo sat up. 'You had an accident?'

'I flew into a barrage balloon. It was the only way I could get down.'

Leo snorted. 'Landing is the hardest part of flying. But we'll come to that later.'

Faye's face lit up. 'You'll teach me?'

Leo waved his hands to calm her down. 'Let's see what you can do. Earlier, I saw you float up and away. Can you steer, or are you like a balloon?'

'I can steer.'

'Show me.' He folded his arms.

'Righto.' Faye lay on her back and closed her eyes. Taking off came easily now, and within moments she was six feet up. She leaned forwards and swooped out through the barn doors.

The summer night air was warm and she was delighted to be out of the chilly barn, at least until she flew into a swarm of midges with an open mouth. She spat them away, wiping her lips. This caused her to start to turn head over heels. She wailed, flapping her arms to right herself, and began to rise. Leo had wanted to see her steer, so she turned in a circle above the barn, but the wind was stronger up here and shoved her about, sending her cartwheeling over the trees. She threw her arms and legs wide, which slowed her down. Her belly was beginning to stir, her lips were cold and she started to feel a little giddy. Time to land. She felt the pull of gravity as she dipped below the trees. She bent at the knees as she landed but tumbled over and collapsed in a heap.

She grinned at Leo who was standing in the barn's doorway. 'Whaddya think?'

'I withdraw my offer.'

'Wait, what?' Faye rearranged her limbs and got to her feet, rushing back into the chill of the barn. 'You said!'

'It's quite simple.' Leo shook his head. 'The human body is not designed for flight, Faye. How do you even move about and steer?'

'I sort of . . . lean.'

'I saw,' Leo said, eyes wide. 'It was a disaster. Your turning circle is as big as the moon. You need to be able to turn on a penny. Like that!' He clapped his hands together, sending one of them banking like an aircraft.

'It's a bit tricky, y'know.' Faye nodded up. 'It's really windy up there.'

'Don't fight the wind,' Leo said. 'Use it!'

'Like a sailing ship?'

'Not exactly. I could try and explain Bernoulli's principle, but I fear I would only add to the likelihood of you perishing in a terrible crash.'

'Bernoulli's principle.' Faye squinted one eye. 'That's where the shape of a wing makes the air move faster over the top and so it gets lift, right?'

Leo looked at her sideways. 'Lucky guess.'

'No. Bertie drew a diagram for me once. But I don't have wings, do I?'

'No,' Leo said. 'You need rudders, ailerons and flaps.'

'I don't rightly know what those are, so you'll have to tell me.'

'You'll need them to steer, and you'll need some sort of craft.' Leo shrugged. 'You're a witch. Get a broomstick.'

'I've been reliably informed that we don't fly on broomsticks. And what good would a stick do anyway? It don't have them flaps and rudders and whatever.'

'True.' A hint of a smile appeared on Leo's face.

'What?'

Leo turned and gestured to all the spare parts piled up in Larry's barn.

'But perhaps we could make one?'

WITCHY STUFF

'Now, promise you won't go half barmy,' Faye said as they approached the barn.

It was almost midnight, and the moon was as gibbous as it got without being full, but the air was still warm and humid. Terrence had been looking forward to getting at least one cryptic clue in his crossword before a good night's sleep. Being dragged all the way to Larry Dell's most rickety barn by his daughter on a mysterious errand was not on the cards. And he wasn't alone. Poor Bertie had been roped into this little jaunt, too. The lad hobbled behind him, panting as he kept up.

'Maybe if you told us what this was about, I could make such a promise.' Terrence batted away a cloud of midges. 'But until I see what kind of palaver you're involved in this time, I'm not promising anything.'

'I promise,' Bertie said, catching his breath.

'Crawler.' Terrence smiled.

They stood before the barn, with Bertie a bit further back than the other two.

'What's up with you?' Terrence asked him.

Bertie shifted about on his feet.

'He had a bad experience here last time,' Faye told Terrence. 'Don't worry, Bertie. He's a lot calmer now. And he's not always there.' Faye peeked inside the doors.

'Faye.' Terrence rested bunched fists on his hips. 'What the bleedin' 'eck are we doing here?'

'I need to show you something. I can't just tell ya. You need to see it.'

Bertie and Terrence shared a look.

'Come on then, what is it?' Terrence said impatiently as he peered over Faye's shoulder. 'Is it in the barn?'

'Dad, Bertie,' Faye said quietly. 'Look at my feet.'

'Your feet?' Terrence wrinkled his face in confusion. 'What about your— Oh, bloody hell!'

Faye's feet weren't touching the ground. They were three inches above it, floating steadily.

Bertie, always one for knowing how things work, circled around Faye looking for mirrors and rope. 'How . . . how'd you do that?'

Terrence knew. 'Witchy stuff?'

'Witchy stuff.' Faye silently rose higher. The magical energy made her want to gasp, but she kept it under control.

'Lumme.' Bertie backed away.

'Your mother couldn't fly.' Terrence narrowed one eye. 'So how come—'

'She said I need to learn.'

Terrence's face froze. 'What? You . . . you spoke to her?'

'Not exactly,' Faye said, regretting she had mentioned her mother in the first place. Her poor father looked like he was about to crumple into tears. 'I got a message. From, y'know, the other side. Sounds silly when I say it out loud, but there we go.'

'How . . . is she?'

'We didn't have a chat, Dad. She just said that I should learn to fly. She left instructions in her book.'

'I thought her book was gone,' Bertie said.

'All up here.' Faye tapped the side of her head. 'Long story, but here's the problem – it's a bugger to steer when you're floating about. I need something that I can sit on and ride and turn.' She drifted closer to the barn, her feet finding the ground again.

Bertie snapped his fingers. 'Like a broomstick.'

'Bingo. Only not just a stick. If I'm going to steer, I need—'

'Rudders, flaps, trim tabs.' Bertie counted them off on his fingers.

'That's the stuff.' Faye smiled. 'Bertie knows.'

'Hang on just a moment.' Terrence stepped between them, still looking a little befuddled. 'I ain't no expert on flying, but I do know it's bloody dangerous, and if you hadn't noticed, there's a war on. I'm not having you whizzing about up there willy-nilly.'

'I have to learn, Dad.' Faye took his hand, and looked from him to Bertie. 'Something's happened to me. I have a lot more power now, and I don't know how to use it properly. It's not just about flying, it's about magic, and learning how to control it. 'Cos if I don't ... I worry that people will get hurt. Or worse. I've tried to ignore it, but one wave of my hand and I might bring the roof down. By helping me with this, you're keeping me safe.'

'It's true, Mr Bright,' Bertie said. 'I've seen some of the stuff she can do and it's proper powerful. I reckon she might be the most powerful witch going.'

'And how many witches do you know, Bertie?' Terrence asked.

Bertie curled his lip as he thought. 'Three at the last count.'

'I'm not the most powerful,' Faye said, thinking of Vera and Otto. 'But it's more power than I'm comfortable with. I need help. I've got the ghost of a Hurricane pilot helping me with the basics. And you two can be my ground crew. So, how about it?'

'I could've had a nice early night.' Terrence pressed the palms of his hands to his eyes. 'Mug of Ovaltine and the crossword. I don't ask for much.'

'I'll help you, Faye. It's a secret project, Mr Bright! We should call it "Code Name: Whirligig".' Bertie smiled proudly.

'Thank you, Bertie, you're a brick.' Faye slapped the lad on the shoulder. 'Dad? You said you needed a hobby.'

Terrence blinked his eyes open. 'I'd ask what we're supposed to make this broomstick out of, but I reckon there's a reason you brung us here.' He gestured at the barn.

Faye swung the barn doors wide.

Bertie had seen it all before, of course, but he still gasped at the display of aircraft parts as the moonlight revealed them in all their glory. The wing parts were all stacked together, and the wheels were in a neat pile. Leo had been busy tidying things away after his last tantrum.

'What the bloody hell?' Terrence stepped into the barn, his mouth open. 'Larry Dell, you crafty old sod.' He turned to Faye. 'This is hoarding. I should report him for this.'

'Ooh, no, don't dob him in,' Bertie said. 'I promised him I wouldn't.'

Faye frowned at her dad. 'You won't, will you?'

'Not till we've sorted you out,' Terrence said, then laughed when he saw Faye and Bertie's concerned faces. 'I promise. I won't turn him in, but I might encourage him to return what's left over.'

Faye smiled. 'So you'll help me?'

Terrence moved to the workbench and inspected a rear-view mirror from a Spitfire. 'I don't know if we have everything we need, but yes, we'll do what we can.'

Faye rushed to Terrence and wrapped her arms around him. 'Thank you, Dad. And you, Bertie.' She smothered the boy, too. His eyes half closed in bliss as he hugged her back.

'This could take ages.' Terrence surveyed the Aladdin's cave of plane parts. 'And I've got a pub to run.'

'I know,' Faye said. 'But it's better than jigsaws and ships in bottles, eh?'

'Can't argue with that.' Terrence smiled.

'Righto.' Faye made for the door. 'I have to go and do ... stuff.'

Terrence frowned. 'At this time of night?'

'Witchy stuff?' Bertie asked.

'Witchy stuff,' Faye said, glad to be keeping it vague. After Martine's injury, Bellamy had sent the witches telegrams, summoning them to an emergency meeting at the stones to 'Recalibrate the ritual'. Faye's gut twisted every time she thought of poor Martine, and what her injury meant for their mission.

'Are you with us, Faye?' Terrence waved his hand in front of her eyes. How long had she been in deep thought? She blinked back to reality.

'Tickety-boo. Will you be all right?'

'As rain,' Terrence said.

Bertie didn't look so sure, peering into the shadows.

'Ah, yes.' Faye picked up the pilot's helmet from the workbench and put it on. 'Leo,' she spoke into the microphone, 'can I rely on you to leave Dad and Bertie to work in peace?'

There was no answer, but Faye noticed her father shudder. The barn grew chill.

'Leo? Promise me you'll be good.'

'Of course,' said a voice beside her ear.

She jolted and turned to see Leo leaning against the barn door.

'Bloody hell!' Terrence cried, and Bertie instinctively grabbed his arm.

'Leo, this is me dad and Bertie. Dad, Bertie, this is Leo.'

Bertie gave a polite smile. 'Yes, we've met.'

'He's a pilot,' Faye told them. 'And, as you can see, he's been in the wars a bit.'

Leo gave them a curt nod.

'How do,' Terrence managed to say.

'If you want to talk with him, you have to use this.' She wriggled the pilot's helmet off and handed it to Bertie. He put it on, a silly grin on his face.

'Roger, wilco!' Bertie jabbed a thumb in the air.

'That's all lovely, then.' Faye clapped her hands together. 'I'll leave you lads to it.' She strode into the moonlight. It glowed blue around her.

'Faye.' Terrence hurried after her. He took her hand.

'What is it, Dad?' Faye asked. His eyes were glistening.

He glanced back at Leo. 'If you speak to your mother again . . . tell her I miss her.' He squeezed Faye's hand.

'I will, Dad.'

'And ask her . . .' Terrence bit his lip and lowered his voice. 'She speaks to me in my dreams. Ask her if it's really her, will ya?'

Faye pulled her father closer and hugged him tight. Her breath shook and she wiped a tear from her eye as she turned and headed towards the wood.

Faye the Dozy Twonk

By the time Faye arrived at the standing stones, the others were all there. All but Martine.

'Ah, Faye, good evening,' Bellamy said, his voice terse. 'We can begin.' He beckoned Faye closer to the circle of witches. She took a place next to Jennifer who was checking herself in her little silver powder mirror. She snapped it shut and smiled at Faye. Jennifer's cat yawned.

Bellamy moved to the head of the slaughter stone, swiping his hand across the moon and veiling them in darkness. He clasped his hands together as he spoke. 'Apologies for the last-minute and clandestine nature of this meeting, but as you may have gathered, Martine has had a little accident.'

Faye blushed and lowered her head, feeling shame and relief that Martine hadn't revealed the real reason for her injury, nor that there might be a spy in their midst.

'The good news is the ankle is only twisted and not broken.'

There came happier murmurs from the others.

'The bad news is that she's not match fit. Not by a long chalk. She will be on scrying duties only.'

'She's one of the best scryers I know,' Mrs Housego said, 'but she can't do it all on her own. She'll be exhausted, poor lass.'

'What does this mean?' Jennifer asked. 'Should we wait? Should we call it off?'

Voices began to overlap as the witches bombarded Bellamy with questions.

'How was this allowed to happen?' Mrs Housego demanded to know.

'You're supposed to be taking care of us, Bellamy,' Jennifer added. 'You're in command. How can you—'

'Don't blame Bellamy,' Faye raised her voice. 'This is all my fault.'

The chattering stopped and all heads turned to Faye.

She set her jaw before speaking. 'I was trying something ... stupid. And it didn't work, and she got hurt. I'm the one to blame.'

'What were you doing?' Mrs Housego asked.

Faye glanced at Mrs Teach and Miss Charlotte, wondering if they were going to chip in with either blame or excuses, but they were trying their best to pretend that they had never met her before.

'I won't say.' Faye reminded herself that Mrs Housego just might be a German spy – one particularly keen on nudity – and she had to watch what she blurted out in the woman's presence. But the thought of this jolly old lady being in league with the Nazis was ridiculous.

Which was, of course, exactly what they would want Faye to think. Faye was getting annoyed by all this double-bluff spy nonsense.

'I want to apologise, and I'm ready for whatever punishment you see fit, Bellamy.'

Bellamy's head twitched at the mention of his name. 'Punishment? Oh, good grief. Are we the navy? Do we flog the lower ranks with a cat-o'-nine-tails? Most certainly not. Faye, I accept your apology. Accidents will happen and all that.' His eyes flicked to Miss Charlotte and Mrs Teach. How much had they told him?

'And the ritual is going ahead,' Charlotte said. It wasn't a question.

Bellamy folded his arms and nodded his head so hard and fast that it became a blur.

'Do we shirk from a challenge? No, we do not.' He turned to address each witch. 'Mrs Housego, Mrs Teach, Faye Bright, Charlotte Southill and Jennifer Gentle. I have come to know you all a little these past few days and my admiration for your skills and power has grown tenfold. In fact, I am so confident in your abilities that were I to choose just one of you –' his gaze briefly fell on Faye '– I think we could still pull this off.'

It took Faye a moment to realise that all the other witches were now looking at her. She tried to smile, but her top lip twitched.

'Ladies, get what rest you can tonight,' Bellamy said. 'We shall meet again at noon tomorrow at Therfield Station, and we will begin our journey to Dover.'

Bellamy raised his arms to the night sky. 'May the wind be at our wings,' he said, and Faye wondered how deliberate his choice of words was. 'For tomorrow we change the course of the war.'

The witches walked back through the moonlit wood, Bellamy leading the way. They were silent, some pondering the sudden reality of their mission, others frostily avoiding one another's gazes. The pubs were closed, but Bellamy had invited them all back to Hayward Lodge for 'a snifter or two'. Faye just wanted to sleep, but she had one last task to do tonight.

'I'll see you there,' Faye said to Mrs Teach and Miss Charlotte, but they didn't reply.

Faye left the main group, taking a path by the Wode River.

Jennifer hurried after her.

'Faye, where are you going?'

'I left me bike further down the path.'

'May I keep you company?' Jennifer asked, her cat darting about in the undergrowth, on the hunt.

Faye wasn't sure she had much of a choice, so agreed.

'I didn't say a word about, you know ...' Jennifer flapped her hands like wings, looking around to make sure no one was following or eavesdropping. 'I promise, Faye, I would never betray your trust like that.'

'Oh, I know.' Faye ducked under a scrum of midges. The grass here was getting taller and thicker and the path was barely wide enough for one. She had to keep looking behind her to speak to Jennifer. 'I'm perfectly capable of making meself look like a fool.'

'I saw the way Bellamy kept glancing at you when he was banging on about skills and power. He has all the subtlety of a bull in a china shop.'

'I wish he wouldn't do that,' Faye admitted. 'Sometimes I wonder if he thinks I can win the war all on my own.'

'He's basking in your reflected glory, Faye. This mission will be a huge success and he'll take all the credit. You see if I'm wrong.'

'I don't care who gets the glory.' Faye parted the hanging branches of a willow tree and held them for Jennifer and her cat to pass. 'So long as we get it done.' They moved away from the river and took a wider path deeper into the wood.

'You're far more forgiving than I, Faye Bright.' Jennifer looked around, then lowered her voice. 'Is what he said true? I know you can fly, but about how powerful you are?'

'Oh, I dunno. It's not like it's a competition.'

'There are plenty of other witches who see it that way.'

'So I've heard.' Faye left the path and ducked under the branches of a sycamore tree. Jennifer jogged after her to catch up.

'Well, I think you're amazing. If it was down to me, you would be High Witch and running the whole show.'

'I don't want to run any show. I just want to be useful.'

'You're so modest.' Jennifer flicked her hair back. 'And that's a good thing, of course. If I had your power—'

'You don't want this power,' Faye said a little snippily.

Jennifer stopped in her tracks, startled.

'Sorry, Jennifer, but something happened to me recently, and I changed. And I'm not sure I like it.'

Jennifer's cat ran up her leg and she embraced her, stroking her and making her purr. 'Changed?'

'I had . . . I had all the power of the moon inside me.' Faye turned her hands over, flexing her fingers. 'The power to move oceans, to blot out the sun, to reach into the minds of others. For a few moments, I could do it all.' She clenched her fists. 'It didn't last, but a lot of that power is still inside me. It never rests. And it wants to get out. That's why I want to learn to fly. It's a good way to use that energy up. Better me whizzing about up there than hurting people down here.'

'Hurting people?' Jennifer inclined her head. 'I thought Martine's ankle was an accident.'

'It was.'

Jennifer gasped. 'You did it? How?'

'I didn't do it on purpose. That's the problem. I'm an accident waiting to happen.' Faye stuck her hands in her pockets. 'If I could give it all away, I think I would.' She turned and resumed walking down the path.

'Golly. Give it to me, why don't you? What I could do with that sort of power.'

'What would you do?' Faye asked.

'Fly to Berlin and biff Herr Hitler on the schnozz, for starters,' she said, getting all excited. 'Then I'd give

Otto Kopp a good thrashing and teach him a lesson for all the rotten things he did to you.'

'If it was that easy, I would've done it already. We're here.' Faye's beloved Pashley Model A rested against the tree where she had left it. She gripped the handlebars, swung her leg over the saddle and kicked the pedals into position. 'Hop on. It's all downhill to the village.'

꩜

They rattled towards Woodville, the cat in the bike's basket, Faye hunched over the handlebars, Jennifer's arms wrapped round her torso, clinging on for dear life.

A thought niggled in Faye's brain. Something wasn't quite right, but she couldn't put her finger on it. Something that Jennifer had said. There was so much nonsense swirling around in her mind that it was becoming impossible to keep track of it all. She yearned for a simpler time when the most complicated thing in her life was bell-ringing.

Faye shook her head clear and concentrated on the road.

This was better than flying. Faye knew this bike like an old friend. If she wanted to steer, she simply had to think it and the bike would respond. As they came to the Old Roman Bridge, Faye spotted a pothole in the road.

'Hold tight,' she called, and pulled on the handlebars.

'What?' Jennifer cried.

The bike skipped over the hole with ease. In fact, it flew. Just for a few seconds. Faye felt a familiar thrill. The cat glanced back at her, ears flapping.

It wasn't long before they found themselves at Edge Road, a short walk for Jennifer to Hayward Lodge and a quick downhill ride for Faye to the Green Man.

'The pub's closed, but you're welcome to come in for a cuppa,' Faye said.

Jennifer held her cat tight, her hair somewhat frazzled after the ride. 'Actually, no. I'm going to pootle off to my lodgings, make a pot of tea and curl up with a good book. Long day tomorrow. Saving the world and all that.'

'Sounds like a good idea,' Faye agreed. 'See you first thing.'

Jennifer dashed forwards, her cat leaping off her to the ground. She took Faye's hand. 'Don't be too quick to give your power away, Faye. So few of us girls have it. And it won't just be useful for tomorrow. There's a whole war to win.' She gave Faye a tight hug, one that lasted just a little too long for comfort, then turned and walked with her cat towards Hayward Lodge.

Faye cycled away, freewheeling down the Wode Road to the pub, trying to sort her thoughts into some sort of order. As she leaned the bike against the pub's wall, she happened to look up and spotted Jennifer ducking down Perry Lane. Faye wondered why the girl and her cat were going in the opposite direction from Hayward Lodge. Jennifer was heading back into the wood. And just how did Jennifer know about Otto?

'Oh, Faye Bright, you dozy twonk,' Faye whispered to herself. 'Jennifer's the bloody spy!'

A Voice from the Past

Faye's first instinct was to fetch the other witches, but they were all at Hayward Lodge. Even if she flew, by the time she got them here she would have lost Jennifer.

Faye stood and looked at the dark pub. Dad and Bertie weren't back yet, probably still working on Code Name: Whirligig, or whatever it was Bertie called the broomstick.

Faye would have to go after Jennifer herself.

She swung a leg over the crossbar of her Pashley Model A, leaned on the pedals and took off after Jennifer.

The night air was warm and sweat clung to Faye's back as she pedalled along woodland paths. She soon spotted Jennifer with her cat draped over her shoulder. But instead of taking a possible left down the long and winding river bridle path – one that might have still taken her to Hayward Lodge – Jennifer kept going up towards the coast.

Faye slowed down, catching her breath and keeping her distance.

Jennifer took her time, stopping to inspect mushrooms, always staying within sight. The path rode up and down the rolling farmland for a mile or so before rising to the cliffs overlooking the sea.

Faye's head bobbed as she cycled up the last stretch, droplets of sweat falling from her brow onto the lenses of her specs. She looked to the horizon, but Jennifer was nowhere to be seen.

'Bugger,' Faye muttered. She stopped the bike. There was only one thing for it. Faye rested the Pashley on the path, closed her eyes and raised her arms to her sides.

Silently, and to the bemusement of a passing nightjar, Faye rose into the air.

The barrage balloons that lined the coast were silhouetted against the moon reflected on the sea. The shoreline was dotted with barbed wire and steel defences. Distant searchlights probed the sky over Margate.

Faye rotated until she was facing east.

She saw Jennifer hurrying along the coastal path to one of the new pillboxes. The girl ducked inside. Faye considered flying there right now, but the thought of abandoning her beloved Pashley again made her wince, so she landed, grabbed the bike by the handlebars and pushed it to the cliffs.

The pillbox was an irregular hexagon, squat and concrete and dotted with loopholes for gun barrels to poke out of. These had popped up all along the coastline in the last month and were designed to take potshots at any invading tanks and soldiers, should the worst happen. Most were manned by the Home Guard, but this one was left empty tonight. Not surprising as there was a bloody great crack up its side. Faye recalled hearing Captain Marshall complaining about it in the pub last week.

Faye left her bike in the tall grass and scurried over to the pillbox, keeping her steps light. She conjured a glamour to blend into the shadows.

There was little noise from inside. Something that sounded like a ceramic plate was being rested on the concrete floor.

Heart thumping, Faye edged closer to the nearest loophole and peered into the darkness.

Jennifer was kneeling on her suede scrying bag. She had arranged wax tablets inscribed with runes on either side of her obsidian mirror. She gently placed a gold disc on the mirror and carefully applied a precise amount of blood on the disc with an amber glass dropper.

The air hummed, and Faye wondered if Mrs Teach's ears were whistling. She wished her friends were with her now.

The blood on the disc fizzed and a voice came from the other side.

Faye's blood ran cold.

She would know that breathy Bavarian voice anywhere.

'Miss Gentle,' Otto Kopp said. 'I have been longing to hear from you.'

'*Mein Herr*, I have very good news.' Jennifer spoke

with a cold deference that Faye had never heard from the girl before. Her intonation was odd. Like she was reciting lines from a play. 'I have the time and location of tomorrow's ritual. Everything you require to wipe them out.'

Faye's mind raced. What magic was in her mother's book to stop this? There was nothing she could recall. She would have to kick the door in and—

Faye noticed a movement on the edge of her vision.

A black blur came at her with teeth and claws and Faye was reminded that glamours didn't work on animals.

Jennifer's cat wailed as it leapt at Faye. She turned, half expecting her face to be scratched, but the cat landed at her feet, hissing as it pawed at her plimsolls. It was almost as if it wanted Faye to follow her.

'What are you trying to—'

The cat saw something behind Faye and darted away.

Faye turned too late as Jennifer rushed her, head down, knocking her over.

Faye's specs fell to the ground. She scrabbled to get them, but a boot landed on her knuckles. Faye looked up into Jennifer's rage-filled face. The girl reached into her pocket and took out a handful of grey powder, flinging it in Faye's eyes.

Faye fell into darkness.

BITTER PILLBOX

Bertie Butterworth's Battle of Britain Diary

Friday 16th August, 1940

*A raid at teatime. Not as bad as in recent days.
Heavy guns at Dover. Faye can fly. Really! Well,
I saw her float and that's practically flying, isn't
it? Me and Mr Bright are working on a Top-Secret
Project for Faye that I cannot divulge in these
pages in case this diary is captured by the Nazis
and taken to Adolf Hitler himself. I should
probably also tear out the page with Mum's recipe
for Spotted Dick as she wouldn't want that falling
into enemy hands.*

Faye woke on a rug. It was dusty, the pattern faded, but
it was the sort of rug you might find before a hearth
in any living room. That was as far as the home com-
forts went.

Faye's eyes were sticky, and even when she managed

to get them open, everything was a blur. It was still dark. How long had she been unconscious? It felt like only a few minutes had passed, but Faye's shoulders ached from sleeping on the thin rug, so maybe she had been out for longer.

Faye sat up, hugging her knees. Her specs were neatly folded and tucked into the breast pocket of her dungarees. She put them on. Not a scratch. The fact that Jennifer hadn't take the opportunity to smash Faye's glasses gave her a strange flutter of hope.

She looked around. The room's walls were red bricks, with some plaster hastily daubed around the steel door in an effort to make it look finished. The big crack she had seen from the outside ran through the bricks inside, too. The floor around the rug was cold concrete with countless shards of brick and stone scattered about. Faye was in the pillbox. The hexagonal shape of the room and the loopholes told her that. In one corner was a deckchair, probably left by whichever member of the Home Guard was here previously. She wondered if they knew their pillbox was being used to send magical communications to the enemy. She wondered when the Home Guard would be back.

Faye groaned her way to her feet and tried the door, which she knew with crushing inevitability would be locked. It was. She shuffled to the nearest loophole, kicking over an empty tin of baked beans on the way.

'Jennifer!' she cried, moving from loophole to loophole. 'Jennifer, let me out!'

Faye looked at the tall grass, still and grey in the

moonlight. Her bicycle was not where she left it, and Jennifer was long gone, as was the cat. The more Faye thought about the cat, the more she wondered if it had been trying to warn her of the attack.

Laughter echoed in the darkness. Faye spun to find Jennifer's little silver powder mirror in the centre of the room. A tiny pool of blood sizzled on the mirror's glass, and the laughter became louder.

'I know that laugh,' Faye muttered to herself.

A white glow from the mirror grew more and more intense until it filled the room.

'Good evening, Faye Bright.' Otto Kopp's breathy voice came from the mirror. 'You snore, by the way. But you must have needed the rest as you've been asleep all day.'

All day? Panic rose in Faye. The ritual started at midnight. She had to get to Dover. She had to warn the others. She gripped the door's handle and pulled hard. It rattled in its frame but remained firmly in place.

'Save your energy, Faye. We have much to discuss.' Behind Otto's voice was a familiar drone. Some sort of engine. Faye couldn't put her finger on it.

'Otto Kopp,' she said. 'Still alive, then?'

'Oh, yes. Very much alive and well, thank you for asking.'

'Last time I saw you, poor old Harry Aston was a demonic dog and was about to bite your head off.'

'Harry's existence as a Jäger was mercifully short.'

Faye felt a pang of sadness for Harry. A fool, to be sure, but no one deserved what happened to him.

She glanced at the powder mirror on the ground, not daring to touch it.

'And how's your best mate, Jennifer?'

'Jennifer is a wise young woman, Faye. I befriended her when no one else would.'

'Befriended? You turned her into a spy and a traitor.'

'Ah, you had to make it political. What a shame.'

Faye could feel the magical energy coming from the tiny mirror and its bond with the aether, the space between places that connected everyone and everything magical. She wondered who else might be listening.

'The truth is, Faye, the British spurned Jennifer. She had nowhere else to go. All I did was offer a sympathetic ear.'

'I bet you did.' Faye returned to the steel door, looking around its edges for weak spots. 'If Jennifer is the traitor, why didn't she kill me?'

'Kill you?' Otto sounded genuinely shocked. 'Jennifer adores you. Worships you, in fact. She could never do you any harm.'

Faye's knuckles were still sore from where Jennifer had trodden on them, so she found that hard to believe.

'Soon this terrible war will be over.' The droning noise at Otto's end grew louder, and yet he decided to lower his voice to a whisper, as if afraid that others might hear him. 'I'm no Nazi, Faye. I've lived a long time, almost as long as your Miss Charlotte, and I've seen tyrants come and go. These fellows are on the winning side, but their Thousand Year Reich is just a dream. They'll self-destruct like all the others, but

I've learned that it's simply prudent to align your banner with the current victors. All I want to do, Faye, is study magic. To pursue its secrets for the benefit of all, so that we can bring peace to the world. Is that so bad?'

'Is that the same twaddle you told Jennifer?' Faye gave up on the door and started looking for loose bricks around the loopholes. 'You must think I'm thick as two short planks to fall for something like that.'

'On the contrary,' Otto said with a chuckle. 'I would have been disappointed if you had. You're a very smart young lady. Pragmatic. Why don't you join me? Be on the winning side?'

'If it's all the same to you, I'd rather stick needles in me eyes.'

'Faye, before breakfast tomorrow the most powerful witches in Britain will be dead. Within days your RAF will be annihilated, and soon after the Channel will be so full of Nazi landing craft you will be able to go from Dover to Calais without getting your feet wet. The war is over. You want peace, don't you?'

'Up yours with knobs on.' It wasn't Faye's most intelligent retort, but it did the job.

'What if ... what if I could give you what you really want, Faye?' Otto mused, his voice taking on a sympathetic tone. 'Time with your mother, hmm? You know I could do it. What would you say to that?'

'I'd say you were a filthy liar,' she said, burying the temptation deep inside her. 'Here's the news, Otto. My mum is gone.' Her voice was shaking, and without any warning a sob bubbled up from inside her. 'Oh, bloody hell.' She sniffed, wiping away a tear.

'Don't cry, you poor lonely little girl,' Otto oozed.

'You think this is a weakness, don't ya?' Faye cleared her throat and took a breath. 'Me, crying. No, matey. It means that someone loved me. And it might cause me pain just to think of 'em, but that ain't a weakness. It's what makes me get up in the mornin'. My mum did good with the time she had, helping those around her, and I intend to do the same. And I ain't lonely. I have a fella, a father and sisters in magic, and we ain't got time for the likes of you.'

'A shame. I had to ask. I was right, though, wasn't I, Faye? Mrs Teach, Miss Charlotte, Vera . . . they're all suspicious of you, aren't they? Even more so now that you recall the wonders in your mother's book.'

'I see you're up to date on all the local gossip.'

'I am, I am.' Otto's voice dripped with glee. 'And a little bird tells me that you can even fly.'

'I dabble,' she said. Though a fat lot of good it was now, stuck inside a squat bunker.

'Oh, such modesty. I do enjoy your flippancy, Faye. It's very refreshing.'

'Oh, do you? Then how about this for flippancy?' Faye then unleashed a tirade of insults that she had learned from an American crime paperback she'd picked up at the church jumble sale last month. It had been quite an eye-opening read, what with the dames with legs from here to ya-ya, a series of cold-blooded murders, and hoods with turns of phrase that would make a docker blush. She had read it twice in quick succession.

'What can I say, Faye? I am shocked. And I thought you were such a nice girl.'

'When we meet again, Otto, I'll show you just how not-nice I can be.'

'Unlike that dreary song, Faye, we shall not meet again. For as much as Jennifer wanted me to let you live, I'm afraid I cannot. Not unless you're absolutely sure that I can't tempt you join the side of the victors?'

'Get stuffed.'

'As I thought. Your powers are such that you represent a danger to my plans. Thus, sadly, if you will not join me, then tonight is the night you die, Faye Bright.'

Faye almost missed his declaration as she finally figured out where she had heard that droning noise before. 'You're on a bomber.'

'Very good, Faye.'

'And Jennifer ... she's with the others at—' Faye stopped herself, not wanting to give away any secrets.

'Dover. I would imagine they're about to start.'

'About to start? It's midnight?' Faye vibrated with anxiety. She had to get out of this concrete prison.

'Almost midnight. It must be chilly on those cliffs.'

'You know about Dover?'

'I know everything.'

Faye imagined Jennifer meeting the others at Therfield Station at noon. 'She's probably told them I'm sick or something, and to go ahead without me.'

'I believe the plan was to tell them you were going

to be a little late,' Otto said. 'Poor, witless Bellamy Dumonde would abandon the ritual if he thought you weren't coming.'

'And Jennifer's told you exactly where they're gathering for the ritual.'

'To the square metre. It transpires she's quite good when it comes to orienteering.'

Faye's voice was as cold as the feeling of dread in her belly. 'And you're going to wipe them out with your bomber at sunrise.'

'The bombardier even said he would let me press the button.' Otto cackled. 'I don't have to be here, of course, but I insisted. Call me sentimental, but I want to feel the warmth of the fire on my face when the most powerful witches in Britain are reduced to charred remains.'

Faye dashed back to the steel door, pulling as hard as she could on the handle.

'Oh, but I did promise Jennifer that I wouldn't harm you, didn't I? Ach. What to do? Hmm. Oh well. You cannot make an omelette without breaking a few eggs, *ja*? I shall break it to her gently. Goodbye, Faye Bright. You were almost a worthy adversary.'

The light of the powder mirror intensified and became so dazzling that Faye had to cover her eyes with her hands. Otto and the droning noise were replaced by a hum that rose and rose in pitch until it was beyond Faye's hearing.

The blood on the mirror had evaporated to nothing. Otto's singular connection over the aether was gone, and the crackle of the universe filled Faye's ears.

And there they were.

Witches.

She couldn't be sure where they were or who they were, but witches were scrying in the aether. Perhaps they were fortune-tellers? Perhaps they were having their own conversations? Faye didn't care. They were her only way of communicating with the world outside this bloody pillbox.

'Dover!' she called out to them. 'Come to the White Cliffs before sunrise. We're summoning a cone of power to repel the invasion and we need your help. We've been betrayed! Please!'

The mirror shattered. There was a moment of darkness, then a ball of flame burst in the air above the rug, which caught fire, filling the room with smoke.

DANDELION DEMOLITION

'Not another blimmin' fire,' Faye grumbled to herself.

She dashed to the rug, grabbed it by the tassels and flipped it over, smothering the flames. The pillbox was still filled with smoke and dust, so Faye hurried to the nearest loophole to gasp in some fresh air.

The fire was out, but she was still stuck in a squat building made of brick with concrete panels bolted to the outside, designed to withstand the impact of tank shells.

'Oh, buggeration.' Faye bit her lip and considered her options. She could wait for the next Home Guard patrol to come along, but she had no idea when that would be. She had to get to Dover before the sun came up again.

The loopholes – designed to poke rifles through – were far too narrow. The door was the only way out. It was one solid sheet of steel. There was no keyhole in the door, so it had to be padlocked from the outside. The hinges were bolted to the door, but the bolts on the hinges had been hammered in. Faye felt the smallest tingle of hope.

She grabbed the empty tin of beans and bashed it

against the bolt, from the bottom up, in the hope that she could dislodge it, then slide it out.

She bashed the tin again and again, but the bolt wouldn't budge and the can crumpled.

'Double buggeration.'

Panic niggled at Faye. Her fingers began to fidget. She was grinding her teeth. Her toes wriggled in her plimsolls.

'What now, what now, what now?' she muttered to herself, walking in little circles.

There was nothing in her mother's book about unlocking doors. From chatting to Mrs Teach and Miss Charlotte, locks were a big blind spot for witches. By all accounts, the wretched things were impervious to any kind of magic.

Faye wondered about generating some kind of magical energy herself. The sort that had brought down that bomber. If she were to unleash anything like that in such a small space, she would almost certainly blast the walls, but Faye herself would end up like an overcooked Christmas turkey.

'What was the point of me learning to fly, Mother, if I just ended up trapped in a concrete bunker, eh?'

Faye backed up against one of the walls. What did she have? A charred rug, some broken glass, a deckchair and a hexagonal room covered in brick dust and bits of plaster, and weeds in every corner.

A little light flickered at the back of Faye's brain.

There *was* something in her mother's book. A short ritual in the forbidden section – an appendix with hastily scribbled warnings of what *not* to do – and it had struck Faye as odd that this particular ritual was not allowed.

It was the ritual for growing plants by talking to them.

Faye recalled a note beneath the ritual explaining that it had been banned after one too many witches used it to win prizes at Harvest Festival vegetable competitions.

There were no vegetables in the pillbox. But there were plenty of weeds. And one in particular caught Faye's eye. A flowering dandelion in the corner opposite the door. It grew close to the big crack in the wall that Captain Marshall was so worried about.

It was well known among gardeners that plants that received regular encouraging chit-chat would grow to be bigger and healthier than most. What was less well known was that there were certain secret words that would lead to sudden and enormous growth.

Faye crouched down beside the dandelion. Drawing on the same simmering energy that she used to fly, she whispered those secret words now. Her voice reverberated off the walls, but the dandelion remained still. For a moment, she began to doubt her memory, wondering if Mrs Housego's soup had done some permanent damage to her mind. Other words jostled for Faye's attention. Words of failure and uncertainty. She ignored them and kept reciting. As she did, a light like the sun burst into life before her.

The dandelion began to twitch.

Faye smiled, not missing a beat as she repeated the words over and over. The tiny sun became brighter.

The dandelion shivered and stretched as it reached up for the light. The yellow petals of its flower bloomed bright. The jagged green leaves billowed like sails. The join between the floor and the wall cracked and spat dust as muscular roots broke through.

Feeling giddy, Faye let the magic wash over her. She backed away a little, noticing that it wasn't just the dandelion that was growing. All the weeds in the pillbox were spiralling up and out. The big crack started to widen as more fissures began to trace across every wall.

Pebbles of concrete dropped on Faye's head from the ceiling. Still reciting the words, she hurried back into the safety of the door frame, ducking under its lintel.

A tiny sun radiated in the centre of the pillbox, all weeds stretching out for it. The first dandelion was the size of a football now, getting bigger and bigger with each passing moment. Lines appeared in the ceiling and great clumps of concrete fell where Faye had been hunched just a few moments ago.

The dandelion was now bigger than a medicine ball and its roots creaked as they broke through the floor.

The far wall with the big crack fell away first, the roof tumbled with it, and the remaining walls were not far behind. The tiny sun vanished, shrinking in on itself with a roar. The dandelion's yellow flowers closed in on themselves, green leaves shutting tight, and then the flower burst open, white seeds exploding into the evening air.

When the air cleared, Faye was left standing in the still-upright doorway of the now destroyed pillbox.

'So, that's how that's done.' Faye puffed out her cheeks, her skin tingling.

She got her bearings, looked to the south, and took to the sky.

THE RITUAL BEGINS ...
EVENTUALLY

Jennifer had heard the phrase 'tearing my hair out' many times but had never thought that she might actually see someone perform the act. Tonight might just be that night.

She and her fellow witches stood by a huge burning bonfire on the cliffs of Dover, on the spot where the ley lines converged and the emanation of magical power made their hair stand on end. But they were not entranced by the magic, the flickering flames or the way the light threw shadows across the grass, or even the curious stillness of the English Channel. No, they were all watching their erstwhile leader, Bellamy Dumonde, negotiating with an elderly man and his dog over by a stile.

'I think you'll find,' the man said, raising his chin, 'that this is a public right of way, and I may come and go as I please.'

He looked like a model for a gentleman's outfitters,

one that supplied nothing but tweed for men of a certain age. Even his terrier wore a little tweed jacket. The dog yapped at Bellamy throughout the entire conversation.

'That might be the case on any other night, sir.' Bellamy did that thing where he arched his spine and placed two hands on the small of his back. It was meant to make him look relaxed, though in truth Jennifer thought that Bellamy was getting ready to headbutt the elderly dog walker. 'But this evening I have a special permit from His Majesty's Government to . . .' Bellamy faltered. Just how did you explain what they planned to do here tonight? 'To . . . work here this evening on a project of vital importance to the war effort. There should have been a couple of soldiers down the path who are under orders to redirect any passers-by to—'

'Oh, them.' The dog-walking gentleman wrinkled his nose. His terrier did the same. 'They kept babbling on about something, but I ignored them. I served at Verdun, you know. Awarded the DSO.'

'Might I enquire why you are walking a dog at this time of night?' Bellamy asked, but the dog-walking gent's voice rose in pitch and he began waving an angry fist.

Their conversation faded to the back of Jennifer's mind. For her part, she was having doubts. After what she had done to Faye, and her beloved bicycle, she felt a niggle of, well, *guilt*. It was an unusual sensation, which made her belly squirm. Even Otto, after all his smarm and charm, had shown himself to be a snippy old so-and-so. She began to wonder if the Nazi occult-ist really had her best interests at heart.

'I didn't fight the Hun to have whippersnappers tell-ing me what to do and where to go.' The gentleman in tweed prodded his walking stick at Bellamy. 'I crawled through the mud and the blood of my brothers so that I can walk Victor at any time of the day or night I please.'

'Victor?' Bellamy asked.

The dog barked, confirming his name.

'I see.' Bellamy pressed his fingers to his head and beckoned the man over the stile. 'Just ... That's it ... If I could ask you to go around? Yes, splendid.'

Victor's owner took his blessed time walking around the bonfire. He gave the gathered women a polite nod and doffed his tweed cap to each of them in turn.

'Good evening, ladies.'

Jennifer couldn't help herself and gave him a little curtsey. Her cat coiled around her ankles, watching Victor with suspicion. She wasn't normally rattled by dogs, but the cat had been hissing and arching its back in a most hostile manner ever since they had left Faye in the cracked pillbox.

'Behave,' Jennifer said to the cat, but it just hissed again.

'I say,' Bellamy called after the man who kept walk-ing. 'Will you be coming back this way? I only ask as it might be quite dangerous, and I wouldn't want you to ...'

The man's head bobbed out of sight as he took a path

down to the shore. As soon as Bellamy was convinced he was out of earshot, he turned to Jennifer.

'You're sure she's coming?' He meant Faye. The idea that she might be even the slightest bit late was driving him to distraction. His hair was wilder than ever, his elbows at right angles.

When Jennifer had told Bellamy that Faye was going to be late – just as the train pulled out of the station – he had trembled and his eyes started to dart about. For a moment, Jennifer had wondered if Otto's plan would fall at the first hurdle and that Bellamy would cancel the ritual there and then, but the train was already chuffing along. Even now, though, he looked ready to pack it all in. Jennifer had to keep him enthused.

'Faye promised that she would be here.' Jennifer picked up her cat, trying to force it to sit on her shoulder. The cat made a retching noise.

'Is it unwell?' Bellamy asked.

'Furballs.' Jennifer noted the eyes of Mrs Teach and Miss Charlotte targeting her. They were no fools. They were suspicious from the off, but they said nothing. It was as if they were waiting for her to slip up. She wouldn't give them the satisfaction.

'It was something about her bicycle,' Jennifer continued, keeping the story as simple as possible. 'She wouldn't elaborate any further, but she did swear blind she would be here, and I know Faye is a gal of her word.'

'What were her exact words?' Bellamy tilted his ear at Jennifer as if hearing the same words from a slightly different angle would give them new meaning.

'Bellamy, darling.' Jennifer softened her voice. 'If you're that concerned then let's wait for her.'

Jennifer meant it. Her mission now was to delay this ritual until sunrise. The first part of her mission had been relatively simple. When they arrived at the battery, she had popped down to use the lavatory and taken the opportunity to contact Otto. Sitting on the lavvy throne with all her scrying equipment on her knees had been most undignified, but it got the job done. Otto curtly acknowledged the message and reminded her to keep Bellamy and the witches there till sunrise. He was coming, and nothing would stop him.

'We're already late starting. We cannot delay.' Bellamy began pacing back and forth. 'Even with a full compliment the ritual can take hours, but without Faye . . .' His voice trailed off as he wrestled with his few remaining options. Jennifer sensed he was on the verge of calling it off.

'Then let's begin. We have everyone else here.' Jennifer gestured at Martine in particular, who had hobbled up and down the cliff paths on crutches. 'Even Martine, who's crippled and said repeatedly that this would be a disaster.'

'I did.' Martine nodded. 'And it still might be, but I will not abandon my fellow witches. If it must be a disaster, we shall face it together.'

What sentimental gibberish, Jennifer thought. 'Jolly good,' Jennifer said aloud, wondering if the French woman's medication had eroded her brain.

Jennifer caught Mrs Teach and Miss Charlotte

357

sharing a look of suspicion. Were they on to her? No. Those stuck-up cows thought they knew everything, but soon they would be gone, and Jennifer would be glad. Mrs Housego and Martine also gave Jennifer the squinty eye of doubt. She smiled back, wishing them both dead.

'I knew it. I blasted well knew it.' Bellamy raised his hands to the overcast sky. '*Should you hinge this entire operation on a slip of a girl? I* asked myself. *Fortune favours the bold,* I told myself. Well, not in this bloody case.' Bellamy kicked at the grass and ground his teeth.

'Then what do we do?' Mrs Housego asked.

'What do we do?' Bellamy nodded then shook his head for a while as if some debating society in his brain was arguing the case for and against. 'We begin,' he concluded and started marching around the bonfire.

'So, we're definitely on?' Jennifer's whole body tensed as she waited for his answer.

'We are indeed.' Bellamy pouted his lips in a manner that was probably meant to convey a Churchillian determination but made him look like a toddler about to have a tantrum. 'You said so yourself, Jennifer. We need to do this tonight. Any abeyance is unacceptable.'

Jennifer exhaled in relief. If Otto were to bomb an empty clifftop, she would have to take the blame and Otto didn't strike her as the forgiving type.

Bellamy was stroking his beard. 'But without Faye Bright here we simply cannot generate the same level of power that we're used to. Unless . . .' He stopped in his tracks, the red glow of the bonfire lighting up his face.

'Oh no,' Mrs Teach muttered, dreading what was coming next.

Jennifer, always on the lookout for anything that could delay the start, blurted, 'Skyclad?'

'Yes!' Bellamy snapped his fingers. 'I think we could do it. You've all improved immensely these past few days, and I am convinced that if we perform the ritual skyclad we will be able to—'

He was unable to finish the sentence as the witches surrounded the man, barracking him like West Ham centre forwards challenging an offside decision.

Only Mrs Housego came to his defence. 'Don't knock it till you try it!'

Jennifer stood back and enjoyed the barracking. Stuck-up, narcissistic witches. Otto didn't need bombs to destroy this lot. Leave them to their own devices for long enough and they would do it themselves.

Martine was yelling at Bellamy now. Mrs Teach and Miss Charlotte harangued him from the sides.

Mrs Housego continued to defend him. 'Goin' skyclad worked for me then, and it'll work for me now!'

'Oh, be quiet, you mad old nudist!' Mrs Teach said.

Bellamy froze. 'N-nudist?' He looked at Mrs Housego. 'You're a nudist? So you're only in favour of a skyclad ritual because you're a bally *nudist*?'

'It's been scientifically proven that nudity is good for one's health—' she began.

'Oh, good grief!' Bellamy clutched his head.

Jennifer let her mind wander. This felt like a big turning point in her life. After this would be a fresh start. A little part of Jennifer wanted to stay and continue to be Faye's friend, a role she had enjoyed playing. Jennifer had even been careful to not smash Faye's glasses to pieces this time, and had placed them carefully in a pocket in her dungarees in a gesture of kindness. But Jennifer had a feeling that after attacking Faye and leaving her at Otto's mercy in the pillbox, the girl would most likely hold a grudge and there would be no more hugging or trusting.

No, Jennifer decided that after Faye and the other witches were dead, a new life was on the cards. America, perhaps? She fancied the glamour of New York or Hollywood. Yes, a girl with her skills could thrive there.

'You wanted this all along, didn't you?' Mrs Teach prodded Bellamy in the chest. 'You dirty little man.'

'How dare you, madam?' Bellamy objected. 'The simple fact is that with Martine injured and Faye absent, performing the ritual skyclad is the only way.'

'I don't think that will be necessary.' A voice cut through the babble. It was a voice that everyone else seemed to recognise. One they all respected and dreaded in equal measure. All except Jennifer, but even she could guess who it was. Jennifer could sense the voice's owner behind her, stepping over the stile with effortless grace. But Jennifer did not want to turn and look, because Jennifer did not want this to be real.

Vera Fivetrees stood by Jennifer's side, her face amber in the light of the bonfire. The flames danced in her eyes. She gently held a red handbag and wore a calm smile that terrified Jennifer more than the thought of any demon from the underworld.

'It would be a shame to see all your good work go to waste, Bellamy,' Vera said. 'With your permission, I should like to offer my services to you and my fellow witches. I come in solidarity and good faith, and I have no wish to undermine your authority here.'

I bet, Jennifer thought to herself.

'Once the task is done, you have my word that I shall return to my secure accommodation.'

Jennifer had to stop herself scoffing at that. But her mind raced as she weighed the pros and cons of Vera's arrival. The good news was her presence here was an unexpected bonus for Otto. Not only would this rabble finally be gone, but their uppity leader would go up in smoke with them. Jennifer wondered if she could convince Otto that this was her idea all along. In the bad news column, Vera was very clearly in charge now and Jennifer's delaying tactics would have to convince one of the sharpest minds in all witchery.

'Vera,' Bellamy began, bewildered. His hands twitched as if he didn't know what to do with them. 'Mrs Fivetrees, I would be honoured.'

'Miss,' she reminded him. 'And call me Vera.' Vera slipped her arm into the crook of Jennifer's. 'Come, child,' she said. 'Let's see if we can thwart an invasion, shall we?'

It was all Jennifer could do not to scream as Vera led her back to the bonfire. Bellamy took out his glowing dagger and the witches held hands in a circle. As he drew sizzling pentagrams in the air, a protective veil descended around them. The cone of power ritual had begun.

DEATH OF A BICYCLE

Immediately upon take-off, Faye began tumbling aimlessly. If she wanted to make the start of the ritual, she had to be in Dover by midnight. And she wasn't going to do that by turning head over heels.

It was cold up here and the air was full of insects whose idea of a really grand night out was to fly directly into Faye's mouth.

She recalled Leo's offer of his flight jacket, helmet and goggles. And, with much stretching of limbs, she changed course and headed for Larry Dell's barn.

As she drifted over the fields, the barn came into view and she could see the warm glow of lamps from inside. Did that mean her dad and Bertie were working there? Had Larry made some kind of peace with Leo? Or was the poltergeist fed up of sitting in the dark? Distracted by these thoughts, she realised too late that she had to slow down, and so she ended up slamming into the corrugated roof of the barn. She rolled off and landed in a cloud of dust before the open doors.

'Faye! Where have you been?'

As Faye got her breath back, she looked up to find her dad and Bertie gawping at her from within the barn.

'Long story.' She got to her feet and patted herself down. 'I've come to borrow—'

Faye stopped. Her feet suddenly felt so heavy that she thought she might never walk again, let alone fly.

There, in the middle of the barn, was a familiar shape.

A bicycle frame. Covered in mud and sand. Without wheels. Without a basket. Without a chain.

Faye staggered to the Pashley Model A, falling to her knees and running a hand along its frame. It was scratched all over with chips in the paint, and it felt cold.

'Constable Muldoon found it in a ditch near Hayward Lodge this morning,' Terrence said. 'He brought it to the pub. At first, we were worried sick.'

Faye glared daggers at her father. 'But not worried enough to look for me.'

'That girl with the cat.' Bertie wrung his hands together. 'She told us *not* to worry. She said you'd got annoyed with the bike, really angry she said, and you were kicking it and you threw the wheels into the sea, and you said you never wanted to see it again.'

'Does that really sound like me?'

Bertie and Terrence were still, apart from their eye-balls, both pairs of which slid towards one another, silently urging the other to speak first.

Terrence cleared his throat. 'You have been known to fly off the handle, Faye.'

'Yes. At you, maybe. Not my bike!' she snapped and both men inched back. 'Why didn't you come looking for me?'

Bertie raised a hand for permission to speak. 'When I asked where you were, she said you were off to Dover. We thought everything was all right. You'd said you had some witchy stuff to do. We thought that was it. Honest.'

Faye turned back to the bike. 'Where are the wheels? The basket?'

'That's how it was found,' Terrence said. 'No chain, either.'

Faye clenched her jaw and breathed in through her nose in big, cleansing breaths.

'Faye, is everything all right?' Bertie asked.

'She breaks my best specs, betrays me, traps me in a burning pillbox and leaves me for dead. That I can understand, but this ... Jennifer Gentle and I will be having words when I next see her.'

'Why did you come here, Faye?' Terrence asked in a quiet voice.

'What's the time?' Faye looked in confusion at her father. 'Who's looking after the pub?'

'Pub's closed and me and Bertie wanted to get on with it, so—'

'The ritual starts at midnight!' Faye shook her head. 'I have to get to Dover.'

'It's long gone midnight, Faye,' Terrence said. 'You've got no chance. There's no trains and buses and even a motorcar wouldn't make it in time.'

'I've got to get there before the ritual ends at sunrise!' Faye made a fist.

'But, Faye—'

'Dad, if I don't, the most powerful witches in the country – and my friends – will be dead.'

'Blimey, Faye, what have you got yourself into this time?'

'You could make it to Dover if you fly,' Bertie suggested.

'Not the way I fly,' Faye said.

'Before you, er, landed, me and Mr Bright were discussing what you need to steer up there. And we reckoned that a seat, handlebars and some sort of frame would do the job, tickety-boo.' Beaming like a circus ringmaster, Bertie threw his hands at the fallen Pashley. 'Ta-da!'

Faye adjusted her old specs. 'You want me to fly on my bicycle?'

'Makes sense.' Terrence moved to the workbench. 'If you hunch over the handlebars, you'll have a low profile and a little less wind resistance. Hardly a Spitfire, but it'll be better than you bouncing through the air like a barrage balloon.'

'Anything's better than that,' Faye conceded, then clapped her hands together. She took rapid breaths as she geed herself up for the long flight. 'Right, okey-dokey. Let's go.' Faye moved towards the remains of the bicycle, only to find Bertie and her father blocking her way.

'Where are you off to?' Terrence asked.

'Dover.'

'Not like that, you're not,' he said.

'It's cold up there,' Bertie agreed. 'And you'll need help steering. The handlebars on the bike won't be enough.'

'We've had a few ideas on how to make you as safe and comfortable as possible.'

'I haven't got time, Dad.'

'Give us an hour,' Bertie begged. 'You can help us.'

'With what?'

※

After Terrence and Bertie had explained their plans to Faye, she agreed to give them an hour. They worked together in silence for the most part. A few grunts and *uhms* when they got stuck. They were right about the steering. Swooping over the barn was one thing, but if she tried to get to Dover without any way to manoeuvre she'd probably end up in Norway before breakfast.

※

A little over an hour passed before Terrence announced they were done.

'Voilà!' With a magician's flourish, he presented Leo's flight helmet to Faye.

They had welded a pair of steering vanes onto the headphone cones. One on either side, making the wearer look like Mercury, the winged messenger. While the solder cooled, Terrence had painted an RAF roundel on each vane, with the letters F and B.

'Faye and Bright,' he said by way of explanation. 'And the vanes are made from the rudder of a Hurricane, so we know they're flight-worthy.'

Faye approached the helmet slowly, looking at it from side to side. She was open-mouthed. She ran a finger along one of the vanes. 'And these ... these will help me steer?'

'Should do,' Terrence said. 'Obviously, they need extensive testing.'

'The boots are ready.' Bertie placed a pair of fur-lined pilot boots on the workbench. These had smaller vanes on the heels. He had painted little bolts of lightning on the vanes. 'They might be a bit big, so I stuffed some cardboard into the toes.'

'Move them together and you should steer a lot more effectively.' Terrence demonstrated with his hands.

Faye lifted the helmet onto her head. 'Bloody hell. It's heavy.'

Terrence stood before her, making adjustments to the chin-strap and lowering the goggles into place. 'We'll look into ways of making it lighter, but once you're up there, whizzing along, it should be easier to move your head. How's that?' He patted the sides of the helmet.

Faye wrapped her arms around him. 'Thanks, Dad.' She waved Bertie over. He shuffled closer, but not close enough, so she had to grab him into the hug. She squeezed them both.

'All right, all right, gerrof.' Terrence wriggled out of the embrace. 'Don't forget, you've got to be in Dover before sunrise.'

Faye strode across the room to take Leo's flight jacket from where it hung on a nail. She reached for it, then stopped herself.

'What's wrong?' Bertie asked.

'I can't just take this. Not without asking.' She raised her head. 'Leo? Are you there?'

'Always,' said a voice, crackling through the helmet's headphones, loud enough for all to hear. The room chilled as Leo appeared in the darkest corner, leaning against one of the barn's beams.

'Leo, I need all your kit. May I?'

'I've been watching.' He smiled at Terrence and Bertie who both shuffled closer to one another. 'Are you going into battle?'

She glanced at her worried father. 'I hope not, but I'm trying to stop a Nazi from doing a very bad thing.'

'Then you have my blessing.' Leo stepped closer to Faye, looking her up and down. 'Hmm. A few tips before you fly, yes?'

'Er, righto.'

'First, never rush in blindly,' Leo said.

'Good advice,' Terrence agreed.

'And stay below four thousand feet if you can.'

'How will I know that?' Faye asked. 'Do I take a very long tape measure with me?'

'Don't be flippant. Stay low. And never fly straight.' Leo zigzagged his hand left and right and up and down to make his point. 'Change course constantly to baffle the gunners.'

'Gunners,' Terrence said, his voice dry. 'Oh dear.'

369

'When you hear any gunfire, turn immediately.'

'Gunfire. Lordy.'

'Conserve ammunition,' Leo said.

Faye shrugged. 'That'll be easy. Don't have any.'

'Your magic, then. Save your energy for when you really need it.' Leo made a plane with his left hand. 'When you attack, find the blind spot.' He moved his right hand towards it from the rear. 'This is the enemy. This is you. Always come from below and behind. They won't see you.'

'Below and behind. Gotcha.' Faye nodded as she committed it to memory.

'Good luck, Faye Bright,' Leo said with a smile. 'I would be honoured if the first witch in the RAF would take my jacket, gloves and boots.'

Faye grinned and hurried to wriggle the boots on. Bertie was right, there was a little cardboard in the toes, but the fur lining was very cosy. Next came the jacket and gloves.

Terrence took off his red neckerchief with the white polka-dots and handed it to Faye. 'The pilots in the pub say these stop your neck getting sore from all that looking about,' he said, and Faye detected a slight wobble in his voice. 'Keep looking about, eh, Faye? Don't put yourself in harm's way if you don't have to.'

'I won't, Dad.'

Faye wrapped the neckerchief in place and was about to stride to the bike when Bertie hobbled over and took her by the shoulders. 'I'm so proud of you,' he managed.

Faye found her heart was pounding in her chest.

'Dad, Leo, will you excuse us?' she said, grabbing Bertie by the wrist and pulling him with her outside and around the side of the barn.

Bertie looked left and right, puzzled. 'Faye, why are we—'

Faye gripped Bertie's lapels and pulled him towards her, pressing her lips against his. He parted his and returned the kiss. She ran her fingers through his hair, and her specs were all askew and steamy.

They broke apart, gasping for air.

'I love you, Bertie Butterworth,' she said.

'I love you, Faye Bright,' he said back.

Faye felt a glow inside of her. A new, earthier kind of magic. 'I could do this all night. But—'

'You need to save the country from the Nazis,' Bertie said. 'Fair enough. There'll be other nights.'

'Not like this.' She kissed him again, then they hurried back to the barn hand in hand.

Terrence was waiting for them with the Pashley. 'When you've quite finished.'

Faye's hand slipped from Bertie's. She swung a leg over the former bicycle's frame, closed her eyes and rose into the air, passing out through the barn doors.

'Oh, one more thing.' Bertie limped after her.

'Bertie, love, I am in a bit of a hurry.'

'I know, I know, but I thought we should give it a name,' Bertie said. 'And seeing as it flies, and seeing as what you're wearing used to belong to Leo ... how about we call it the Griffin?'

Faye smiled. 'The Griffin? I like that, Bertie. I like that very much.' Faye leaned over the handlebars. 'Come on, Griffin, let's get to Dover by sunrise,' she said, and the Griffin soared high into the night sky.

FLIGHT OF THE GRIFFIN

Faye Bright was orbiting the Earth. She was jolly close to the surface of the Earth compared to the great stone satellite that hung in orbit, but both were tethered by the invisible and mysterious force known as gravity all the same.

What she was *not* doing was flying. Not in the traditional sense. Doctor Jacob Bernoulli's theorems of flight were not what kept this Kentish girl in the air tonight.

Faye recalled the notes from her mother's book on how this kind of magical aerial movement was mastered by the ancient Persian scholars of sorcery. They would pootle about on carpets that not only gave them a more stable flight, but also somewhere comfortable to sit and chat upon landing. She had thought about using the rug in the pillbox, but it was so dusty and threadbare she doubted it would last the journey, and she didn't much fancy digging it out of the rubble. She also briefly considered pinching the rug that lay before the hearth in the living room behind the pub, but she knew that Dad would go spare.

The Griffin was her magic carpet, and it flew like a beauty. The air roared around her. The wind gave her a nudge from side to side now and then as she hurtled along, but she was able to keep a straight course. The steering vanes on the sides of her helmet and boots helped when she leaned into a turn. Pulling on the handlebars gave her lift, and tipping herself forwards took her into a dive. The big disadvantage of the steering vanes was that whenever she looked around she tended to waver, but she soon got the hang of it.

She was thankful for Leo's flight jacket and boots, too. Any bare skin was soon wet and cold at this height. Her chin and lips were made fat and numb and she had to pull her father's neckerchief over her nose to warm them up again. Her specs rattled behind the goggles, and the edges occasionally steamed up, but visibility was good.

Kent was dark. A county in blackout, huddled in the night from the threat of invasion. She spotted the odd lamp flickering in a window, but it was an otherwise silent and unknowable landscape below. Which meant she was lost. She thought she was heading due south, but she couldn't be entirely sure. Faye hadn't spotted a recognisable landmark for ages.

Beyond the slumbering land was the indigo blue of the North Sea. It would take longer, but she could follow the coastline to Dover without fear of going the wrong way. Faye leaned on the Griffin, moved her head and boots, and turned in a graceful arc towards the silent water.

She made a mental note to ask Bertie and her dad for a few modifications on her return. The handles could be closer together, and it would be helpful if both the pedals could be fixed at the same height, and the saddle needed to be lower. She could probably do with a compass and a watch of some kind, too.

Faye scoffed at herself. *If* she returned. She had no idea what she was flying into.

She found the coastline and flew low enough to hear the waves lapping on the sands. High above her, bombers made their way to London and she felt sick at the thought that there was nothing she could do to stop them. She kept on course, putting them out of her mind.

It wasn't long before she saw the familiar sight of Deal Castle. With six semicircular bastions, from the air it resembled the shape of a Tudor Rose. Built on the orders of Henry the Eighth to protect against invasion, it did the same job now. Six-inch guns pointed to sea and in the grounds were army trucks and dormant searchlights.

Faye heard shouts from the castle's crenellations and the searchlights burst into life, punching through the air and swinging in her direction.

'Oh, blimmin' 'eck.' Faye's first instinct was to pull up, but the beams were too quick and caught her, refracting in her goggles and almost blinding her. She leaned left, then right, dodging them, but they were fast to find her again. Even with the wind rushing around Faye, she could hear orders being given in loud, if slightly baffled, voices.

They were trying to figure out what she was.

A *rat-a-tat* split the air. A short burst of exploratory gunfire to see how this strange flying object would react.

'Bloody hell, I'm on your side, you pillocks!' she yelled as the unseen shells whizzed by her, but her words were lost to the sea.

She recalled Leo's advice. When you hear gunfire, turn immediately. She zigzagged a bit more, rising and sinking, hoping to make herself a less appealing target.

She wondered if it was too late to conjure a glamour. It was much more difficult to pretend not to be there when you've already been spotted. And all of Faye's concentration was focused on flying and not being shot out of the air.

White-hot streaks of tracer bullets burst ahead of her, leaving jagged lines dancing on her retinas.

The cloud cover above was too high for her to hide in. She dived so fast that her ears popped. The white foam from lapping waves suddenly looked very close. Faye pulled up, feeling the spray lash against her flight jacket. The horizon returned to its rightful place and the gunfire had stopped. Faye dared to glance back, the steering vanes on her helmet making her shimmy, but Deal Castle was behind her, its searchlights still probing the blanket of clouds. She wondered how they would make sense of this in their reports. A flock of birds, perhaps? Or bats? She knew from her own work with the ARP that any sightings and use of weapons would need to be logged and reported. The RAF might even send a plane to investigate.

So it came as no surprise, as she passed Walmer Castle on her right, that she heard the drone of fighter engines ahead of her. But this wasn't the roar of a Spitfire's Merlin engine. This was the relentless growl of a Luftwaffe plane. And more than one of them.

Faye raised her head to see three Bf 109s in formation above her. The tone of their engines changed as the revolutions of their propellers intensified, becoming a deathly drone. One by one, their wings tipped over as they began to dive towards her.

OUT TO SEA

Faye zigzagged but, unlike the gunners at Deal Castle, the Luftwaffe pilots had no doubt that she was a target. They unleashed salvos of fire from their guns, the tracer bullets whizzing around Faye. She heard them hiss as they punched into the waves.

Faye's heart nearly shot up through her gullet, and her breathing was like one of Mrs Pritchett's dogs after chasing a rabbit. There was no room for any thought other than to keep moving, keep dodging, stay alive. She tried to recall more of Leo's advice. Something about blind spots and angles and it had all sounded so easy when standing in Larry Dell's barn, but out here in the dark, over the North Sea, with three Luftwaffe fighters on her tail, Faye's mind could not stray, because to think of anything else would be an invitation to panic.

As she rounded the coast over St. Margaret's Bay, she spotted a familiar shape. Through the dots of sea spray on Faye's goggles, it came into focus. The South Foreland lighthouse. Faye had found them.

Another rattle of fire from the Bf 109s sent a jolt of fear through her.

If she had found Bellamy and the witches, then so had the Luftwaffe. The bonfire's light was made diffuse by Bellamy's protective veil, like a dying candle through frosted glass, but it was the only light for miles and if she headed towards it now the Luftwaffe would follow.

She had to draw the fighters away and give them a better target. Herself.

Faye closed her eyes, concentrating furiously as she attempted to both fly and conjure a glamour. She wasn't trying to hide this time. She wanted to be seen. She wanted those pilots above to see a target that was irresistible. A Spitfire. A wounded one, with smoke roiling from its engine, limping back to base alone. Yes, that's what she would put in the minds of those pilots.

Faye turned and headed out over the Channel, and she smiled when she heard the pitch of the fighters' engines change as they banked to pursue her.

ꝏ

The protective veil around the witches crackled with energy. Jennifer felt it emanating from the other witches as the cone of power ritual finally found its rhythm. Martine had volunteered to scry alone – it was all she was good for with a manky ankle, after all – and so Jennifer, Mrs Housego, Mrs Teach, Miss Charlotte and Vera Fivetrees danced around the bonfire. Bellamy played his cursed concertina, having repaired the bloody thing and somehow made it louder and more grating than ever before.

It wasn't just her fellow witches' energy that she could feel. Mrs Teach and Miss Charlotte were radiating glares of suspicion at Jennifer all through the dance. She took delight in their paranoia, knowing they couldn't prove a thing. If anything, it made her dance all the harder, despite her weary muscles and her mind scrabbling to think of how she could get away before sunrise.

They had been at it for hours now, though no one knew exactly how long. Bellamy had banned watches of all kinds. They would be led by the rising sun, he had told them. If they didn't generate enough magical energy before sunrise, then the moon's protective veil would fade, they would return to the Earthly plane and be exposed to the enemy's bombs.

Jennifer glanced to the east. The world beyond the protective veil was monochrome, like a silent movie projected onto cloud. Nevertheless, she could make out the faintest glimmer of daylight on the horizon.

Even with Vera, the power they were generating didn't come anywhere close to what they had with Faye, and she could see in Bellamy's pained expression that the ritual was failing.

'Roit, soddit.' Mrs Housego stepped away from the dance circle and began unbuttoning the front of her long black dress.

Bellamy looked up from playing his concertina. 'Mrs Housego, what are you doing?'

The others looked on, continuing to scry and dance as Mrs Housego's dress fell away. Beneath it she wore a long white slip.

'You ain't got the power you need to make this work, young Bellamy.' She wriggled her slip off over her head. 'I reckon you need at least one of us skyclad.' She hopped about as she took off her bloomers. 'And it ain't right to ask these modest young ladies. Me, I'm beyond caring about what I looks like. I got skin like a tobacco leaf, and me bosoms are like onions in a sock, so I reckon if anyone should go skyclad, it should be me.' She kicked off her shoes and rejoined the dance around the bonfire.

She spun without a care, raising her bare arms to the night, her grey hair whipping across her face, her gnarled feet padding nimbly on the grass.

Jennifer braced for some kind of magical energy surge from Mrs Housego's skyclad form. If the stories were true, then the old shrew could single-handedly bat aircraft out of the sky.

Not a sausage.

If anything, the ritual's magical energy diminished as the old woman started to turn blue and her dancing slowed.

She wasn't the only one flagging. Bellamy's concertina lost time as he played with the enthusiasm of a condemned man. His face sagged as his master plan failed before his very eyes.

Through the veil, Jennifer could hear the muffled drone of bomber engines in the darkness before anyone else.

Otto. It had to be Otto. Soon the sun would rise, and the bombs would be dropped, and they would all be ashes.

Jennifer, too, if she didn't figure out a way to leave sharpish. She considered running as the bombs started to fall, but Otto had told her the amount of ordnance he was carrying could level a city, so she didn't much fancy her chances. She had to delay the ritual one last time and get as far away from here as possible. All kinds of mad ideas had passed through her mind as she danced, but in the end she decided to keep it simple.

She fainted.

Jennifer gave a little whimper and fell back on the ground, eyes closed. She heard Martine make a startled sound, and Bellamy's concertina wheezed to a stop.

'Oh, what now?'

Good, Jennifer thought. He'd see her as a liability and send her away. He might need convincing. Jennifer reckoned she could play possum for another minute or so, complain of giddiness, then ask for a rest in the shelter. That place looked pretty solid. Plenty of concrete between her and the blast. She would be safe in there, while the others were vanquished by Otto.

'Keep dancing, keep dancing!' Bellamy cried to the others as he hurried to her side. 'Jennifer? Jennifer?' Bellamy nudged her arm, trying to wake her.

'She looked fine a minute ago,' Martine said, with little concern in her voice.

'Some people will do anything to get out of work.' Miss Charlotte's breathless voice whooshed by as she danced in a circle.

Jennifer hardly expected a mass outpouring of sympathy from this lot, but was a smidgen of concern too much to ask for?

'She's up to something,' Mrs Teach whispered as she passed.

'I've been watching her all this time,' Martine added. 'She's been distracted since she got here. Always looking around like she wants to escape. Something's not right.'

Even Jennifer's cat wasn't impressed with her. The vicious little puss scratched at her arm. It took every ounce of self-control Jennifer had not to bat the bloody thing away.

'What's that?' Vera's voice came around the bonfire. She had heard the engines, too. They were much closer.

Jennifer's limbs began to tremble. She had to get up and run. Now.

'Sounds like Bf 109s.' Bellamy, like every other overgrown boy these days, had developed a fine ear for identifying aircraft engine noises. 'Three of them.'

Three? That wasn't right, surely? Otto said he was coming in a bomber. One. Singular. And the sun wasn't quite up yet. Was he early?

'Could be an advance party for a raid,' Bellamy said. 'They do that sometimes. Fighters first to clear a path for the bombers.'

Bomber, Jennifer thought. *Just the one, and it's coming for you.*

'Look!' Martine said. Jennifer could sense her hobbling up on her one good foot. 'On the horizon.'

Jennifer desperately wanted to open her eyes. It had to be Otto's bomber.

'It's ...' Bellamy began, his concertina playing a bum note. 'It's someone flying.'

The air echoed with the rattle of Luftwaffe gunfire.

'They're shooting at them!' the still-naked Mrs Housego cried as she danced.

'It must be one of ours,' Bellamy said. 'There's another. Coming from the south. A bomber.'

That was it. Jennifer jumped to her feet. The cat hissed a warning to the others, and Jennifer made a mental note to wring the neck of the ungrateful little traitor at the first opportunity.

Jennifer turned on her heels, running straight into Charlotte's arms.

'Going somewhere?' Charlotte's blood-red smile stretched wide. Jennifer wriggled in her grip. 'I think we've found our spy.'

DOGFIGHT

Faye had imagined the English Channel as a vast no man's land. A gulf between two warring factions. But as the first light of dawn began to glow across the water, dispersing a misty canopy, Faye saw convoys of ships, fishing boats and patrols of aircraft going about their perilous business. The Channel was a front line and a very dangerous place to be.

The air rattled as the pursuing fighters took more shots at Faye as she swayed left and right. The shells punched into water ahead of her, sending up spurts of spray in neat, regular lines. Their aim was getting better.

Faye corkscrewed up, leading them out to sea, and further away from her friends on the cliffs of Dover.

Another salvo came from the 109s, whistling by her ears. Faye turned again, glimpsing the formation of fighters. They were right on top of her, and she had unwittingly arced directly into the range of their guns. She held her breath, ready for the worst.

More guns fired, but the lead fighter flashed and

smoke began to belch from its engine. The other fighters scattered and turned about, their engines straining with the effort.

The familiar roar of Rolls-Royce Merlin engines snarled around Faye and she glanced up to find six RAF aircraft diving to put themselves between her and the Luftwaffe planes.

They looked a little like Spitfires, but these had additional glass bubbles behind the cockpit: gun turrets with a battery of four barrels spitting fire at the enemy. Boulton Paul Defiants, one of Bertie's favourites, and a rarity in the skies as he made a point of singling them out whenever he saw them.

As the 109s circled around to regroup, the Defiants made two formations of three. Arrowheads with propellers and Browning machine guns. Faye pulled up alongside the cockpit of the lead aircraft and gave the pilot a salute. The dawn sun glinted off his goggles so she couldn't see the expression on his face, but he looked at her for what felt like an extraordinarily long time before raising a hesitant hand to wave back. His gunner in the bubble was similarly gobsmacked.

Faye leaned forwards on the Griffin and accelerated for the cliffs. Now that the 109s had been scared off, she had to warn the others that Otto was coming. As she did so, one of the Defiants flashed in flame as bullets ripped across its wing and engine. Smoke swirled from the plane as it fell from the formation.

Faye's heart paradiddled like a drum as a new sound split the air.

A shadow swept over them all, and she looked up to discover a lone Dornier Do 17 bomber, tracer fire thumping from the machine gun in the cockpit bubble on its nose. The remaining 109s whirled around it in dogfights with the Defiants, and suddenly the air was filled with bullets.

The Dornier stayed on course, its engines steady and relentless. It was heading for Dover. For Bellamy's bonfire. Otto had to be on that bomber, and Faye had to—

The air burst in a flower of fire and smoke. Faye, ears ringing, was thrown across the sky. The Griffin tumbled into the sea, landing with an insignificant splash and slipping beneath the surface in the blink of an eye. Faye followed it moments after, slapping ungracefully on the water, then plunging down. As the waves sloshed over Faye, she gulped a mouthful of brine. She wondered how it could feel so warm in her mouth when the rest of the sea was so cold. The weight of her wet flight jacket dragged her down. The Channel, polluted by convoy fuel and oil, was a grey soup leaking into her goggles.

Something glinted in the murk.

The handlebars of a Pashley Model A bicycle.

Defying every instinct to climb for the surface, Faye swam down. Further and further she went, kicking as her lungs burned, reaching, fingers cold in her gloves, stretching. The Griffin's handlebars bumped against the tips of her fingers, then drifted further away.

Head pounding, Faye gave one last kick.

✄

Squadron Leader Andrew Bowden didn't quite know what he was going to put in his report when he returned to base later that morning. Seeing what appeared to be a young woman flying on a wheel-less bicycle frame over the Channel was one thing, but what happened after that was altogether more extraordinary. His squadron was coming to the end of their coastal night patrol when they engaged a trio of Bf 109s accompanying a single Dornier Do 17 on a dawn raid. This was unusual in itself. Most Dorniers came by the dozen and flew at twelve thousand feet. This one was on its own and flew so low that Bowden's usual strategy of attacking from the blind spot on its rear was completely redundant. The commander of the bomber was either utterly clueless or a genius. Bowden ordered his squadron to form up, then circle above the Dornier's tail before opening fire.

That's when he saw the girl. She pulled up beside his cockpit and gave him a jolly wave like she was on her way to the butcher's to pick up her ration. And he knew it was a girl because of the way her ponytail flapped out of the back of her flight helmet. Which, he eventually noticed, had steering vanes welded onto its sides, decorated with RAF roundels.

Andrew blinked and waved back. He asked Roger in the bubble if he was seeing the same thing, and when Roger eventually found his voice he replied that he did. That was something. It wasn't just Andrew losing his marbles. Perhaps both of them were? It had been an exhausting patrol, coming after a series of long days and nights battling the Luftwaffe. He felt the weight of exhaustion in his bones and wouldn't be surprised if they were all seeing things by now. Speak to any pilot down the pub and after a few pints, they would confess to seeing strange lights and objects in the sky, but not the sort of thing they would put in any report for fear of being grounded on account of being a sandwich short of a picnic.

The air filled with flak. Freddie, Andrew's wingman, was hit and started limping back to Blighty. Instinct took over and Andrew and his squadron repositioned to counter-attack, the horizon spinning around them. Another 109 fell into the Channel, and the third curved up into the clouds.

The girl on the bike took a blow, spun through the air and fell into the water. As the battle continued, Andrew almost forgot about her. There was no room for such fancies in the heat of the fight. He was ready to dismiss her as a vision brought on by exhaustion.

Then she burst out of the sea, riding her bicycle frame, flying faster than any plane he had ever seen. There was a glow about her, like a rainbow. No. An unearthly, iridescent glow. Like the light of the moon.

That was exactly how Squadron Leader Andrew Bowden later described it to the man from the Special Operations Executive.

He told Squadron Leader Andrew Bowden never to

mention it to anyone for as long as he lived on pain of execution.

Andrew kept his word. Though he did describe the event in a private journal, later discovered by his puzzled grandchildren in the year 1982.

A Witch of Woodville

Faye spat a mouthful of warm, salty water back into the Channel where it belonged. Her head was thumping after going so deep and without air. Her vision was still blurred, though getting better, and her ears were ringing as liquid sloshed around inside them. She took a croaky breath as she rose from the waves. She was wet, cold and covered in some sort of slimy gunk. This was not how she wanted her day to begin, and she vowed never to half drown in the English Channel again. All in all, a very bad idea.

She got her bearings. The sun was yet to fully rise, but the moon was fading. The chatter of machine-gun fire echoed around her as the Defiants and 109s continued their deadly battle.

The Dornier was still heading for the cliffs.

Faye could feel the pull of the moon. A fellow satellite in orbit. Faye might not have all of its might, but she was the more agile of the two. She leaned forwards and chased after the bomber.

As the sea rushed beneath her, she considered her options. The Dornier had guns pointing in every direction, and even now it was blasting at her. She thought about boarding the plane and convincing the crew that Otto was a very rotten egg, and what they were up to was generally a bad idea, and they should all go back to their families in Germany and be nice to other people. Even Faye wasn't naïve enough to think this would work. Especially with Otto onboard ordering them to ignore her, and her German was all but non-existent, but she entertained the idea for a few blissful seconds.

Her reverie was broken by the whistle of shells as the Dornier came horribly close to taking her out.

'Blimmin' cheek!' she said with a gasp.

Faye stayed close to the surface of the Channel, weaving from side to side.

A trio of Defiants moved into position over the Dornier, their guns blazing fire. But their tracer bullets moved in strange arcs, as if an invisible hand was batting them away.

Otto was protecting the bomber.

She had to make the most of her one advantage. She was fast. She was also completely knackered after a night of flying, but she would ask the moon for one last boon. She would race the bomber to the cliffs.

✒

Jennifer wriggled. Her hands were tied behind her back, her ankles bound together with string from Mrs Teach's handbag.

'Never leave home without a length of string,' the dotty old bat had boasted as Charlotte tied Jennifer in knots. They were good knots. Jennifer wasn't going anywhere. She was going to die here with these loons. Even that bloody cat had turned against her. The wretched moggy had attached herself to Bellamy, rubbing up against his ankles.

'I thought I recognised you.' Bellamy tickled behind the cat's ears. 'You're Dolly's cat, aren't you? Yes, of course. That was your big mistake, Jennifer. Dolly's cat was always very loyal. She was just waiting for the right moment to turn you in.'

Jennifer sneered. Betrayed by a moggy. Of all the ridiculous ways she could have met her end, this was the most humiliating. Of course, it needn't be this way.

'I'll tell you everything,' she blurted. 'Otto is coming. Otto Kopp. He's coming in a bomber, and as soon as the sun is up ...' Jennifer's voice trailed off as the sun's light reached them. The protective power of the moon weakened and the veil around them faded. Streaks of pink washed across the sky, the grass under their feet was bright green once more, and the Channel sparkled blue.

'It's gone. The moon's protection is gone.' Jennifer kicked her bound legs in a futile effort to get away. 'We're done for. Enough bombs are about to be dropped on this spot to send the White Cliffs tumbling into the sea. Now, for goodness' sake untie me and we can all get to the shelter.'

'Shelter?' a new voice said. 'Not bloody likely.'

Jennifer rolled over to see Faye Bright, glowing in the amber of dawn as she stood on the edge of the cliffs. She was astride the remains of her bicycle, and it looked like she was wearing a pilot's flight helmet with little wings attached to its sides. Jennifer couldn't fathom how Faye had escaped the concrete pillbox, let alone Otto's wrath, but here she was, and Jennifer found herself surprisingly thrilled to see her.

Faye removed the helmet and dropped it on the ground, running her hands through her hair, squeezing water from it, then adjusting her old specs. Her shoulders rounded and her knees bent, she looked fit to drop. It didn't help that she was covered in green slime. Had she been for a swim? She wore a scowl that would turn lesser folk to stone.

'She's right,' Faye said, dismounting the bike and shrugging off her soaked flight jacket. 'Otto is on his way in a bloody great bomber.' She pointed out to sea, but Jennifer couldn't spot the aircraft yet in the brightness of the sunrise. 'He's protected it with his magic. We have to stop him, and we have to do it together.'

'Faye, if I may?' Bellamy said, nodding to Jennifer. 'If she's correct, then I vote for taking shelter.'

'This is a chance to defeat Otto.' Faye stood her ground. 'We won't get another like it. And besides, I don't want to give the hateful old coot the satisfaction of seeing me run. Anyone else feel the same?'

Jennifer saw the others hesitate. Of course they wouldn't help. They were all out to save their own skins. Look at them. They could talk about sacrifice all they wanted, but in the end, even with all their magic, they were just as scared as the rest of us.

'I stand with Faye.' Vera Fivetrees stepped forward.

Jennifer groaned inwardly.

'When I heard about what she had done on this very spot a few days ago, how she harnessed raw magical power with her bare hands, I must confess I struggled to believe it, despite the eyewitness accounts from Miss Charlotte and Mrs Teach. I even tried to recreate it myself.' She turned to Faye. 'The lights you saw coming from Miss Charlotte's cottage.' Vera smiled. 'And now she can fly. But even so, she's right. She cannot do this on her own. None of us can. Only together. Who will join me? Who will join Faye?'

'I will.' Martine limped forwards on her crutches.

'Count me in.' Miss Charlotte rolled up her sleeves.

'Jolly good,' Mrs Teach said, no less determined.

'Roit behind you, girl,' Mrs Housego cheered.

'Blinkin' flip, you haven't got a stitch on!' Faye said.

'It's all right,' Mrs Housego said. 'I prefer it like this.'

'Yes, but let's not have a repeat of Lady Sage's fate, eh?' Faye shook the excess water from her pilot's jacket and wrapped it around Mrs Housego, then moved her closer to the warmth of the bonfire.

'Bless you, Faye.' Mrs Housego rubbed her hands together.

'Jennifer, what about you?' Faye asked.

'What?' Bellamy objected, and the others joined him in a babble of rage.

'We need to do this together.' Faye raised her voice,

and to Jennifer's astonishment, the others shut up. 'I'm too cream-crackered to take Otto down on my own, and we need all the power we can get. If we don't include Jennifer, we won't be able to do it and he will have won. And might I remind you that bloody bomber is minutes away and we ain't got time to be faffing about arguing the toss. So form a bloody circle and get to it.'

'I shall do no such thing.' Jennifer's voice took a turn for the shrill. 'What have you lot ever done for me, hmm? When I was a young witch I wrote to dozens of you for advice and guidance and not one of you wrote back. You're nothing but a petty clique of chattering harpies.'

'Who did you write to?' Mrs Teach looked around at her fellow witches. 'I never got a letter, and I always write back to young witches.'

'My mother had a list of the country's most esteemed witches—'

'Who?' Vera asked.

Jennifer's eyes slid about as she tried to remember. 'Jessica Boyce, Diana Dee, Maggy Henry, Lizzie Wagner, Mary Denslow—'

'They're all dead, poppet,' Mrs Teach said. 'Most of them before the Great War. Any more?'

'Daisy Dent?' There was a wobble of uncertainty in Jennifer's voice.

'She died in nineteen twenty-nine trying to make her cat sing.' Mrs Teach grimaced at the memory. 'Quite batty.'

'Lilith Collier.'

'Bitten by a snake in an erotic liaison that went horribly wrong,' Vera said.

'You!' Jennifer clenched her teeth and pointed at Miss Charlotte. 'I wrote to you and you're still here, worse luck.'

Miss Charlotte folded her arms. 'I have a policy never to answer fan mail.'

'It's true.' Mrs Teach shook her head with disapproval. 'She never even sends me a Christmas card. Jennifer, dear, it sounds like your mother's list was a wee bit out of date and Otto took advantage of that.'

Jennifer felt the world tilt around her. She had been played for a fool and everyone knew it. She wanted to be sick.

'Ladies, we don't have time for this.' Faye hunkered down by Jennifer and inspected the knots. 'Miss Charlotte, have you got a knife to cut these?'

Charlotte handed over a folding knife. 'She'll betray us, Faye.'

'I don't think she will.' Faye looked Jennifer in the eye. ''Cos you've been betrayed yourself, haven't you, Jennifer? Otto's left you right in the lurch here. You've done what he needed you to do. You've served your purpose and that's it. He's going to let you die here with the rest of us.'

Jennifer wanted to deny it, but under Faye's gaze she couldn't find the words. It wasn't the steely kind of gaze that she might've received from Vera or Charlotte. This was a look of pure truth, and it was far more powerful than any hate or malice. Jennifer didn't want to give them the pleasure of being right, but she found herself nodding all the same.

Faye cut Jennifer's bonds, then stood and extended her hand. 'Join us. I hereby make you an honorary member of the Witches of Woodville.'

'Is that what we're calling ourselves?' Mrs Teach asked with a wince.

'We most certainly are not,' Miss Charlotte replied.

'Bellamy, Vera, Martine and Mrs Housego, you're all one of us, too,' Faye added, getting smiles from them and scowls from Mrs Teach and Miss Charlotte.

Jennifer felt lost. All of her certainties had fallen away and now the one person she was trying to kill was offering her a hand in friendship.

'I don't know what to think any more.' Jennifer's voice cracked.

'Don't think,' Faye said. 'Dance.'

Jennifer set her jaw, took Faye's hand and was pulled to her feet. She didn't want to let go, even though Faye's hand was still wet and clammy from the sea. Faye gently released her grip, giving Jennifer's hand a little squeeze before she did so.

'Stand at the northernmost point of the circle,' Faye told Jennifer. 'Right before the flaming bonfire.'

As she did so, Jennifer looked up and saw movement on the cliff paths.

'What . . . what's that?' She pointed and the others looked.

There were people coming up the path. Dozens of them.

'More bloody dog walkers?' Bellamy wondered.

'No.' Charlotte stepped forwards, getting a better look. 'Witches.'

She was right. They marched alone, in pairs, in threes and more. Women of magic all stomping towards the bonfire.

'They came,' Faye said, almost breathless. 'I used your little mirror,' she told Jennifer, a big smile on her face. 'I called out to them and they came.'

'Busloads,' said Mrs Teach.

The first witches clambered over the stile and Vera greeted them by name. More followed, more than Jennifer could count.

'Form a circle, ladies!' Faye cried to them and they hurried into place, holding hands.

'We don't have the moon, Faye.' Bellamy sidled up to her. 'Without it's protection—'

'I'll protect you. Whatever happens, keep dancing.' Faye moved to face the Channel, fists clenched. 'Let's begin.'

WHITE CLIFFS, ORANGE FLAMES

Jennifer had never known anything like it. The power surging within her made scrying look positively feeble. One of the witches played a fiddle, another banged a drum. As the mass of witches danced around them, Bellamy hurried from Jennifer to Faye to Charlotte and to Mrs Teach, drawing a sparkling pentangle before each of them. The hairs on Jennifer's arms stood on end. The very air was charged. Not with the cold power of the moon, but the fiery heart of the sun. Flames leapt from the bonfire and began to swirl around the witches, weaving in-between them. Jennifer tensed, expecting the agony of burning, but none came. Instead, she could feel the relentlessness of Mrs Teach, the ambition of Bellamy, the wisdom of Vera, the ruthlessness of Charlotte, the passion of Martine, the warmth of Mrs Housego and, most powerful of all, Faye's pure heart.

Jennifer could move mountains with power like this,

but it had never been in her reach because she had never known what to look for, and yet the source of her own power had been there in front of her all the time.

Some called it fanaticism. She called it gusto.

Her concentration was broken by the deadly drilling of a machine gun. She opened her eyes to see the bomber closing in fast, light flashing from the gun in the cockpit, its bullets kicking up soil, grass and chalk as they headed straight for her. Jennifer wanted to run, but her feet were rooted in place, so she braced for death.

Faye hurried to place herself between them and the bullets, reaching out with both hands.

They swerved around Faye, whizzing through the air and thumping harmlessly into the ground behind the dancers.

Jennifer wanted to thank Faye, but she was trembling so much she could barely speak. Faye was right. Otto didn't care if Jennifer lived or died.

'What's happened?' It was Bellamy. His voice wobbled more than usual. 'Where is it?'

Where's what? Jennifer wondered. Then she realised that the firestorm that had been whirling around them was gone. She turned to the bonfire, but it was gutted. A pile of smouldering, ashen sticks. But still there was a flickering glow of flame. Where was that coming from?

It was only when Jennifer saw the other witches all staring at her in horror that she realised the light was coming from her.

Consumed from head to toe in raging fire, Jennifer

Gentle was a human bonfire. She felt no pain, only the power of those around her. It rippled through her body, making every hair stand on end. Her skin tingled and she wanted to weep in ecstasy.

Faye was shouting something at her. Jennifer couldn't hear the words, blood rushing in her ears, but she followed where Faye was pointing and saw the bomber rising over the cliffs, almost directly above them, its bay doors swinging open. Time slowed for Jennifer. She knew what to do. She would take her desire for vengeance and use it. Jennifer Gentle would show that bastard Otto Kopp what kind of witch she was.

ø

They were done for and it was all Faye's fault. She had brought Jennifer into the cone of power and now all of its might was channelled through the girl. If Jennifer held a grudge – and who wouldn't after being tied up like a hog? – she could wipe them all out in an instant.

Jennifer glowed like a candle, her eyes brightest of all. She looked directly at Faye. And she smiled.

Jennifer Gentle raised her arms and threw a string of fire from where she stood to the bomber. It slammed into the cockpit, melting the glass. The propellers bent back on themselves and the aircraft came to a stop, suspended in the air like one of the model aircraft Bertie hung on string in his room.

Jennifer moved a hand and the bomber tipped back on itself. Over the roar of the flames, Faye could hear startled cries from inside. At the rear of the plane, a hatch opened and the crew leapt from the plane onto the grass of the cliffs. She heard a few snaps as legs and ankles were broken, but she guessed that was far more preferable to perishing in a burning aircraft.

A final surge of power burst from Jennifer. The bomber exploded in a boiling ball of flame, and countless pieces of it tumbled onto the grass or clattered down the face of the white cliffs and onto the chalky shore.

Jennifer gave a gasp and tumbled to the ground.

One figure did not fall. A short, bald man dressed in a Luftwaffe flight suit slowly rose above the bomber. The air around him shimmered, his legs were crossed, his arms held out before him.

'As you can see, Faye Bright,' Otto Kopp called to her from on high, 'you are not the only one who can fly.' All looked on in silent awe as he turned his head to the flaming witch beside her. 'Jennifer Gentle, you have betrayed me. After all I have done for you. My retribution will be long and—'

A flying concertina pinwheeled into Otto's face, breaking his nose.

'*Scheisse!*'

The ancient Druid dropped like a stone, landing awkwardly on the cliff's edge.

'What are you all waiting for?' cried Charlotte, the flinger of the accordion. 'Get him!'

A cliff full of witches – a busload, in fact – roared and charged at Otto Kopp.

Faye almost felt sorry for him as he watched on his

hands and knees, nose bloody and bent, as the witches closed in on him. His eyes darted about, looking for a way out, but his choices were limited to the witches and the long drop off the cliff.

Wincing, he got to his feet. He raised his left hand which burst into blue flame. Screaming in agony, he drew a rune before him and vanished.

The charging witches staggered to a halt.

'Bugger me, not again,' Charlotte cursed, looking at the spot where Otto vanished.

Faye was about to ask what she meant, but there were shouts from British army soldiers and Military Police officers. They aimed their rifles at the bomber crew who raised their hands in surrender.

℘

Jennifer curled into a ball on the grass as she felt the power drain from her.

'I ... I want it back.' Her voice was thin. 'Please, I'm ... I'm nothing without it.' She looked to the others, ready to beg.

Then she saw something in Vera's face she had never seen from another witch before. The woman pursed her lips and raised her chin in respect. Bellamy was smiling and dancing about, giddy as a schoolboy. Mrs Teach, Miss Charlotte, Martine and Mrs Housego stood by in silent admiration. Faye was utterly speechless, grinning as she caught her breath.

Around them, the other witches burst into applause.

'That was extraordinary,' Vera said.

'Incredible power,' Mrs Teach agreed. 'And handled with both grace and ferocity.'

'Sublime,' Miss Charlotte said.

'*Magnifique,*' Martine whispered.

Jennifer felt an unfamiliar sensation welling up inside her. She thought it might be pride. Mixed, perhaps, with a sense of belonging.

Jennifer sobbed again, but these were joyful tears and she let them streak down her cheeks as she smiled and reached out to the others.

She was about to get to her feet when she felt a meaty hand grip her shoulder. She looked up into the ruddy face of a Military Police officer. He was flanked by two others.

'Officer,' Vera said in a calm voice. 'Place Jennifer Gentle under arrest, on suspicion of treason and passing information to the enemy.'

'What?' Jennifer screeched. 'Didn't you see? I just saved you all.'

Vera continued in that deadened voice. 'She is to be placed under my supervision and guard with immediate effect.'

'No! I saved you, you ungrateful old hag!'

Faye hurried to Vera's side. 'Vera, look at what she did. We'd all be dead if it wasn't for her. She saved us.'

Vera remained unmoved. 'If it wasn't for her, we wouldn't have needed saving. There will be a trial. A fair one. You may testify on her behalf, if you wish?'

'I will. Jennifer, I promise, I will.'

Faye continued to make empty promises, but

Jennifer's rage blocked out the rest. She kicked and thrashed and screamed and swore bloody murder on all of them. The traitorous cat watched impassively as the MPs dragged her away.

Charlotte strolled over to them and reached into one of her pockets. She took a handful of ash and blew it into Jennifer's face.

The witch welcomed the peace of the darkness.

THE CONE OF POWER

Bellamy waited until Jennifer was gone before announcing that they still had a ritual to complete. 'We have no time to waste!' He raised his hands to the brightening sky. The moon was still visible in the pinks and purples of sunrise.

Bellamy looked around for his concertina, only to find that it had been trampled in the kerfuffle of Jennifer's arrest. Mrs Teach and Miss Charlotte stood close by, looking guilty despite their impassive faces. There would be time for an investigation later.

Bellamy was about to ask if someone could strike up some music, but one witch was already banging a drum. Another played her fiddle. The other witches began dancing in circles. They knew exactly what to do.

Bellamy rushed to his concertina case and took out the photographs of Hitler, Göring and Raeder and held them high.

'As one, ladies,' he cried over the music. 'You cannot cross the sea, you cannot cross the sea, you cannot cross the sea!'

411

'*Sie können das Meer nicht überqueren*!' Martine corrected him, leading the chorus.

They sang as they danced, their voices harmonising into something wonderful. The ground crackled with magic. Faye rose up, the air around her vibrating as she stretched her arms wide. The sky, all of it, flashed white, leaving dots dancing on Bellamy's retinas. The sun turned the sea silver and the ritual was ended.

ß

Faye and the witches lay exhausted on the grass as the morning drew on. Bellamy stroked Dolly's anonymous cat, the crafty little minx having snuggled up to him in the aftermath of its previous owner's arrest. Bellamy and the cat would make a fine pair.

Already, Faye could feel the magical energy returning. It would always be there, and it was something she would have to learn to live with. After all, she was a witch now. Faye looked up at the slowly drifting clouds. Now and then, distant engines growled and gunfire disturbed the peace, but they felt safe here on the cliffs.

Faye couldn't stop thinking about Jennifer and how she would try and help her the best she could. Even if she had locked Faye in a pillbox, left her to die and smashed up her bike. But we would all do mad things if we let the likes of Otto Kopp into our heads.

Faye had no doubt that Otto would want his vengeance, but his failure would probably put him in Adolf Hitler's bad books, and that was good enough for Faye.

'Ladies, I should like to thank you all from the

bottom of my heart.' Bellamy stood, brushing grass from his knees. 'Would this ritual have been an utter disaster without your sterling work? I rather think it would have been. And I shall never forget your dedication and passion.'

'Don't get carried away,' Miss Charlotte muttered, still lying on the grass with her eyes closed. 'We did what we had to.'

Mrs Housego raised herself in careful stages. 'But we done it well enough.'

'And there were not too many captains,' Martine said, lighting a cigarette. 'Just witches.'

'Crazy witches?' Mrs Teach asked with a naughty grin.

'The craziest.' Martine smiled and winked.

'Indeed.' Bellamy flexed his fingers and shuffled before Vera, clutching Jennifer's cat as a furry shield. 'I believe I owe you my sincerest apologies. My actions have put a stain on your reputation that was not deserved. Can you ever forgive me?'

Faye wondered if this would be the moment when Vera would reveal to Bellamy that she had been playing him all along, masterminding the entire operation to expose the spy among their ranks.

Instead, Vera simply said, 'Apology accepted, Bellamy Dumonde. Let's return to London and discuss how we can better work together in the future, shall we?'

She extended the crook of her arm and Bellamy took it, the two of them looking for all the world like a couple out for a stroll.

'I think that's a simply splendid idea.' Bellamy inclined his head in deference.

As the other witches got to their feet, chatting about the night's strange events and preparing to return home, a voice came hollering across the breeze.

'What in the blazes is this?' There stood an elderly gent draped in tweed. His terrier wore a matching jacket. The man was red-faced at the sight of so many women in one spot. 'What kind of nefarious activity are you suffragette delinquents up to, eh? I shall report you all. This is a disgrace.'

As he ranted, Bellamy turned wearily to Miss Charlotte. 'I don't suppose you have any left, do you?'

Charlotte took a handful of black powder from her pocket. 'Leave this to me,' she said, strolling over to the ranting man with a wicked smile on her face.

THE GHOST OF IVY BARN

Bertie Butterworth's Battle of Britain Diary

Saturday 17th August, 1940

One hell of a battle over Dover. Probably shouldn't put any detail here as I've signed the Official Secrets Act, but I will say that the Griffin's first flight was a success. Made a walnut cake to celebrate. Oh, and Faye said she loves me. Now I think I can fly.

Faye discovered the truth about Otto when she returned to Ivy Barn the next morning. She brought the Griffin in for a soft descent by the barn doors. She was finally getting the hang of landings.

'Someone called Otto left a message.' Leo was waiting for her in the centre of the barn, his usual chill emanating around him. 'I am not your messenger boy,' he added.

At the mention of Otto's name, Faye felt a creeping

sensation tingle between her shoulder blades. 'What did he say?'

'Something about revenge, and having nowhere to hide.' Leo sneered in disapproval. 'He was raving mad, frankly.'

'You have no idea.' Faye leaned the Griffin against the barn doors.

'How did it fly?' Leo asked.

'Like a dream.' Faye patted it on the handlebars. 'It even functioned as a submarine for a short while.' She filled Leo in on yesterday's extraordinary adventures, and she enjoyed seeing him smile as she took him through every twist and turn of the dogfight over the Channel.

'And here we are,' she said, letting her hand slap against her legs. 'You're still stuck in this barn, and I'm still trying to get you out. But I reckon I had this all the wrong way around.'

'What do you mean?'

'When you passed on that message from my mum, when she said I needed to learn to fly, I was so wrapped up in me own head that I thought she was trying to help me catch a spy. But Mum never had no interest in spies and such. If I've learned anything from having every word of her book plonked in my head, it's that she was more concerned about helping her neighbours than anything else. She was telling me to learn to fly to help you.'

'Me?' Leo frowned. 'How will you flying help me?'

'I've had some thoughts about that, and there's something I want to try out, and . . .' Faye trailed off, distracted by a noise from the path to the village. 'Hold your horses. Here they come.'

Larry was ambling down the path, accompanied by Mrs Teach. Miss Charlotte came hand in hand with Martine. Behind them trailed Bertie and Terrence, the ranks of the Woodville Village Home Guard, Reverend Jacobs, Mrs Pritchett and her dogs, and countless villagers.

They gathered around the barn door, and Faye craned her neck to see those standing at the back. Bertie shuffled to find an apple cart for her to stand on, and he moved it in front of the barn. Faye stepped up onto it.

'Morning all,' she said, raising her voice. 'Can you hear me at the back?'

She got a few affirmative cheers in reply.

'I'll take that as a yes.' Faye took a breath, adjusted her specs and started to speak. 'I reckon there's half the village here. Those that couldn't make it are most probably on some duty or other, doing their bit to keep us all safe, but you're all welcome here this morning and probably wondering why I asked you all to come.'

Faye noticed a few looks of astonishment in the crowd. They weren't looking at her, but at what was behind her. She glanced back to see Leo peering out of the darkness, the burns on his face still glistening.

'Leo, don't be shy, mate.' Faye beckoned him forward.

He did so, though kept part of himself in the shadows of the barn.

Faye turned back to the crowd. 'This here is Flight Officer Leopold Byk, 145 Squadron. He lost everything.

His home, his country, his family. And his life.' Faye let that sink in for a moment. If anyone in the audience was still shocked that they were looking at a ghost, they didn't show it. Most were still craning their necks to get a better look at the pilot. 'I know many of us have lost loved ones in this bloody war. I know most of us have someone away serving and risking their lives. And we do these things 'cos this is our home, our neighbours and our families, and we'd like to keep it that way, thank you very much.' She looked back at Leo again. 'Leo didn't have to fight for us, but he did so just the same.' Faye shrugged. 'And yeah, he's doing it 'cos he's after a bit of the ole retribution on those that took all he had. I don't think anyone here will begrudge him that. But he was also fighting because he knows what's right. He was fighting because he didn't want any of you lot to go through what he's suffered. And for that, he ended up giving his life.'

Faye could see it in their faces now. They were beginning to understand what they were witnessing.

'This is Larry's barn, of course.' Faye gestured to the dent-headed farmer. He turned and gave the crowd a wave. 'And since he told me that he had a ghost in his barn, I've been trying to give Leo the peace he deserves, but I could never work out what it was that he needed. Leo blames himself for making mistakes. For not doing enough. I think he's wrong about that. I think we here just need to show Leo a bit of gratitude.'

Faye stepped off the apple box and turned to Leo. She gave him a salute.

418

'Thank you, Leo, for your service and sacrifice, and for teaching me to fly.'

Behind her, Faye heard the rustle of clothes. She looked back to see everyone in the village saluting.

Terrence was the first to step forward and address Leo. 'Thank you, son. Whatever happens, we won't forget what you did. Not ever.'

Bertie was next, still a little apprehensive of the poltergeist. Larry stood by his side. 'I've been chatting with Larry here,' Bertie said, 'and though we both love all these plane parts, we realise they're not doing any good stuck in a barn. I'm going to help Larry get them properly sorted so they can be used for the war effort. All this scrap –' Bertie gestured around the barn '– will be used to fight the Nazis, Leo. I hope that meets with your approval.'

A smile broke across Leo's face and he gave Bertie a salute. Bertie, eyes glistening, saluted back.

One by one the villagers offered their quiet thanks, and one by one they drifted back down the path to the village.

Later, they would remember the peculiar encounter in their own particular way. Reverend Jacobs would mention meeting a Polish pilot in his sermon in Sunday. For years to come, Milly Baxter would wistfully reminisce about a passing meeting with a dashing airman from Gdansk.

Larry, however, had become used to the idea of a poltergeist in his barn. He was the last to thank the pilot. 'You're welcome to stay, sir.' He scratched at the dent in his head.

'Actually, Larry,' Faye said, 'I think it's time for Leo to go.'

As she spoke, Mrs Teach, Miss Charlotte and Martine moved silently into the barn, each holding a bundle of sage. Miss Charlotte lit hers and Martine's, then Mrs Teach's, and they began to waft them about.

'Go?' The pilot's voice came over the helmet radio for the first time since Faye had thanked him. His voice was tight with emotion. He chose his words carefully for fear of losing them to tears. 'Go where?'

'Hop on.' Faye gestured to the Griffin leaning against the barn door. She wriggled her flight goggles into place over her specs. 'Get on the saddle. You're coming with me.'

'I . . . I can't leave the barn. We've tried, we—'

'If I'm right about Mum, then I think this will work.' Faye took the handlebars and swung a leg over the crossbar. 'It's not enough for you to walk out of here. You need to fly.'

'This is crazy,' Leo said, positioning himself over the Griffin's saddle. 'I'm a ghost, it's not possible for me to— Oh!'

As the Griffin rose from the ground, so did Leo.

Faye beamed, balancing her feet on the pedals. 'Ladies, I'll see you at the stones tomorrow, shall I?'

'You shall indeed,' Mrs Teach replied, shrouded in sage smoke.

'Don't be late,' Miss Charlotte warned, swiping her sage about with Martine at her side.

Faye rolled her eyes. 'Dad, Bertie, I'll see you back at the pub.'

'Righto,' Bertie replied. Faye registered the hint of envy in his eyes, and she knew she would be taking him for a special moonlit flight tonight.

Terrence gave a wave. 'Happy landings.'

'Hold tight,' she told Leo, feeling a strange light sensation as the ghost wrapped his arms around her waist.

Without a sound they left the Earth behind.

⌀

Faye created a glamour. Anyone looking up would only see a strange shining star in the sky, an optical illusion, a trick of the light. They soared over Kent's patchwork of farms and fields, pulling up alongside a trio of RAF Hurricanes on patrol.

Leo's hand came into Faye's field of view. He was pointing to move closer to the lead plane. She nodded, leaning to steer the Griffin, bringing it alongside the fuselage of the Hurricane. The noise of the Merlin engines was incredible, the air reeked of hot oil. They were so close they could almost touch it, but the pilot remained blissfully unaware of their presence.

Leo's hand pointed again, this time at the section behind the cockpit. There was an emblem just above the RAF roundel. Faye didn't recognise it, she hadn't seen it on any other RAF fighters. Next to it, someone had written the words 'The Polish Squadron'.

Even with all the noise, Faye could hear Leo laughing, whooping with joy. She laughed with him, but his chuckles blended with the whirring of the Hurricane's propellers.

The lead aircraft peeled away, and the others followed. Off on their next mission and glowing with a new light.

Faye gave them a salute, and when she looked over her shoulder for Leo, he was gone.

THE WITCHES OF WOODVILLE
WILL RETURN ...

ACKNOWLEDGEMENTS

On behalf of the Woodville Village Council, the author should like to offer thanks to . . .

Bethan Jones and all at Simon & Schuster for their ongoing faith in the witches.

Lisa Rogers for her astonishing ability to keep track of the wheres and whens.

Ed Wilson and the team and Johnson & Alcock for being such a lovely bunch.

Julian Barr and Ian Sainsbury for cheerily taking my early drafts down a back alley and giving them a good kicking.

Mel Melcer, Chris Stay, Robyn Sarty, Anna Chabowska, and Kasia Lasinska for helping to polish my Polish.

Dominic Currie for giving me a copy of *The Ancient's Book of Magic* by Lewis de Claremont, which inspired the Zadoc Brown book that Bertie gives to Faye.

Duncan Moyse's advice on barrage balloons was invaluable.

Christopher Wills and Chandra Finaughty's advice on strychnine was given a little too gleefully, but thanks all the same.

Thanks to Sage Gordon-Davis for the name.

And last but by no means least, my eternal thanks to Mark Desvaux, the BXP Team, Bestseller Academy members and Bestseller Experiment podcast listeners for all their support over the years.

JOIN THE WOODVILLE VILLAGE LIBRARY AND GET FREE STORIES

Head Librarian, Araminta Cranberry, welcomes all applications to join the village library. There you will find free stories featuring secret histories of Mrs Teach and Miss Charlotte, a tale from ancient Britain with a cameo from Julius Caesar, and a recipe for Jam Roly Poly, with more to come ...

Simply sign up for the Woodville Village Newsletter here:

https://witchesofwoodville.com/#library